A Realm of Dark Fury

The Lost Heirs

Book One

RD Baker

Cover Art by Stephen Rocktaschel

Map Designed by Robbie Corlett

ISBN: 978-0-6458207-8-2

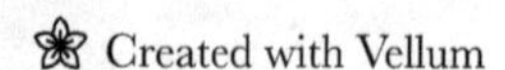

For everyone who was ever told "You can't"

You have, you are and you will

Show those fuckers just how wrong they were

Content warnings

The following book contains extremely dark themes that some readers may find distressing. Please be aware of the following content:

-Explicit depictions of sex

-Graphic depictions of violence, gore and permanent injuries

-Themes of enslavement, forced servitude and imprisonment

-Death of infants

-Death of children

-Abuse and mutilation of a corpse

-Loss of a loved one

-Sexual assault, on page and discussed as a past event (not involving the MMC)

-Forced marriage

-Kidnapping

-Torture; physical and psychological

-Psychological manipulation and gaslighting

-Violation of consent and sexual harassment

Your mental health matters.
Be kind to yourself, always.

Religious Acknowledgment

The lore and mythology in this book borrows heavily from Slavic Paganism. It is an inspiration and by no means a faithful retelling. All figures are used with the utmost respect and acknowledgment to culture and history.

Spotify Playlist

Half Life
Livingston

Chokehold
Sleep Token

FU In My Head
Cloudy June

De Selby (Part 2)
Hozier

Someone Else
Loveless

Daylight
David Kushner

Running Up That Hill (A Deal with God)
Loveless

Without Me
Dayseeker

Under The Influence
Joel Sunny

MIDDLE OF THE NIGHT
Elley Duhe

Dangerous Hands
Austin Giorgio

Take Me Back To Eden
Sleep Token

Underneath
Cobi

In the Name of Love
Martin Garrix, Bebe Rexha

MIDDLE OF THE NIGHT
Loveless

Never Let Me Go
Florence and The Machine

Dynasty
MIIA

The Other Side
Ruelle

The Last Day on Earth
Kate Miller-Heidke, Marcus Bridge

Pronunciation Guide

People

Elara Osunon - Eh-lah-ruh Oh-soo-non
Rook Norahi - Roohk Nooh-rah-hee
Theron - Thay-ron
Regan - Ree-gen
Keir - Keer
Drusilla - Drew-sill-uh
Nesryn - Nez-reen
Vayr - Vay-uh
Osayr - Oh-sair
Thalassa - The-lass-uh
Caedmon - Cayd-men
Celeste - Sell-est
Orion - Oh-ry-an
Hipatia - Hy-pay-sha
Tannis - Tann-iss

Places

Korbiriya - Core-bih-ree-ya

Veles - Vehl-ess
Peryrus - Pay-roohs
Isambard - Ee-sam-bard
Jerindos - Jay-rin-dohs
Yuarian Mountains - You-are-ree-en Mountains
Grixos - Gricks-oss

Deities
Mokosh - Moh-kosh
Lada - Lah-duh
Peyrun - Pay-ruhn
Nav- Nahv (Home of the Gods/Place of the Afterlife)

Dragon Territory
The Scale
Jerindos
Isambard
Korbiriya

Argamentine Forest
The Scalp
xos
Tethus mts
The Wastes
Fiachra

Prologue

I'm going to die today.

I drag myself across the battlefield, the chainmail biting into my neck. My helmet disappeared hours ago, my hair matted to my head, a combination of sweat and blood sticking it to my scalp like a shell. The sword of Arankos hums in my hand, as though it can sense that the last of my bloodline is holding it. As though it can sense my impending death.

A Velesian soldier rushes me, and I lunge at him, my sword clanging against the armor enveloping him. It merely sends him stumbling, but I continue on, unconcerned with killing. I have to find Keir.

If I'm going to die, I'm going to die beside him. Like I swore to.

"Keir!" My voice is weak, barely audible over the worn battle raging around me.

I stumble over the endless bodies of the fallen, some still skewered with spears, bleeding into the earth at my feet.

Perhaps, Keir is one of them. Perhaps, he has already died. Perhaps, he has already left me alone.

I blink the sweat out of my eyes and focus. No, Keir is still alive. I can still feel him, still feel that thrumming warmth in my chest. He's here, somewhere.

Another soldier runs at me, swinging his blade. My sword clashes with his, and my arms barely have the strength to hold him back. He knocks my blade away, the tip of his sword striking me across the face. Pain blooms in my ear and jaw. He comes at me again, but this time my blade surprises him, impaling him from below, and he falls back, clutching at the fountain of blood that has burst forth from his neck.

I keep moving, keep pressing on. "Keir!" Blood runs down my neck, and I reach up to feel that my ear is flapping loose from my head.

It doesn't matter. I'm about to die.

We've lost. The Peyrusian House will fall today. I will take my family name to Nav with me.

Through the melee, I see him, still fighting, still swinging his sword as the Veles soldiers close in on him. Keir's face is splattered with blood and filth.

The soldiers are not expecting me, and I bear down on them both, my sword removing an uncovered head before tearing open the other one's throat.

Keir's eyes meet mine for only a split second, before we continue to fight together. My arms ache as I swing Arankos. I want nothing more than to lie down and give up. But Keir fights on, so I must too. I can't let him down. Not now.

A soldier charges from the left, and I cry out to warn Keir, but I'm too late. The blow lands in Keir's side, tearing through his tattered armor. Keir's eyes widen, a blur of white in his grimy face. My blade slices open the soldier's neck, and he falls away, body convulsing, as death takes him.

Keir's hand is clutched to his side, blood spewing from the wound. He drops to his knees, and I land in front of him, dropping Arankos to the blood-soaked ground. I take his face in my hands, my thumbs trying to wipe away the sweat and the dirt.

"We've lost," I say to him.

He grimaces, attempting a smile. "At least we die together." He sags against me, his breathing shallow. "I love you, Elara. I hope you know that."

Tears bite at my eyes, and I press my forehead to his. "Yes, I know that."

Keir's shoulders jerk as a short laugh escapes him, and his blue eyes look into mine. "Even when we're about to die, you can't say it."

"I'll say it in my next life, when we are farmers, tending to our crops, surrounded by laughing children, remember?"

He raises a hand, pushing a strand of blood-stained hair out of my face. "Until our next life then, Elara." I can taste the blood, dirt and sweat as he kisses me tenderly.

Even though I know this is inevitable, even though I know what is coming, I still cry out as he slumps against me with a strangled gasp.

"Keir, no. No." Tears slowly roll down my cheeks.

"Don't cry," he says, his eyes fluttering closed. "Don't cry, jewel. You never cry."

Thundering hooves reverberate through the ground below us. I clutch Keir to my chest as his breathing slows. "Wait for me." I brush his mottled blond hair from his forehead. "Wait for me by the Gates in Nav."

"I'll see you soon," he whispers.

I hold him close, feeling his body go still. He breathes his last, and then I am alone on the battlefield, rocking his body back and forth gently. I grit my teeth as I feel the warmth in my chest burn up, like the dying embers of a fire. Keir's bond to me withers and dies, tearing from beneath my ribcage with a sharp snap.

I howl as I press my cheek against his.

Please, won't someone kill me? Why is no one killing me?

The thundering hooves come closer, and I close my eyes. The riders are here. The riders of Veles will strike me any moment, and I will join Keir in Nav. It will all be over soon. A breeze blows across my face, cool and fresh. I take one last deep breath as voices sound at my back.

I hold Keir's body tightly, tilting my head up to the smoke-filled sky. *Kill me. Take me back to him.*

Something hard strikes me in the back of the head, and I welcome the warm darkness that takes me.

It's over.

It's finally over.

Chapter 1

Elara

"A Peyrusian Princess, you say?" The voice was distant, muffled.

"Mmm, indeed." Another voice. Closer this time.

"I never understood why these royal houses send their princesses into battle. What good is a woman on the battlefield?"

The owner of the other voice chuckled. "The Fae, there's no explanation for their ways. Insufferable creatures." Footsteps sounded close to my head. "By all accounts she fought bravely though. Her mate died in her arms."

"Oh, how tragic," the voice replied, so disdainful I could almost hear him sneering. Anger prickled at my throat as I willed myself awake.

Awake? Where was I? I had to be dead. I was dead in Nav, and Keir was waiting for me somewhere. But I sucked in a breath, my chest aching as my lungs expanded, and I was sure that there was no pain in Nav.

"Pretty thing, isn't she?" There was a creak of leather as

someone crouched beside me. "Aside from the missing ear, of course."

"Too bad it was so torn up, I would have liked one of those pointy things as a pendant." Their hearty laughter echoed around the room. They were mocking me.

"Wonder what the King will say when he sees his pretty little trophy all cut up like this?"

I groaned, rolling on to my side, pain gnawing at my ribs.

"Oh, watch out. She's awake." More laughter. "How are you feeling, fairy?"

"Where. Am. I?" The words got caught by each ragged breath. My vision swam as I opened my eyes. As I struggled to focus, I made out two blurry figures standing over me.

"You're in Veles." There was something white floating around his face, a beard perhaps? "Fresh from the battlefield. And a sad and sorry sight you are, too."

I tried to push myself up on my hands, my head throbbing as blood began to circulate around my aching body. "No." I gritted my teeth as I rose into a sitting position. "I died. The Riders came for me."

"You're gonna wish you had, fairy," the other one said, the one whose blurry image was dark, clothed in green. "You are now the honored guest of His Majesty, King Theron of Veles."

"Lucky indeed." The bearded one leaned in closer, and a grimy hand grabbed my chin. "Looks almost like an angel, doesn't she? That golden hair."

I shoved his hand away. "Don't touch me." My hand shot to my side, instinctively reaching for my sword. I clenched my teeth together when I realized it was gone. Of course they hadn't left me armed. I glared up at them, blinking, trying to fill my lungs with air. "You're lucky they took away my weapon."

More disdainful laughter. "Now, now, is that any way for a lady to address her hosts?"

A door swung open, the hinges creaking heavily, and hurried footsteps approached. "Get away from her, you beasts." It was a woman's voice, older, stern. "I said out, now."

"Oh, now Drusilla, calm down," the bearded man said jovially. "We were just welcoming our guest after waking up."

"You're animals, the both of you." Drusilla walked over to me, leaning down to look at my face. She tutted, shaking her head. "Oh now, they've done a number on you, my dear." She looked over her shoulder at the leering soldiers, and waved her hand sharply. "I said fuck off."

They both broke into breathless laughter, trying to remain cavalier while clearly caught off guard by this woman cursing at them. They backed away to the door slowly. "Yes, alright," the one clothed in green said with a chuckle. "We'll leave you two alone."

Drusilla waited for them to leave with a tapping foot, her hands firmly on her hips. She didn't move until the door closed behind them and their abashed laughter faded. She smiled softly as she turned back to me, her golden eyes sparkling above her rosy cheeks.

"Now, my name is Drusilla. I am to be your maid while you are here."

I shook my head. "Why would I need a maid?" My fingers clawed into the floor, the feeling of the hard stones unyielding beneath them. The room slowly came into focus. I was in a tower, or a round room at least, with arched windows at three points around me, letting in brilliant sunlight. It was so jarring - expecting death, and instead I was lying in a sun-bathed room on a warm afternoon.

"The King has insisted a princess needs a maid." Drusilla offered me her arm. "Now come, let's get you up off this filthy floor and into your room. I've drawn you a bath."

I was tempted, for a fleeting moment, to run. To shove this kind woman into the wall and hope she hit her head against the craggy stone, incapacitating her long enough for me to flee. But as I took her arm, the rush of blood to my head sent stars into my vision, and I swayed as though I was caught in the gale of a winter storm.

I was unarmed and injured. Wherever I was, there were sure to be plenty of guards, which meant escape wouldn't be possible. Drusilla tutted and fussed as I found my bearings, so sweetly and with such concern, that I felt a stab of guilt at my plan to hurt her. She was a servant, a slave no doubt. She had no part in any of this.

I allowed her to shepherd me to the door, out into a long passageway - heavily guarded, as suspected. The guards watched me curiously as I limped on the arm of the woman who would not stop sucking on her teeth, grimacing with every gasp of pain that left my body.

"Oh, my lamb," she said softly as I stopped, leaning with one hand on my knee, trying to catch my breath. "I'd heard you Fae healed quickly."

"We do. I mean, we can… I'm just…" I inhaled deeply through my nose as a wave of nausea washed over me. "Don't worry about me. I'll be alright."

Her brow furrowed. "I certainly hope so."

We continued along the passageway, keeping a slow pace. Pain shot through my legs with every step, like a thousand needles stabbing me at once. I looked down to see my leathers torn to shreds. This was the first chance I'd had to properly note my appearance. I raised my free hand to see it was covered in blood, congealed, settled between my fingers, caked underneath my fingernails.

Keir's blood. The last trace of him. The last tangible essence that he'd ever existed. Soon it would be gone. *He'd* be gone. I closed my hand, squeezing hard, as though I could hold onto him, imprint that blood on my skin forever. I let out a breathless sob as we stopped walking again, and pressed a hand to the hollow place in my chest that had torn open when Keir died in my arms.

I gritted my teeth to stop the tears flowing, wincing as pain tore through my cheek.

My ear.

My hand flew up to the side of my face, and I felt a patch of gauze. And underneath it? I touched carefully, wincing as I prepared myself. My ear was gone. I ran my fingers further down, over the gash in my jaw, and I clenched my eyes shut as the sting of my filthy hands shot through the wound.

Drusilla took my hand and guided it away from my face. "Now, my lamb, you'll just get yourself an infection." She gave me a small smile. "I'm sure there's a very pretty girl under all that blood and grime." She squeezed my arm and we kept walking, kept limping together down that endless fucking passageway.

Finally, *finally*, we reached a door where Drusilla stopped, pushing down an enormous brass handle. It gave way, opening to a grand bedroom, housing a four poster bed dressed with gossamer curtains and thick layers of linens on the mattress. A fire roared in an imposing stone hearth, and there was a large bay window that ran the length of the opposite wall, stained glass depicting angels with enormous golden wings - the Seraphim, of course.

My simple little bedroom back home in Peyrus had not been this ornate.

My home. My chest ached as I wondered what had happened to them all. Had the Velesian forces made their way into the city? My mother. My father. What would Theron do to them?

As we stepped into the room, my feet landed on thick rugs. Even in the throes of the pain, I wanted nothing more than to tear off my shoes and feel those rugs against my bare feet. My shoulders heaved at the thought, at performing such a simple action after months and months of war.

I could hear Keir chuckling. *Going soft, jewel? Crying over rugs?* I smiled despite myself, dashing my tears away with the back of my hand.

I staggered away from Drusilla's supporting arm, to an armchair by the fire, and collapsed into it.

"Now, now, My Lady. Let's get you out of these clothes." Drusilla rushed over, kneeling before me to undo the straps on my boots.

"I don't think you'll be able to get them off," I told her. "They're like a second skin by now."

Her nimble fingers worked up the lengths of the knee high boots, and her eyes flashed upwards briefly as she began to pull one of them from my foot. I winced, my fingers digging into the armchair. The boot stuck to me, several layers of grime and sweat, and all that fucking blood acting like plaster. But Drusilla kept at it, working back and forth gently, easing the shoe from my leg. It still felt as though she was taking off several layers of skin with it.

"I'm sorry, My Lady," she said as I hissed in a sharp breath.

I bit my lip and shook my head. "Please call me Elara."

Drusilla laughed out loud. "Now that would not be fitting." Finally, with an insistent tug, the boot came loose from my aching leg. "I've never called any of the ladies I've been charged with by their first name."

"Were any of them prisoners, Drusilla?" I looked down at

her through the narrow gaze afforded me as my head remained tipped back.

"You're a princess, it wouldn't be right," Drusilla said softly.

I scoffed, leaning my head back against the warm leather of the armchair. "I am no princess here."

Drusilla began on the other boot and smiled. "If you insist, Elara. I'd be glad to call you by your name."

The second boot hurt as much, if not more, than the first, and tears bit at my eyes as it was eased from my calf. I looked down at my feet, encased now in filthy woolen socks. I had been wearing those boots and those fucking itchy socks for two weeks straight. I almost whimpered with relief as Drusilla peeled the sodden lengths from my feet, fresh air touching my skin.

I sat up and pushed my bare feet into the rug beneath me, then slumped sideways in the chair. "Oh Gods, that feels good."

"You're lucky you didn't get bloody trench foot." Drusilla clicked her tongue, regarding the socks with a wrinkled nose before tossing them into the fire. "Luckily your body was able to heal fast enough to avoid that. Now." She regarded me with a kind smile. "Shall I help you with the rest too, My La - Elara?"

I nodded and rose from the armchair, sighing again as my gloriously bare feet sank into the silken pile. "The bindings here." I gestured to my back. "I need help. The rest I can manage. I hope."

Drusilla freed me from the leather bodice, of which there was precious little left. It fell apart in her hands as she unfurled it from my body.

"My - my Mate," I said, the word tasting sour in my mouth. "What did they do with his body? Do you know?"

Drusilla tutted softly. "I'm afraid I don't know, my lamb. I'm very sorry you lost him."

My throat threatened to swell closed as I imagined Keir waiting for me, betrayal crossing his face as he realized I did not die as I'd promised to. As I'd sworn to. And now I'd possibly never know what had happened to him; whether he'd been given a proper burial, or if his body would simply rot away on that battlefield in Grixos, surrounded by fallen Velesians and the remainder of the Peyrusian forces. As though he'd been nothing. As though he'd been no one. As though he hadn't been mine, my Bonded.

Drusilla's warm hands gently squeezed my shoulders. "Come now, Elara, let's get the rest of these mucky clothes off you and get you into that warm bath."

I nodded weakly, and Drusilla proceeded to undress me as though I was a small child. I raised my arms to let my camisole be pulled over my head, and the gashes in my back stung as they yawned open with the movement.

Drusilla wrapped me in a fine silk robe that was cool against my skin and led me into an adjoining room, where a copper tub stood in the middle. A series of golden taps were arranged over the bath, and a heavy scent of lavender hung in the air. A large armoire stood against the wall, holding jars of herbs and tinctures. At least my wounds would be well tended to.

I sucked in a breath through my gritted teeth as I lowered myself into the steaming water. My bones protested, and the water washed over every wound like acid. I slumped against the side of the tub, and Drusilla knelt beside me, removing the gauze from the side of my face.

"My ear," I said quietly. "My ear's gone, isn't it?" I knew it was. I had felt it. But I hadn't yet looked in a mirror. I hadn't seen it myself yet.

"Yes, my lamb." She didn't say anything else, she didn't have to. What more was there to say. She dabbed some ointment onto the gashes on my face, the smell of marigolds wafting into my nose.

I closed my eyes as Drusilla unpicked my hair, taking out the braids that had kept it plastered to my head. Once the braids were undone, she lifted a jug of warm water to wash my hair, carefully tipping my head back so it didn't run over the open wounds on my jaw. I could feel my magic returning slowly, knitting the broken skin back together. It would, however, take days for me to heal completely. I was simply too weak.

"The King," I said finally, "what does he want with me?"

Drusilla puffed out a breath. "Oh, Elara, I wish I knew."

I turned my head, resting it on my arms on the edge of the tub, and eyed her carefully. She wasn't old, maybe in her 40s. Her brown skin was weather-worn, as though she had spent a lot of time outside in the sun. The wrinkles around her eyes spoke of joy and laughter. Her golden eyes glowed as she met my gaze.

"There were whispers," she said in a low voice, her eyes darting around the room, as though the very walls might have ears. "I shouldn't tell you this, My Lady. But there was a whisper that he meant to make you his bride."

A laugh rippled through me. "Me? His bride?" I scoffed, turning my head to look out the window, the light of the day fading slowly into dusk. "Why would the Velesian King want a Fae bride?"

"I don't know," Drusilla replied. "It was just what the court was saying."

Of course they were. The only explanation they could give themselves for the Velesian King to claim a half-dead Fae from the battlefield was to imagine he was claiming her for himself. Nothing could have been further from the truth, I was sure of it. The Seraph detested the Fae, and always had.

Another thought snaked through me, cold and vicious. Perhaps he wanted to claim me, but not as his bride. Theron's reputation as a defiler of the daughters of the rival royal houses was not a wild fiction, but the truth. My hands clenched into fists on the edge of the copper tub, and I knew that if he so much as fucking breathed near me, I would tear him into bloody ribbons.

"There now," Drusilla announced with all the warmth of a proud mother. "I can see your pretty face, and all that blood's out of your hair." She began to comb the pale length of my hair, and the action made my chest ache as I thought of my mother. My sweet mother, sitting behind me, singing as she combed and combed until my hair gleamed. *Like corn silk*, she'd say.

I lowered my hands into the water, raising them again to watch the rusty pink rivulets run down my skin. *Goodbye, Keir.* I bit back my tears, sure I would put a hole in my lip as my teeth clenched down on it.

Don't cry. You never cry.

I wondered how long it would be before I would start.

Chapter 2

Elara

The curtains were thrown open, and the harsh sunlight streaming into the room made my eyes water.

"Now, my girl, it's really time you wake up for some food," Drusilla said, standing beside the bed, her hands clasped in front of her.

I raised my head, looking around. Of course, the ornate room. The stained glass. I let my head drop back to the pillow, burying my face in the soft linen, shielding my eyes from that bright fucking sunshine.

"How long have I been asleep?"

Drusilla chuckled. "Two days, my lamb."

My head shot up from the pillow again. "Two days?" Of course I slept for two days. I hadn't slept properly in weeks. In months. The last time I'd slept had been in that fucking tent on the sodden ground in Keir's arms....

I quashed the feeling that arose. No. Not now. There was plenty of time to mourn in the deep of the night.

Drusilla moved to the table underneath the window, where

she'd placed a tray of food. My stomach constricted longingly at the smell of fresh bread, and the sweet scent of jam that wafted over to the bed. Gods, I was hungry.

"Come now," she said, gesturing to me as I rose from the bed.

I padded across the floor, and sat down to the most luxurious food I'd seen in ages. I tried not to sigh too happily as the taste of strawberry jam filled my mouth, but Drusilla's guffaw told me I wasn't hiding my emotions very well.

"Hungry?"

I nodded, washing the bread down with a large gulp of yellow juice that was sweet and sharp. "I haven't eaten anything but gruel and dried bread for months."

Drusilla tutted her disapproval. "What was a princess doing out on the battlefield?"

I shook my head, looking out the window. "It's not unusual in Peyrus." It was a lie. But Drusilla wouldn't have known that. They would believe what I said, and have no reason to think I was lying.

"I still don't think it's right," she said. "A girl, as young as you."

"I'm 22. I'm hardly a girl."

"A girl in my books." She rose from her chair and made for the armoire in the far corner of the room, opening it to reveal cascading silks and satins in every shade imaginable. "Now, what shall we dress you in today?"

"Is something special happening today?" I asked, spreading another slice of that delightful bread with more of the jam. I felt like I'd never tasted a strawberry in my life before today.

"The King wants to see you."

The loss of my appetite was almost instant. I let the slice of bread drop to the plate and watched as Drusilla pulled out a green gown, shaking her head and replacing it, before pulling out a blue gown, the color of a soft summer dawn.

"Ah yes," she said, turning to me with a wide smile. "This is perfect. It matches your eyes."

"Why does the King want to see me?" I asked.

"Because you are his guest."

His guest, yes, of course I was. His *guest.*

A knock on the door interrupted my thoughts, and Drusilla opened it to reveal a man so tall he had to bend considerably to enter the room. He straightened up, revealing an angular face with a sharp nose in the middle of it, his thinning blonde hair pulled back, making his forehead appear even higher than it was. He wore robes of black, with a frothy white collar that bubbled up around his thin neck.

He bowed deeply to me. "Princess Elara, you are most welcome here in Veles." When his eyes met mine again, I saw they were the most extraordinary shade of gray, like a burgeoning storm. "I am Regan, advisor to the King. I am sorry to bother you at breakfast, but the King has been most anxious for news of your recovery. He has sent me to see how you were feeling."

"I've been asleep since my arrival." I attempted a smile. An ache burst through my jaw and I winced, reaching up to where the wounds had been. Raised skin remained, a gnarled scar, but it had healed. My fingers traced further, knowing what they would find. Or not find. Of course my ear was still gone. It was ridiculous to wish that it had magically grown back, I knew that wasn't possible.

Regan's eyes crinkled with concern. "I'd heard you'd sustained a rather serious injury."

"Just an ear," I replied lightly, "Mokosh blessed me with two."

Regan chuckled, a little awkwardly. "Ah, a sense of humor, Your Highness. What a quality."

"The Velesian women aren't blessed with humor, sir?" I lifted my eyebrows as I gave him my sweetest smile.

I heard Drusilla suppress a laugh behind me, rasping deep in her throat. Regan's smile faded slightly as his brow furrowed, and he eyed me with uncertainty before forcing a wide smile back onto his face.

"Ah." He wagged his finger at me. "I'd heard you Fae could be devilish, Your Highness. Well done."

Devilish Fae. I resisted the urge to roll my eyes.

"Perhaps you could explain to me why the King has invited me here as his guest," I said, draping my arms over my lap. "The daughter of his arch enemy who was killing his soldiers on the battlefield does seem an odd choice of house guest."

"His Majesty is well aware of the needs of war, Your Highness." Regan strode a little further into the room, his hands behind his back. "He bears you no ill will for your actions."

"How good of him." I didn't mean to sneer, but the rage swelling in my chest made it hard to swallow the snide tone in my voice. Fuck Theron. Fuck his good will.

Regan cleared his throat when I said nothing further. "Well then, Your Highness, I shall leave you to prepare for your audience with the King, and will return to fetch you in a while."

"Thank you." I rose to my feet. "I look forward to meeting the King in the flesh."

"Indeed." Regan bowed and left the room.

I exhaled heavily, and looked over to see Drusilla clutching the blue dress and shaking her head at me, an almost admiring look on her face.

"Oh Elara," she said with a short laugh, "you certainly aren't afraid of anyone, are you?"

I shrugged. "Of course I am. I've just become very good at not letting anyone know it."

"Well, you're certainly braver than I would be in your position." She laid the dress out on the bed. "Now, have you finished with your breakfast?"

I cast a look over the table, over the food that lay there, and grimaced. My stomach felt heavy, and acid crept up my throat. "Yes, I have."

"Then, let us start on your hair, shall we?" She walked to the dressing table and stretched out a hand, gesturing for me to sit down in front of the mirror.

I sat on the blue velvet stool and saw my reflection for the first time. My face didn't betray the wrench of shock that wove through me. The scar that ran along my jawline up to my left ear - where my ear had been - was thick, an angry shade of crimson. I turned my head slightly to see what remained of my ear, which was merely a hole surrounded by raised red bumps. My eyes flashed up to meet Drusilla's in the mirror, and she squeezed my shoulders gently as she gave me a sad smile.

"Now, my lamb, you're a beauty. We'll do your hair so it's draped over that side of your face, yes? We'll hide it."

I wanted to protest, I wanted Theron to see exactly what had happened, exactly what his soldiers had done to me. But the shock kept me still, and I merely nodded, allowing Drusilla to comb out the length of my hair. It hung in long waves to my waist. I couldn't remember the last time I had cut it.

"And look at your rosy cheeks," Drusilla said as her fingers flew along the length of my hair, braiding it with expertise won from years as a lady's maid. "You look so well now, sleep and food have done you good."

I didn't especially care whether I looked good, or pretty. I had no desire to impress Theron, or any of the courtiers. I was glad for *myself* that I no longer looked like a wretched ghost.

Drusilla skillfully draped the braids she'd created over the left side of my face, pulled back on the right side to reveal the pointed ear that remained. She opened a box on the dresser and retrieved a pair of long, sparkly earrings, encrusted with diamonds. She held out her hand, and the smile dropped instantly. She looked downright horrified. "I'm so sorry, my lamb, how insensitive of me."

I shook my head and took the earring from her hand. "Not at all, perhaps I'll start a new fashion at court."

She laughed awkwardly. "Perhaps you will."

I clipped the earring to my ear, and despite myself, I was pleased with what I saw. I looked regal, and I wanted Theron to see exactly that. I wouldn't be cowed by a fucking Seraph. I rose to my feet and followed Drusilla to the bed, where she set about binding me into the silky blue dress. The bodice wrapped around my waist and sat low on the shoulders, flaring into a cape and a long, trailing skirt.

"Now, my lamb," she said as she sank to her knees, helping me into a pair of blue satin shoes, "you are ready for your audience." There was concern in her eyes, crinkling the corners of those amber eyes as they met mine.

"What kind of King is he?"

Drusilla's brows drew together. "He is fierce."

A knock sounded at the door, and I straightened my shoulders. I readied myself for the audience with my captor.

Fierce.

I would give him fierce.

Regan led me down endless passageways and stairwells that told me exactly how far I was being kept from the fearsome King. The guards lined the hallways, a silent sentry of black armor, heads covered in strange domed helmets. They all watched me with varying expressions of curiosity and disgust. A filthy Fae, in their castle. A female, who'd lain waste to their own. I suppressed a smirk.

"The King is greatly anticipating this meeting," Regan said as he hurried along beside me. He seemed to have trouble keeping pace, sweat breaking out across his brow.

"Am I walking too fast, sir?" I asked him when he stopped and leaned against the wall, trying to catch his breath.

"Madam, you do have a certain speed about you." He gave a short laugh before inhaling deeply, straightening to continue down the stone corridor lined with brightly coloured stained-glass windows.

I stole a gaze outside, at the city that sprawled off into the distance, a mass of brown buildings that ended abruptly at the foot of lush green mountains. Beyond that, the very tips of the enormous mountain range that separated Veles from the southern Realm were visible, frosted in snow. So different to Peyrus, all the way in the icy north, the flatlands and dark forests I had grown up in.

We descended a grand sweeping staircase and crossed a hall in which hung flags and tapestries. The crests and emblems of the important families of Veles, those that had retained Theron's favor at least. There were suddenly many more guards, armed with spears and dressed in armor of shiny Velesian steel, glinting black in the sunlight that poured in through the windows.

Theron was clearly afraid of me. What had those two assholes said when I woke? I had fought bravely? I wondered what other stories had circulated about me in the Velesian court that had Theron this spooked. The thought had me squaring my shoulders, even though my hands were still shaking.

Two enormous oak doors ended the passageway and two guards stepped forward to open them for Regan and me. I took a deep breath, clenching my back teeth to stop my jaw trembling.

I am not afraid. I am not afraid.

The throne room was draped with the red and black colors of the Velesian house, a carved ebony throne perched on a grand dais dominating the room. Courtiers stood to either side, dressed in varying shades of burgundy, red, and black. They all fell utterly silent as Regan led me into the room. I kept my gaze firmly ahead on the figure who sat in the ebony throne.

The figure adorned with the most towering golden wings I'd ever seen in my life.

Theron watched me with amusement as I approached, leaning casually to one side of his throne, chin resting in his hand. His fingers rubbed back and forth across his lips, his eyes looking me up and down. He was younger than I expected, surely no more than 25. A black crown sat atop hair the color of rust. His skin was a warm, rich gold, and made his green cat-like eyes even more startling.

He would certainly be thought of as handsome, his regal black velvet garb unable to disguise a strong physique. A sharp jawline jutted out over the high collar of his jacket. But his gaze was terrifying - cold and calculating, as though he was thinking of a million different ways in which he could either devour me or murder me.

I moved through the sea of red and black, feeling like a beacon amongst so much darkness. The Velesians were dressed in finery like none I had seen before - thick gold chains, black shimmering lace, heavy burgundy satins. And all this fuss to watch a simple Fae princess meet the King? It somehow made the scene even more unnerving.

Theron rose to his feet suddenly, and Regan dropped into a deep bow.

"Majesty," he said, "I present to you, Princess Elara of Peyrus."

I bowed my head, refusing to curtsey. Princesses didn't fucking curtsey.

"Your Majesty," I said, and a gasp rose from the crowd, Regan's eyes widened as he gave me a side glance from his bowed position.

Theron laughed heartily. "You have shocked my courtiers already, Your Highness."

"And how have I done that, Your Majesty?"

"By speaking before I spoke to you." Theron replied.

"What a boring way to live." I cocked an eyebrow haughtily. "I imagine starting every single conversation you have becomes tiresome after a while."

Regan had gone a strange shade of purple, still bowed and staring at the floor. He made a strangled sound, and Theron seemed to become aware of his presence for the first time.

"Oh Regan," he said with a wave of his hand, "do get up now."

Regan straightened with an audible creak, making me wonder just how old he was. "I do apologize, Your Majesty, I didn't brief Her Highness on Velesian etiquette."

Theron rolled his eyes and sighed loudly. "I don't think we

need to worry about the manners of a Peyrusian Princess." His gaze returned to me, and he grinned. "I'm sure Her Highness has excellent manners." Even though that almost lecherous gaze made me deeply uncomfortable, I kept my face neutral, my eyes staying on his. He broke away first, taking in my figure with an upturn of his lips. "Do you like the dresses I sent up for you?"

"You seem to, Majesty."

The courtiers gasped again, and I couldn't help the small smirk that traced over my lips. Theron raised his eyebrows at me, throwing himself back down into his black throne. "Do you always speak so freely, madam?"

"I do apologize, Your Majesty, all those weeks and months on the battlefield have turned me into something of a savage." My voice was high-pitched with cynicism.

Theron burst out laughing, his teeth a bright white flash as he threw his head back. "I made a wise decision in not killing you. You're delightful."

"I am sorry to have fooled you so, Your Majesty, I can assure you I am nothing of the sort."

He laughed again, and Regan looked as though he was about to faint or burst into tears of frustration.

"Well, I do hope we will get to know each other better, now you are here to stay with us."

I cleared my throat, feeling suddenly parched as the eyes of the courtiers bore down on me. "Did any of my kin survive the battle?"

Theron's lips twitched pensively. "That is something to be discussed another day."

"And my Mate?" Bile rose in my throat at the word. "He fell beside me, on the battlefield. What was done with his body?"

Theron waved his hands dismissively. "Again, a matter for another day."

"Very well." I shifted on my feet. "May I ask what you intend to do with me?"

"Why, have you here as my guest, Your Highness." His grin was venomous. "A beauty like you should be exposed to the world, not hidden away in Peyrus. Especially not the state it finds itself in now."

My throat tightened. "And what state is that?"

"You may imagine I don't take kindly to rebellions." His golden wings rustled as he spread them over the sides of the throne. "I can't let betrayal go unpunished."

"You struck the first blow, Sire."

"Your parents knew the price of rebellion, madam." His smile had dissolved. "Your father had faced me once before and made the right decision. This time, he was not so wise."

My palms broke out in sweat, and I prayed they wouldn't stain the silky fabric I clutched in my fingers and betray my anxiety. "A good ruler must also know when to show mercy."

Theron's hand slammed into the throne, and the courtiers around me collectively jumped. He rose to his feet, his golden wings spread wide. "Mercy?" His green eyes blazed. "The same mercy you showed to the troops whose heads you took with your sword? You, madam, are solely blessed with the gift of a weapon, intended for what? Mercy?"

I willed my breathing to remain steady, even in the face of my greatest enemy and the fury in his face. "I did what I had to in order to survive."

"You're a soldier, Elara." It was the first time he'd used my name, and hearing it from his lips sent a shiver of pure ice and dread down my spine. "You're a warrior, and a ruthless killer. I've had my reports from the battlefield, and I know you swung Arankos into the necks of many of my kinsmen. That is your mercy, is it?"

"What would you have had me do, Sire?"

"I would have had you speak some sense to your fucking father, you stupid girl."

"I am not a stupid girl!" I couldn't stop myself, and the shock on his face at being spoken to like this was well worth it. "I am Elara Osunon, Princess of Peyrus, wielder of Arankos and I will slice you limb from limb given half the fucking chance."

The courtiers burst into outraged chatter, heaving like a dark sea around me. But all I focused on was Theron, whose expression shifted from shock to amusement in the blink of an eye.

If he killed me now, I didn't care. I wouldn't die afraid of him, and I would let him know. But my rage was interrupted by the oak door at the far end of the throne room being thrown open.

All eyes turned away from me and fixed on the man striding in, hauling a serpent's head the size of a horse behind him.

Chapter 3

Elara

The man was covered in blood, from the top of his head down to the boots that encased his muscular legs. He wore black leather armor that was shredded across the chest. He dragged the serpent's head across the throne room as easily as if he was dragging a blanket behind him. The courtiers swiftly stepped aside, grimacing at the greenish-black trail of serpent blood the man left in his wake.

He wasn't Fae, nor was he a Seraph. He had no wings, none that I could see in any case. His eyes gleamed turquoise blue in his face, and the flecks of skin I could see through the serpent blood were a deep brown, darker than Theron's.

He stalked right towards me and I was too dumbfounded to move. I merely watched him approach, until he was right beside me. He looked me up and down, then turned to Theron hurling the serpent head to the base of the throne podium.

"It's done," he said.

"So I see," Theron said admiringly. "Was it difficult?"

"No." That was all he said. He rolled his shoulders as he

clasped his hands behind his back and I gave him a sideways glance.

I was tall for a woman, standing just shy of six feet, but this man still towered head and shoulders above me. And it wasn't just his height that was intimidating - it was his size. He was a tower of sheer muscle, a broad back and thick arms. His dark hair was plastered to his head, but I supposed it hung to his shoulders when it wasn't encrusted with serpent blood.

He seemed to notice me inspecting him and he turned to look down at me. His glowing blue eyes narrowed as he took me in. "So, is this the Peyrusian bitch?"

My mouth fell open, and my cheeks burned with outrage. "What the fuck did you just call me?"

He leaned down closer to me. "I asked, are you the Peyrusian bitch?" He raised his voice, and spoke slowly, deliberately.

Theron chuckled. "I'd be careful what you say to this one, she's a venomous little asp."

"I kill asps." The man's eyes flickered briefly to the serpent's head before us. "I appear to be rather good at it.

"And I kill Velesians." I replied, holding his gaze. "I'm very, *very* good at that."

"Good thing I'm not Velesian."

"Perhaps I'll just have to expand my repertoire."

Theron's laughter echoed across the throne room. "Oh, you two are going to be good friends!" He cried, clapping his hands together like a fucking child. "Elara, this is Rook Norahi, my personal assassin."

Rook spat at my feet, sneering. "Looks like I got your dress dirty, Highness."

I glanced down to see serpents blood seeping into the blue silk that trailed to the floor. I smiled as I met Rook's eyes. "Theron picked it out, it's not really my style."

"You probably prefer blood red, hmm?" Rook grinned.

"Soaked in the blood of my enemies, perhaps."

"Well, your kind certainly has plenty of those." His lips curled back revealing a mouth of gleaming white teeth.

Theron clapped again, delighting in the scene playing out before him. "Yes!" He threw his hands into the air. "Oh, do you know, I've had a wonderful idea."

Rook and I both turned to look back at Theron, who was now nodding enthusiastically. "Rook," Theron said, "you will train with this delightful creature."

"Train?" Rook and I both said the word at the same time.

"Yes, train!" Theron gave us both a wide smile. "I have some very amusing plans for our esteemed royal guest, and since she's a great warrior, it would make sense for her to train with my greatest warrior, wouldn't you agree, Rook?"

I could practically hear Rooks' jaw clench and flex. "Your Majesty, I wouldn't want to hurt your fragile little guest."

"Oh, I assure you, you won't." I scoffed.

"I don't beat women," he said, looking down at me.

I returned his cynical gaze with a glare. "No, males like you probably just rape them."

Rook's eyes widened with rage, and he took a step towards me. I didn't even flinch, pure fury keeping me rooted to the spot. And then I saw it. The elongated knot glowing underneath the serpent's blood, a shimmering silver mark on the man's forearm. The mark of a slave, forced onto all those who had found themselves on the wrong side of the Uprising five years ago.

This man was a Night Demon.

"Rook." Theron's voice was a sharp bark that had Rook instantly freeze. "Now, you two, I think this will be the most advantageous training environment. We wouldn't want the Princess's skills to become rusty." He walked down the stairs of the dais, and approached his assassin, "I trust you will train her well, and sharpen her already formidable skills, won't you?"

Rook inhaled through his nose, his jaw feathering violently. "Yes, Your Majesty."

Theron clapped him on the shoulder, grimacing as his hand landed in the serpent blood with a wet slap. "Then why don't you go and get all cleaned up. You can both start tomorrow." He waved for a servant, who came rushing forward to wipe the green sludge from Theron's hand with a white cloth.

"As you wish, Sire." I replied. "Only, I do wonder where my weapon is?"

"Ah, of course, Arankos. Took some work to bring that back from Grixos, let me tell you." He shook his head. "That weapon really does only answer to you."

"You have heard the stories then, Sire." I suppressed a smirk. "I do hope none of your guards were stupid enough to touch it."

Theron sucked on his teeth, throwing his hands up. "Oh, Highness, let me say we learned a lesson or two in how to deal with that monstrosity."

I quirked an eyebrow. "Is he still alive?"

Rook grunted next to me, shifting on his feet, and I cast him a brief sideways glance.

"The guard who dared touch the famed Malakh steel did, unfortunately, succumb." Theron's cat eyes flashed with irritation, even as his lips twisted into another unsettling grin.

"Well, now at least you know the fables to be true, Sire. Only the Peyrusian heir may wield that weapon." I smiled sweetly.

"Is that why your fucking father sent his only child out onto the battlefield?" Theron asked me, his eyebrows raised. "Was his hope that this cursed blade would defeat the Seraphim forces?"

I clenched my teeth together. They still didn't know. "My father believed in my skill."

"Your father is a fool." All eyes turned to Rook as the words fell from his mouth.

"Don't you dare talk about my father," I snapped.

"Or what?" Rook's gaze was murderous.

"You want to ask the Velesians what I did to their men on that battlefield?" We were almost chest to chest now. "I'd be happy to offer you a demonstration."

Rook lowered his head. "Your father is a fucking *fool*."

"Alright!" Theron clapped loudly, and Rook straightened, his gaze staying on me. "As much as I would love to watch this verbal sparring match continue, we do have other business to attend to."

I turned back to Theron. "I ask you again, Sire, where is my weapon?"

"You will train with a regular sword, Your Highness." Theron turned his back, waving his hand dismissively. "We will discuss your personal weapon another day."

Rook gave a brief bow to Theron's back and stalked out of the throne room. I watched him leave, his hulking figure moving through the dark crush of courtiers.

"Regan, take her back to her chambers," Theron ordered, sinking back into the ebony throne, stretching his golden wings. "We will speak tomorrow after your training, Highness."

I had more I wanted to know, more I wanted to ask, but Theron had made it clear no further questions would be welcomed. I bowed my head and followed Regan from the throne room. My head was throbbing.

No one knew. They mustn't have captured my parents yet. If they were still asking why my parents had sent me onto the battlefield, they'd not yet spoken to them, nor met with confusion when they posed them the same question.

My heart swelled a little, knowing they were safe. And cracked at the same time as I wondered when, if ever, I would see them again.

Drusilla and I ate supper in front of the open window with the warm summer breeze washing in over us. She was chattering away about something to do with the other maids, some terribly dramatic moment involving a silk dress and an overheated press.

I wasn't paying attention. My mind kept wandering back to the Night Demon, Rook. I'd only seen them once before when I was a child and only from afar. Besides that I'd only heard the stories, the terrible stories. The warnings to not stray too far from light after sundown, to keep your windows locked at night. Lest a Night Demon fly into your room and…

"Drusilla," I said, interrupting her mid-sentence. "Why does Theron have a Night Demon here at court?"

"Oh, you mean Rook?" She said lightly, spreading more butter onto the thick piece of dark bread on her plate. "He's a slave."

"Yes I know, I saw the mark. But why would Theron have such a dangerous creature here?"

"Dangerous? Rook?" Drusilla laughed and gave me an indulgent look. "Dangerous like the Malakh you mean?"

My cheeks flushed with shame. "You mean to say - those stories, they're all-"

"Lies?" Drusilla nodded emphatically. "My lamb, you are young, and you've been hidden away in Peyrus all your life. Now, that's not to say that the stories you've heard about all the truly terrifying creatures in this kingdom haven't been believed by others too." She gave her shoulders a shake and clicked her tongue. "But much like the Malakh were villainized, so too were the Night Demons. But I can assure you, those monstrous tales were borne of nothing but jealousy and ignorance."

I dipped my head. "I'm sorry."

"No need to apologize to me, Elara. As I said, you are not the only one who believed it." Drusilla shook her head, gazing out the window at the deep pink and purple sunset. "The uproar amongst the courtiers and the maids was enormous the day they dragged Rook in here."

Dragged? I quashed the question, the image of Rook being dragged into Veles in chains. It was too awful to contemplate. "So what was Theron's motivation? Did he merely want Rook's strength for himself?"

Drusilla sighed. "Rook is a strong warrior, and has served Theron well. But it's much more than that, my lamb. After the Uprising, Theron demanded a life from each of the royal houses that he deposed, but not just any life. He demanded their heirs."

Bile rose in my throat at the thought of what this decree would have meant for me. Five years ago, my parents had saved me from slavery. And this also meant - *oh Gods*. Rook wasn't just a Night Demon.

He was their fucking Prince.

"Rook quickly became a favorite of Theron's though," Drusilla went on, "he's loyal and strong, Theron trusts him completely. And he's never been any sort of trouble. In fact..." Her voice broke off into a low chuckle and her cheeks flushed a little. "I mean, I know the Accord doesn't allow it, but..."

"What's the Accord?"

"It's the restrictions the Night Demons were placed under after the Uprising," Drusilla explained, pouring me another cup of tea. "Theron placed them under something called The Accord. They're not allowed to leave Isambard, they're not allowed to fly, they're not allowed to breed -"

"Not allowed to *breed*?" My eyebrows shot up in shock. "You mean... you mean, they're not allowed to - to -" I couldn't speak it out. The very idea was so barbaric.

"They're not allowed to... go to bed with another, no." Drusilla said carefully, pursing her lips as she gave me a meaningful glance. "Theron didn't want to risk the continuation of the race. But..." She chuckled. "Rook doesn't always pay attention to that."

I felt a violent flush rise in my cheeks. "You mean, he - he takes people to bed?"

Drusilla nodded, covering her mouth to hide her grin. "I've heard some very interesting whisperings about his skills in the kitchens, let me tell you."

I shifted in my chair. I wanted to scold her for talking about something so depraved, so incredibly intimate, something illegal, as it was... And I was also ashamed of the curiosity that coursed through me. Why was I so fucking nosy? Why did I care that this blood-soaked brute took females to bed?

"His skills?" My voice had dropped to a low whisper.

Drusilla giggled. "Oh Your Highness, I do apologize. I shouldn't discuss such things with a young maid like you."

A maid. Well, she wasn't entirely wrong. Keir and I had engaged in plenty of fumblings, plenty of touching, some caressing and moaning, but never actually done... that. I wasn't sure why now. What had we been waiting for? I leaned back in my chair with a sigh.

"Have I upset you, my lamb?" Drusilla asked.

I shook my head. "No, not at all." I hesitated, measuring my next words. "What is Rook like? The King wants him to train with me, and I'd like to know what I'm getting myself into."

Drusilla puffed out a breath, her eyes rolling to the ceiling pensively. "Well now, I suppose he's a quiet kind of person. He keeps to himself, always watching from the shadows. But he's not cruel, or vicious, from what I understand."

"He doesn't seem to like me much." I mused. "He called me a bitch and spat at my feet."

Drusilla choked on her tea, her eyes wide as she spluttered. "He didn't!"

I nodded. "Oh he did."

"And Theron wants to send you into the training ring with him?" Drusilla tutted her disapproval. "Anger and weapons, that's a bad combination. And you're so much smaller than him!"

I chuckled. "I can best him." I couldn't, Gods did I know I couldn't. The only advantage I'd have over Rook was speed.

Drusilla shook her head, and smiled. "I suppose I had best get your leathers ready for tomorrow then, hadn't I?"

I gazed out the window at the darkening sky, the soft evening breeze blowing in over my face. I wondered whether Rook was down there somewhere in the castle seething, determined to show me what a mistake it was to square up to him. I wondered whether he would hold back tomorrow or if I would bear the full brunt of the hatred he clearly felt for me.

I dreamed that night that he climbed in through my window, his teeth gleaming in the moonlight. He tossed a serpent's head onto the floor before he climbed into my bed, leering down at me as blood dripped onto my face.

"Are you pleased to see me, my love?" He whispered, before his teeth seized my throat.

Rook was already in the enclosed courtyard that held the training arena when I arrived the next morning. I padded down the steps, feeling exposed in the linen camisole and brown leather vest I wore. At least the leather pants sat snugly and gave me some feeling of security. But fighting without my armor was a strange sensation.

Rook was even more exposed, wearing only a pair of black pants, his feet bare. He had his back to me, a battle ax in his hands, swinging it with great skill at an unseen enemy. The muscles on his back rippled, his many scars undulating over his brown skin. His hair was tied up at the back of his head, revealing a tattoo that snaked from the base of his neck over his left shoulder, a series of lines and dots with a script I couldn't decipher threaded through them.

I had seen a tattoo like that once before, when my parents had been visited by emissaries from Isambard. I'd only been small, but I remembered those elegant tattoos that adorned the arms of the beautiful woman who'd been at our court. Her brown skin and thick black hair had entranced me, so unlike any of the fair-haired, fair-skinned Fae.

Rook held the ax with two hands and lifted it above his head. My mouth dropped open as he swung it forward, one-handed, into the sandy ground with such force that I felt it reverberate under my feet.

I'd never seen anyone wield a weapon like that before.

He seemed to sense my stare, and turned to look at me over his shoulder. "Good morning, princess," he said, pulling the ax from the ground and turning to watch me approach.

He spun it so it stood, pommel down, his muscular arms draped over the double-headed blade. The damned thing had to be as tall as I was, and the gleaming crescent blades were wider than Rook's shoulders. The head was etched with markings similar to those that decorated Rook's skin. The wooden haft was stained dark from blood and sweat, making it impossible to tell what kind of wood it was. Two feet of the handle, from pommel up, were woven with a thick black leather braid.

As I approached, he lifted it, swinging it in his hands with ease, around and around, as though it was weightless before arcing it over his shoulder one last time and slamming it into the ground in a shower of dust. He was showing off, certainly, his self-assured smirk was evidence of that. The way he used it, as easily as though it was a part of his body, was downright elegant. This was his favored weapon, and I'd never fought against one like it before.

I moved my gaze from the ax to its owner, who was still watching me with that self-assured and smug look. Now that I could see Rook properly, and not covered in serpent's blood, I noted that he was quite young, probably only a handful of years older than me. His eyes were not as iridescent as they had been yesterday, but the shocking blue was only accentuated by the deep golden brown hue of his skin. Sweat gleamed on his stomach in the sunlight, the muscles there contracting with every breath he took.

His lips curled into a cruel grin as though he'd noted me taking in his state of undress. "I started without you, I hope you don't mind."

"It's fine," I replied lightly, "I wouldn't want you to have to face me when you weren't adequately warmed up."

"I'm certain I have much to fear with your skills, princess." He scoffed as he said it.

"You certainly do, *prince*."

His eyes flashed when I said the word. "Don't call me that."

"Why not?" I asked, holding his gaze. "It's true, isn't it?"

"You don't know a fucking thing about me." His voice was a low snarl.

"And you don't know a fucking thing about me," I replied. "But I can tell you, I'm not fucking afraid of you."

"That is a shame. You Fae do make such a sweet little squeaking noise when you run away from a fight." He cocked an eyebrow. "Which the Fae just so happen to do rather regularly."

"Not this Fae."

"Oh no?" He leaned down over me, trying to use his height and sheer fucking size to intimidate me. "And what sets you apart from your sniveling, pathetic kin?"

I swung my fist, my knuckles screaming in protest as they connected with his cheekbone that felt like fucking steel. I didn't let my pain show though, because the look of surprise on Rook's face when he turned to face me sent a thrill through me, better than any healing tincture.

"Rage," I replied through gritted teeth. "I'm not fucking afraid of you."

"You fucking should be." He rushed at me, reaching out to grab me with both his hands, but I ducked out of reach and spun away from him. Standing behind him, I kicked him in the back, sending him stumbling forward, but my kick wasn't enough to incapacitate him. He turned on me, and with a lunge he'd grappled me, knocking me to the floor.

"Well now," he said, leering down at me, "thought you'd get one over on me, hmm?"

I bucked underneath him. "Get the fuck off me."

"Not so easy to *not be afraid* when I've got you pinned to the ground." He lowered his face to mine, baring his teeth in a grin. "Your move, princess."

I drove my knee up into his groin, and he sucked in a heavy breath. His hands released me for just long enough, and I slammed my fist into his throat. He rolled off me with a rasping cough, and I sprang to my feet, waiting for him to recover. Instead, he lay in the dust and dirt, throwing his hands out to either side of him - and *laughed.*

I resisted the urge to jump on him and crack his fucking ribs. Instead, I crossed my arms over my chest and tapped my foot. "Are you just going to lie there and laugh all day or are we *training*?"

He put a hand behind his head, tilting so he could look directly at me. "Want some more, do you?"

I rolled my eyes. "Unless you're already too tired -"

My sentence was cut off as he ducked into a sudden roll towards me, catching me by the legs and flinging me flat on my back into the dirt. I gasped as the air was knocked from my lungs, but managed to lift my legs before Rook could crawl over me again and wrapped my thighs around his neck. I squeezed with all my might, but he wrapped those enormous hands around my thighs, wrenching them apart and flipping me onto my stomach.

He threw himself down on top of me, twisting my arms behind my back. I flailed under him like a fish out of water.

"You're quick, I'll give you that." He sniggered into my ear. "But being quick isn't enough."

"Get off me." I hissed.

"Oh, but we're training, remember? Now, how would you

get out of this situation on the battlefield?" His grip on my arms tightened.

Gods, he was so fucking heavy.

"*Get. Off. Me.*" I bucked again, my cheek connecting with the ground, sending dust into my eyes. I blinked it away, sweat running down my temple.

"Is that what you would do on the battlefield, princess? Demand the attacking soldier get off you and expect him to obey?" His breath was hot on the side of my face, washing over the sensitive patch of skin my missing ear had left behind. It sent goosebumps cascading down my shoulders. "You know that right now, if this was a real battle, you'd be dead, right?"

I craned my neck to look at him over my shoulder, meeting those glowing blue eyes. "If this was a battle, I'd have ended you with my sword already."

His eyebrows shot up. "Is that so?" He pushed against my back, his weight crushing me. "Too bad you don't have that fucking sword then."

"Get the fuck off me."

He relented and unhanded me, rising to his feet and brushing his hands together as though to remove the feeling of my skin. He grinned cynically as I got up and met his gaze.

"You're weak, princess. Weak and feeble."

"I'm a warrior."

"You're a sacrifice," he countered, his hands on his hips. "You were sent out to battle by your dim-witted father and left to the slaughter. Everyone knows he didn't want you."

The words stung, like a freshly slapped cheek. I swallowed hard. "At least my father didn't abandon me to Theron at the end of the Uprising."

Rook's eyes widened and he rushed at me, towering over me. "You shut your mouth you fucking bitch or I'll -"

"What?" I squared up to him, full of fury as I gazed up at

him. "You'll beat me? You'll change into some horrid winged dragon and fly up to my window and rape me?"

Suddenly, he had me by the upper arms, and he'd hoisted me into the air so I was face to face with him. "You say that again, and next time I won't let you up. I'll make sure you fucking *stay down there*."

I spat in his face, and he jerked back, his eyes flickering shut for a moment. "Fuck you, Rook. Put me down."

His blue eyes were lit with rage when he looked back at me. His lip curled back in a snarl, and then he simply let me go, letting me fall to the floor. I landed painfully, right on my ass, dust flying up around me. Rook gave me an exaggerated bow. "If you're done for today, *princess*, I hope you'll excuse me."

"Had enough already?" I asked, coughing as dust crept down my throat.

"I'd say you've had more than enough." He turned on his heel and stalked across the arena. "If you're brave enough to come back to face me, don't waste my fucking time again."

I watched him leave, rage rolling through me. *Fuck you*, I thought to myself, rising to my feet. *Next time I'll show you exactly what I'm made of.*

Chapter 4

Rook

"And next time, I'm going to make sure you stay down." My skin was hot, slick against hers and she raised her head, a moan leaving her lips.

"Is that so?" Her hips rolled underneath me, pressing her ass against my throbbing cock.

"Mmmm, and you'd enjoy it, princess." My tongue traced the length of her delicate ear and she shivered.

I jolted awake, the feeling of sweat and naked skin so overwhelming that I reached around me in the bed to make sure I was, in fact, still alone. My chest pounded with the exertion of breathing. *Fuck, Fuck. Why the fuck am I dreaming about this bitch*?

I was painfully hard and with a frustrated grunt I threw back the covers. I stalked across the moonlit chamber to the basin, plunging my hands into it, and splashing cool water over my face. I wouldn't have been surprised if steam had risen from my skin. I felt like my entire body was on fire. My chest ached in a strange way and I rubbed a hand across it. There was a warmth there, low and humming. I shook my shoulders, willing it to stop.

Fucking bitch.

When Theron had told me he'd retrieved the Peyrusian Princess from the battlefield, I'd hoped he'd just have her killed. What good was she to any of us? A stupid, weak, useless Fae. Her father had been a coward, and his daughter was just like him.

But no, Theron had kept her alive. And not only was I being forced to train with her, now I was having fucking *dreams* about her.

The feeling of her skin and the smell of her sweat remained on me like a curse. The dawn was only just breaking over the mountains, the barest hint of purple coloring the night sky. I was still hard and for a moment I considered fucking my fist to relieve the tension that held my whole body in its web. But not to her, not to the thought of her body underneath me, that perfect ass -

FUCK. I raked my hands through my hair. She'd cast a spell on me. That had to be it. She was invading my dreams.

I pulled on a pair of black pants and tied my hair back. I needed to move. I needed to run. I needed to wear my body out so I wouldn't dream of her. I slammed my fist against the door to my chamber twice and after a moment a guard opened it.

"I need to train," I told him.

He rolled his eyes. "It's barely morning, Norahi. Go back to sleep."

"I said I need to train." I leaned on the door frame, towering over him. "Now, get out of my way."

The guard considered protesting for a moment, his lips pulled into a taut, white line. With a jerk of his head he gestured for me to leave the chamber. I walked out onto the cold stones, my feet bare. I moved down the passageway towards the heavy oak door and tore it open before the guard could even move in its direction.

The sky had lightened a little more, and I took a deep breath of the fresh morning air. The day would be hot, but now it was temperate. I stepped onto the dewy grass, flexing my toes before I broke into a run. I dashed the length of the palace wall before turning the corner and crossing the open green. The gardens passed me in a blur, the air rushing past my ears mingling with the sounds of the birds' early morning calls.

The palace grounds were too small. I ran the length of the grey stone walls four times over, desperate for an open space. For sand under my feet. For salt water…

I came to a stop when my lungs began to scream at me, the muscles in my legs burning. I threw my head back, my shoulders heaving. The lust and desire that had chased me from sleep had abated somewhat. But that warmth in my chest remained, clawing at my collarbone and winding around my ribcage. Not unpleasant, but foreign enough to bother me.

What the fuck was wrong with me?

I wondered if she'd be brave enough to face me again. The day before she'd surprised me with her grit, the punch she'd thrown at me catching me off guard. She wasn't strong, but she *was* determined, and indeed filled with rage. But rage was volatile, and made her an easy target. She would need to learn to harness it before she -

I broke that train of thought instantly. I didn't *want* her to become a better fighter, and I sure as fuck didn't want to spend my time babysitting a fucking Fae princess. Fucking Theron. Pushing her on to me like some kind of sick joke.

No, if she returned to face me, I'd make sure she didn't get up again.

To my combined relief and irritation, Elara didn't show up in the training arena that day. Irritation because I'd wanted the chance to kick her ass permanently and relief because… well, I didn't know that dreaming about her moaning underneath me wouldn't make seeing her rather uncomfortable.

Gods, I fucking hated this.

I'd trained with my ax until my shoulders ached and my body was drenched in sweat. I was determined to push my body to the point of exhaustion, hoping that with enough exertion my sleep would be dreamless.

I dragged myself back to my chambers as the sun went down and pushed the door closed behind me. In the semi-darkness, I drew myself a bath to wash off the sweat, dust and filth. I lay my head back against the edge of the tub and closed my eyes. That odd thrumming sensation in my chest shifted a little, spreading across my body. I was too tired to fight it. I drifted away on it, letting my mind wander as the steam rose around me.

"Is that good?" Her blue eyes gazed up at me as her hand pumped up and down my length.

I gasped. "Fuck. Yes."

She moaned as I pushed my cock down her throat, and my hands threaded through her hair.

"I love fucking your mouth," I said.

My eyes flew open. I'd fucking fallen asleep, the water around me now tepid. And I was fucking hard *again,* after dreaming about her *again.*

I got out of the tub and rubbed my body down, every

nerve on fucking edge. *Fuck fuck FUCK.* This was wicked Fae magic. I was going to fucking strangle her. I had to break this fucking spell. But right now, I had a throbbing cock that needed seeing to and my hand wasn't going to suffice.

I pulled on my clothes and boots, then slapped my door with an open palm. "Open up!"

The guard opened the door with an exasperated sigh, pushing his ridiculous helmet back from a sweaty brow.. "Now what?"

"I'm going to the tavern." I pushed past him, ignoring his protests and insistence he had to check with Regan first. I wasn't in the mood to wait. I had to get this bitch out of my head, I had to erase the feeling of her mouth and her hands and her skin and -

NOT HELPING, ROOK.

I bit back a groan as I moved on, through the Palace grounds and down the narrow road that led to the village. I ignored the filthy looks as I passed, the Velesians in their finery staring me down. These were not my people. I hated them as much as they hated me. To them I was a monster, nothing but a horrific myth they warned their daughters about. I didn't care. I wasn't here for them.

The road narrowed further, becoming muddy and uneven underfoot. It twisted between the houses that were smaller now, shoved together in a haphazard arrangement of broken tiles and crumbling plaster. Most of Veles was refined and polished, boasting fine houses with large windows and perfectly kept green gardens.

This end of town, and the tavern I was headed to, most certainly were not.

I heard and smelled the tavern before it came into view, a cacophony of music, laughter and bare-fisted brawls. Maids with dresses so tight their breasts practically spilled out the top sat on the window sills outside, flirting outrageously with the males who were several pints of ale into the evening.

I passed them all, entering the dimly lit room, dripping candles set in the window frames and on rickety shelves, the perfect light for hiding all the dark deeds that went on within its walls.

I saw several faces I knew from the palace, eyes averted in the unspoken agreement that *No You Did Not See Me Here Finger-fucking the Maid.* Everyone was here to escape servitude for just a few hours, just like me. Except now it wasn't just servitude to a Seraph King. Now, it was servitude to a pair of blue eyes and a rosy pair of lips and the most perfect ass I'd ever seen in my life.

"An ale, if you will," I said to the barkeep, whose name I knew but never uttered. We rarely used names here. There was no point. Names meant nothing here. He gave me a curt nod, drawing me a pint and slamming the wooden pitcher down unceremoniously in front of me. I threw a few coins down onto the stained counter, taking my drink and heading deeper into the tavern.

There was debauchery at every turn if you cared to lift your eyes from the floor long enough to see it. I finally found a quiet corner free of bare skin and unfettered moans, and placed myself down in the shadows. I took a long sip of the bitter ale while wondering how much of it I would have to drink to fall into my bed in a drunken stupor.

"Hello Rook." The soft voice purred beside me and there was a rustle of skirts as the owner of the voice sat down.

"Hello there," I replied, taking in the long curly red hair and the bust that was practically bursting from the bodice of the green dress she was wearing. "You're one of the kitchen maids, aren't you?"

She nodded, fluttering her long eyelashes at me. "Ivy. My friend told me all about you."

I leaned forward, resting one hand on my knee. "Oh she did, did she?"

Ivy bit her lip and nodded.

I reached out, tracing a finger down her cheek. "And what did your friend have to say?"

Ivy huffed out a little breath as my finger continued down her throat. "That she couldn't walk for a day afterwards."

I smiled. "Only a day? Hmmm." My eyes dropped to her breasts, which were now heaving in her dress. "I'm sure I can do much better than that."

Yes. I'd come here for a reason.

I grabbed Ivy by the waist and pulled her on top of me. She rucked her skirts up around her waist and my hands moved underneath, running up her thighs. I growled as my hands found her bare ass under all those layers of petticoat.

"Filthy girl," I breathed against her ear. "Not wearing any underthings." I gripped her hair, yanking her head back, her breathing speeding up as her eyes met mine. "Were you hoping to meet me, were you?"

She grinned, nodding. "I followed you here."

"Filthy, filthy girl." I groaned as she ground herself against me. "You're not even shy about fucking me in a tavern, are you?" I tore down the bodice of her dress, exposing a pebbled brown nipple, and sucked it into my mouth.

She bucked on top of me, her fingers scrambling against my scalp as she inhaled sharply. "Ouch!" I released her, and she slapped the back of my head. "I didn't say to stop, did I?"

Fucking females. I went back to her nipple, sucking on it as I freed my needy cock from my pants. I heard her make a sound of surprise as I pressed against her thigh, a high-pitched *Oh.*

"Bigger than you expected?" I murmured into her neck.

"I don't think you can fit," she panted, wriggling her hips.

"We'll make it fit, sweetheart, don't you worry." I spat in my hand, rubbing it along my length as she watched with raised eyebrows. I gripped her hips, guiding her on top of me. We both moaned as she rolled her hips, once, then twice, before I was seated fully inside her.

She let out a little squeak, her body not ready for my size. Her eyes rolled back, fluttering shut as she moved slowly, grinding herself up and down. I hissed in a breath through gritted teeth. I needed more, I needed her to ride me hard. I needed release, *now*.

"Oh gods, oh fucking *gods*. The girls were right." She lifted her hips, rocking herself on me, stroking my throbbing cock with her hot cunt. "They said… They said your cock was special."

"Oh, it's very special," I said, leaning back to watch her fuck me. "It's made just for filthy girls like you. Just so you can rub this slippery cunt up and down me to make yourself scream."

My words had her gasping, riding me harder. Those enormous tits were bouncing in my face, and I seized her nipples between my fingers. I pinched hard, earning me another surprised little squeak and a clench of her cunt which nearly dragged me over the edge.

I tipped my head back against the wall, feeling myself rise. There was raucous laughter nearby, but I didn't care, and Ivy didn't stop. This wouldn't be the first time someone had seen me openly violate the Accord. Let them tell Theron. He didn't give a shit.

Ivy whimpered, pounding herself down on to me, becoming tighter as she neared her climax. I closed my eyes, surrendering to the feeling and aching for release.

"It's happening." She gripped onto my shoulders. "Oh

fuck it's -" She broke off in a strangled moan, pulsating around my cock as I gritted out a groan. The rush of relief as I spilled inside her left me breathless for a moment, and I looked up at her with a satisfied grin that she matched.

She shifted her head, tipping it to the side as she laughed and for a split second, her hair was back-lit, glowing like a golden halo. And then all I could see was Elara, all I could smell was her sweat as she collapsed against me.

"Oh Gods," she sighed, and it was *her fucking voice.*

I grabbed Ivy's arms and pulled her back up, staring into a confused set of amber coloured eyes. "Is something wrong?" She asked me, frowning.

I didn't know what to say. This was supposed to make me feel better. This was supposed to *relieve* my fucking tension. Instead, I was growing hard again as the image of the Peyrusian Princess, perched on top of me in a wench's dress with her breasts exposed, swam before me.

Fucking Gods, why are you cursing me like this?

Ivy looked down at my cock and let out a disbelieving giggle. "You Night Demons really do have an appetite, don't you?"

I hurriedly tucked myself away, pushing her off me. She yelped as she tumbled onto the wooden bench, sending curses at my back as I strode out of the tavern, into the humid night. Rain had started to fall, the unpaved road beneath my feet turning sodden, the smell of mud rising to meet me.

"Norahi!" One of the guards barked at me as I walked into the Palace. When I ignored him and kept moving, he was at my back poking me with a spear. "You were told to stay put."

I spun on him, tearing the spear from his hand easily, snapping it over my knee, and throwing the pieces down at his feet. "Fuck off if you know what's good for you." He didn't follow me as I went back into my room.

I wanted to get drunk. I wanted this strange feeling in my chest to go away. I wanted to ensure I didn't fucking dream of her. I decided there and then that I'd kill her in the training arena the next time I saw her. I didn't care what Theron had planned for her. I didn't care that she was a princess. She was a witch, invading my dreams, stealing my fucking soul, and I would make sure she'd stop.

And, of course, that night I dreamed of her. Of her riding me, of me gripping her hips as I whispered in her ear, *You take me so fucking well, princess.* And she didn't even care that we were in a crowded tavern while it happened.

I felt groggy in the training arena the next day, the sunlight stinging my eyes. The foulest mood had overtaken me and when I heard footsteps behind me, I gripped my ax in my hand. Ready to end it. Ready to end this fucking torment.

When I turned to face her, she was already armed, a long sword in her right hand.

And she was fucking glaring at me.

"Morning." I said.

"An astute observation." She lifted an eyebrow.

I nodded down towards the sword. "Came prepared today, did we?"

She brandished the weapon, the sunlight catching its gleaming blade. "I did."

"Too bad it won't do you much good." I lunged at her, sparks flying as my ax ran the length of her blade. She spun the sword in her hand, deflecting my ax, striking me back when I tried to advance on her.

"You're especially slow today," she said with a sneer, "too much ale at the tavern last night?"

I laughed as we circled each other, her cheeks flushed. "I spent the night in the arms of a rather pleasing maiden if you must know."

"Let me guess." More clashing of the ax and the sword, more sparks. "A redhead with big tits?"

"It's always a redhead with big tits." I grinned, baring my teeth. "Jealous, little Fae?"

She scoffed. "Of what?"

I rushed at her, locking her sword against the handle of my ax with the curved underside of one of my blades. Her eyes were wide and full of fury as she stared up at me. "Of the fair maiden who knew my cock, of course."

"You're a pig." She let her hand fall from the sword so it dropped beneath my blade, and swiftly grabbed it again with her other hand. "I would only *pity* her."

"Pity her?" I threw my ax back and forth between my hands. "She was making sounds you could only dream of making."

That hit a nerve. With a loud cry, she launched herself at me, and I was a little surprised at the height she gained. Her speed gave her leverage that my cloudy head wasn't prepared for, and the arc of her sword sent me stumbling. I laughed as I righted myself, meeting those furious blue eyes.

"What's wrong, princess?" I spun the haft in my hand. "That little Fae cunt of yours in need, is it?"

"Certainly not."

The sounds of our weapons clashing drowned out her words, but then we were face to face again, and I heard her very clearly.

"My *cunt* would never have need of a depraved cock like yours."

"It's probably worn out from servicing all your kinsmen in camp."

She pushed back against me, but with a sharp jolt of my ax I'd torn the sword from her hand. I swung the haft around her, and yanked her back against me. She flailed against the pressure on her throat, choking and garbling incoherently.

"What was that, little Fae?" I pressed harder and her ribcage contracted as she gasped for air. "Oh, you want me to let you go?"

She drove a booted heel into my shin, but I held fast. She stomped on my foot, and I gritted my teeth, but did not let go. I was going to squeeze the fucking life from her. A few of the guards eyed me with alarm, and a few began to move forward.

"You fucking little witch," I hissed in her ear. "You'll have no hold over me anymore."

She jerked her head back, and hit me square in the nose. I staggered, releasing my grip enough for her to drop down into a lunge, and she scrambled for her sword. I could taste blood as I went after her, grabbing her by the ankle and pulling her back towards me.

"Let me go!" She spun onto her back, trying to kick me with her other foot, but I kneeled down on her leg, and she let out a howl of pain. "*You're hurting me*!"

"Good!" I crawled over her, curling my hand around her throat and slamming her head into the ground. Her face went slack for a moment, her eyes unfocused as she looked up at me. "And what now, princess?" Blood was dripping from my nose onto her pale skin. "Are you ready to die? Because I'm going to kill you."

Her eyes fluttered closed, her breathing shallow. She

squirmed a little under me, her hips pressing against me as she tried to move. "Is that so?"

Her words had me instantly release the pressure on her throat. Suddenly, all I could feel was the warmth of her breath on me, the feeling of her skin, and that fucking humming in my chest. I stared down at her, and when her eyes opened, she looked at me with confusion.

"I thought you were going to kill me," she said weakly. And then a tear rolled down the side of her face. She closed her eyes again and sighed heavily, making a sound almost like a sob. "Just do it."

"You're going to give up that easily, are you?" I wanted to taunt her. I wanted to sneer at her. I wanted to beat the shit out of her. But then another tear rolled from between her lashes, and Gods if I didn't reach out with my thumb and wipe it away.

She jerked at the touch, her eyes flying open, filled with fear. She wriggled underneath me, bucking me off with her hips. "Don't fucking touch me," she said, trying to turn onto her stomach, trying to escape me. I rose to my knees, letting her go. She scrambled for her sword and then she was on her feet. She held the sword out towards me, her hand shaking. "Don't *ever* touch me."

"Why would I want to?" I eyed the gleaming blade. "Are you going to kill me now?"

"Yes." Her shoulders were heaving.

"Well, go on then."

She dashed the back of her hand across her eyes, sniffling as she held the trembling blade out in front of her. "I fucking hate you."

"The feeling is mutual." I stayed on my knees, eyes locked with hers, daring her to do it. Daring her to plunge that blade into my chest. "Go on then, you coward."

"Fuck you!" Her voice broke, her chest quivering as she tried to breathe. "I just want to be free of you!"

"And I of you!" I bared my teeth at her. "You fucking witch, invading my fucking dreams."

Her eyes widened and she stumbled backwards. "Wh-what?"

I rose to my feet. "You heard me. You and your wicked Fae magic. Stay out of my head."

She shook her head adamantly. "No, no, *you're* the one, you, you're fucking *evil.*"

The guards had all assembled at the edge of the training ring, completely absorbed in the scene unfolding before them. They began to murmur to each other and Elara looked side to side, brushing her long pale hair from her face before looking back at me.

I rushed at her, and she dropped her sword as my fingers dug into her arms. "Stay out of my head, or I'll tear that pretty head of *yours* clean from your body, do you understand me?"

"I said don't touch me." She writhed in my arms. "Get the fuck off me."

I lowered my mouth to her ear. "I told you, I don't want you in my dreams."

"I don't know what the fuck you're talking about!" Her eyes were wild as she thrashed in my grasp. "*You're* the one sending me depraved fantasies of fucking me in a tavern. You fucking pig." She spat in my face.

I shoved her away from me and she hesitated for only a moment before she ran from the arena. The guards all craned their necks to watch her leave, then turned back to me.

"What the fuck are you all looking at?" I wiped the back of my hand across my mouth, feeling the blood that had started to dry there. The guards dispersed, back to their posts.

She was lying. She had to be. She was trying to trick me. But that look in her eyes, that hopelessness. That defeat. And that *fear*. Either she was a very good actress or it was real. I ran a hand across my chest, across that humming warmth. Gods, what the fuck was this?

I went back to my chambers, slamming the door behind me and wishing I could make this entire palace disappear. I stalked the length of my room for far too long, trying to make sense of it. Trying to understand.

But there was no understanding of it. And even after I went back out into the hot sun, even after I punished my body with more training, even after the sunset and I dragged my aching body back to my chambers, I still dreamed of her.

Chapter 5

Elara

"You're trembling." Drusilla's eyes met mine in the mirror as she finished pinning my hair up into soft curls.

I looked down at my hands, which were pale and cold in my lap. I shook my head, not meeting her gaze. "I'm alright."

"What happened to the Fae who gave the king guff in a throne room full of Velesians?" Drusilla's warm hands clasped my shoulders. "Hmm? Last time you were going to meet the King you strode out of here with your head held high and now you're a quivering bundle of nerves."

"I'm fine. Really. Just tired." I gave her a weak smile, and her concerned gaze moved from my eyes to the purple bruise around my neck.

"Tired. Yes." She gave my shoulders a maternal rub, and my stomach wrenched. It took all my strength not to throw my arms around Drusilla's waist and cry into her skirts. I wanted nothing more than to have my mother hold me, to stroke my hair and tell me everything was going to be alright.

But instead I blinked away my anguish, taking a deep breath as a knock sounded at the door.

"She's coming!" Drusilla called, wringing her hands as she looked at me. "Now, if I may give you some advice - no sass. I can see that you've perhaps had the sass beaten out of you, but if you want to do what I think you're about to do, putting up a front won't get you far with the king."

I nodded, wincing at her words. "Yes, of course." I swallowed hard, trying my best to give her a confident smile but I could feel my lips trembling as I approached the door. The sass had well and truly been beaten out of me.

"The King is in the library," the guard said over his shoulder, already heading off down the cold passageway ahead of me. I fell into step behind him, rehearsing over and over in my head what I wanted to say to the king - that I no longer wished to be anywhere near Rook.

Rook. I'd dreamed of him, of course. The same heady, passionate dreams I'd had every night. He'd held me and kissed me and bitten my neck, his tongue moving over the bruise his hand had left behind in our waking hours. He'd whispered apologies and told me how perfect I was as he kissed my scars. He'd told me *You're mine* over and over again, until the words pursued me from sleep as I'd woken, sobbing into my pillow.

The Rook from my dreams and the Rook who'd tried to kill me were oceans apart.

Suddenly we were at a large double door, and the guard pushed it open, holding on to the brass handle as he jerked his head.

"In you go." He wouldn't look at me. "King's waiting for you."

I nodded my thanks and walked slowly into the library. Black shelves towered either side of me, almost reaching the cavernous ceiling, holding shelf after shelf of brightly bound books. Under normal circumstances, this room would have thrilled me. I'd have spent hours exploring, reading, marveling at the artworks and the beautiful stained-glass windows.

But today, it simply felt as though I was on a death march. Panic rang in my ears as I rounded the corner and spotted Theron sitting at a deep mahogany desk. His brow was furrowed as he inspected the papers scattered before him, and if he heard my approach, he didn't acknowledge it at all.

I moved to the edge of the desk, pausing for a moment before I dropped into a brief curtsey. *No sass. Remember your manners. Don't put up a front.*

"Your Majesty," I said quietly. "I hope I am not disturbing you."

Theron huffed out a breath, pushing the papers aside and looking up at me. "Certainly not, dear one. I am more than happy to make time for you." He looked me up and down, leaning back in his leather chair. "Are you quite well? You look rather drawn."

"I'm not sleeping well, Sire."

Theron frowned. "I'm sorry to hear that. May I be of some assistance?"

I shifted on my feet, taking a shaky breath. "I don't wish to train with Norahi anymore."

Theron's eyebrows shot up, and he rose from the chair. "Is that so? May I know the reason why?"

"He tried to kill me." I replied. I pulled aside the shawl I had slung around my shoulders, to show him the enormous purple hand mark on my neck. "He called me a witch and said he wanted to be free of me, then he tried to kill me."

Theron's lips twitched pensively as he clasped his hands behind his back. "It's a lovely room, isn't it?"

I blinked, the sudden change in topic catching me off guard. "I-I'm sorry, I don't -"

"The library." He gestured grandly around the room we found ourselves in. "It is such an inspirational space, don't you think?"

"I-I... Yes, it's lovely." My head was still swimming after Rook had slammed it into the ground the day before, the residual headache lingering. "But I don't understand what the library has to do with Norahi."

"Did you know he speaks 5 languages?" Theron opened a book, flicking absently through its pages. "The Night Demons, they're incredibly well educated. Not that you'd know it." He laughed cynically as he slammed the book shut. "Barbarians." He muttered the word so quietly I barely heard it, and his eyes narrowed as he looked back at me. "So, he tried to kill you, did he?"

"Yes."

"And how did he do this?"

I swallowed hard. "He-he slammed my head into the ground, then he tried to strangle me." I bit down on my lip as it trembled, determined not to show just how shaken I was. I'd engaged in combat before. I'd looked death in the eye plenty of times. But for some reason, being face to face with *Rook*, having him spit blood in my face as he declared his intention to end me, had shaken me so violently to my core that I could scarcely look at Theron as I recounted it. "H-he said he'd tear my head off, if he got the chance."

Theron exhaled heavily, steepling his hands before him. "Gods. You really got under his skin, didn't you?"

"I seem to have, yes."

"The guards have reported his odd behavior to me," Theron said, walking to a tall window that looked out over the neatly trimmed palace gardens that sprawled below. "Training at all hours of the morning, pacing his chambers for hours at a time. Like a caged animal." He turned, spreading his wings behind him as he leaned against the window frame. "He seems rather unraveled since you arrived."

"He -"

"Perhaps you are a witch." Theron crossed his arms over his chest. "Perhaps you have cast some horrid Fae spell on him, to drive your enemy insane."

"Rook is not my enemy." I said it too quickly, and didn't even know why. I picked at my nails, trying to find the right words. "I-I have no quarrel with him. Not directly."

Theron rolled his eyes. "Yes, you would think that."

"What do you -"

"And what did you do, in this supposed attempt on your life?" He interjected. "Did you stand idly by, or did you fight back?"

"I-I fought back." I drew in a short breath. "I mean… I thought he had the upper hand, and I…"

"You gave up." Theron finished when I would not go on, dipping his head to meet my eyes. "I'm told you begged for death."

"I'm tired, Sire." My voice cracked as I said it. "I'm tired, and I was sure he'd end me. He's so much stronger than me."

Theron's brow furrowed, and he nodded slowly. "Yes, he is, isn't he? Although I'm told you threatened to kill him, and he also welcomed death."

I blinked, shaking my head. "He-he was going to -"

"What?" Theron looked at me expectantly. "He was going to let you kill him?"

"No."

"But you were going to let him kill you?"

My head was starting to throb again. "No. I mean… No. I fought back."

"Shall I tell you what the guards observed?"

"The guards?" My voice was failing me, faltering as fast as my resolve under his withering gaze.

"Yes, the guards." His gaze darkened. "The guards told me they saw two warriors ready to tear each other limb from limb but neither took the chance when offered. This tells me you and Norahi know very well what you are doing down in that arena, that you are more than capable, and you are simply playing the part of the damsel in distress in order to gain my pity."

"He tried to kill me!" Angry tears bit at my eyes as I took two stumbling steps towards him. "He was going to -"

"He wiped your tears from your face, madam. The guards told me *everything*." He laughed, shaking his head. "I'm told he dreams of you. And that you dream of him? Is that right?"

My cheeks burned as my eyes dropped to the floor. "I don't know what you're talking about."

His footsteps thundered across the floor towards me, and his green cat eyes narrowed as he towered over me. "Do not lie to me. You said you dreamed of him, and he of you, is that so?"

"I dreamed he tried to kill me." It wasn't a lie. I had dreamed he'd torn my throat out… Hadn't I? His teeth had been on my throat… He'd tried to kill me in *that* dream. I clenched my eyes shut as I tried to remember. "I dreamed-"

"I don't care," Theron said, and I opened my eyes to meet his again. "Are you strong enough to face him again?"

My throat went dry. I didn't want to admit any weakness. I didn't want, under any circumstances, to let Rook know he'd won. That he'd scared me off. Because Theron clearly didn't care enough about my life to ward off a demon who meant to end it. Of course he didn't. I was a fucking fool.

When I didn't respond, Theron lifted an eyebrow, turning

away from me to walk over to a low, round upon which a chess set was laid out. He picked up the ivory Queen, turning the piece in his fingers. "Do you play, madam?"

"I do." When his eyes flickered to mine, I cleared my throat. "I mean, I do, Sire."

"Then you know how games are played. If you do not guard yourself, and do not put the pieces into motion, then you give your enemy an in." He put the Queen down in the center of the board and turned back to face me. "If you tell me you are too weak to face Norahi, then I will find you another guard to fight. And I will be sure to let Norahi know that within these walls, there is a little Fae Princess whose fear makes her an easy target for his rage." He blindly reached behind him, and flicked the ivory Queen to the floor, where the piece rolled in aimless circles. "*Or...*" He walked towards me, cocking his head. "You face Norahi in that arena, and continue to show him that you are not afraid of him, and allow him to prepare you for what lies ahead. Because believe me, dear one, he is the least of your worries right now."

I took in a shuddering breath, my hands clasped so hard my fingertips were going numb. "Are you threatening me, Sire?"

He gave me a crooked smile. "Oh no, I would never dream of it. I am merely *challenging* you. Are you up for it?"

The chess piece came to a stop against the leg of a chair. I looked at it, lying on its side, unmoving. This was a game to him. Nothing more than a game. I needed to guard myself before one of his pieces charged across the board and claimed me.

I squared my shoulders, looking him in the eye. "I am, Sire. Forgive my intrusion."

The corner of his mouth quirked, and he was clearly proud of himself. "Always a pleasure to see you, madam."

I bowed my head, and turned to walk out of the library.

"Do let me know how training goes!" Theron called after me, and I took a deep breath as I thought of facing Rook in that arena again.

He groaned underneath me. "That's my girl. Fuck, that's it."

I rode him harder, my climax building so intensely it almost hurt. "Rook, I'm going to -"

"Come for me. Good girl." His thumb circled my clit. "Come on my cock, that's it."

I woke up shuddering, the blanket clenched between my thighs as I ground my hips against the bed. My climax shattered through me, and I moaned into my pillow. I was panting, drenched in sweat, and the overwhelming feeling of lips and teeth and fingertips all of my body lingered.

The early light of the dawn was coloring the sky outside, and I rolled onto my back, trying to breathe, trying to blink away the image of Rook beneath me. *Fucking monster.* Tears of rage bit at my eyes. I'd never once been told that a Night Demon could do this, that they had the power to invade your very dreams and assault you while you slept.

The tears fell harder as my body subsided, because it didn't fucking *feel* like an assault. I hated how good he made me feel in these dreams. I hated that the Rook of my dreams was a generous lover who drove my body to peaks of desire that left the heat of his body branded on my skin when I woke. These dreams felt so real, *he* felt so fucking *real.* I wanted to be free of him. I just wanted this all to end.

The door to Drusilla's chamber opened, and I buried my

face in my pillow, feigning sleep so she wouldn't see my flushed face. She moved quietly about the room, stoking the fire and opening the windows to let in the fresh morning air. I rolled over slowly, my breathing finally steady.

Drusilla smiled at me as she approached the bedside. "Good morning, my lamb. Did you sleep well?"

I shook my head. "Bad dreams."

"Oh dear, I am sorry. I'll have the healer make you a calming tea, to drink before bed. It will do you good."

Will it make me immune to demon curses? "Yes, thank you, that would be wonderful." I pushed back the covers and sat up, rubbing my face. I glanced out the window, at the rising sun. "More training today, then."

Drusilla tutted disapprovingly. "I spoke to Regan, and said you and Rook should be kept away from each other. He said he couldn't go against the King's orders."

"It's alright, I can handle Rook." I swung my legs over the side of the bed, my toes curling a little as they hit the cold floor.

"You can *not*," Drusilla said with a scoff. "He almost killed you both times you faced him."

"I almost had him last time." I gave her a weak smile. "He doesn't want to kill me"

Drusilla let out a throaty laugh. "Oh no? Then what is he trying to do?"

"He just wants to scare me."

"And you?" She raised her eyebrows. "What are you hoping to do in all of this?"

"I-I don't know." I walked to the basin and washed my face in the cool water. I let the droplets run off my cheeks, falling back into the basin, my reflection swimming in the ripples. "I don't know what I feel towards him. He makes me *angry*. He's so full of hatred."

Drusilla sighed heavily, and handed me a linen cloth to dry up. "He and your family are enemies, he shouldn't take that out on you."

"In matters of war, there is no gray, Drusilla." I gave a short laugh. "Only black and white. Rook sees my kin as his enemies, therefore I am his enemy."

"It's ridiculous." Drusilla ushered me to the stool in front of the dressing table, and began winding my hair up into braids on top of my head. "He has no business beating the living shi-I mean, the spit out of a *princess*."

"The king assured me that Rook is the least of my worries," I told her, and her amber eyes flashed with alarm as they met mine in the mirror.

She shook her head, and forced a smile onto her face. "Come now, let's get you all ready for your day, it's going to be hot again, I can feel it." On cue, thunder rumbled in the distance, and dark clouds began to gather on the horizon as Drusilla helped me into my camisole and leathers.

A maid brought me breakfast, and she stared at my scars and missing ear openly, her mouth falling open in shock. I held her gaze, and Drusilla slapped her over the back of the head before sending her out of the room with a string of curses in a language I didn't understand.

"Sorry, Your Highness," Drusilla said, sitting down at the table opposite me and pouring me a steaming cup of strong-smelling tea. "These young girls from the flatlands, they come here and have never seen the world and have no manners at all."

"I'd noticed Theron doesn't have any Seraph in his service." I spread honey onto my bread, allowing myself a small moment of pleasure when my teeth tore through the crust. Bread had never tasted this good back in Peyrus.

Drusilla sighed heavily and poured her own tea. "Yes, he

does have a very strong sense of hierarchy. He believes in the superiority of the Seraph race."

I rolled my eyes. "I'm sure he does."

"Most of the servants are Cinder Elves or half-Seraph offspring, brought here by the soldiers." Drusilla leaned back in her chair and stretched her tanned arms over her head, adjusting the rusty brown turban that held her curly brown hair on top of her head. "I'm part Cinder Elf myself, my father was a Seraph general."

My eyebrows shot up in surprise. "What's the daughter of a Seraph general doing as lady's maid in the palace?"

Drusilla laughed. "Oh my lamb, believe me, being a Cinder Elf weighs more heavily than who my father was."

I drank my tea, thinking back on everything I knew about the Cinder Elves. They had been almost wiped out during the Uprising, a peaceful race of forest dwellers. *The little brown tree people*, my mother had called them. They lived in Jerindos, beyond the Yuairan mountains, far away from Peyrus. They'd been drawn into the Uprising and had paid the price dearly, much like the Malakh and the Night Demons.

The Night Demons. I suppressed a groan as I thought of Rook, and then my cheeks fucking burned as *I thought of Rook*.

Drusilla's eyebrows flicked with concern as she looked over her tea cup at me. "Everything alright?"

I nodded. "Just preparing myself for more pain today." Before Drusilla could express any more concern or make me any more uneasy about my skills in the arena, I pushed away from the table and rose to my feet. "Anyway, I should go down and warm up before Rook graces me with his presence."

"Elara -" Drusilla got to her feet.

"It's alright." I cut her off quickly, pulling on my boots. "Really. I just need to get down there and move. I'll feel much better for it."

Three harsh raps on the door, and a guard opened it for me. With a jerk of his head, he gestured for me to leave the room, and I walked the now-familiar path through the passageways down to the training arena. My heart was pummeling my ribcage, and I huffed out a curse at myself. *Stay fucking calm.*

When I reached the training arena, it was mercifully quiet. I let out a heavy sigh of relief. I needed to gather myself before I faced him again. I laughed bitterly at myself - this was his intention. That was why he was doing this. Gods, I was so *stupid.* He was hoping to muddle my head with ridiculous dreams of him, because that was the only way he knew how to handle a female. *Idiot.*

My heart continued to buzz in my chest, humming with warmth, and I ran my hand over it, almost expecting the heat to be palpable. It felt strange, yet familiar. My heart jumped suddenly, hammering against my palm, and I spun around to see Rook crossing the training arena towards me.

"Good morning," I said.

He scoffed. "Is it?" He stopped halfway, tilting his head back a little as he narrowed his eyes at me. "That's what you like, is it?"

I shook my head. "What are you talking about?"

"These fucking dreams, little Fae." He crossed his arms over his chest. "Is that what you desire of me, is it? To eat that fucking cunt of yours, hmm?"

My cheeks flushed so violently that my mouth went dry. "I don't desire anything of you." I almost sounded sure. I almost *felt* sure. I didn't like the feelings that coursed through my belly at his words.

"I told you what would happen if you didn't stay out of my head, witch." He stalked to the wooden rack against the wall, and heaved his ax from the stand. He pointed it at me as he approached me. "I warned you, and you didn't listen."

"I fucking told you, I'm not *in* your head." I backed away from him, holding up my hands. "I'm unarmed, and you're going to attack me?"

"I want to kill you, you fucking little witch. Why would I want you armed?"

Thunder rumbled overhead as he rushed at me, and I leapt out of the reach of his ax, rolling across the hard ground. I lurched up into a crouch as Rook spun on me, his ax whirring through the air as he ran at me. I was only a few feet from the rack holding all manner of weapons, but he moved faster than I was expecting. I wouldn't reach it in time.

I sprang over his flying weapon, and laced my fingers under his chin, flinging myself onto his back. I wrenched him backwards, but he was ready for me and threw himself down, crushing me under him. All the air was pressed out of my body, and my lungs rasped loudly as I tried to suck in a breath.

He tried to get up, but I regained enough of my senses to slam my still-interlocked fingers into his throat, surprising him enough to roll away from me. I half-crawled across the ground into a sprint, his hand brushing against my ankle as he tried to grab me and haul me back to him.

I made it to the rack, pulling a sword from it, swinging it around to face him just in time to see the ax flying through the air towards me, glinting in the sunlight. The flat of the blade caught me in the torso, and I was sent back into the dirt on my back. Rook pursued me immediately, arcing the ax towards me.

It came to a stop right at my throat. Rook's chest was heaving as he leered down at me, breathing through his gritted teeth. "And, you're dead. Again."

"So are you."

He looked down to see my sword pointed at his stomach, the barest whisper of the blade against his skin. His eyes met mine, that glowing iridescent blue boring right into me, as though he could see into my very being.

"Go on, then." His mouth set in a hard line, his jaw feathering violently.

I pressed the blade against him, feeling the resistance of his flesh. My heart was hammering in my chest.

"*Go on.*" The challenge in his voice gave me goosebumps.

"Why do you want to kill me, Rook?"

His eyes widened at the question, catching him off guard. He quickly drew his eyebrows together again. "Your kind are traitors, liars, and thieves."

"Why do you want to kill *me*, Rook?"

We stared at each other for what felt like an age, our weapons still trained on each other.

"I want you out of my head." Rook's voice was low, his chest still pounding as he drew breath. "I want you gone. Since you got here, since you walked into this fucking palace-"

"I was dragged here, just like you."

"Nothing like me!" He bellowed.

"I'm a captive, just like you." I held his gaze, and lowered my sword. His eyes flickered downward for a moment, noting the movement, and then flashed back up to mine, pressing the blade of his ax harder into my throat. "Are you going to kill me now?"

His eyes widened with rage. "Yes."

The humming in my chest was so loud now, my jaw began to tremble along with it. I put a hand on his chest, over his heart. "Then do it."

He cried out as though I'd burned him, staggering away from me. He put a hand to where I'd touched him, looking down as though he expected to see a mark. His wild eyes moved back to me.

"What the fuck did you do to me?"

I pushed myself up on my hands slowly. "I did nothing."

"You stay the fuck away from me." He pointed the ax at me again. "You- you fucking *witch*, you stay the fuck away from me, do you understand?"

"You're in my dreams, and I am in yours." I got to my feet, his eyes fixed on my every move. "And we both say we're not doing it to one another."

Rook scoffed, and spat into the dirt. "Why would I want to have dreams like that about *you*? A fucking traitorous fucking Fae bitch?"

"And you believe I'd want to dream such things about you?" I took a step towards him. "You could have killed me, and you chose not to."

"And I could say the same for you." He lowered the ax, letting the head butt into the ground with a soft thump. "I told you to, I *challenged* you to, you coward, and-"

"You don't want to kill me."

He jerked back a little. "What?"

"You don't want to kill me, any more than I want to kill you."

I became aware of the guards at the perimeter of the training yard, leaning on their spears, watching us intently. They would convey every word of this conversation back to Theron. Rook sneered at me, as though coming up with a snide remark to throw my way, but then his face dissolved into something else, something I couldn't quite read. He rolled his shoulders, averting his eyes, lifting the ax and swinging it onto his shoulder.

"You swear you're not casting a spell on me?"

I shook my head. "No. I wouldn't even know how. I-I can't

do that." I paused for a moment, watching him shift on his feet. "And you?"

"Me what?"

"You're not -"

"No," he snapped, and his eyes met mine again. "All those stories, they're all lies. I don't do that. I've *never* done that."

"I believe you."

He snorted. "I don't really fucking care if you do." He gestured around us. "My father did not abandon me to this. My father is *nothing* like yours. Do you understand?"

"I understand."

"And you and I are nothing alike." He swallowed hard, and he huffed out a breath. "You know nothing about me, and I don't want to know anything about you. We train, *here*, and that's all. That is *all*, do you understand?"

I nodded. I clenched my hand, the one I'd lain on his chest, at the same time as he put a hand over his heart, rubbing as though trying to erase a stain. He shook his head, and without another word he strode from the arena, hurling his weapon into the wooden rack on his way.

I watched him leave, the feeling of his skin burning on my hand and that humming in my chest getting louder and louder.

Chapter 6

Rook

The laughter of the war council tore me from my thoughts. I looked around the room, at the self-aggrandising shoulder claps and indulgent smiles of the Seraph generals, at Theron's own smug grin, and wondered what joke I had missed.

Theron's eyes landed on me, and he grinned. "What do you have to say about it, Rook?"

I cleared my throat, leaning forward on the table. "I beg your pardon, Sire, what were you saying?"

The room broke into guffaws again.

Theron lifted an eyebrow. "Where are you, my friend? You seem eons away at the moment."

"I am sorry, Sire, the heat, it's, uh, making it hard to sleep."

"The heat." He scoffed. "Yes, the *heat*." More guffaws around me. "I would have trouble sleeping too if I had that Fae Princess pinned under me every day."

"What?" I snapped too quickly, and the council was stunned into silence. *Shit*. Of course Theron didn't know about my dreams, that's not what he meant. I was becoming paranoid. Gods, I needed to calm down. "I'm so sorry, Sire, I'm somewhat agitated."

Theron snapped his fingers, his eyes staying on me. "Wine for my friend."

A servant rushed forward with a goblet of wine, placing it in front of me with a curt nod. I gulped it down, hating the dry, bitter taste of the pig swill Velesians called wine, but hoping the alcohol would calm my nerves enough that I could function again.

Satisfied that I was doing as I was told, Theron spread his wings, leaning back in the oversized oak chair at the head of the long table, and drummed his fingers on its surface. "What I was saying was, the Princess is rather pleasing on the eyes."

"Even deformed as she is." One of the council members leaned towards his neighbor and muttered the words furtively, but loud enough for us to hear.

"Watch your mouth." Theron and I regarded each other with surprise as soon as the words left our mouths. He laughed jovially after a moment.

"Become protective of her, have we?" His smile dissolved as his gaze settled back on the offending council member. "Speak of the Princess like that again and I will have you deposed and claim your lands, do you understand?"

The council members tittered nervously, anxious to show their solidarity with the King, and I took another hefty gulp of wine. *Fucking Fae.* Now I was here defending her, to the council. She had sounded so sincere when she had said she couldn't cast any magic. And I had no reason to doubt her - I knew the Fae magic was old and weak. They'd lost their wings centuries ago. Their numbers had dwindled until their kind was reduced to nothing but a tiny kingdom in Peyrus. She shouldn't have been able to cast a spell on me.

And yet…

I ran a hand over my chest, where that warmth remained, clutching my heart in a fist of glowering embers. When she'd touched me there, her hand splayed on my skin, it had been like lightning.

The most beautiful lightning I'd ever felt. Warm and sweet, almost soothing in its suddenness.

I took down another gulp of wine, the chatter of the council members once again fading as my thoughts engulfed me.

I'd accepted my fate long ago. I'd been Theron's thug, his assassin, his loyal servant for all these years, without question. There was no point in questioning. I was a slave. Nothing more.

And now, the creeping feeling of renewal had washed over me, and I could feel myself becoming addicted to it. Elara's touch had been like the first cool morning after a summer of unbearable heat. The first sip of water after a day spent under the punishing sun. I could still feel the warmth of her body, unsure now whether it was the specter of my dreams haunting me into my waking hours, or whether it was the memory of her against me as she fought to stay alive in that training arena.

And of course, she was right.

I didn't want to kill her. The final swing of my ax towards her throat had been the last stumbling step into an abyss I'd never navigated before. Seeing the terror in her eyes had caused me physical pain. And then a little voice crept into my mind, repeating that singular thought over and over until my skull had throbbed - *I never want her to be afraid of me again.*

I chewed my lip, staring at the dull surface of the table before me, tracing the wood grain with my eyes. Like a map that led nowhere. Like the very one I was trying to traverse now. It wasn't possible for me to feel anything for her. I didn't want it to be.

But even as the council laughed heartily around me, even as my head began to swim as I held up my goblet for a second glass of wine, I knew it - I was in deep shit. The second I had laid eyes on her in that throne room, watching me drag the serpent's head towards her, when I'd seen those scars on her face that told me she was a warrior who would never run from a fight - I'd already known then I was done for.

And it wasn't just that she was beautiful. She was, of course. Delicate, regal, tall and lithe, soft golden hair that I wanted to bury my face in. She smelled wonderful, I was sure of it. Her face had felt like silk under my thumb the day I'd chased away that stray tear. Her beauty was one thing - but the overwhelming possessiveness I felt for her was another.

Oh fucking Gods, Rook. What have you done?

I pushed myself away from the table with a groan, unable to stand the sheer volume of the banter and laughter surrounding me. War council meetings - they were a joke. They always descended into men speaking dirty fantasies about the maids and nothing more. I walked out onto the balcony, looking out over the gardens, bathed in warm golden light as the sun crept slowly to rest behind the mountains.

I needed to get away from her. Even though the thought of not seeing her would cause me pain, I had to get away from her. The thought of touching her, even in combat, was too much. I'd tumble further and further into this abyss, into this chasm of longing.

And the last thing I wanted was to long for a Fae.

"Problems, Rook?" Theron's voice sounded behind me, languid footsteps approaching me.

I leaned on the railing and exhaled heavily. "Just… trying to gather my thoughts, Sire."

"Mmm." Theron came to stop beside me, his gaze sweeping out over the gardens below. "You seem rather undone since the Princess arrived, my friend. Is it bad memories?" He gave me a sideways glance. "Or something else you'd rather not give a voice to?"

"I don't want to train with her anymore." I said it quickly, biting out the words before my ridiculous heart could pull them back down my throat and bury them.

Theron laughed, lifting an eyebrow as he turned to face me. "You know, she told me the exact same thing."

"She did?"

Theron nodded. "It seems neither one of you feels the other is a suitable training partner."

"She's weak."

"No, she's not." Theron's response came like the snap of a whip.

"I'm going to hurt her." I was scrambling for an excuse now.

"You haven't so far."

Fucking Nav, why was he doing this. "Sire, I cannot -"

"She lost her Mate." Theron's gaze remained neutral as I met it. With a subtle lift of his eyebrows, he took another sip of wine and sighed lightly. "He was dead in her arms when the Riders found her."

My throat constricted, and the whirlwind of emotions in my belly combined with drinking too much of that fucking wine had me sucking in a sharp breath. "I had no idea."

"It would seem she fought her way across the battlefield to die alongside him." Theron sounded almost admiring. "She took down one Seraph after another without hesitation, and then she held him in her arms, welcoming death."

"That's how she got those scars?" *Fierce little Fae*. I had to suppress a smile. Oh Gods, I was fucking *proud* of her now.

Theron swirled the goblet in his hand, looking back out over the gardens. "Yes, she lost the ear to one of my own soldiers. But he lost his life to her blade."

"I see." I didn't know what else to say. I was overcome with a feeling of shame and guilt. *I'm just like you.* And she was, in a way she didn't even know or understand. And I'd mocked her, chided her, told her we were nothing alike.

"Are you still dreaming of her?" Theron asked, gazing absently into his goblet.

I tried not to let my surprise show. "How did you know about that?"

"The guards informed me of your… disagreement with the Princess. It seems you are both dreaming of the other and convinced some wicked magic is at play." He grinned at me, his green eyes dancing, clearly enjoying this game of his. "You are sure she is a witch sent to ensorcel you, and she is certain you are nothing but a vicious Night Demon straight from the nightmarish tales of her girlhood."

I clenched my teeth. "They are just dreams."

"Indeed." Theron looked up at the darkening sky. "Perhaps now you know that she has more in common with you than you could have ever supposed. You will find it within yourself to be a little kinder to the Princess. Nav knows she is going to need all the help she can get."

Anger prickled at the back of my neck, souring my tongue. "What do you have planned for her?"

Theron clapped me on the shoulder, giving me an amicable smile. "Oh, just a little fun. Sometimes, females need motivation to realize which path they should choose."

The wicked glint in his eyes made my skin crawl. With a swish of his wings he swept back into the council chamber, leaving me alone on the balcony.

I waited only a few more minutes before I made my

excuses and sought a quieter place to clear my head and think about how I was going to dig myself out of the situation I'd been forced into.

I shouldn't feel anything for her. I *couldn't.*

But I did.

Back in my chamber I threw open the windows, letting in the evening air that was finally turning cool after another stifling summer's day. I undressed, my clothes suddenly feeling like a yoke around my neck, and washed myself down with cool water from the basin.

Theron's words played over and over in my mind. Nav knows she is going to need all the help she can get.

I knew better than anyone just how twisted Theron was, the depths he was willing to trawl in order to hurt, bend, and break. I'd heard enough terrified screams, seen enough acts performed in his name, to know that whatever he was going to do to Elara was going to be terrible.

But I also knew that he underestimated folk too easily, and something told me Elara would shock him at every turn.

Elara.

I hung my head, raking my hands through my hair. Fucking Gods, what had this female done to me? I couldn't describe the strange sense of relief I felt knowing I'd see her again. Knowing that I'd be in that training arena with her. It wasn't necessarily that knowing of her Mate's death had softened me further - no, I was already drowning too deeply in the abyss for that - but it somehow reassured me that I had tried to get away. That I had *tried* to distance myself.

And I'd failed. If Theron pushed us together like this, then it was beyond my power to fight it.

The image of her holding her Mate, wailing as he died in her arms, made me both mournful and envious. Mournful, for so many reasons, and most of them I didn't want to acknowledge.

And envious because I was a fucking lunatic over a dead Fae who'd been the last male to hold her in his arms, to kiss her lips. I was a fool. The deep simmering heat in my chest leapt like a flame, up my throat, and was accompanied by the strangest, yet most comforting thought I'd had in a long time - *She's mine.*

I grunted out my frustration as I pushed myself away from the basin. I was becoming possessive over a female I'd just tried to kill. I was having jealous thoughts of her dead Mate. And I felt something else. Something even more terrifying.

I *cared* for her.

That night, I surrendered to the dreams when they inevitably came. I relished every second in that state, feeling her skin, tasting her sweat, biting that silky flesh as she moaned and writhed underneath me.

And when I woke in the morning, for the first time in years, it was with a smile on my lips.

Because I would see her.

Chapter 7

Rook

The sun was already high in the sky by the time Elara appeared in the training arena. I felt her presence before I saw her, a prickling warmth on my shoulders that felt nothing like sunlight. When I turned to face her, she'd stopped a few feet away from me, her expression unreadable.

"Hello."

I bowed my head briefly. "Hello, princess."

She raised an eyebrow, and opened her mouth to speak, but quickly closed it again and shook her head. "We're here to train, aren't we?" She strode over to the weapons, pulling down two swords. When I didn't respond she stalked back towards me, and threw one of the swords to me. "That's what you said, isn't it? We're training, and nothing more."

"I did say that." I spun the hilt of the sword in my hand, settling its weight in my hand, keeping my eyes on her. "Elara-"

"Come on, then." She raised her weapon, ready to attack, waiting for me to be ready. "That's what you said."

I took a step towards her, my hand raised, but she swung for me, and I was forced to deflect her blade. She didn't let up, coming at me again and again. She didn't want to talk. She was adhering to the exact warning I had issued her the last time we met. Warnings that I no longer cared for.

"Elara-"

My words were cut off by yet another parry, another attack, and Gods, she was moving quickly. I could see now exactly what Theron had meant when he said she wasn't weak. I could see now how she'd made her way across that battlefield. She was a skilled fighter.

"Elara, wait." Our blades were joined, hers holding mine in a vice grip, and her eyes were almost wild when they met mine. "I'm sorry about what I-"

She spun the blade and released me, backing away from me. "You said you didn't want to talk."

"I was wrong."

She scoffed, and ran a hand across her brow, where tiny beads of sweat glimmered in the sunlight. "We're here to train, so let's train."

"It doesn't have to be like this." I lowered my sword and raised my hand again. "I'm sorry, I was wrong. I was too harsh with you. I didn't know..."

"Didn't know what?" Both hands were back on the hilt of her sword, and she eyed me with something akin to distrust.

"I didn't know about your Mate."

She dropped her sword as though it had suddenly become a flame in her hand, and clutched a hand to her stomach. Her mouth set in a hard line as her head fell back, and she took a deep breath. "I thought you didn't want to know anything about me." She turned away from me, her shoulders hunched.

"Theron told me." I approached her back slowly.

She glanced over her shoulder at me and laughed bitterly. "So, you thought you'd find it within yourself to stop trying to kill me, because I'm in mourning? How big of you Rook."

Her words stung, but I kept moving towards her. "You said we were the same. And I rejected that idea. But you're right. We are. I was just too jaded to acknowledge it." I reached her side, and wanted nothing more than to put a hand on her shoulder, but her eyes were blazing when they flashed up to mine, shining with tears, and I knew that touching her at that moment would probably just end up with me getting a black eye or a blade in my stomach. Instead, I gave her a sympathetic smile. "I'm so sorry you lost him."

Her face crumpled, and her shoulders began to shake. She put a hand over her mouth, and I wanted to take her into my arms so fucking badly.

"Losing a Mate must be -"

"Stop calling him that," she snapped, her voice cracking as she inhaled sharply.

"Stop calling him what?"

"Mate." She dashed her wrist against her eyes. "I hate that word."

I shook my head. "Why?"

"Because I'm not a fucking animal!" She rounded on me and shoved me in the chest. "I don't *mate.*" Another shove to my chest. "I don't *breed.* I'm not a fu-fucking ani-" She broke off as she shoved me weakly, one last time, and fell to her knees. She cradled her head in her trembling hands, and let out something like a howl.

I dropped to my knees in front of her. "I meant no offense, I'm so sorry."

She turned away from me, sniffling. "It doesn't fucking matter. Just leave it."

I sat in the dirt beside her for an age, not sure what to say, watching her shoulders shake and listening to her sniffle as she tried not to cry. Finally, she looked over her shoulder at me, her eyes red-rimmed.

"Do you have any idea what it was like to lose him and then have those - those dreams of you?" Her lip quivered. "I had *just lost him*, and then I was… I was dreaming of you, of doing those things with *you*."

"Elara-"

"I wake up soaked in your scent." Her voice took on an edge of hysteria, splintering at the edges as tears threatened to break over those thick black lashes. "I can *smell* you, everywhere, that's how… That's…" She broke off as her breath hitched in her throat, shaking her head.

"I promise you, that wasn't me." I reached out without thinking, and took her hand. She flinched for a split second, but didn't try to pull it away. "I swear to you, it wasn't me. And I'm so sorry for it." I was overcome with shame. I'd woken that morning, smiling after dreaming of her, while she'd no doubt been wracked with guilt.

I moved closer to her, and her brow furrowed. But she didn't look frightened. Gods, she wasn't afraid of me. I tightened my hand around hers.

"I have a feeling you're about to get some bad news," I told her quietly, "and I want to assure you I'll do whatever I can to help you."

"Bad news?" Her eyes widened a little. "What do you mean?"

"Whatever Theron has planned for you." My eyes flicked around us, at the guards, then back to her. "But you're strong, and you're fast, and I think you'll shock the ever-living shit out of him."

Her eyebrows lifted for a moment, and then her face broke

into a smile. She covered her face with her free hand, laughing breathlessly. "You think that, do you?"

"I know it." I returned her smile as she raised her gaze back to me.

"I thought you hated me." Her smile changed to a crooked grin, and she pushed the hair out of her face. "You're being rather amicable towards someone you hate."

"I don't hate you, Elara." I shrugged when she regarded me with surprise. "I thought I did. But I don't."

"All this because you found out Keir died?"

I shook my head. "No. It's more than that." I realized I was leaning closer to her, her face only inches from mine. Her surprise had dissolved into curiosity, and her fingers shifted in my hand, reminding me I was still clutching them tightly. I caught myself, clearing my throat and straightening a little. "Come on now, we're going to get you ready. Not that you need much help." I rose to my feet and pulled her up with me.

She bumped into me a little as we stood, and her blue eyes fixed on me for a moment. She lifted her hand, as though to touch me, and I readied myself for that lightning, that sweet sharp sensation of her hand on my chest.

But instead she balled that hand into a fist, and let it drop. She averted her eyes, and nodded.

"Alright then, Rook. Let's train."

It wasn't much. But it was something.

Theron regarded me with a grin as he stripped off his armor, dismissing his sparring partner with a wave of his hand. He stretched his wings wide at the same time as his arms, and gestured for me to leave my place at the edge of the training room.

"Well, my friend, how are things?" He asked, running a hand through his sweat-soaked hair.

I nodded, my hands in my pockets. "Good. She's doing extremely well."

Theron quirked an eyebrow. "I find it incredible how you assume I meant her."

"I simply thought you wanted an update on her training." I rolled my shoulders, clasping my hands behind my back.

Theron sighed. "Go on then."

"She's doing exceedingly well. I can't say I'm not surprised. I never expected her to be so…"

"So?" Theron repeated when I did not continue. "So, what? So unlike all the other Fae you have ever known?"

I cleared my throat. "I suppose so, yes."

He threw back his head and laughed, clapping me on the shoulder and jovially shoving me towards a table where servants were pouring out water and wine. "You seem rather taken with her."

"She's a Fae, Sire. I have no interest in her beyond training her." The lie made my tongue feel as heavy as lead.

Theron took a huge gulp of water, pouring the rest of the contents of the cup over his head, shaking the droplets out of his hair with a heavy exhale. "Mmm, yes you said that you don't find the Fae attractive." He ran a hand over his face. "But *she* is rather extraordinary, don't you think?"

"Her skill and bravery are to be admired." I grabbed a goblet of wine, and Gods, I was drinking too much, but my nerves were on edge under Theron's gaze.

Theron guffawed, crossing his arms over his chest. "Would you stop being so fucking stoic and be a male for once? Come on, even you aren't immune to her charms if you've been having dreams about her." He leaned in, lowering his voice conspiratorially. "What do you think she'd be like in bed?"

I had to swallow down the words *Don't you fucking talk about her like that* swiftly with another gulp of wine. I shrugged casually. "She's probably the kind to just lie there and not do a great deal."

Theron laughed loudly. "Do you really think so? A warrior like her?"

I clenched my teeth together as heat flooded my face. In my dreams she certainly didn't just lie there and take it. In my dreams she was fucking extraordinary. Theron was regarding me with a lifted eyebrow, and I cleared my throat quickly.

"The battlefield and the bedroom are hardly one and the same."

"No, I suppose not." Theron rubbed his chin thoughtfully. "But a female like that, I have no doubt that with some proper training she'd be, well, she'd be a lot of fun."

I suppressed a growl. "Training?"

"I wonder if she's pure." Theron snapped his fingers, and a servant hurriedly placed a goblet in his waiting hand. "What a prize *that* would be."

I was becoming increasingly incensed, and shifted on my feet. "Indeed."

Theron's eyes fell on me again, and his lips turned up into a grin. "You, my friend, are tense. You need some relief."

"I don't know what you-"

"Come now." He clapped an arm around my shoulders and guided me out of the training room. A servant appeared at his side with a shirt, which Theron draped over his arm, continuing down the passageway in only his black trousers. "I have had some distraction ordered to my chambers, and I'd like you to come and partake."

The servants threw open the doors to the foreroom of

Theron's wing to a scene of wild debauchery. The darkened room was lit with candles, and members of Theron's council were everywhere, surrounded by females in tight dresses that left nothing to the imagination. Theron's vizier was already under the ample thighs of a female Elf on the red velvet couch as we passed, and Theron laughed out loud.

"This is what you need," he said, gesturing around the room. His green eyes were blazing when they met mine. "I do wonder how an Elf cunt compares to a Fae's."

I swallowed hard, and all I could think of was my dreams. I averted my eyes, as though Theron would have been able to read those visions straight from my fucking eyeballs.

"I-I don't think there's much difference, is there?" I attempted to sound jovial. "A cunt is a cunt."

Theron laughed out loud, throwing his head back. "A cunt is a cunt indeed." He punched me lightly in the arm and raised his eyebrows. "Go, have fun." He seized a buxom black-haired Elf in his arms, who squealed delightedly as his hands encircled her waist. He dragged her off into a dark corner, and I was left alone in the middle of the room, watching the scene unfold around me.

A few weeks ago, this would have been welcome to me. I would have surrendered to it and thought nothing more of it. I would have enjoyed every scandalous moment.

Now, my head was swimming as soon as I caught sight of a head of blonde hair, my head snapping in its direction as I stupidly wondered if it was her. *Of course it fucking well isn't.*

A servant passed me with a tray of tiny glasses, holding the ridiculously strong liquor the Seraph favored, the name of which always eluded me. I grabbed two and threw them back, sucking in a breath through gritted teeth because fucking Gods, it was strong. I was instantly overcome with a warm haze, the room becoming a little fuzzy.

Arms were around my waist then, soft lips moving over my back, fingers tracing into the collar of my shirt.. I glanced over my shoulder, and my breath caught in my throat as I saw the blonde head of hair again. Hands moved over my hips, into the waistband of my pants.

"Shall I make you feel good?" The voice wasn't hers, but it didn't matter. She tightened her grip around me, guiding me towards the darkness, and I let her. I turned around to look at her, my back flush with the wall, and in the dim light I took her in. Her skin was darker than Elara's, and her eyes were the wrong color. But it didn't matter. Here, in the haze of alcohol and the darkness of the corner, I could pretend.

I spun her around, and then pushed her against the wall, her back to me as she writhed under my grasp. I threaded my fingers through that blonde hair, pulling her head back to bite the delicate skin at the base of her neck. She let out a little squeak of surprise, her hands behind her as she tried to free my cock from my trousers.

I ran my tongue over her skin, soothing the bite. She was pulling her skirt up, and I eagerly helped her. Her head fell back against my chest as my fingers moved between her thighs.

"Is that good?" I asked as my finger began to stroke her clit.

She nodded against my chest. "Mmmm." She turned her head, seeking out my mouth, which I quickly avoided, sinking my lips into the flesh of her shoulder. She finally managed to undo my trousers, my cock pressed against her ass. I groaned as I felt the heat of her cunt, so fucking close.

She gasped a little, her hand wrapping around the base of my cock."Ooh, you're huge aren't you?"

I didn't want to speak. I clenched my eyes shut, and then all I saw was Elara. The slope of her back, beads of sweat running down her pale skin. Her ass, pink and tender from the strike of my hand that had left her moaning and begging for more.

"Fuck me, My Lord." The Elf's voice was ragged with desire, teetering on the edge of her climax as my finger continued to stroke her. "Oh please, fuck me."

Rook, please. Please fuck me. Elara's voice drowned out the Elf's, her scent overwhelming me. *Oh gods, I need you. Please. I need you.*

"Oh fuck." The Elf's shriek shattered through the fantasy that had me grinding my hips against her. I was panting, sweat running down the back of my neck.

I put my hand over hers on the wall, leaning my forehead against the back of her head, against that soft blonde hair... And with a heavy sigh I realized I didn't want this. I didn't want her. I didn't want *her*.

I stopped my movements, and she held her breath, tensing a little against me.

"My Lord?" She tried to turn to look at me, but my body was still holding her in place. "Why did you stop? What's wrong with you?"

I let go of her, pulling her dress down as she protested. I ignored her words, adjusting my own clothing and striding from Theron's chambers, my eyes fixed on the floor. I left the laughter, the moans and the drunkenness behind me, my hands aching from being balled into fists at my side.

I was shaking by the time I was back in my chambers. A ribbon of heat had wound itself around my ribs, and now that I was alone, it pulled tight. Every time I closed my eyes, every time I fucking blinked, images of Elara flashed and stuttered behind my eyelids. I sank on to my bed, trying to steady my breathing, scraping my hands along my thighs as I attempted to regain some sense of equilibrium.

As night fell, the tension began to ebb from my body. The moon shone through the window, casting beacons of light along the stone floor. Finally, I was able to move again, and I walked to the window, looking out over the gardens. The lights of the town twinkled in the distance. The tips of the mountains were illuminated in the moonlit night sky.

The southern star shone brightly, pointing towards home. *What do I do?* I asked desperately. *What can I do?*

The night did not answer, merely left me alone with my thoughts and my fantasies and the coil of heat that continued to snake its way around my ribs.

This was going to drive me mad.

Chapter 8

Elara

"How is training going?" Theron asked me, his eyes staying on me as we were served our supper.

I shifted in my seat, the tight bodice of my lilac dress pressing into my ribs. They still bore a bruise from where Rook had blind-sided me with his ax, and breathing was a little painful. Especially in these dresses that Theron continued to insist I be dressed in every day.

"It's going well, I suppose." I replied, nodding to the servant who filled my goblet with wine.

"Rook tells me you're a rather formidable fighter," Theron said with a level of enthusiasm that made me feel a little uneasy. "And trust me, if Rook says that, it must be true."

"That is flattering," I said, taking a sip of my wine. "He's even tried to teach me how to use a battle ax."

Theron chuckled. "And, how did that go?"

"Not especially well." I smiled, hoping it appeared sincere. "I was trained with a long sword and it's such a different weapon."

"You were trained with a long sword?" Theron gestured

to me with the hand holding his goblet, looking me up and down with disbelief. "*YOU,* My Lady, trained with a long sword?"

"Yes, Sire. Arankos is a long sword. It only made sense for me to train with the use of such a weapon if I was to wield it." I took another sip of my wine, his wide eyes and shocked expression giving me much more satisfaction than they should.

"I am surprised King Vayr allowed his daughter to be trained at all," Theron said with a quirk of his lips. "Or was that perhaps the good Queen Thalass's influence. Your mother comes from a line of warrior princesses, does she not?"

No matter how much I managed to surprise him, he was always a step ahead. The knowledge of my family's lineage was certainly no secret, but it unnerved me just how much he knew about me, and I so little about him.

I attempted a nonchalant smile. "Indeed. My mother was a skilled fighter, until…" *She had me.* I swallowed the words down. It still hurt me that my mother's pregnancy had weakened her so much that she had never been able to pick up a sword again. She had always insisted it wasn't my fault, and yet I couldn't shake the deep feeling of guilt.

Theron was watching my face intently, then smiled. "And so, the battle ax," he said, mercifully not pressing me for more details. "How do you find it?"

"Heavy." I met his eyes as I said it, and the look he was giving me made the hairs on the back of my neck stand up. But my discomfort was quickly followed by another idea. A stupid one, perhaps. But once it had landed in my head, it would not let me go.

"So, you won't be slicing me limb from limb any time soon then?" Theron's lips twitched into a devilish grin. His green eyes strayed over my neckline, moving languidly back up to my face, pausing for far too long on my lips.

I gave him a slow smile, smoothing the satin of my dress over my legs. "I suppose it will have to wait a little longer, Sire." When I looked back up at him, he was leaning on the table on his elbows, his hands steepled before him.

"Elara." He was just saying it, testing how it sounded on his lips, his green cat eyes fixed on me.

The dangerous idea whirred around my head like a trapped sparrow. If I committed to it, perhaps I could gain my freedom. I hoped he did not see the movement of my throat as I swallowed hard, biting back the anxiety that sent needles prickling at the base of my neck.

"Do you enjoy looking at me, Sire?" I asked. "You seem to do it a great deal."

He rubbed his hands together slowly. "A traitorous, mutilated Fae? Why would I be looking at you?"

"Why else would you dress a filthy, mutilated Fae in fine silks and satins if you did not wish to look at her?" I hid the sting his words had unexpectedly dealt me. But he was playing into my game, and I played on. I could use this to my advantage. "You've dressed me up like your own little doll, showing all the curves and edges you want to see, Theron."

His eyes widened a little when I used his name, his hands clasped together so hard his knuckles went white. "I gave you pretty dresses because that's what all princesses want. Or would you rather I dressed you in rags?"

"You may do what you like," I replied, leaning back in my chair, my arms draped casually beside me. "But I know that look on a man's face, and I know what it means."

Theron chuckled. "Do enlighten me, dear one."

"It means you lie in your chamber at night and imagine unwrapping me like your own little prize." I traced a finger along my collarbone, his eyes following it, so predictably. It was working. Of course it was, he was a male after all. They were all the same. "Is that what you do, Theron? What do you do with your tongue while I am lying in your bed with you?"

He charged at me, his hands slamming down either side of me on the arms of the chair. His face was only an inch from mine, and he was breathing heavily.

"Do you wish to be in my bed, madam?" His voice hoarse with desire.

"Me?" I asked, my eyes moving over his face, lingering on his quivering lips. "A traitorous, mutilated Fae?" I looked into his green eyes and smiled. "Why ever would you desire such a thing?" *Play the game. Get into his bed. And fucking murder him when he least expects it.* In bed, I could have the upper hand. He'd be unarmed, vulnerable. It was the perfect opportunity.

He lowered his mouth, closer, closer, until our lips were almost touching, and I felt almost triumphant as his sharp, clean breath washed over my lips.

And then he grinned.

"Oh Elara," he said, shaking his head and growling low in his throat. He stood, straightening his black velvet jacket. He offered a hand to me. "Come, let me show you something."

I hesitated for a moment before I took his hand, but I smiled and took it. *Keep playing the game. Just keep playing the game.* His hand was cold, despite the warm evening, but I forced myself not to recoil.

He led me down the passageway, through an open door that led outside into a courtyard with torches lighting the path. The guards watched us pass, their gazes lingering on me longer than should have been decent, and the tight dress had suddenly made me desperately self-conscious.

We rounded a corner, and there stood a brightly lit temple,

gold and blue spires glowing in the fading light of the summer sky.

"Are you of the Faith?" Theron asked me, his grip on my hand remaining tight.

"I am, Sire."

"I always admired it." He swung my hand back and forth as though we were merely lovers out for a stroll. "My mother, well, the woman I was told was my mother, she insisted on it, she was incredibly devout, had us praying to Mokosh every night, asking for blessings."

"Your mother was not your mother?"

Theron ignored me and went on. "She was a strange woman in that way I suppose, so insistent on faith and praying to the Mother Goddess, while being a terrible mother herself. To me at least."

We walked up the three sandstone steps into the chapel, which smelled heavily of incense. The wooden altar at the end of the chamber was lit with dripping white candles and draped with blue silk.

Out of habit I dipped to my knees, mumbling the blessing that I had spoken since I was a child. "Great Mother and Father, you bless us with your love."

Theron keeping a hold of my hand. He laughed softly. "Such piety, madam." I looked up at him and he grinned. "Though seeing you down there on your knees does give me a certain thrill."

I quickly rose back to my feet, the prickling, creeping anxiety snaking further up my back. What had I been thinking? Well, I knew exactly what I'd been thinking. Get into his bed, get him into a vulnerable position, and kill him. I was such an idiot.

Theron pulled me further into the temple, to the golden steps below Mokosh's altar. "To answer your question, no, my mother was not my mother." He looked up at the ceiling, adorned with a majestic mosaic of gold and blue. "But she raised me, and it is in her memory that I keep this temple lit up, decorated."

"Who was your mother?"

Theron looked down at the steps we stood on, and pointed with the hand that wasn't holding mine. "There."

I looked at the spot by my feet with a frown, shaking my head. "I beg your pardon?"

Theron chuckled, releasing my hand to walk around the temple, gazing again at the ceiling. "I was taken from the arms of my own mother, when I was mere minutes old." He sighed. "My father, the old philanderer, had fucked every chambermaid in the palace, and well, one of them inevitably fell pregnant with his bastard. Now, he couldn't possibly leave a son of his in the care of a mere maid, so he had me taken from her, and placed into the arms of his beloved, Queen Eloise."

"You were born a bastard?"

Theron nodded as his gaze moved to the murals on the walls, depicting Mokosh and Perun, the mother and father god, creating the earth through their lovemaking. He ran a finger along the base of one of the murals, and chuckled.

"Ironic, isn't it? A place of worship and it has these sorts of pictures on the walls." He looked back at me. "Are you still pure, Elara?"

Pure? I frowned. The Seraph were obsessed with the idea of "purity". I was so intensely uncomfortable with his question I remained silent, avoiding his eyes. But Theron was not going to let the topic go.

"Of course you are, the way you tried to seduce me up there, tells me you're extremely pure, dear one." His brow furrowed for a moment. "Although, you did have your mate in your arms when we found you. So, perhaps I am wrong? Or did his Fae cock not satisfy you, which is why you sought out mine?"

I didn't want him to know that panic had turned my stomach into a pit of ice. "I merely thought - I thought you liked me."

"I do *like* you, Elara." He narrowed his eyes. "Now, if you would be so kind as to answer the question."

"Which question?"

"About your purity." He pointed to the altar. "And remember, the Mother Goddess is listening. She'll hear it if you lie."

My eyes darted for a moment to the picture of Mokosh and Perun, their faces frozen in the throes of ecstasy, and swallowed hard. "I am."

"You're what?"

"Pure." I looked up at him, my cheeks burning. "My... mate and I, we never..."

Theron said nothing, merely watched my face, his green cat eyes positively glowing.

"What did you do with his body?" I finally asked, realizing I had a tight grip on the skirt of my dress, crinkling the fabric in my sweaty palm.

"You'll see." His words dripped with menace, and I felt nausea wash over me. "Now, where was I?" Theron rubbed his chin thoughtfully. "Ah, yes, of course, Queen Eloise. She had a son already, my older brother. Only six months separated us, but it may as well have been a century. I was merely the bastard, and he was the crown prince. And Eloise, loving mother as she was, never let me forget it,"

I wanted to ask what had happened to his brother, but I kept quiet, not wanting to make a sound. I felt like I was trapped in a cage with a viper.

"The evening we learned of the Uprising, Eloise came rushing in here." Theron gestured around the room scornfully.

"She raced in here, begging Mokosh for power, for mercy." He laughed maniacally. "So sad for her that she did not find it."

"What did she find?"

Theron slinked towards me. "She found me."

I willed my breathing to stay even, as he walked right up to me. His gaze darkened as it fell upon my face, and he raised an eyebrow.

"She looked at me, much as you are looking at me now." He raised a hand to my cheek, stroking it gently with his cold fingers. "Such confusion. How could her son, her beloved son, be standing over her, threatening her life?"

"You killed your own mother?"

His hand gripped my throat suddenly, and his eyes narrowed. "Not my mother. Just the bitch who told me I was worthless my whole life. Who made me pay the price for my father's infidelity."

I couldn't make a sound as his hand wrapped itself tighter around my neck, just held the gaze of those terrifying green eyes.

"Oh yes," Theron said with a heavy breath, "right over there, on those steps, I stomped her fucking head in. I pounded her into the stones until there was nothing left but blood and bone fragments, and then I found my father and cut his fucking throat." He lowered his mouth to my jawline. "Do you doubt me?"

I shook my head, my jaw trembling so violently my teeth were chattering. "N-No."

Theron hissed in a triumphant breath. "Good." His eyes met mine again. "Your little performance up there, dear one, that was most impressive. And as much as I'd love to be the first one to claim that perfect little Fae cunt, I have much more interesting plans for you." His mouth moved to my ear. "By the time I am done with you, you will be begging to be in my bed, believe me." He shoved me away suddenly, and I nearly lost my footing as my shoe caught in the hemline of the dress, the satin sliding against the floor beneath me.

"Go to bed, Elara." He commanded. "Go to bed, and prepare for the days ahead. I'm sure you'll find it all very amusing." He stalked out of the temple, into the warm summer evening.

I sank to my knees, my hand rubbing my neck, still feeling the icy grip of his hands. His parting words sent shocks of horror down my spine, and I wondered just how bad things were about to get.

Chapter 9

Elara

The flat of Rook's sword caught me in the side, and I hit the ground hard, dust flying into my eyes and nose. I spluttered, my fingers flexing around the hilt of my sword.

"What the fuck was that?" Rook asked, walking around me, his bare feet padding through the dirt. "Where are you today?"

"I didn't sleep well." I pulled myself into a crouch and rose to my feet. "I'm just tired."

It had been a week since my interlude in the temple with Theron, and I'd barely slept since that night. Every time I closed my eyes, terror took over. Nightmares plagued me. Intermingled with the dreams of Rook that left me waking soaked in sweat and cheeks burning with shame, now I was pursued through the darkness by Theron, watching him murder his mother over and over again. And every dream ended the same way - him pointing at me with blood-stained hands, telling me *You're next.*

I was clinging on to my sanity by my fingertips, petrified each and every day that something awful was coming.

Rook shook his head and sighed loudly. "Tired gets you killed."

"Oh fuck off," I muttered, rubbing my hip, which throbbed from the impact of the ground.

Rook leaned down over me, his blue eyes blazing. "What was that, princess?"

"Stop fucking calling me that!" I lashed out, shoving my hand square into his chest and pushing him away from me. I swung the sword, rage coursing through me, and he brought up his own in time to deflect my strike away from his neck.

"Are you crazy?"

I lunged at him, bellowing as I did, all the rage and fear and panic welling up in me. Rook sprang aside, deflecting my wild swing and knocking my sword to the ground. I heard his own sword drop, and suddenly his arms were around me, and he was pressed against my back. I writhed in his grasp, his calloused hands gripping my arms against my body.

"Let me go!" I screamed.

"I'm not doing that until you calm down." His voice was low, just as it was in all those fucking sweaty dreams I kept having about him.

"Fuck you!" I kicked my legs in the air, trying to get out of his grasp. "Let me go!"

"Elara. I need you to calm down."

Tears bit at my eyes. I shook my head, thrashing again, weaker this time, the fight leaving my body. "Fuck you, Rook."

"I'm not fighting you while you're like this." His mouth was right by my ear. "Anger and fear are deadly. You need to calm down."

I sagged in his arms, and I didn't even care that my hair

was sticking to the sweat on his chest. I merely stayed there, trying to steady my breathing, trying not to think about how nice it was to just be fucking held by someone.

"Did something happen?" He asked me quietly.

I bit my lip, willing myself not to cry. "I'm afraid."

Rook gently turned me around in his arms, and tipped my head back. His eyes searched my face, and I was shocked at the tenderness I saw there. "I know you are. And I wish I could say you didn't have reason to be."

My head fell against him, and I wasn't sure if I could keep breathing. "Rook-" I gasped. "Please... I can't... I can't..." My shoulders heaved, my throat suddenly dry and raw.

His arms went around me then, pulling me in to his chest. He stroked my hair, and tears bit at my eyes. This was my first tender interaction in weeks, and it was with the Night Demon who'd tried to kill me when I first arrived. Who *I'd* tried to kill when I first arrived. And now he cradled my head against his chest, waiting patiently until I could breathe again.

"This is a change from calling me an evil witch," I said after a while, and Rook laughed. He notched two fingers under my chin and looked into my eyes, smiling, and I saw for the first time the dimples set in his cheeks.

"A pleasant change, I hope."

I sniffled. "Careful, you might find yourself giving a shit about a Fae."

"You're unlike any Fae I've ever met before, princess, and, I'm sure, I shall ever meet again."

"How so?"

He shrugged. "You just are. A fierce little Fae."

"Sorry I nearly decapitated you."

"I was well ready for you, don't worry." He traced the tip of his index finger along my scar. His eyes moved along it, his smile melting into something soft and tender, before his gaze met mine again.

I tried not to cringe. "It's bad, isn't it?"

He shook his head. "Not at all. Reminds me just how tough you really are, princess."

Our eyes were locked on each other, and my heart was suddenly caught in a warm glow that was so strange it was almost painful.

"The guards will be reporting back on this," he murmured, his finger continuing to caress my jawline.

"Let them, Theron can't possibly do any worse than he already has."

"Oh well now, looks like you two are getting on famously!"

The voice sent a cascade of ice down my back, and Rook stepped away from me instantly. I hurriedly wiped my face, hoping my cheeks weren't too flushed.

Theron sidled down the steps into the training arena, his hands behind his back. "Things going well, Rook?" He walked around us slowly.

Rook cleared his throat. "The princess was upset, Sire."

"About what?" Theron asked.

"Her - her situation, Sire. It's causing her some anxiety."

Theron stopped in front of Rook and grinned. "Her situation?"

Rook's shoulders tensed. "The - the loss of her betrothed."

"Rook knows all about loss, princess." Theron said, his green eyes moving to me. "He'll no doubt tell you the story some time." His gaze moved back to Rook. "Touch her like that again, and I'll be out of an assassin, do you understand me?"

Rook's eyes were looking over Theron's head, his jaw set like a steel trap. He merely nodded, his fists balled at his side.

"I said, do you understand me?" Theron's eyes flamed.

"I understand, Sire."

"She's. Not. For. You." Theron snarled. "I won't have her sullied by some fucking Night Demon." He looked over at me, pleased to see me standing with my hands clutched to my mouth. "Now, Your Highness, perhaps you and your training partner would like to come into the Throne Room. I have an announcement that I'm sure you'll both be very interested in."

Chapter 10

Elara

Rook and I looked out of place in the throne room, disheveled in our training clothes amongst the burgundy and black sea of courtiers. He and I stood side by side before the ebony throne, Theron watching us both with a predatory smile.

"Now, our esteemed royal guest has been here a number of weeks," Theron said, "and I believe she has been training well alongside our very own Rook, is that not so?"

Rook shifted beside me. "Yes, Sire. She is fast, and strong. She is a fine warrior."

"Excellent. I trust your judgment, my friend." Theron rose to his feet. "Princess Elara, my people should be shown your skill. Indeed, if you can hold your own against my assassin, I believe you'll provide an excellent spectacle."

"Spectacle, Sire?" I asked, trying to keep my tone light.

"Yes, a spectacle, Princess." Theron snapped his fingers, and a servant rushed forward. In his hands, he held a Peyrusian banner, the crest of my family emblazoned on it. A white iris in the beak of a Phoenix. And it was covered in blood.

Theron took the banner from the servant, holding it out in his hands, his cat eyes positively gleaming as he cast his gaze to my face. "Now, Your Highness, I'd like you to tell me where this came from."

"From my home." Rook shifted beside me as I spoke, and he inched closer to me, only fractionally, so it was barely noticeable to anyone but me. "That is the banner of my people."

"We got it from your throne room, in fact." Theron said, his words dripping with delight. My lungs wouldn't fill with air. Panic burned at the back of my eyeballs, sweat breaking out on my top lip.

"Is that so, Sire?" He'd stormed Peyrus. He'd destroyed it. The banner was covered in blood. Oh Gods, what had happened to my parents?

"It is indeed, dear one." Theron replied. "Now, I would like to make you an offer. I would like you to partake in a series of games, for the amusement of my people, and for you to show off your formidable skills."

"Forgive me, Sire, what kind of games?" I asked.

"Trials, I suppose you might call them." Theron turned the banner over in his hands, inspecting the crimson stains. "A tournament, if you will. I will come up with a series of trials for you to complete, and since you are indeed so strong and fast, I'm sure it will not be a problem for you."

"You said you would make me an offer, Your Majesty." My fingernails were biting into the palm of my hand. "What would I receive in exchange for completing these trials?"

Theron tossed the banner at my feet. "The opportunity to save your kingdom, your home, piece by piece." He snapped his fingers again, and two guards marched out of the throne room. He looked us both over as we all waited for what was coming, and he gave us an indulgent smile. "It was rather heartwarming to see you two embracing this afternoon. I was sure you'd have killed her by now, Rook. Seeing as you've had ample opportunity."

"I wouldn't do that, Your Majesty." Rook replied.

"You wouldn't kill your greatest enemy?"

Rook gave me a side glance. "The Princess isn't my greatest enemy."

"She's the entire fucking reason you're here!" Theron was almost gleeful as he said it.

My head snapped over to look at the demon beside me. "I'm what?"

Rook's eyes met mine, but then I saw him freeze as his gaze moved over my shoulder. I spun around to see the guard hauling in a person - a woman - limp and bleeding. She was filthy, as though she'd been dragged along the road, blood and dirt mixed on her face in a terrible raw mass.

My stomach dropped.

"Esther!" I lurched forward. "Oh Gods, what have you done to her?" My nursemaid, the woman who'd cared for me since childhood, who'd been a second mother to me, now lay between two Velesian guards. She wasn't moving, and I wondered if she was already dead. "What have you done?" I cried as the guards stepped forward and stopped me getting any closer. "What have you done?" I railed against them, grabbing at the spears they held to block my way. "Esther! Esther!" She didn't move, didn't respond.

Theron was pacing slowly back and forth in front of the throne as I turned to him. "Now now, dear one, calm down."

"What have you done?" I flew at him, but hands were suddenly on me, holding me back, and I looked over my shoulder to see Rook. I jerked my shoulders, fighting against his grasp. "Let me go! She's my family!" My eyes flew back to Theron. "What are you going to do to her?"

"My lady, as I said, I am giving you the opportunity to win your lands back, your family back, piece by piece." The smile on his face was infuriating, and he rubbed his hands together. "Now, I was going to have this woman who meant so much to you be the first trial, be your first opportunity to earn back a small part of Peyrus and the royal house. But then -" His eyes moved over my shoulder to Rook. "Then I saw something I did not quite approve of. So now you have, unfortunately, forfeited that chance."

"Wh - what do you mean?" I looked from Esther back to Theron, over my shoulder at Rook and back again. "What have I forfeited?"

"You attempted to seduce me a week ago," Theron announced loudly to shocked, theatrical gasps from the courtiers. "You invited me to your bed, did you not?"

I felt Rook tense behind me, his fingers flexing as they continued to hold my arms. "I most certainly did not!" I protested. Esther moved, one arm reaching out, trying to lift herself from the ground. "I did no such thing!"

"You attempted to seduce me and then you did the same thing with the very man I assigned to train you today, did you not?" Theron's voice was growing ever louder, whipping up the courtiers into a frenzy around us.

"She did not." Rook's booming voice caught me by surprise, and I jumped.

Theron raised his eyebrows. "Oh is that so? Is that why I caught you in a lover's embrace in the training arena today?"

"He was comforting me!" My voice had taken on an edge of desperation, almost cracking as the words tumbled out of me. "He was just comforting me because I lost my betrothed! We weren't doing anything!"

"I assure you, Sire, there was nothing untoward going on."

Rook's hands dropped from my arms. "I would never touch a Fae, you know that."

"Even one as beautiful as this one, Rook?" Theron sneered. "Even one whose body is pressed against yours in combat, dripping in sweat? Even one who haunts your dreams and has you moaning so loudly in your chamber that the fucking guards can hear you?"

"I assure you, your majesty, it's nothing." Rook's eyes moved from me back to Theron, his hands spread. "I have no control over my dreams. They mean nothing."

Esther groaned from across the room. I again moved towards her, trying to reach her and comfort her, to make sure she was alright. The guards stood in my way, their spears pushing me back.

"Esther! Esther! It's me, it's Elara! I'm here!"

The old woman raised her head, her violet eyes glowing in amongst the soft papery wrinkles of her skin. Her soft milky skin which was now covered in blood and filth. Her lips moved, but her voice was so faint I couldn't hear what she was saying. Her hand reached out to me.

"It's alright," I assured her, "it's alright, I'm here. I'm here."

"Rook!" Theron called. "Kill her."

I spun around, thinking he meant me. I was ready to fight. I was ready to claw Rook's fucking eyes out if he came anywhere near me. But then I met his eyes and saw the tortured look on his face, and his shoulders slumped a little.

"Sire, this isn't necessary." He said, his voice full of defeat.

Theron's eyes blazed. "I order you to kill this woman." He pointed at Esther.

"No!" I flew at Rook, my fists slamming into his chest, beating at him, clawing at him. He merely stood there, taking every one of my strikes, his eyes full of sadness. "Don't you fucking touch her! Don't you fucking go anywhere near her! I swear to the Gods I will end you! I will end -" I was torn away from him by two pairs of hands, away from Rook. I flailed and kicked against them, crying and screaming as a guard brought Rook his ax.

Theron stood at the base of the throne podium, leering at me. "I told you, you forfeited your chance to earn her life back. You do not touch anyone, nor is anyone permitted to touch you, do you understand me?"

Rook walked towards Esther, who was still barely moving on the ground, his ax in his hand.

"Don't you touch her, Rook!" I writhed in the hands of the guards. "You touch her and I will kill you! I will fucking kill you, Rook!"

The two guards hauled Esther from her slumped position on the floor, forcing her on to her knees. An enormous oak tree round was rolled in, and Esther's head was placed upon it. My screaming was totally incoherent now, the guards drawing blood from my arms as their fingers cut into me.

Esther's hands hung limply on either side of her. Rook stood beside her, then dropped down to one knee, putting a hand on her head. His eyes lifted to meet mine. "I'm sorry." He said to her, as well as to me.

Then he rose to his feet, lifted his ax, and lined it up with Esther's neck. His mouth set in a hard line, and then he swung.

I didn't hear the impact of the ax over my screams, and the tears in my eyes blurred what happened. But I saw the wild spurt of blood as Rook removed Esther's head from her body, sending it rolling away from the oak tree round. I doubled over, the air draining from my lungs, my throat raw from screaming. Disbelief flooded me.

He'd killed her. He'd fucking killed her.

"I hope we all understand our positions now, Your Highness," Theron said, his footsteps echoing across the now silent throne room. "I provided you with a partner to train with, and you violated my trust. You attempted to seduce my loyal servant and convince him to violate the Accord."

"I didn't," I gasped. "I didn't."

"Silence!" His feet were right in front of me. "I know what I saw and I will not be made a fool of." He seized my face in his hand, forcing me to look at him, to look into his evil cat eyes. "Now, hear me - you will be given the chance to save others you love, but one single discrepancy, one single fucking foot out of line, and I will lay waste to everything and everyone you hold dear, do you understand me?"

"Fuck you, Theron."

He slapped me so hard my head snapped into the shoulder of the guard beside me, raw heat spreading across my cheek. I tasted blood, could feel it pooling in my cheek.

"Take her back to her room." He said. "And she's only to leave it to train for the tournament."

I looked back across the room as I was hauled out, and Rook watched me mournfully, the ax in his hand dripping Esther's blood to the floor.

"You don't have to worry, you know." Keir stroked my hair as my head lay on his chest.

"About what?" I asked.

"Me." He smiled as I gazed up at him. "I'll be alright."

I nuzzled into him. "Are you sure?"

"You know me, jewel." He kissed the top of my head. "I'm always

fine. You go on ahead. You did always love the sunshine."

When I looked up again, it was Rook's chest I was lying on.

I started up in the bed, throwing my hands out.

I was alone in my room, the floor illuminated blue from the light of the full moon. The sheets around me were cold, the breeze blowing in through the open window carrying a scent of fresh grass and gardenias.

My nightshirt was sticking to my back, I was so bathed in sweat. Gods I was so fucking tired of this. I pressed my knuckles into the corners of my eyes, dashing away stinging tears.

I don't want to dream of him, I told Lada. *Why do you keep making me dream of him?*

I clambered out of the bed and stumbled across the room to the window, gulping down the warm summer air. Only when my hands touched the frame did it occur to me that the window was open. These enormous windows, wide enough to fit a person.

The windows that were always latched at night. Always.

I spun around and a hand clapped over my mouth.

Rook's features were illuminated by the moonlight, his eyes wide and urgent as he looked down at me.

"Shhhh." He cocked his head, as though listening. I tried to push him away and he held my mouth tighter. "Shhh." He hissed again. "Just stop it. You'll wake your maid and then we'll both be in trouble." He raised his eyebrows. "Alright? You'll be quiet?"

I gave a brief nod, and he moved his hand slowly from my mouth.

"What the fuck are you doing here?"

"I had to come and see you, after what happened." He shook his head, his brow furrowing. "I'm sorry, I'm so sorry. I had no choice."

I shoved him in the chest, and his hands seized my arms again. "Fuck you, Rook."

"Will you keep your fucking voice down?" His hands squeezed gently. "I'm risking my life to come and apologize to you, alright?" His hands slid on my skin, and he drew back a little. "You're all sweaty, are you sick?"

"No, I was having another fucking dream about you."

He winced. "Oh. I'm sorry."

"Fuck off." I shoved him away. "You're lucky I'm not tossing you out of this tower right now, you fucking ghoul."

"I told you, I had no choice." His voice was almost breaking, and I couldn't tell if it was because he had to keep quiet or if it was because of pure emotion. "You think I enjoy killing old defenseless women who've been half beaten to death? You think I can sleep at night knowing I did that?"

"I don't care how you sleep, you fucking murderer," I hit back, unable to stop myself hammering my fist into his chest. I sucked in a heavy breath as I looked up at him. "How can you do this? How can you kill like this, for him?"

"I told you, I don't have a fucking choice." He leaned over me, backing me against the window frame. "I'm his slave, and he tells me what to do. And if your fucking Father hadn't betrayed my people I wouldn't be here, so blame him."

I shook my head. "What are you talking about?"

"The Fae abandoned my people during the Uprising," he replied, his features becoming ever sharper as my eyes adjusted to the half-darkness. "They knew the Velesians would call in a debt of the Heirs, and your father decided to betray us rather than risk you." His lips pulled back in a sneer. "Not that it did you a lot of good I suppose, you ended up here anyway."

"That's why you hated me? *That's* why you wanted to kill me? Because of what my father did?"

"I lost *everything*." The last word was seared with pain as it emerged from his gritted teeth. His hand balled into a fist against the wall beside me. He lowered his head a little, and took a deep breath. "I lost everything." He said again, quieter this time, his voice heavy with defeat. "Who was she?"

I scoffed. "What do you care?"

His jaw feathered violently, his eyes glowing as he glared at me. "Who. Was. She?"

"You cut her fucking head off and now you want to know who she was? What does that change?"

He lunged at me, caging me in with his arms. "Because it lets me hold on to some tiny fucking shred of who I used to be. Not the fucking thug he's made me. Not the monster you see when you look at me now." His head dropped a little. "Please, just tell me who she was."

"My nursemaid," I replied slowly. "She looked after me when I was a child."

Rook nodded, stepping away from me to lean on the window sill. "She didn't deserve to die like that. And I need you to understand that… I have no choice. No matter what you might think of me, no matter…" He looked at me mournfully. "I'm sorry."

"Sorry won't bring her back."

Rook flinched. "You honestly think I'd do something like that of my own free will?"

"How should I fucking know!" I caught myself, and we fell silent, listening for any hint of Drusilla, any sign that the guards had heard me. We both finally exhaled, and I looked back at him. "All I saw in that moment was you, threatening to kill me. Your anger and your hatred."

"It wasn't like that, I swear to you. I *swear* it. Please tell me you believe me."

I couldn't ignore the pain in his voice, and I knew he

meant it. "I believe you."

"I'm a killer, his own personal thug, and I have to live with that." He gave me a sideways glance as I moved to stand beside him at the window. "I'm so sorry you had to see that. I'm so fucking sorry, Elara."

I took in his profile in the moonlight, the pain etched on his face obvious even in the half-light of the moon. After a while I reached out, and for a reason I couldn't quite explain, I placed my hand over his. He hissed in a breath when I touched him, but didn't move away. "Are you alright?" I asked softly.

He laughed bitterly. "You don't have to worry about me."

"Are you alright?"

He rubbed his other hand over his mouth, shifting on his feet but not moving his hand out from under mine. "No. No, I'm not alright. I wasn't always like this. But this is what he's made me. I hate myself for it."

Without thinking I leaned my head against his arm, clasping his hand even tighter, my fingers entwining with his. "I'm sorry, Rook."

"It's not your fault." He huffed out a breath. "I know that now. It's not your fault. You're as much a victim of your father's weakness as I am."

I didn't know how to answer that, because Rook still didn't know the truth. I bit it back, and simply stayed like that, with my head against him. We stood in silence, looking out over the gardens of the prison that held us both as the stars twinkled overhead.

"I can't believe Theron is jealous," I said.

Rook scoffed. "Me neither." He looked down at me, cocking an eyebrow. "Although if we're both locked up in our rooms having sweaty dreams about the other then perhaps he has reason to be."

"Don't flatter yourself." I was intensely relieved he couldn't see the flush in my cheeks. "Not *all* the dreams I have about you are… like that."

"Oh no?" He huffed out a little breath. "That's disappointing. What do I do in the other dreams?"

I rolled my eyes. "Crawl into my bed and ask if I'm happy to see you before you tear my throat out."

"Well if that's how you Peyrusians do it then no wonder you're dying out." He chuckled softly when he saw me glare at him. "I promise if I ever crawl into your bed, I won't tear your throat out."

"Well that's a relief, I can sleep easier now."

"I mean, not unless you want me to."

My eyes flashed up to his, and I shivered a little. "Penchant for biting, Rook?"

"Depends on where. And why." He glanced over his shoulder at the enormous bed. "Plenty of room for me in there I suppose."

I swatted him in the chest. "I won't be responsible for you violating the Accord."

He grinned, his teeth a bright white flash in the moonlight. He lowered his mouth to my ear. "You think I pay attention to that?"

"I thought you don't fuck Fae?"

"That was then. This is now."

I drew back from him a little, and as I looked at his face in the moonlight I told myself it was merely loneliness, nothing else that made my eyes linger on his lips, wondering what they would feel like. It was grief and loneliness and a desire to feel anything but what had consumed me for weeks, for all the days since I'd been hauled away from Keir, that made me even consider for a moment inviting Rook into my bed and forgetting everything.

But even as I tried to convince myself of the lie, the whisper of heat in my chest grew, like a flame exposed to fresh air. It was accompanied by a sliver of fear. It couldn't mean that. It couldn't be…

Rook's eyes searched my face, and he raised a hand to my cheek. "I'm glad I came up here tonight."

"Me too." I leaned my head against his chest, and his arms moved around me, easily and naturally, just like they had in the training arena earlier that day. His fingers traced over the back of my neck, and I knew if we didn't stop now, if one of us didn't pull back -

Heavy footsteps sounded in the passageway outside, tearing us both out of the moment. Rook pulled away from me, leaping onto the window frame much more nimbly than a man of his size should have been able to. His eyes fixed on me for a second, and then he dropped down the tower wall, out of sight.

I waited for the footsteps outside to fade, the guard moving away. When I went to the open window, Rook was gone, like a shadow into the night. I clutched a hand to my chest for a moment, my heart thundering.

A few weeks ago Rook and I had sworn we were enemies, we had tried to kill each other. Tonight I'd wanted to take him to bed. Tonight my body had called for him in a strange and comforting way that I could not make sense of. My mind was racing. Everything was too confusing.

I closed the window, leaving the latch open. I didn't know why. Maybe I secretly hoped he'd come back, climbing the tower again, risking his life to come and lie down beside me and take me in his arms. I crawled into bed, knowing sleep wouldn't come for a long time. And even when it did, I'd dream of him.

Chapter 11

Elara

Training became agony. For too many reasons to count.

Every day that passed was fraught with terror, wondering if today was the day that Theron would announce the first trial, the first chance for me to earn back my home. I was sure he had more people I loved hidden away in the dungeons, and the thought of my parents hidden away down there while I slept far above them in a four poster bed and fine linens kept me awake most nights.

When I did finally sleep, the nightmares returned, Theron pursuing me with his bloody hands. I lay awake begging Lada for dreams of Rook, when days before I had been begging her to take them away. But now dreaming of Rook whispering filthy words in my ear while I moaned underneath him was far more favorable than dreaming of Theron coming after me and threatening me with a grim demise.

My fighting became sloppy because I was so tired. I made mistakes, got hurt, over and over. Rook began to hold back, too much, and it made it so much worse, for us both. His frustration was palpable, and although I knew it was simply because he wanted me to be ready for whatever Theron was going to throw at me, my anxiety peaked all the same.

The sun beat down on us one hot summer's morning, and I could feel my arms becoming weak as I tried to fight him off, to fight back, to fucking hold my own. But it was no use, and my blade slipped, hitting the ground and sending me into Rook's sword. He gasped as it grazed my stomach, drawing a dotted line of blood through my camisole.

"I told you to leave that fucking vest on," he scolded me, throwing his sword aside and dropping to his knees in front of me.

"It was too hot." I watched as he yanked the camisole loose from my leather pants, pulling it up and inspecting the thin wound. I was keenly aware of the boring eyes of the guards around us. I was so delirious from sleeplessness that I didn't even care if they saw Rook undressing me anymore. Let us draw Theron's ire. If we died, then we died. I giggled and Rook's eyes flashed up to me, his brow furrowing into a heavy frown.

"Are you drunk?"

I shook my head. "Of course not."

"Then, what's wrong with you?"

Suddenly, tears were rolling down my cheeks, and I covered my face with my hands. Oh Gods, I was *crying.* I was so exhausted and taut with terror that I was crying. *You never cry.*

Rook was on his feet, his hands clasping my arms. "Elara, what's wrong?"

"I'm tired. I can't sleep. I have endless nightmares and then I can't stop thinking about these trials and -" I broke off, knowing if I went on I would throw myself at him and land him in trouble and possibly get someone I loved killed again.

This same thought didn't seem to occur to Rook, who swept me up in his arms in one fluid movement and carried me out of the training arena.

"Rook, what the fuck are you doing?" I asked as a sob hiccuped out of my throat.

"I'm taking you to bed."

I gasped and pushed my hands against his chest as we passed the guards. "Are you cra-"

"To sleep, you fucking idiot." He tossed me in his arms to adjust his grip, holding me tighter. "Now shut up and let me help you."

We passed the open mouths of the guards, and then Regan appeared before us at the bottom of the sweeping staircase that led up into the tower.

"What is the meaning of this, Rook?" He asked sternly.

"She's hurt, and she's exhausted." Rook replied. "She's been making too many mistakes during training and she needs to sleep. It's a hot day and she's no good to me out there like this, I'm going to kill her."

Regan's eyebrows betrayed his surprise for only a moment before he stepped aside and let us pass. "I'll inform the King."

"Do that." Rook barked over his shoulder, starting up the stairs.

I slumped against his chest, smelling leather and perspiration and underneath it a scent of salt, like the sea. Or at least what I'd been told the sea smelled like. I sighed, the warmth of his arms making me sleepy already.

"You smell so nice," I murmured.

"Oh fucking Gods, you certainly sound drunk."

"Have you ever had Fae wine?" I asked. "It's strong. Makes you do silly things."

"We'll have to try it sometime when you're not delirious with exhaustion."

We reached the door to my room, and he kicked it in with his foot.

Drusilla exclaimed as the door flew open, dropping the clothes she had in her hands. "We have door handles you know, you moron!"

"And I have my hands full with your mistress here," Rook said, depositing me on the bed. "She's exhausted, she needs a sleeping draught or she's going to lose her fucking mind."

Drusilla's face quickly shifted from irritation to concern, and she rushed over to me, stroking my forehead with her cool fingers. "Oh my lamb, you're pale." She looked up at Rook. "I'll go and see the Healer, and bring back a draught for her. Stay with her, make sure she stays lying down." She hurried out, the door swinging shut behind her.

Rook poured me a cup of water and sat down beside me on the bed. "Do you need me to hold your head up or can you drink?"

I glared at him, sitting up and taking the cup from him. I took a sip, then held out the cup for him to take again.

"Drink." He ordered, pointing his finger at me. "All of it."

"You're impossible, you know that?" I downed the cup, water dribbling down my chin. I wiped it away with the back of my hand as I gave the cup to him, and laid back down on the bed.

"At least you listen sometimes," he said, placing the cup on the nightstand. He leaned over me, pushing the camisole up again to reveal the cut on my stomach, which had started to sting. "Next time, leave your fucking armour on when I tell you to."

"Are you always like this?" I threw my arms up over my head.

"What? Logical? Intelligent? I'd like to fucking hope so." His fingers traced underneath the cut, and his eyes flashed up to my face as I quivered under his touch. "Sorry, am I eliciting some unwelcome feelings?"

"No." I rolled on to my side, facing him. "I wish you could sleep with me."

His eyes widened with surprise. "I beg your pardon?"

I shook my head quickly. Gods, I really was tired. "No, I don't mean - oh fuck." I threw myself onto my back as Rook chuckled. "I just mean, I sleep better when someone is in the bed with me. I haven't slept alone in a long time."

"Ah." He reached over and pushed a strand of hair out of my face. "I understand that. Not that I've slept with anyone in a very, very long time."

"But what about the redhead with the big tits?" I bit my lip to suppress a smile.

"That's a bit different to sleeping with someone though, wouldn't you say?" He grinned. "A fuck in the back alley behind the tavern as opposed to sleeping in a bed with a woman you've been able to enjoy for hours, well that's quite a different story."

"I wouldn't know."

He cocked an eyebrow. "I don't believe that for a moment."

"Believe it." I said with a shrug. "I've never - well, never…" I trailed off, and he moved closer to me.

"You're very, very tired if you're telling me all this." He leaned on an elbow beside me, his calloused fingers brushing against my cheek.

"Do you really fuck the kitchenmaids behind the tavern?" I asked him.

Rook burst out laughing, those dimples in his cheeks

appearing again. "That's what you want to know is it? You're rather nosy for an innocent princess."

"Just because I haven't done that doesn't mean I'm innocent." I wriggled closer to him.

"Well, to answer your question, yes." He rolled his eyes with a quirk of his lips. "I mean, strictly speaking not *behind* the tavern. *Inside* the tavern more accurately." His blue eyes bored into mine. "But you already knew that."

"I thought maybe you were just taunting me."

"Mmmm… you did seem a little taunted." His fingers traced up and down my back, and I sighed. "Oh you like that, do you?"

I nodded. "Feels nice."

"I assure you," he said, his breath warming the shell of my ear, "you have nothing to be jealous of."

I gazed up at him. "Wasn't she any good?"

He shrugged. "She was alright. Made a lot of noise."

"Doesn't that mean you were good?" I asked, putting my hands against his chest, closing my eyes.

"I suppose it does." He pulled me tighter against him.

"Would you like to do it again?"

His lips turned up in a smile as he lowered his mouth to my cheek. "Is that an invitation?"

"Might help me sleep better."

Rook laughed, a deep, pleasing sound that made goosebumps break out over my shoulders. "Mmm, I suppose it might." He kissed my cheek then, and not just a tender, elusive brush. He pressed those soft lips against my skin, and if I hadn't been so tired I would have turned my head immediately to try and catch his mouth with my own.

"So, you definitely don't hate me anymore then, Rook?" My voice became heavy as sleep crept over me.

"No, Elara." His fingers traced up and down my back

again, and he growled low in his throat as a small moan left my lips. "I definitely don't hate you."

"You'd violate the Accord for me?"

His lips brushed against my neck, his hand wandering further down my back. "I don't give a shit about the Accord."

"I had that dream, you know. About the tavern." I yawned. "You. And me."

"I know. You told me." He kissed my neck. "I did, too."

The door flew open behind us, and Rook quickly straightened up from beside me.

"Getting cozy, Rook?" Drusilla's voice was filled with displeasure.

"She wanted to be warm," he replied, rising to his feet and crossing his arms over his chest."And said she felt safer with me being there."

"I'm sure." Drusilla eyed him suspiciously, then turned to me, her expression changing instantly to one of concern. "Now, my lamb, I have this for you." She held up a small brown vial topped with a cork. "It'll help you rest."

"No nightmares?" I asked, and Rook flinched.

"You have nightmares?" Drusilla asked, sitting down beside me. "Oh, I had no idea, you poor thing."

"She wakes up screaming." Rook's indignant tone faded quickly as the words left his mouth.

Drusilla's head snapped towards him. "And how do you know that?"

"She told me." His eyes flickered to me. "And anyone with any sense would know, after what she's been through."

"Yes, yes, alright." Drusilla turned back to me, pulling the cork and handing me the vial. "Here, my lamb, drink it up, it's a little bitter but it works fast."

I downed the liquid in one gulp, and it enveloped the back

of my throat with a deep bitterness that made my toes curl. I grimaced and Rook laughed.

"You can go now, Rook." Drusilla said sternly.

"No." I reached out for him. "Please, just stay until I'm asleep."

Drusilla rolled her eyes. "You're going to pull me into all this trouble now too, aren't you?"

Rook sat down on my other side, and I took his hand. "There's no trouble, Drusilla, just calm yourself." He looked down at me, stroking my cheek with the backs of his fingers. "You sleep, and tomorrow, we'll see how the world looks, ey?"

I clasped on to his fingers as a fog descended over me. "Til tomorrow." I murmured, and then, mercifully, I slept.

And all I dreamed of was a warm bed, and two strong hands caressing my back.

Chapter 12

Elara

Rook watched me walk into the training arena with a wide smile, his arms crossed over his chest. "You look like a Fae instead of a ghost."

"After sleeping for three days I'd want to hope so." I walked across the arena, and he uncrossed his arms, almost as if he wanted to embrace me, then stopped himself. We both looked around at the guards, then smiled at each other.

"Sorry if I garbled rubbish when you carried me upstairs." I said sheepishly.

"You didn't." He assured me. "I hope I wasn't too - um. Too affectionate."

I shook my head. "I dreamed of it actually."

"What?"

"Your -" I cast a quick glance at the guards, whose eyes were fixed on us with icy stares. "You, touching my back."

"Better than tearing your throat out I suppose." He said with a crooked grin. "Now, shall we get some training done, get some blood pumping in those stagnant limbs of yours?"

"Sure."

He walked over to the wooden rack. "And your weapon of choice today, madam?"

"Hands."

Rook turned to me slowly with a cocked eyebrow. "What's that?"

I gave him a small smile. "Hand to hand combat. That's an important skill, isn't it?"

He laughed. "Yes it is."

"And you were rather adamant last time we engaged in hand to hand combat that I had no idea what I was doing and was wasting your time."

He rolled his eyes. "I suppose perhaps I did say that, didn't I?" He cocked his head. "It's true though."

"Well then," I said with a shrug, "shall you see what you might teach me?"

"I'm a little worried I'll hurt you." He pushed away the strands of hair that had escaped the black tie holding his curls out of his face.

"I'm well-rested and ready for you." I raised my fists in front of me. "Go on then."

Rook rolled his eyes. "Oh, for fuck's sake." He walked around behind me. "First of all, thumbs go IN." He tucked my thumbs along my fingers. "You punch with a thumb pointing out like that and it'll be shattered." One arm went around my waist, and his foot knocked my back leg towards him. "Back leg goes back, or you'll have no leverage. And you swing from here." He ran his hand across my hips. "Don't just throw your arm, throw with your body. You're small and you want to make the most impact."

"I am not small." I said, looking over my shoulder at him.

"You're smaller than me, and I'm who you're fighting." He put his hands over mine, leaning against my back. "Now, you want one small punch, to disarm, and then a big one, to knock him on his ass." He moved my left hand in the air, and then swung my right hard. "And then draw back." He pulled my right hand back, and I looked over my shoulder at him. His mouth was so incredibly close we both started a little.

"I know what you're doing," he said in a low growl. "I'm not stupid."

"I have no idea what you mean."

"Pretending not to know how to throw a punch?" His hand moved from holding mine up to back around my waist. "What are you trying to tell me?"

"A lady surely shouldn't have to be quite so forthcoming?" I grinned at him, and his eyes narrowed a little as he shook his head.

"Maybe the lady should show me what she's made of." He spun me around to face him and took a step back, arms spread wide. "Now then, do your worst."

"I'll hurt you." I raised my fists.

"Maybe I'll like it." Rook gave me a satisfied smirk.

"Biting *and* hitting." I took a step sideways, and Rook matched my step so we began to circle each other. "You really do have some interesting habits, don't you?"

"I wouldn't call it *hitting*." He chuckled, flashing his mouthful of white teeth. "Spanking perhaps." He leaned a little closer. "And only when you've been a very bad girl."

"I thought I was the one doing the hitting." We kept circling each other, like a dance, eyes locked on each other.

"Right now all you're doing is flirting. Used this method on the battlefield a lot, did you?"

My punch caught him off guard, sending him stumbling, but his recovery was quick and his arm flew over my head to grapple me. I was too fast for him, ducking out of his reach and shoving him forwards. He spun on me, lunging at me, and I leapt onto his arm, using it as a springboard to fling myself onto his back. I laced my fingers under his chin and pulled backwards, leaping out of the way into a crouch as he hit the ground.

He turned over onto his stomach, grinning at me.

"Well, my lady, I think you've learned a lot more than how to throw a good punch."

I laughed. "You underestimate me."

"Never." He shook his head, pushing himself up into a sitting position, tilting his head as he smiled at me. "You're a lot better at hand to hand combat than I gave you credit for."

"Why thank you." I pushed my hair out of my face, wiping the sweat from my brow with the back of my hand. "You're a lot easier to get on your back than I thought you'd be."

Rook threw his head back and laughed out loud, gaining a surprised turning of heads from all the guards encircling the arena. Rook's turquoise eyes were sparkling when they met mine.

"Maybe I should climb up that tower again, hmm?" He lowered his voice, leaning closer to me. "See how easily you get me on my back again."

I raised my eyebrows. "Risky."

He growled low in his throat, his eyes moving to my lips. "Worth it."

"Rook!" Regan's voice rang across the training arena, and we sprang to our feet as the spindly man made his way towards us. "I see training is going well?"

"Hand to hand combat, sir." Rook said. "The princess felt it was an important skill."

"Well, how lucky you were here to help her." Regan shook his head. "The King made it clear that you aren't to touch her."

"Then the King doesn't understand how combat training

works." I replied, and both men looked at me. "How is someone supposed to train with me and not touch me?"

Regan sighed, raising his shoulders theatrically with the breath, his skinny neck making him appear like a turtle retreating into its shell. "Your Highness, what I just saw was not training."

"Then have someone else do it." I said, crossing my arms over my chest, and Rook gave me a dismayed glance.

Regan's eyes moved from Rook to me and back again. "Rook is the finest warrior we have, and Theron wants you well-prepared."

"Then you all need to stop complaining. Now, if you don't mind. I would like to resume my training."

"I'm sorry, Your Highness, but Theron has requested your presence in the throne room." Regan said. "He's announcing the first trial."

My stomach dropped, and sweat broke out over my palms. "Yes, of course." I replied, my voice wavering. "Finally." I tried to sound jovial, because part of me was in fact relieved. But terror clawed at the back of my throat. No, I could be brave. I wouldn't let them see my fear.

My eyes met Rook's and he nodded. He turned to pull on a linen shirt, and followed Regan and I out of the training arena. My head roared as we walked, and I started counting my breaths to try and keep my bearings.

Every step closer to that throne room became heavier. Became more drowned in dread. I began to lag back a little, wondering if I maybe stopped walking, everything would be alright. All of this would go away. I'd wake up in my room in Peyrus, and this would have all been a bad dream. My steps faltered.

Then Rook's hand splayed gently across the small of my

back. "Come on now, love." He whispered, pressing me gently forward. "You can do this."

Yes. I could. I squared my shoulders and kept walking, his hand staying on my back until we reached the doors of the throne room. It fell away as I stepped in, and I walked through the crowd of courtiers, the fucking courtiers who seemed to just stand in here all day with nothing else to do.

Theron sat on his black throne, an eagle perched on the armrest beside him. "You look well, Your Highness."

I'd not seen him since he'd had Esther killed, and fury welled up inside me.

"Thank you, Sire." I replied, keeping my hands at my sides.

"I'd heard you'd had some trouble sleeping?" He stroked the eagle's feathered breast with the back of his finger. "I do hope that has been remedied."

"It has, Your Majesty." I didn't want to talk to him. I just wanted to know what I had to do.

"Excellent, you'll be needing your sleep." Theron rose to his feet, offering his arm to the eagle, who opened his wings and fluttered, landing on the leather glove on his master's arm. "I have decided on the first trial, dear one. Now, are you aware of the rather impressive arena we have for just such an event as this?"

"I'm not, Sire." I replied. "Is it very large?"

"Oh, it is indeed." Theron chortled. "We call it the Pit."

"How creative." The courtiers murmured amongst themselves at my insolence. I didn't care. I wanted this over with.

Theron chuckled, stroking the eagle again gently. "Yes, sometimes simple is better. Now, this will be the first trial, so I thought we'd have something special for you. A cousin of this creature in fact." His head nodded to the eagle who remained perched on his arm.

My brow furrowed as I tried to make sense of what he was saying. "You mean for me to fight… a bird?"

Theron laughed heartily. "Oh no, something much more interesting than that. Have you ever seen a griffin?" The courtiers burst into excited chatter around us.

"I've never seen one up close, Sire." I replied. A griffin. I could do that. I'd managed worse. They weren't that big, were they?

Theron gestured to the window. "Why don't you go and see?"

I heard a screeching coming from outside. It was so loud it was audible over the teeming crowd of courtiers, their excitement rising to fever pitch as the griffin outside let out a high-pitched roar.

I walked slowly to the window, willing my breathing to remain steady. It was alright, the creature couldn't be that big. I'd taken down a bear before, single-handedly. I could handle this strange roaring creature.

I reached the window and my stomach dropped. The creature was so large that at first I didn't even notice the iron cage it found itself in, nor the guards that stood around it, bellowing and poking it with spears every time it thrashed against the bars.

It was twice the size of a work horse, if not even larger, easily reaching 12 feet at its full height. Its beak was large enough to fit around my waist and snap me in two. I could see its yellow eyes, cold and calculating, planning escape. The cage, even as large as it was, rocked from side to side as the creature spread its brown feathered wings, shrieking and squawking wildly. The griffin was angry, and even that enormous cage could barely contain it.

A guard lunged forward to poke his spear between the bars, shouting at the raging creature. The griffin ripped the spear out of his grasp, yanking his arms within the confines of the cage.

My heart stopped as the griffin tore those arms off with one pass of its beak.

I didn't stand a fucking chance against this thing.

"What say you, Your Highness?" Theron called across the room. "You defeat this creature, and you earn back the first part of your kingdom."

I watched as the guard was carried away. He was completely silent, leaving a trail of blood behind him in the courtyard. The griffin tossed the arms to the ground, turning its head to eye them, before it descended on the severed limbs, swallowing them down. I could hear the bones crunching, even from this distance.

I walked back to the throne, slowly. "What part of my kingdom will I earn back with my victory?"

"I'd like that to remain a mystery, if it's all the same to you." Theron waved his hand. "Now, off you go, you must prepare. The trial will begin tomorrow morning at 9 o'clock."

I ended up back in the training arena even though I didn't remember walking there. I was suddenly back in the sunshine, and Rook was standing in front of me, talking. I didn't hear a word. Panic roared in my ears. I'd never fought alone before, totally alone.

"Hey!" Rook grabbed my shoulders, shaking me. "You need to listen to me, or that thing is going to take off your head."

"I can't do this." I said. "I can't do this."

"Yes, you can." Rook raised his eyebrows. "Are you fucking joking? You fought your way across Grixos all by yourself just to die with the man you loved, and you think you can't take on one single griffin?"

"Th-that was different. Did you see the size of that thing?"

Rook let out an exasperated sigh. "I know, it looks huge but-"

"I can't do this Rook. I can't."

"Yes, you can." His brow furrowed. "You need to breathe."

I shook my head. "I c-can't. I can't do this. That thing tore that guard's arms off, as th-though they were nothing." I was breathing so fast now that my lungs hurt, and I felt dizzy. "Rook, I'm going to-"

He grabbed my arms. "You're not going to faint. Deep breaths."

"I'm going to die." I was shaking violently now, feeling cold despite the burning sun. "You wanted me to die, and n-now you'll get your wish."

He growled out a breath through gritted teeth. "I *do not* want you to die."

"B-but why?" I clawed my fingers into his shirt. "Why do you like me all of a s-sudden?"

"Elara, for *fuck's sake*-"

"*Why?*" I felt on the verge of tears again. It didn't matter. It shouldn't have mattered. But Rook and Drusilla had become my whole world these past few weeks, and I had to know. I had to make sense of the world I now found myself in, even if I would be leaving it in less than a day.

Rook sighed heavily. "This isn't helpful."

"I'm going to d-die. I'm going to fucking d-die." Grey clawed at the edges of my vision, and I slumped forward against him. *Stupid, stupid little girl.* Hopelessness crashed into me.

"Elara, breathe." Rook's mouth was right by my ear. "I need you to listen to me, and to breathe. You're not going to die. *Breathe*. You're not going to die. Alright?" He pressed me tighter to him as I trembled. "You're strong. And brave. And you are not going to die. Breathe. Listen to me, and breathe. I'm here." His fingers traced circles over the back of my neck, and a tear ran down my cheek. "I know you're scared. But we're going to overcome that."

"H-how?"

"Simple. You are Elara Osunon. Remember what you told me? How good you are at killing Velesians? Well, now you're going to be good at killing griffins."

I closed my eyes, focusing on the feeling of his rough fingertips on the base of my neck. "Elara O-Osunon, slayer of gr-griffins, hmm?"

Rook chuckled. "See? You're a warrior." He drew back from me and gave me a smile. "You're going to walk into the Pit, and you're going to walk right back out of it. Alright?"

I nodded, balling my shaking hands into fists on his chest. "I bet you're never frightened, are you?"

"Of course I am. You're fucking terrifying."

A breathless laugh broke from me. "Oh yes, the quivering Fae princess, you must be shaking in your boots."

"On a daily basis." He put a finger under my chin. "I don't want you to die. Are you ready to listen to me, so we can get you ready for this?"

I took a shaky breath. "Alright. So how does the Pit work? What is it?"

"It's an arena, a huge arena, and Theron uses magic to change the environment." Rook explained. "He's going to have some bait, something there for you to reach, I don't know what. You need to get across the obstacles, and then that griffin will be in there as well. They're not easy to kill, but it's not impossible."

"So what do I need to know?"

Rook stepped back from me, and ran his hand along his ribcage. "So along here, the griffin doesn't have ribs, they have a chest plate, it's like steel. Do not hit it there, you'll waste energy and risk losing your weapon."

"Right, avoid the chest."

Rook's hand moved under his arm. "At the top of the chest plate is a membrane, and it's soft. There's no protection under here. You want to stick your sword in there, and when you think you've hit what you need to, keep going. To the hilt, alright?"

I nodded. "Yes, understood."

He sighed, "Other than that, be fast. Move quick. The griffin can move about as fast as you can, but you're more nimble than it."

"What kind of arena will Theron have?"

Rook shrugged. "He likes jungles and forests, lots of trees, lots of places for the predator to hide."

"Alright. So let's train."

Rook shook his head. "No, you've had enough training and I don't want to risk you getting hurt today. You need to stretch and rest and prepare yourself mentally."

"Alright." I didn't want to leave him yet, not yet. I wanted to stay with him as long as I could. I knew he wouldn't come up the tower to see me that night because I should be resting. "You didn't answer my question."

"Which one?"

"Why you like me all of a sudden." I felt shy suddenly, wanting to hear the answer but also worried that maybe it was nothing more than pity or loneliness that had brought about Rook's change of heart. "So, why do you?"

"Like you?" He rubbed his chin, narrowing his eyes. "Well, it was your ass really. It's fantastic."

I burst out laughing, covering my face with my hands as my cheeks flushed what I was sure was a violent shade of crimson. "I can't believe you just said that."

He stepped closer to me, and as he brushed a loose strand of hair from my face the guards around us became insignificant. All I could focus on was the kindness in his eyes, and his lips as he smiled down at me.

"So you'd be sad then? If I died?"

"You know I would." His brow furrowed for a moment. "You need to trust yourself. Don't wallow in that head of yours. Don't play over everything that can go wrong."

I nodded. His finger was still resting against my cheek. "Did you mean it when you said you'd climb my tower again?"

He lowered his mouth a little. "I know what you're asking me, and… and I-" He broke off, shaking his head. "It's going to distract us right now. You have to fight that thing tomorrow, and I don't want to see you get shredded." His eyes gazed deeply into mine. "Right now you need to survive. *I* need you to survive, alright?"

I nodded. "Alright." I wrapped my fingers around his under my chin. "Alright. Survive first. Fantastic ass later."

He laughed, those dimples showing again. "That's right." He swept his fingers over his lips swiftly, so quickly the guards wouldn't have noticed the kiss he placed on them, and stroked them over my cheek. "We'll have time after all this, love. Go and rest. You need it."

I watched Rook walk out of the training arena. "Your tattoo." I called after him.

He stopped and turned back to look at me. "What about it?"

"What does it mean? What does the script say?"

He touched his hand to his lips then his forehead, then held it out as he bowed to me. "Heir to the Moon and Stars, princess." He rose. "And yours?"

I tensed. How had he seen my tattoo? My cheeks burned

as I remembered him pushing up my camisole after he'd accidentally cut me. He must have seen it then.

"I'll tell you after the tournament." I replied. "I'll need to explain it to you, so I'll have to show you."

Rook laughed. "I look forward to it." He turned and left the arena, his hulking back disappearing down the passageway.

My hand went to my sternum, where my etched tattoo of a rising sun hid beneath my clothing.

Chapter 13

Elara

I'd been afraid I wouldn't be able to sleep, the fear of the trial and the possibility of failure sure to keep me awake all night.

But, I had slept.

I knew I had, because the dreams of Rook's lips tracing over my tattoo lingered on my skin as I opened my eyes. I stared at the ceiling as the sunlight began to change over me, and my fingers gripped into the sheets as the longing subsided.

I felt a pang as I thought of Keir. Keir, who I had loved so much, and mere weeks after his death I was dreaming of another man, wishing another man into my bed. I rolled on to my side. Nothing about this situation was normal. Nothing about what I felt or thought or wanted was normal anymore.

The door to Drusilla's chamber opened, and she hurried in, my black leathers draped over her arm. "Time to rise, my lamb. I've had them make you a special breakfast to give you your strength today."

"Thank you, Drusilla." I said, sitting up in bed. "A good final meal, ey."

Drusilla eyed me with alarm. "Now, don't be saying things like that. It's just a griffin, you can best it. They're vicious creatures, but stupid. Throw a rock and it'll chase it long enough for you to take its head off."

"Fought many griffins in your time, have you, Drusilla?"

"I'm from Jerindos," she replied, "that's where the griffins come from. They used to chase us as children, through the fields. Had to be quick to get away from them, let me tell you."

Rook had told me to be quick. I could move fast. I'd be able to do that.

There was a knock on the door, and Drusilla let in the kitchen maid, who carried the tray laden with steaming plates across the room. She deposited it on the table, and I noticed her red hair straying out from under her cap. Red hair, and big tits. The stab of jealousy I felt at that moment was so ridiculous it made my cheeks burn.

The kitchen maid gave me a quick curtsey. "Your breakfast, madam."

I glared at her, and her brow furrowed a little before she quickly backed out of the room. Gods, I was a brat. But the thought that she'd had Rook and I was about to perhaps die and never have him made my toes curl with envy.

Drusilla frowned but said nothing as I moved from the bed to the table. "Now, eat up," she said, "I know you probably don't feel like it but you'll need your -" she paused as I began to shovel the food into my mouth. "Strength."

"What?" I asked, as I put another forkful of eggs in my mouth.

"I thought you'd be nervous and simpering and telling me you couldn't possibly eat, or something else like that." Drusilla sank into the chair opposite me and chuckled. "But you're here eating like one of the knights."

"I'm not stupid," I said, taking a sip of the sharp, sweet yellow juice. "You have to eat before you fight."

"Did you sleep well?"

My cheeks burned. "Yes, just fine, thank you."

"No nightmares?" She asked with a smile. "I heard you cry out once but you didn't sound frightened."

"No, no nightmares." My cheeks were positively flaming. My dreams had made me cry out, and it hadn't been out of fear. Gods, how *embarrassing.*

"Good. So you'll be well rested and well fed for the trial today." She gave me a reassuring smile. "You'll make it through, I promise. Theron doesn't want you to fail."

This was a new thought that should have occurred to me much earlier. Drusilla was right - Theron wanted me weak and tortured, and desperate for his mercy. Not dead. I breathed a little sigh of relief, as unwarranted as it perhaps was. The trial wouldn't be impossible.

Drusilla began to braid my hair as I finished my breakfast, and not a strand was out of place when she was done.

"If you're done, we can get you into your leathers now," she said.

"Wait." I said, going to the dressing table. I sat down in front of the mirror, and picked up the soft kohl pencil. I smudged black onto my eyelids and underneath my eyes along the lash line.

"Why are you doing that?" Drusilla asked. "You look like one of those northerners now."

"I am one of those Northerners, Drusilla."

She shook her head. "I still don't understand why you're doing that."

I turned to smile at her. "It makes me look fierce. And I

feel it too."

"Very well, if you're done making yourself look like a Malakh, let's get you dressed." She gestured for me to stand up, and I pulled off my nightgown.

It wasn't until I was in my full leathers and Drusilla was adjusting the bodice that I allowed myself to remember what I was about to do. I was going to win back part of my kingdom today. I had no idea what, or who, it would be, but I was going to do it.

Drusilla nodded her approval. "You look good," she said, looking me up and down. "Very fierce indeed."

A sharp rap sounded at the door, and Regan stepped into my chamber. He looked me up and down with a nod. "Ready, Your Highness?"

"Certainly, but for my weapon. Where is it?"

"You will be provided your weapon in the arena," he replied, "no one can touch that beastly thing, so it's been placed in a case in the armory, you will be allowed to retrieve it from there under watch before you're escorted in."

"Why thank you."

Regan stepped aside and gestured to the door. "Well, if you're ready, madam, they are all waiting for you."

I kept my head high as I strode down the passageway alongside Regan. I was a warrior. I was a fighter. I would show them just what I could do. I wouldn't be cowed by the looks of these guards, by any fucking Velesian I passed.

We descended into the hall and crossed it out into the open. Already I could hear the roaring of the crowd in the distance. The breeze blew through the thick green foliage above me, and I breathed it in deeply.

Three guards flanked us as we walked, and then there were suddenly six. I suppressed a smirk.

"Good morning." A deep voice sounded beside me, and I

looked up into Rook's face. His hair was pulled back, and he was dressed much more formally than I'd seen him before, a fine linen shirt tucked into black trousers. He carried his ax in his right hand, and gave me a smile. "I've been sent to make sure you and Arankos don't lay waste to Veles as soon as it's in your hands again."

"Foiling my plans again," I said, rolling my eyes with a smile.

Rook chuckled, tossing the ax handle in his grip. "You're in remarkably good spirits, did you have pleasant dreams?" He gave me a side glance, his eyebrow cocked.

I felt my cheeks once again erupt with heat. "I had very pleasant dreams," I replied, "about kittens and meadows of flowers."

Rook laughed out loud. "Well that sounds delightful."

"And you?"

"Oh yes, I did have a nice dream." He stroked his chin thoughtfully. "I can't quite remember it in detail. I think I was licking something rather delicious?"

I wheezed as I tried to hold back my abashed giggles.

"If you don't mind," Regan snapped over his shoulder.

Rook and I exchanged a quick glance and both suppressed laughter. "How do you do that?" I asked.

"What?"

"I'm about to walk into an arena of death and I'm laughing with you."

"It's because you know you're going to win." He swung his hand, brushing against mine for the briefest of moments. "It has nothing to do with me."

The towering walls of the Pit came into view over the tops of the oak trees. We descended a set of stone stairs, where more guards joined us, and I began to wonder just how frightened the Velesians were of me.

The tall wooden door to the armory was thrown open to allow us entry, and the sounds coming from the arena were so loud I was sure all of Veles had shown up. Shown up to watch the Peyrusian Princess get torn to pieces by a griffin. I gave myself a shake. No, I wouldn't be getting eaten up by a fucking griffin today. I was going to win.

The guards followed us into the armory, and there, in an open chest, lay Arankos, its blue hilt gleaming in the light that flooded in from gaps near the roof. It began to hum as I approached, and the guards all backed away as though it was about to explode. I knelt and put my hand on the blade. The humming reached a crescendo, and then died down. The guards muttered amongst themselves, and I couldn't help but grin.

"Happy to see you, ey?" Rook asked, leaning on his ax.

"I'd say so." I picked it up, the hilt warm in my hand, fitting perfectly as though it had been made just for me. I exhaled slowly. "Hello, old friend." I said softly. It felt better than I had expected, to have my weapon in my hands again. I gave Rook a smile. "Do I look ready?"

"You look incredible." He gestured to my eyes. "Especially that. I like that a lot."

"Thank you." Panic began to take over again as I heard the crowd above us cheer.

Rook cast a quick glance upwards then advanced on me. "Remember, to the hilt, yes?"

I nodded, and my breathing quickened. "I'm scared."

"I know." He put a hand on my shoulder. "But you'll be alright."

"Will you kiss me if I win?" I was desperate for anything. I needed something tangible to focus on, even if it was stupid and frivolous.

He gave me a crooked grin. "Yes, I will." He gave my

shoulder a squeeze, and then the guards ordered him to step back. "You're Elara Osunon," he said as he was escorted out, "slayer of griffins, remember that."

I took a deep breath. Yes, I was. I could do this.

The guard escorted me down into a tunnel, a half rounded steel door at the end of it. The iron gate slammed shut behind me, and I was alone in the tunnel. I gripped Arankos in my hand, and took another deep breath.

The steel door raised upwards from the floor, disappearing into the wall, and all I could see was green, thick and lush. I advanced out of the tunnel, and was standing in a jungle. Fine mist rained down on my face, and the air was sticky, clinging to my cheeks.

"Princess!"

I turned to the voice behind me, and saw Theron in the stands above. The crowd cheered wildly as he raised his arms. Rook stood beside him, his eyes fixed on me, his brow furrowed. He looked worried, but gave me a small smile, and a nod.

"Princess Elara!" Theron announced, beckoning for the teeming crowd to fall silent. "You have been given the chance to earn back your kingdom, piece by piece, and today is the first trial! Your target is at the end of this impressive arena, and you will need to pass the obstacles in place in order to reach it."

"What is my target, Sire?" I asked.

The scream I heard made my blood run cold. Rook's head jerked in its direction, and his mouth set in a hard line. He looked back at me, his brow furrowed.

"Your target has been secured, madam." Theron said.

"I ask again, Sire, what is my target?"

Theron grinned. "Why, your own dear mother."

My hands began to shake, and I willed my breathing to

stay steady. Just stay steady. I had to stay focused. But then there was another scream, and it was my mother screaming, and I felt panic rising again. Oh Gods, what were they doing to her?

"Either you reach her, or the griffin does," Theron said. "The stakes are quite simple, my dear. Now, I would hurry if I was you." He clapped twice, and the crowd erupted.

I spun and sprinted through the jungle in the direction of the screaming. My mother. She was screaming. She was here. I had to reach her. As I ran, the canopy above me opened, following my path, affording the screaming, wild crowds of Veles the best view as the Peyrusian princess tried to rescue the Queen.

The ground underfoot was like a swamp, giving way easily, and I broke into a heavy sweat within seconds in the hot, humid air. My mother screamed again, and I willed myself to move faster, to get there quicker.

Something slammed into me, sending me flying, my torso connecting with a thick tree trunk. I sucked in a breath, trying to refill my lungs as something thundered towards me. The griffin shrieked as it approached. I hadn't been careful, I'd just run, run with no eyes around me. I knew better than that. But my mother screamed again and my brain wouldn't stop repeating the single thought to just get to her, *GET TO HER NOW.*

The griffin slowed its pace as it approached me, and then shrieked again. I got to my feet quickly, wielding my blade in front of me. The griffin pawed at the ground, then rushed at me with a roar. I leaped over its bowed neck, my sword striking it in the back of the head.

Rook was right, their bones were like steel, and Arankos bounced off the griffin's skull with an audible clang. But it was enough to disorient the creature long enough for me to begin running again, towards my mother.

She'd fallen silent, and my heart hammered in my chest. Had they hurt her? Had they killed her? I almost wished she'd scream again so I'd know she was still alive, still breathing. The squelch of the wet ground under me was almost inaudible over the noise of the crowd around me.

I pelted into a clearing, and didn't even have time to gasp as the floor gave way beneath me. I tumbled into a deep pit, landing heavily on my side, my sword flying out of my hand. The crowd let out a collective *Ooh*.

Pain shot through my side as I struggled to my feet. I hoped I hadn't broken a rib. I snatched up my sword from the ground, and looked up the steep walls surrounding me. They were lined with a black, sticky substance, which gleamed blue in the sunlight. It looked like tar, but smelled like rotten flesh.

I heard the griffin shrieking nearby. I had to get out, now. I sheathed Arankos on my back, and dug my hands into the slimy walls of the pit, trying to get a foothold to get myself up. I was moving too slowly, it was taking an age, and I wished I could fucking fly. I gritted my teeth as I willed the ground under my hands and feet not to give way, to just stay long enough for me to make it up. The slime stuck to my armor, to my face, and it smelled so awful. I retched, trying to breathe through my mouth, my eyes watering.

My mother screamed again, and my heart leapt in my chest. I had almost reached the top when I heard the griffin's thundering hooves. *Move, move, fucking MOVE.* With a growl I launched myself up over the edge of the pit, landing on the ground, shoulders heaving and ribs aching. Dirt stuck to the foul-smelling slime that now covered me. *What the fuck is this?*

And then I saw the dead griffin baby at the far edge of the pit.

It's blue black blood running out of the gash in its throat. I looked down at myself. *Fuck.* I was covered in the baby's blood. *Fuck fuck FUCK.* The thundering hooves came closer and I pushed myself off the ground, breaking into a sprint. I had to get away.

The griffin came from my left, screeching wildly, roaring as it got closer and smelled its baby's blood all over me. I turned and arced my sword, missing, because I was swinging wildly and in no way targeted. I had to focus.

The griffin pulled its head back and then launched itself at me, snapping its beak inches from my face. I rolled underneath it, seeing the rippling breastplate. It turned, looking for me, snapping at my feet. I rose to my knees under its left foreleg, and sank my sword into the soft membrane, which gave way with a loud sucking noise.

The griffin roared, flailing its neck about, more blue black blood pouring over my arm. The griffin lifted its leg and kicked me hard in the side of the head, and my vision went cloudy as I stumbled away. The wound under the foreleg made another terrible sucking noise as my sword was pulled from it, and in the distance my mother began screaming again.

I ran, as fast as I could through the white spots in my vision. The trees began to give way, and the ground underfoot became firmer. I had to be close, I could hear my mother weeping now.

"Mama!" I called out as I ran.

"Elara?" The voice was halting at first, then suddenly became urgent. "Elara! Elara, I'm here!" I pushed through the low underbrush, sharp-edged leaves slicing my face. I reached a clearing, and there she was. Chained to a wooden podium at the end of the Pit, stood my mother. Her eyes widened when she saw me running towards her. "Elara!" Tears were running down her cheeks, and her face was red from crying. "Elara, oh Gods, Elara!"

I had almost reached her. I had almost done it. Suddenly her face distorted with terror. "*LOOK OUT!*" She screamed.

Too late.

The griffin landed on me, right on my back, knocking me to the ground. My sword clattered away from me, and I turned over as the creature raised itself, in time to see that enormous beak come flying right for my face. I dodged one strike, then another, the beak thundering into the ground either side of my head with such force the earth shook.

When it raised its head again, I scrambled along the ground on my back for my sword, but I wasn't fast enough, and the beak came down on my thigh. I cried out, sure I felt bones give way. My hand shot out, nothing but pure instinct driving me, and my fingers landed in the gelatinous mass of the griffin's eyes. It squawked and shook its head, clambering away from me.

I shuffled towards my sword, feeling the warm hilt in my grasp just as the griffin turned its good eye towards me and shrieked again. It charged me, and I raised my sword as it landed on me, praying I wasn't about to hit sheer steel.

But I heard a sickening, wet slap, and blood cascaded over me. I pushed the sword in, harder still, and only stopped when my hand was almost submerged in the wound. The griffin gurgled, and flailed for only a moment, before it went still, collapsing on my legs.

I clawed my way out from underneath it, struggling back to my feet. Searing pain shot through my thigh, and I gritted my teeth as I limped towards my mother. The crowd began to cheer, which caught me so violently off guard, I stopped and looked up into the stands around me. I gave myself a shake and kept moving, dragging my leg as I approached her.

Sobs shook her shoulders as I reached her. Her hair, darker than mine, hung down her back in a messy braid, and her violet eyes were filled with tears.

"Elara," she said as I put my arms around her. She was still chained, so all she could do was bury her face into the crook of my neck. "Oh my darling girl, where have you been?"

"I'm sorry, Mama." I felt tears welling up, but pushed them away, pushed them down. *Not now.* I couldn't cry here. "I'm so sorry."

"I was out of my mind for months." Her lip quivered as she stared at me, shaking her head. "My precious girl, what happened?"

Pain was starting to muddy my thoughts. "I'm sorry, Mama."

Applause sounded beside us, and I looked up to see Theron and his entourage approach. "Well done, Princess." He said, his gaze moving to my mother with a sneer. "You defeated it. Granted, it was an easy trial. But I must say I am impressed."

"Will you release her?" I asked.

Theron nodded. "But of course, dear one. That was the arrangement. Your mother may go home, as we agreed." He gave me a smile that was almost kind. "I am a man of my word, Elara."

I bowed my head. "Thank you, Sire."

My mother sobbed quietly. "May I have a moment with my daughter out of these chains?"

Theron gestured to a guard, who stepped forward, and I released my mother as he unlocked the chains binding her down. As soon as she was free, she threw herself on me, sobbing again as she held me close.

"What happened, my darling?" She whispered.

"I went with Keir," I told her. "I'm sorry, I never should have left, I'm sorry."

"Are you alright?" She asked, taking my face in her hands, her hand straying over the side of my face, her eyes widening. "Oh Gods, Elara -"

"It's... it's alright." I felt faint, and swayed a little as I tried to stay upright in front of her.

"Your ear, your face -" She broke off as another sob tore through her, and she clutched me to her. "Oh, my darling girl."

"Alright, that will do," Theron said suddenly, and stepped forward. "Your mother has a long journey back to Peyrus ahead of her, and I wouldn't want her return delayed."

"No!" My mother clung to me desperately. "You can't keep her here! Please!"

But she was yanked out of my arms, out of my grasp, and I merely slumped to the ground as she was dragged away, screaming my name, fighting against the iron grip of the guards.

Theron looked down at me, and nodded. "We'll have you seen to." He snapped his fingers, and guards rushed forward to help me to my feet. "Take her to the infirmary."

The guards wanted to carry me out on a stretcher, but I refused. I'd walk out of the Pit if it was the last thing I did. I limped along as the crowd cheered, my mother's screams echoing through my head as the Pit around me changed from a lush jungle into a simple, bare arena with a sandy floor.

I was led through a tunnel, into a stone-walled chamber where a bed stood in the middle. I sat down heavily, staring at the floor.

"The healer will be along," the guard told me, hurrying to the door, leaving me alone. I looked at my hands, covered in griffin blood. I realized I didn't know what had happened to

Arankos. I assumed they would find it and lock it up again, until the next trial.

My breath caught in my throat, as the weight of what had happened bore down on me. I'd survived. I'd saved my mother. But this was the first trial. I'd have to do this again. Something else, like this, again.

"You fucking idiot!" Rook's voice thundered as he stormed into the infirmary. "I told you to push that sword in, further than you needed to."

"The griffin kicked me," I replied weakly. "I couldn't-"

"It nearly killed you!" His eyes were wild. "You nearly had your fucking throat torn out!"

"Nearly." I gave him a weak smile.

He shook his head and rushed at me, stopping short, his arms tense as though he wanted to take me into them. "Nearly. Fucking Nav, nearly." He looked down at me, taking my face in his hands. "I thought…" He leaned closer to me, then swallowed hard, his brow furrowed. "I thought I was about to watch you die."

"Too determined for that kiss." I replied.

Rook rolled his eyes and gave me a crooked smile. "You smell like a rotting corpse."

"So do you now."

"Well then you'll have to wait until later, I want to do it properly, when we don't both smell of death." There was movement outside, and Rook stepped back from me quickly. "I have to go."

"Climb my tower, would you?" I asked, wincing as I shifted my leg, pain shooting into my hip.

Rook hesitated, and his expression spoke a thousand words in just a second. I could see he didn't want to leave, but he gave me a quick nod, and hurried out of the room.

Chapter 14

Elara

I lay awake in my bed, every crackle of the fire sending my nerves on edge, waiting for my window to open. I'd almost given up, my eyes becoming heavy, when I heard the scrape and soft creak as the frame gave way.

I sat up and watched Rook climb in noiselessly, putting his feet down on the floor. He smiled at me, his eyes glowing in the dim light of the fire. "Hello, love."

"I thought you weren't coming."

He crossed the room, coming to sit beside me on the bed. "Not easy sneaking around here, you know, trying not to get myself killed." He raised a hand to my cheek and raised his eyebrows. "Now, do you want to tell me why your mother was so surprised to see you here?"

I shook my head. "No. I want you to kiss me and maybe fuck me and that's all."

Rook let out a choked laugh. "Fucking Nav, princess."

"What?" I asked, trying to stay nonchalant. "I was promised a kiss."

Rook shook his head, his thumb tracing my lower lip, and

just that touch sent it quivering. Rook frowned. "Ah. It's like that is it?"

I shook my head as the lump in my throat made speaking impossible.

Rook shuffled closer with a sigh, and put his arms around me. "I thought so."

I wanted to pretend I didn't know what he was talking about. I wanted to insist all I wanted was for him to push me down on the bed and put his mouth on all the places I'd dreamed of him putting it. But his fingers brushed over my bare shoulders, and his tenderness sent me over the edge. I quaked against him as silent sobs escaped me, tears spilling down my cheeks.

Rook held me close, letting me cry, his chin resting gently atop my head. I clawed my fingers into his shirt, feeling the warmth seeping from his skin. I pressed my cheek harder into him, wanting all that warmth for myself. Why, fucking, WHY did I feel so safe with him? It made me almost angry, that he'd been so cruel, so vicious when we'd first met, and now he was holding me in my bed. I was crying into his chest and wanting nothing more than for him to kiss me and to help me forget just what a fucking terrible situation I was in.

"I ran away," I said finally, my throat raw from holding all the sobs in.

Rook lifted my face to look up at him. "You ran away from Peyrus?"

I sat up, pulling my knees to my chest, whimpering as the pain shot through my leg. The griffin had left behind a really decent bruise, but no broken bones thankfully. Rook started forward, concern furrowing his brow, but I waved him off.

"It's alright, just my leg."

He shook his head. "I'm not surprised, the way that

fucking griffin pounded you into the ground." He reached over and took my hand. "So, you ran away?"

"Yes. Six months ago. My parents had no idea - well, I mean, they figured it out, obviously, that I'd run off, but they've not known this whole time what happened to me."

"Gods, Elara, why?" Rook asked.

"Because Keir and I made a vow, we'd said we wouldn't be separated, and so I didn't let myself be separated from him. He was sent to the fight, and I went with him. I told my parents I was accompanying him to the borderlands, to say goodbye, but I went with him instead. Snuck Arankos out of the palace, and just left."

"They didn't send anyone after you?"

"No." I gripped his hand tighter. "By the time they'd figured it out, the battle made extraction impossible. Keir and I had promised that we would wait for each other at the gates in Nav when we died."

"Fucking children." He was almost scolding. "What a thing to promise each other. He should have wanted you safe, not dying next to him on a battlefield."

I yanked my hand away from his. "You wouldn't understand."

"No, you're right, I don't." He leaned forward, the fire-light making his brown skin look even warmer, as though lit from within. "In Isambard, we don't endanger the people we love."

"It was my choice." I spat back. "I'm not some simpering little girl."

"That's not the point." Rook moved closer to me. "You're fierce, and you're a fighter, but if you were mine -"

"Well, I'm not!"

"Keep your fucking voice down, or we both die."

"Good." I felt tears forming in my eyes again.

Rook growled through gritted teeth. "Maybe you are just a stupid little girl."

"Get out of my room." I hissed, kicking my legs out at him. "Go away."

Rook rose from the bed but didn't move any further, leaning one hand against a bed post. "You risked your life to die next to the man you loved, that was it?"

"What would you understand about it?"

"Everything," he snarled. "I would never place the woman I love in that kind of danger, for some stupid fucking vow."

"Are we still talking about me?" I asked him, climbing off the bed and looking up at him in the half-light. "Because you seem very eager to tell me what you would have done, like that matters."

"It *does* fucking matter."

"Why?" I shoved him in the chest.

"Because it doesn't make any fucking sense." He sucked in a rasping breath. "Fucking *gods.* You want a man who'd be happy to watch you die in front of him, is that it?"

I slapped him hard across the face, the sound ringing shrilly through the room. "How fucking *dare you.*"

Rook leaned down over me, his face less than an inch from mine. "Where is he now, Elara? Hmm? He died and left you here, to fight this shit on your own. That's his bond to you, is it?"

"Get out of my room." I pushed against his chest, but he didn't move, didn't budge at all. "I said, get the fuck out of my room, you fucking brute."

Rook seized my arms, pulling me against his chest. His eyes glowed, searing blue, and yet not at all cold. His heart thundered between us, the heat from his skin seeping against me. "You asked me up here for a kiss, remember?"

"You can fuck off with your kiss." But I didn't fight him. I stayed there, cursing myself for the desire that still coursed through me.

Rook's mouth twitched at the corner, into a small crooked grin. "Wouldn't want to kiss you right now anyhow, you stubborn little bitch." But he still didn't let me go. Finally, his grip on me relaxed, and the tension of rage left my body. We both sighed, almost at the same time, and his head dropped a little. "I'm sorry."

"Don't be. You're right. It was stupid of me." I gazed up at him, raising a hand to his cheek. "When you said you understood me, what did you mean? Theron said you knew all about loss."

"That's a story for another time, love. After what you went through today, I don't want to tell you..." He trailed off, and he lowered his mouth to my cheek. "I'm sorry about your mother."

I leaned against him, feeling his lips, his warm breath washing over my skin. "It's alright, I saved her." I murmured. "She's safe now, back home."

"Mmm." His hands moved, from holding mine to his chest, to around my shoulders. His mouth moved along my jawline, along my scars, and his fingers caressed my back. He growled, low in his throat, when I shivered against him. "Watching you fight down there, alone, it fucking kills me."

My fingers flexed on his chest as my head tipped back, letting his mouth explore more of my neck. "It does?"

"I don't do well watching people I care -" He broke off, and a strangled breath passed between his lips. He crushed me against him, and I balked for only a split second as I felt the hard heat of his arousal through his clothes. "Fucking Nav, Elara. You're going to drive me mad."

"You care for me?"

"The first person I've cared about in years." His hands

moved lower, down my back, to my ass. His touch was light, still questioning, but that somehow just made the longing pulling my stomach taut even more acute.

"Why is this happening to us?" I asked as I wound my arms around his neck. It didn't matter, it didn't fucking matter why, oh Gods I just wanted him to throw me on the bed. I wanted to feel his body, all of it, all of it against me. The scent of his skin, that soothing freshness and saltiness, was intensified as his blood heated his body.

"You've cast a spell on me," he murmured, his hands working at my nightgown, fisting it and pulling it up my legs. "Some wicked fucking Fae magic. All I can think about is your eyes and your hair and your hands, and every fucking thing else." He pulled back from me suddenly, panting. "Fuck, not like this." He leaned against the bedpost, shaking his head. "I don't want it to be like this."

"Like what?" I put my arms around myself, his retreat leaving me cold. "Don't you want me?"

He let out a choked laugh. "Princess, you have no idea just how much I want you."

"So, why did you stop? Is it because - because I'm still pure?" Fuck I hated that word, but I didn't know how else to say it.

Even in the half-light of the bedroom I could see his surprise, his eyebrows shooting up. "You're still what?"

I felt immediately self-conscious. *Idiot.*

"You're still what?" He asked, stepping closer again.

"Pure. You know what I mean. I - I told you I'd never…" I was sure my cheeks were glowing visibly, the hot flush so violent it almost made my eyes water. "I just thought maybe, maybe it put you off."

"That's not it, at all." He said. "I wouldn't, I mean, that wouldn't stop me."

"So, what *is* stopping you?" The jealousy I'd felt that morning in my room when the pretty redhead with the big tits had served me breakfast rushed through me full force. "Is it because I'm not some scullery maid you can just fuck and leave?"

Rook scoffed. "Oh come now, don't do that."

I stuck my chin out at him, feeling stupidly hurt by all this. "Am I too noble for you, is that it? You can use the body of some maid but with me you suddenly feel bound by honor?"

"Elara." His voice was low, and hearing him say my name sent a rush down my back, a shiver so intense it made his rejection of me even worse. "Don't do that. That's not what this is."

"Then what is it?" I was almost desperate now, the stinging, the unbearable fucking stinging at the back of my eyeballs making my eyes water. "Why don't you want to take me to bed?"

"Because I don't want this to be some pity fuck." His hands grasped my shoulders. "I don't want this to be two people desperate for someone. I care for you, and I want you, but I don't want it to be meaningless. My life has been meaningless for too long."

"You need to love me first, is that it?" I couldn't help but sneer. "So all those women, all those scullery maids you violated the Accord for, they were all meaningless?"

"You think I meant anything to them?" The pain in his voice took me by surprise. "You think any one of them fucked me out of anything more than curiosity? Seeing if the stories about the Night Demons were true?"

I flinched, cursing my insensitivity. "Rook, I'm so sorry-"

"I told you," he interjected, taking my face in his hands, "you're the first person to look at me in years. The first person to speak to me, who wasn't afraid of me, who didn't treat me like a criminal or a freak."

"I just tried to kill you instead."

Rook chuckled, and leaned his forehead against mine. "We need to get you through all of this," he said, "I want to help you. I want to see you through it all, because then, you'll be free."

Realization dawned on me. I had the chance to earn what Rook would never have - freedom. And then I would be gone, and he'd still be here. Still enslaved. Still trapped. And he'd lose something else. I was just one more thing for him to lose.

I stepped back from him, despite the urge to throw myself into his arms, to comfort him. Fuck, to comfort myself. His hands lingered on my shoulders as I moved away. "I'm so sorry. I wasn't thinking."

He shook his head. "No, it's alright. You're alone, and you're a prisoner. I understand you, better than anyone else ever will." He backed away slowly. "I should go before anyone notices I'm here."

"I'll see you at training tomorrow."

"No you won't." He shook his head. "Fucking Gods, you need to recover first. Let that leg heal. Then we'll train together again."

"So I won't see you until then?"

He hesitated, and ran a hand through his hair. "I-I don't know, love. Just... just get better, alright? Rest."

He paused on the window sill, the evening breeze catching his hair, shimmering blue-black in the moonlight. "I mean it. If you were mine, I'd make sure you were safe. I'd die to make sure you were safe."

"And so would I."

"Then the Gods help the world if we ever fall in love." He

gave me one last smile before lowering himself out of the window.

I stood in the room alone, listening to the fire crackling, waiting for my heart to stop thundering against my ribcage. I ran a hand over the warmth in my chest and thought back on the bond I'd shared with Keir. The silver threads that pulled us together. The space in our souls that we'd occupied in one another.

Now that bond was gone - and as the darkness grew around me, I felt those threads growing again, unfurling and snaking their way through the air, following the Night Demon prince as he crept away from my room. I've tried to deny it for weeks now. I'd tried to tell myself the dreams were meaningless. I'd tried to tell myself that that longing I felt for Rook, that the comfort I found only in his presence, was nothing more than loneliness.

But now I knew - Rook's soul was bonded to mine.

I'd never been able to explain the Bonds to myself, why they formed, why Lada chose the ones she did. But as I lay down in my bed, I knew that Rook had been brought into my life for a reason.

I just hoped we both lived long enough to discover it.

Chapter 15

Rook

W*ell, fuck.*

I stared at the ceiling of my chamber as the moonlight gave way to the dawn, my hand on my chest, feeling the thud of my heartbeat as it was enveloped by the roiling warmth I'd felt for weeks but not been able to explain to myself.

But now it was joined by something else, a sense of a second heart, beating right alongside it, in perfect rhythm. When I inhaled, my lungs filled with her breath.

There was no denying it any longer.

I'd not been raised in the Faith, but I knew enough of it from myth and legend to know the stories of a Ladaian Bond. Two souls, bound to one another, for all eternity, only separated by death. Night Demons scoffed at it, saying it was a denial of free will. I'd never thought to question it, much less thought that it would ever fucking happen to me.

And now I was lying here, glowing with… Love. For a fucking Fae princess.

With a grunt, I kicked the blankets off me, sitting up to

watch the first raindrops patter against my window. The sky outside darkened, the air becoming thick as a storm rolled in. I dressed quickly, tying back my hair, wondering how much longer Theron would let it get before he had me shorn again.

I pushed through the door, out into the passageway. The guards protested for a moment, but I ignored them, heading out into the rain just as the first rumble of thunder sounded overhead. It was terrible weather for running, but run I did. I ran the perimeter of the castle grounds twice, then headed down the path into town.

The streets were empty, and any passers-by saw me coming and quickly ducked into the next welcoming door. Rain beat against my face, dripping into my eyes, and I blinked it away furiously.

How the fuck had this happened?

Of all the beings in the realm, of all the fucking females there were - it had to be her. The daughter of the man who'd betrayed me. The daughter of the man who'd cost me everything. Fuck fuck *fuck*.

And she'd wanted me in her bed. I gritted my teeth in frustration. Why hadn't I just fucked her? It would have been the ultimate revenge. Fucking the Fae princess, and somehow letting Vayr know that his offspring had lost her purity to a Night Demon; the thought should have brought me satisfaction.

Instead, I was overcome with shame. Because I didn't want to just *fuck* her. I didn't want to use her for revenge, I wanted her to be *mine.* I wanted to join my body with hers. I wanted to feel her skin and hear her moans and *fuck it all.* I was ruined.

The rain was falling harder as I left the quiet streets of town and sprinted back up the hill to the palace. I kept running along the palace wall, through the gardens, and across the sodden lawn.

I slowed my pace as the temple came into view. *Keep running*. But I stopped at the bottom of the steps and looked up at the golden spires. The heavy smell of incense wafted from inside, and warm candlelight spilled from the doorways.

I placed a foot on the lower step, then withdrew it and turned sharply away. I wasn't going in there. But something stopped me, like a heavy hand on my shoulder, and I found myself at the top of steps, shoulders heaving from my run, the smell of incense filling my nose. I took a tentative step closer to the door.

Suddenly an old woman dressed in blue robes appeared, gazing at me curiously with large, silvery eyes. "Can I help you, my child?" She didn't appear afraid of me, merely curious, surely wondering what the sopping wet Night Demon struggling to catch his breath was doing on the steps of her temple. I considered turning away for a moment, but the soft brown skin around her eyes crinkled as she smiled at me, and she extended a hand. "Won't you come in?"

I hesitated before I waved her off. "No, I wouldn't want to get your tiles all wet." I tried to smile amicably, but I was feeling tense and uncertain. "I had - I mean, I was wondering… Ummm…. There was something I needed some… advice on."

She laced her fingers together, and nodded. "But of course, if I can help I will."

"Do you know anything about - I mean, what is there you can tell me about…" I broke off, running a hand through my hair and laughing awkwardly. "Sorry, I've been rather -"

"Tired?" She lifted her eyebrows.

"I beg your pardon?"

She gestured to the gardens behind me. "I have seen you

running almost every day, as though you are trying to escape something. And the fact it has brought you here tells me it has caught you."

Caught me. Yes it had. "I've been having rather wild dreams." I stretched my hands, the roiling warmth in my chest clutching at the base of my throat.

"That is usually how it starts." She gave me a knowing smile, tucking a strand of white hair behind her ear. She took a deep breath of the cool, wet air that surrounded us. "Now, what is it you would like to know?"

"A Ladaian love bond," I said quickly, before I thought better of it. "Do you, I mean, can you tell me anything about it?"

"But of course, I am the High Priestess of this Temple." She laughed when I bowed my head. "Oh we do not require such formality here, my child. What would you like to know?"

Thunder rumbled loudly overhead, the rain pelting down in heavy sheets. I took a deep breath.

"How does it form?" I asked, running a hand over my chest without thinking. "I mean, why does it happen?"

The priestess shrugged. "That I cannot answer. Lada's ways are not to be explained."

"But it *is* a love bond?"

"Certainly. Two souls, bound for all eternity, separated only by death."

I gave a short laugh. "Yes, I know the stories. Is there any other way… Can it be forced, by magic?"

The priestess shook her head emphatically. "No. A true Ladaian Bond is one of the few forces of this Realm that not even the Seraph have been able to corrupt. There are love spells that can mimic aspects of the Bond, but a true Bond, where both parties feel the other's heart and breath in their body - that cannot be made by magic."

The combination of relief and irritation I felt at that moment almost knocked me off my feet. So this was real. It wasn't evil Fae magic. It was *real.* I was bonded to a Fae princess who I wanted to protect with my life. She *was* mine. Fucking gods.

"And is it normal to want to… Do… Things?" Gods I was blushing. I was asking an ancient priestess if it was normal to want to fuck someone I was bonded to and it was the most awkward thing I'd ever experienced in my life. I wanted the ground to swallow me up. "I mean… you know…"

"You mean sex?" The priestess laughed lightly. "Is that what you are asking? If it is normal to want a physical as well as a spiritual connection with your Bonded."

"Not *my* Bonded." I almost stumbled over the words, bouncing nervously on the balls of my feet. "I'm just asking, in general terms."

"Of course you are." The priestess nodded, and if she doubted me she didn't show it. "All acts of love are sacred in the eyes of the Goddess. So yes, it is perfectly normal to want to have those experiences with your Bonded, if that is what you both desire."

"And I can't break it?"

She cocked an eyebrow. "You?"

Fuck. "Not me, obviously. I mean, I'm asking if it can't be broken, in general."

"Would you want it to be?"

No. The last thing I wanted was for it to be gone. Where that heat holding my heart had driven me mad at first, the thought of it being gone now was too much to bear. She had anchored herself within my soul, within my very being, and to tear that out of my ribcage now - the thought made me shudder.

"I can't imagine anyone would want it to go away," the

priestess said when I remained silent. "It is nothing to fear. Even if the reason is not clear at first, even if the choice is unexpected, there is joy to be found in a Bond with another."

"Joy. Yes."

She took a step closer to me, her eyes darting around for a moment, as though to check we were truly alone. "Fighting it does not make it any easier."

I didn't want to tell her that giving in to it would make my life vastly more difficult. I didn't even know if giving in to it was a choice I had to make. But that was all too difficult - and too dangerous - to explain to a priestess in a temple in Veles. Instead, I gave her a nod and a brief smile. "Thank you for your help."

"Any time, my child." She waved as I left, back into the pouring rain.

I didn't run back to my chamber. Instead, I walked slowly across the sodden grass. I dug my toes into the ground, and took deep breaths. And all the while that warmth crept through my veins, heating my blood as my heart beat in rhythm with hers.

Thunder crashed overhead as I drew myself a bath. I lowered myself into the warm water, washing away the mud and cold sweat. I closed my eyes, leaning my head against the edge of the tub. *Fighting it does not make it any easier.*

I didn't want to fight it. I wanted nothing more than to give in to everything I felt, to climb that tower again and climb into Elara's bed. I wanted to crush those rosy lips under mine, hear her sigh as my hands moved over her body, over the body that was now mine.

But it wasn't that simple.

I lifted my arm, looking at the glowing silver mark etched into my skin. I wondered that Theron hadn't forced one on to Elara yet. The very thought had rage boiling at the base of my throat. The thought of him hurting her, touching a single hair on her head… I slammed my fist into the water.

Fuck it all.

Rain pelted against the window, the drumming almost deafening. There would be no further relief to be found outside today, no distraction to be found in a sodden training arena. Not that I even wanted to wear myself out to avoid thinking of her anymore.

With a heavy sigh I hauled myself out of the water and dried myself. I'd need to find distraction elsewhere in the castle today. Anything to try and move my focus from the coil that pulled tighter every time I thought of her.

Chapter 16

Rook

I knew the minute I'd stepped foot into the library that I wasn't alone. Over the scent of wood and paper, there was another one, one that rendered me weak and useless.

Elara was here.

Of course she was. Of course my feet had carried me to her without even thinking. The coil that held my heart captive beside hers had led me straight to her side.

There was no fighting it. Even if I'd wanted to. I was utterly, completely ruined for her.

I rounded the corner of towering shelves, and there she was, sitting at a chess board, frowning and chewing her lip as she looked down at the pieces in front of her. She was wearing a blue gown, the same color as her eyes, and her hair hung over her shoulder in a loose braid. She lifted a hand to rub her delicate fingers across her chin, and leaned back in the chair with a sigh.

"Stuck?" I asked, and her eyes darted over to where I stood.

Her face broke into a soft smile. "I am rather. Do you play?"

I walked over to her slowly. "I do. Poorly, but I do." I sat down opposite her, her eyes remaining on me. "I'm not much of a strategist you see."

She lifted an eyebrow. "No?"

"No. More of an In the Moment sort, I suppose. I can't always see what's lying ahead."

Elara laughed softly, stroking the length of her braid. "Yes, sometimes the moves that lie ahead can catch us off guard." She picked up one of the castles, rolling it between her fingers. "Where I come from, these are called Towers. But in some cultures they're called rooks, did you know that?"

I nodded. "I did."

"The pieces that can surprise you the most, ironically enough." The corners of her mouth twitched as she put the Tower back on the board, and she lifted her chin, gesturing to the board. "Your move."

I looked down at the pieces on the board, trying to figure out how she'd gotten to this point. I picked up the knight, moving him towards her Queen, and Elara sucked on her teeth.

"You really aren't a strategist," she said with a small laugh.

"I did tell you." I feigned a groan and threw my hands up as she moved her tower to claim my knight. "So how did you become so good at it?"

"All those lonely, frozen winters in the North. A child has to find a way to entertain herself."

"And you chose chess?" I chuckled. "I can see it now, the studious little princess, plotting war after war on the board in front of her."

She raised an eyebrow. "Well, I never won a war, but I did always manage to win the battles."

"That you did."

Her eyes moved over the board only to meet mine again, the smile still on her face, dropping slightly as she opened her mouth to speak. "I am sorry."

"For what?"

"Last night." She shook her head. "I wasn't thinking. It was wrong of me."

"You don't need to apologize. I don't want you to think… I don't want to give you the impression that I…" I broke off, looking back down at the scattered pieces on the chessboard. "Can I ask you something?"

"Of course."

"Your Mate - I mean, your- The one who-"

"Keir," she interjected, eyeing me curiously. "What about him?"

"How did you know?" I gestured to her with my hand. "I mean, that he was… yours?"

"You want to know about Keir?" She asked a little incredulously, exhaling heavily as she looked out the window at the unrelenting rain. "I mean… I just knew. We looked at each other one day, and it was just… there. There was no explaining it."

"But you and he… You never…" I coughed, laughing awkwardly. "Sorry, this is definitely none of my business."

Elara covered her mouth as she laughed, her cheeks flushing the sweetest shade of pink. "It's alright. I mean, I *did* tell you. There were moments where I thought we would, but…" She shrugged. "I loved him, but it was… different. I wanted to be close to him, and … But… It was different. To anything I've ever felt before."

I met her eyes, and I knew she felt it too. I put a hand to

my chest, and her eyes dropped to it for only a moment before rising back to meet mine. "Different?" I asked slowly.

She nodded. "I can't explain it."

"Did you ever dream of him?" *Like you dream of me.* I didn't have to say the words, I could see from the flicker of her jaw that she knew what I meant.

She shook her head slowly, reaching out to move her King forward one square. "No. That's only ever happened... with you."

"Every night." I reached out and put my fingers around my Queen, holding Elara's gaze. I didn't have to say anything else. She understood completely.

"Every night." She repeated, before nodding. "Yes. I never knew I could feel this way."

I wanted to say something cruel then, shaming her dead Bonded for the danger he'd put her in. Shaming him for not laying down his life to protect her, for dragging her onto the battlefield with him for some stupid, childish vow. Of course she'd never felt anything like this, because no one had ever cared for her like I did.

But I bit the words back. I didn't want to hurt her. Not now. Not when those blue eyes were fixed on me with softness and the barest hint of desire, open and honest and piercing me to my very core.

I looked down at her hand, still on her King, and smiled. "The King is my favorite piece."

She let out a laugh mixed with a scoff, and tossed her braid over her shoulder. "Of course it is."

"Not for the reason you think," I replied.

She cocked an eyebrow. "Is that so?"

"It's the most self-aware piece on the board."

"Self-aware?"

I looked into her eyes, feeling her heartbeat in my very own chest. "He knows he's nothing without his Queen."

Elara sucked in a small, shaky breath. I let the Queen go, moving my hand across the board to brush my fingers against hers. Her eyes were locked on mine, her lip trembling ever so slightly, and fucking gods I wanted to kiss her. Why hadn't I kissed her the night before? Why hadn't I seized her in my arms and let her claim me completely?

"Rook." Her little finger wrapped around mine.

"Yes?"

"I'm afraid I'm very selfish when it comes to you."

"What do you mean, princess?"

"Because even though you said, last night. You said that it…" She cleared her throat, her gaze determined. "It wouldn't have been meaningless."

Gods, I was a fool. Of course it wouldn't have been. Nothing about sinking into her body and joining myself with her would have been meaningless. It would have been *everything*.

"I know, love." I placed my other hand over hers, knowing guards were probably watching from some shadowed corner of the library, ready to report back to Theron. But she was all I could focus on, her very being tearing my mind from every other thought. "And I wish now I'd not been so stupid."

"I want you to say those things to me." Her voice dropped low. "I want you to whisper those things to me, the things you say in my dreams."

My heart was threatening to pound its way directly out of my ribcage. Fucking gods, how had this innocent little Fae princess turned the tables on me like this, that I was now melting under her gaze, fighting the urge to drag her off into a dark corner of the library and give in to her.

"You can't say things like that to me here," I said, attempting a small grin. "You're going to drive me mad."

Her gaze intensified, and I was keenly aware of the rise and fall of her breasts, her nipples peaking under the silk of her dress. Her hand was hot between mine, and my whole body was tense with longing. The storm raged outside, but neither of us were paying any attention to it anymore. The tempest of lust that was rampaging through my blood was more than enough to distract me.

"Rook," she murmured, and one of her feet rubbed against my leg under the table.

How the fuck could just the touch of a foot send heat flooding my groin? I suppressed a groan, gripping on to her hand.

"It wouldn't be meaningless," she said again.

I couldn't stand it any more. I pushed out of my chair, sending it toppling to the floor with a crash. Elara watched me with hooded eyes and parted lips as I fell to my knees beside her, yanking her chair out from underneath the chess table. I pulled her towards me, her legs parting so we were chest to chest. Her breathing was rapid as my hands gripped the back of her chair, caging her in. Her lips were mere inches from mine.

"Norahi!"

The sharp call of the guard shattered the moment in an instant. I backed away from Elara, who was flushed and in disarray in her chair as the guard approached.

"What is the meaning of this?" The guard snapped, looking from me to Elara.

I rose to my feet slowly. "It's none of your concern."

"Looks to me like you were trying to have your way with the Princess here," the guard said with a sneer, pointing his spear at my face.

"I was frightened," Elara said, smoothing the silk of her dress back over her legs.

"Frightened?" The guard asked incredulously. "Of what?"

Elara gestured to the window as lightning flashed. "The storm. It's especially violent today, and I was afraid. Norahi thought I was about to faint. Didn't you?" Her eyes flashed up to mine.

I nodded. "Yes. She looked as though she was in need of assistance, nothing more."

The guard lowered his spear, digging it into the shiny wood floor thoughtlessly as he leaned on it, eyeing us suspiciously. "You watch yourself, Norahi."

"You watch *your*self." I waved him off. "Now leave us alone."

The guard walked off with a huff, grumbling to himself about insolence and *fucking Night Demons*. I waited until he was well out of earshot before I looked back down at Elara, who was sitting primly in the chair, her hands clasped in her lap.

"Sorry," she murmured. "That was so stupid of me."

I lifted my hand to touch her, then quickly pulled it back, letting it drop. I couldn't touch her. If I touched her now that barely-contained monsoon of longing would take over again. She gazed up at me with a sigh.

"I should go back to my room," she said softly, getting to her feet. She paused in front of me, her head lowered. Her breath shuddered as she turned her head ever so slightly. "Thank you for the chess game."

"We didn't finish." I gestured to the board. "Perhaps you can beat me at it another time."

She let out a short laugh. "Yes. Perhaps."

Neither of us moved, just wanting to stay close, just wanting to feel the other's presence. Her hand stretched a little, as though reaching out for me. She let out a frustrated sigh, stepping away from me.

"I'll see you at training," she said, before spinning on her heel and walking quickly out of the library. The door closed in the distance, and I was left alone.

I looked down at the chess board, at the ivory Queen and the ebony King, standing beside each other, and couldn't help but smile. I scooped the pieces into my hand, tucking them away in my pocket, and went back to my chambers.

A King is nothing without his Queen. Without her, everything is meaningless.

Chapter 17

Elara

A knock on my door brought an unexpected visitor. Theron's wings were held close to his back as he walked into my chamber, and I rose to my feet, bowing my head. Drusilla dropped into a low curtsey, and remained there until I started speaking.

"Your Majesty, you've come to visit me?" I didn't smile as my eyes met his. "To what do I owe this pleasure? Have you come to announce the next trial?"

Theron's eyes fixed on Drusilla as she cleared the plates from the table. "You, you can go." His voice was cold. "I need to speak to the Princess alone."

Drusilla eyed me with uncertainty for a split second, before bobbing her knees and scurrying out of the room. Theron's gaze stayed on me, and I held it, unwavering. The door closed behind Drusilla, and Theron's mouth twitched into a smile.

"Alone at last, dear one."

"So it would seem." I replied.

"How have you been?" He asked. " I do hope the griffin didn't leave any permanent damage on those legs of yours."

I shook my head and gave him a small smile. "Certainly not, Sire. I've healed rather well, thankfully."

Theron nodded, and strolled across the room. "Excellent. I've always admired the healing powers of the Fae."

"Was my mother returned safely to Peyrus?"

"Mmm." Theron walked past me, seeming to admire the stained glass windows beside him. "Everything is well, no need to worry."

"I thank you."

"The next trial will not be as easy," he warned me, his bright white teeth drawn into a wide smile.

"I'm not afraid." I was grateful my voice didn't waver.

"No, I can see that." He sat down on the window and stretched his wings out either side of him. "Have you seen Rook at all?"

The question sent both a bolt of warmth into my chest and a knot of concern into my stomach. Theron knew everything that went on in this palace, and there was no doubt in my mind that he knew about the chess game that had taken place the day before.

"Yes," I said nonchalantly. "We had the pleasure of indulging in a game of chess together. A different kind of training, I suppose."

"Keeping the mind sharp is just as important as keeping the body strong." Theron regarded me warmly, looking me up and down. "You do know who Rook is, don't you? I'm sure he's told you by now."

"He is the Prince of Isambard." Gods, I hated his baiting. With Theron I always felt I was two steps behind, unsure of which direction he intended to take.

Theron nodded slowly. "Do you know much about the Night Demons? About their powers?"

"I-I know they can turn into dragons."

"A *sort* of dragon, I suppose, yes." A golden feather dislodged itself from his wing, and he picked it up from where it had fluttered to land on his thigh. He twirled it in his fingers. "But they can do much more than that. Rook, in particular, he has - well, he *had* incredible command of powers I'd never seen before."

"Is that so?"

"Oh yes." Theron grinned. "He can summon the darkness to do his bidding."

Grim fascination overtook me. If it had been anyone but Theron telling me this, I would have been entranced, determined to know more. Shadow magic was something I'd only ever heard of in stories. But I was reluctant to ask Theron for more details, simply because I wanted him to stop talking and leave me alone.

Theron lifted an eyebrow when I didn't respond. "Rook was truly gifted. It was a shame to take all that away from him, but I had to rely on his strength to serve me. Leaving my enemy with such a command of the shadows would have been foolish." He looked out the window at the warm morning light, rubbing his hands together lightly. "He is the greatest prize I could have hoped to seize. I'll have to show you his hair sometime."

"His hair?" I asked. "What do you mean?"

Theron's eyes rolled pensively to the ceiling. "I have quite the collection. You see, he's the only one of the heirs that survived. The others were all weak, all died within months of coming here to Veles. I collected 6 heirs from the kingdoms, and was left with only one."

"What does that have to do with his hair?" I lowered myself into the chair, my back straight as a rod, as though I was waiting for Theron to strike at any moment.

"The kingdoms all had something that was special, something that was significant in their culture," Theron went on, his eyes still fixed on the garden that sprawled below us, his fingers tapping against each other. His wings rustled quietly in the morning breeze. "For the Hux, it was the strangest thing, their pinky fingers." He turned to look at me, raising a hand, extending only the smallest finger. "Such a silly thing."

I tried not to let my breathing betray me, to let him know how barbaric I found this conversation. "Imagine." It was all I could say.

"They truly believed the source of their power lay in these pinky fingers." Theron curled the finger back and forth. "So, I cut it off and put it in a little glass case in my study."

My stomach turned. "The poor Hux Princess."

"Indeed." His gaze shifted for a moment to my missing ear. "I suppose it's a shame someone beat me to that, a pretty Fae ear would have been a valuable contribution to my collection."

"Our ears hold no power," I said flatly.

"No, but they are so very pretty." Theron grinned. "Anyhow, the Isambardians all have long hair. Oh, you should have seen Rook in his prime, what a sight to behold. Long, flowing, curly black hair, down to his waist. A truly regal Prince."

"And you cut it off?" I asked. "To spite your captive?"

Theron shrugged. "Spite, power, who can tell in times of war." His eyes narrowed slightly. "I have his hair in a braid, hanging over my desk. As a reminder of everything I have claimed, and all that is mine."

"But it didn't weaken him, did it?"

Theron laughed. "There was some talk of a belief they hold, that the longer their hair is the closer they are in spirit to their dragon selves. But since Rook cannot change into one any longer, I've not been able to test that theory. Perhaps the

Night Demons are simply more superstitious than they'd like to admit."

I swallowed down my disgust at his sneering. "So, you have a finger and a length of hair, what other wonderful trophies did you collect?" I didn't really want to know, but my anger wouldn't allow me to let him just pass this subject over as though it was nothing.

"A finger, hair." He counted them off on his fingers. "Skin bearing a tattoo, a necklace which was a little boring honestly, and two sets of eyes."

Eyes. My stomach turned even more violently. "Eyes? You took their eyes and wondered that they died?"

Theron chuckled. "Those two shouldn't have been a surprise, certainly."

"And what happened to the others?"

"One killed herself, flung herself off the tower." He gestured above us with a wave of his hand. "Couldn't take it evidently. Then, one turned out to have been pregnant, and she died giving birth to the babe." His lips curled as he looked at my face. "Especially tragic, indeed."

"And the others?" Gods, my father had saved me from this. I wanted to think I'd have survived, that I would have been tough like Rook, that I would have seen it through, but Mokosh knew I probably would have ended like the other heirs.

"They got sick, or became careless, and…" He shrugged, throwing his hands into the air. "And I was left only with Rook." Theron smiled at me. "He says you're training extremely well. I shouldn't be surprised. Seeing you take on that griffin, that was quite something."

"Thank you, Sire." My back was still ramrod straight, my whole body on alert as the golden wings spread even wider.

"I trust Rook completely," he went on, dusting his fingers

over his velvet trousers absently. "I even look the other way when he fucks the scullery maids, though it's against the Accord." He chuckled. "The stories that have circulated at court, the things I have seen myself." He raised his gaze back to meet mine. "Would you like to know?"

I shook my head. "It's none of my business."

"One night," Theron said, leaning back against the window frame, his eyes fixed upwards. "Oh , it was a ball or something here, I saw him fuck some lady from the flatlands outside the Great Hall, and my goodness." Theron laughed heartily. "The sounds she was making! In the absolute fucking throes of passion!"

"How wonderful for her." I wished he'd go away. I didn't want to talk about this, and I certainly didn't want to talk about this to Theron.

"Yes, definitely." Theron leaned forward, his green cat eyes glinting. "They have special anatomy, you see. The Night Demon cock is equipped with a series of bumps and ridges, made especially to elicit the most pleasure from a female when he fucks her."

Sweat formed on the back of my neck, a combination of extreme discomfort at Theron's words, and anxiety over having Rook in my bed, knowing so much about him now, such intimate things about him. I shook my head. "I had no idea, how fascinating."

"Indeed." Theron grinned. "Do you touch yourself, Elara?"

My cheeks burned, and my eyes dropped to my lap. "Sire, I'm sure I don't know how to answer that."

"That's a yes then." Theron laughed heartily. "Of course you do, lying up here alone, after all those… dreams you have of our very own Isambardian prince. You must need to release all that tension somehow."

My fingers were digging so hard into one another it hurt, clasped in my lap. I refused to look up. I didn't want him to suspect for one moment something had happened, something was going on, endangering Rook or me.

"When will you announce the next trial?" I asked in a small voice.

Theron said nothing, and it took two minutes of deeply uncomfortable silence for me to raise my eyes to meet his, to see if he was even going to respond. He smirked at me. "The next trial is in four days," he said, rising to his feet, "and you will be good and ready by then I hope."

"Is it my father? Please, at least tell me that."

Theron approached me slowly, slinking across the room towards me. He stopped in front of me, and raised an icy hand to my face. He gently traced his fingers along the scar on my jaw. His eyes were almost kind for a moment, just a moment. "You are beautiful, dear one. So tender, so fragile."

I said nothing, willing myself, telling myself not to react. I stayed perfectly still.

"It is your father." He said finally. "Let us hope you can win his freedom just as you did for your mother." He turned on his heel and left the room without another word.

I slumped down in my chair, exhaling heavily. My father. He had my father. I had a chance to save my father now, and I would be more careful this time. More alert. I'd be able to save him.

Just like I'd saved my mother.

Chapter 18

Elara

Rook laughed as I landed on top of him with a heavy thud. "Well done! Got me again."

I leaned down over him, lowering my mouth to his ear. "I know you're letting me win."

"And why would I do that, princess?"

"So you end up under me like this." I squeezed him with my thighs.

He sucked in a breath. "You're going to get me in trouble with the guards if you keep doing that."

I shook my head and climbed off him. "I can't be rolling around with you like this. The trial's tomorrow." I rose to my feet and eyed the battle ax leaning against the wall. "How do you swing that thing one-handed?"

Rook shrugged. "I'm strong."

I rolled my eyes. "Lots of warriors are strong. It has to be a skill, how did you learn to do it?"

Rook walked over to the ax, picking it up and swinging it deftly in his hand. "Balance. Knowing where the center of your weapon lies is important. You trained with a long sword, you should know that."

"Arankos and your ax are not the same, the ax is much heavier."

"Ah, but that's not what you asked," Rook said with a grin. "You asked how I wield my weapon one-handed, meaning you want to know how to wield yours one-handed."

"Didn't have you pegged as a pedant, Rook." I crossed my arms over my chest. "So all I need to do is balance Arankos in my hand, and I'll be able to wield it one-handed?"

"More or less." Rook swung the ax, twice, three times, then slammed it down into the ground, the impact sending the muscles in his arms and back rippling. "You need to trust your weapon, and trust yourself."

"Trust myself," I sighed. "Yes."

"You still don't." Rook narrowed his eyes. "You took off into battle without a second thought, and you still stand here and wonder whether you could do it. Whether you're strong enough, or brave enough."

"I'm afraid, alright?"

"Fear is one thing," Rook said, taking a few steps towards me. "Trusting yourself is another."

I looked up at him, at the beads of sweat that shimmered on his brow in the brilliant summer sunlight. "It's my father." I didn't know if he already knew, somehow.

"Ah." Rook grimaced a little. "Sorry. Bad memories."

I swallowed hard. "Yes, I had wondered how it would feel for you."

"You don't need to think about that right now." Rook ran his hands through his hair and shook his head.

"Well, I do." I wanted to reach out and touch him, but the guards seemed even more attentive than usual. I had to wonder if our chess game in the library had done the rounds in palace gossip. Theron's performance in my room had spooked me, and I didn't want to give anyone any ammunition. But Rook's face was overcome with pain, and I couldn't stand it. "I'm sorry. For what my father did. For abandoning you, your people."

Rook gave me a sad smile, and reached a hand out, his fingertips brushing my jaw for a moment. "Don't apologize for him. He was a father trying to protect his child."

"At the cost of a whole kingdom?" I shook my head. "That's not good enough. Your people suffered, you lost your freedom. You might have won if he'd stayed."

"Keep your voice down." Rook's eyes flashed around us. "That's treason right there, princess."

"I don't care." I stepped closer to him, our bodies almost touching. "I'm sorry. It should never have happened. You said you lost everything."

"You need to train." Rook walked away from me, to the wooden rack holding the weapons, and took two swords down. "I want you ready so I don't have to watch you die tomorrow."

"You're avoiding the conversation." I said as he handed me a weapon.

"Fucking right I am." He brandished his sword, his blue eyes fixed on me. "Now, hit me with everything you have."

I knew what he was doing. Exactly what I had done, the night he'd asked about my mother. I didn't want to cause him pain, so I did what he wanted. I took a deep breath, and rushed at him, swinging the blade into his.

It was like a dance, and he moved so lightly on his feet, in a way no one would ever suspect looking at him. Our swords clanged against each other, long scrapes as we deflected one hit after another.

"You're good." Rook grinned at me.

"You keep telling me I am."

"You just need to believe it." Our blades crossed, and he pushed against mine, our faces only a few inches apart. "You can do this. No matter what he throws at you, you can do it."

I broke his hold on my weapon, spinning my back to him and striking backwards. He laughed as he dodged me, and I spun the sword in my hand to come to land at the base of his throat as he moved around in front of me.

He looked down at the sword, holding his arms out beside him. "And I'm dead."

"Yes you are."

He cocked an eyebrow. "You're extraordinary."

I threw the sword down. "No I'm not." I stalked away and he was right on my heels.

"What's this now?"" He reached out and took my arm, spinning me to look at him. "Hey, what's this?"

"You think Theron is going to make these trials easier? You think he's just going to send me in with a single griffin each time?"

"Of course he won't."

I threw my hands up. "Exactly. I have no idea what's coming, and I'm supposed to prepare for that?" I turned away and stormed into the stables adjoining the training arena, stopping by the guard at the door. "Don't fucking follow me in there." I said to him, pointing my finger in his face. He was so shocked he merely nodded.

Rook's heavy footfalls pursued me into the stable. "Elara, you're going to be alright."

"And I might not be. I might die tomorrow."

Rook's hand was on my arm again, spinning me to face him. "Stop saying that."

"Why?" I shook my head. "What chance do I have?"

"Every fucking chance!" Rook grasped my shoulders. "You need to stop thinking about everything you don't know and start thinking about everything you do."

"And what do I know, Rook?"

"You're fast," he said, "you're incredibly fast. You can jump high, long distances. I saw it, you jumped right over that griffin's head, like it was nothing."

"What if I can't use either of those skills?"

With a frustrated growl he pushed me back against the wall of the stable, pressing his body against me. "Gods fucking sake." His chest heaved as he looked down at me, his hands splayed across my shoulders. "Listen to me now. You stop looking for the faults, and start looking for the gains. You recognise those strengths. You draw on them. If you tell yourself you can't do something, you're right. If you tell yourself you can do something, you're right, do you understand me?"

"But if I don't know my enemy?"

"Then you think fast." His eyes moved over my face, flickering over my lips. "You didn't hesitate to think about the strength and weakness of each soldier you faced on the battlefield, you thought about what you had to do to take them down. And you did. To the bitter end."

"This is different."

He shook his head. "No, princess. It's just a battle, like any other."

I slumped against the wall. "I'm tired, Rook. I'm so fucking tired."

His gaze softened. "Still not sleeping well?"

"It's more than that. It's the fear, the anticipation, the never knowing what will come next." I sagged into his arms, and he held me tightly against him. "I wish you could pick me up, and fly me away from all this. Just take me far away."

"So do I, princess. More than anything. But I-I need..." He broke off, burying his face in my hair. "I need you to stop talking about dying. I can't take it."

"What's this then?" A guard's voice sounded from the door of the stable.

"Fuck off." Rook's voice was sharp like the crack of a whip.

"You step away from her now." The guard was moving closer.

Rook kept his arms around me as he turned to look over his shoulder. "I said, fuck off."

"You're not to touch her," the guard said, his lip curling into a cocky grin.

"If I wanted to fuck her in here I would, now I told you to fuck off." Rook's arms remained around me.

The guard drew his sword, and pointed it at us. "You want to give me reason to use this then?"

"Rook," I said, trying to move out his grasp. "Don't do this, just let me go."

"No." His voice was a low snarl. "You want me to let her go, you come over here and make me."

The guard moved closer, his grin getting wider. "Always wanted to see what a Night Demon looks like on the inside." He chuckled. "Going to cut that famous cock of yours off and put it up on my wall."

"Is that right?" Rook's arms around me were like iron. "Would have thought you'd want it so you could fuck yourself with it, you pathetic little shit."

The guard rushed at him, and Rook let go of me to spin around, reaching past the advancing blade as it missed its target. He grabbed a hold of the guard, whose eyes widened with surprise, and seized him by the throat. He lifted him off his feet, the guard spluttering wildly as his hands flailed at Rook's arm.

"Rook, stop it." I put my hands on his back. "Put him down, this is going to land you in trouble." But he wasn't listening to me, his whole body tense as he held the guard in the air. "Rook!" I moved to his side, putting my hands on his arm. "Please, put him down." Rook's eyes were glowing, fixed on the guard.

"No one tells me not to touch her." He snarled. The guard was going purple, spittle foaming at his lips.

I put my hand on Rook's cheek, and he inhaled sharply, his eyes flashing to mine.

"Put him down," I said. "Please, put him down."

Rook looked at me, his shoulders heaving. His brow furrowed for a moment, and he lowered his arm, slowly. The guard's feet swung back and forth, trying desperately to find the ground. Rook's grip eased, and the guard gasped in a breath, his face bright red.

"You're insane," he spluttered, his voice rasping. "You're fucking insane, Norahi."

Rook turned on him again, his teeth bared. "Watch your fucking mouth." He shoved the guard away, sending him stumbling. "Now fuck off like I told you to."

The guard scrambled out of the stable, Rook watching him leave. The door of the stable slammed shut, and Rook looked down at me. I stepped forward to put my hands on his face.

"What was that?" I asked.

He closed his eyes, putting his hand over mine, turning his face to press his mouth into my palm. "Elara, you've ruined me" He murmured into my hand. He took my arm and pulled me close to him, putting his arms around me. "I felt it the other night." He looked down at me, with his glowing blue eyes. "Did you feel it too?"

I nodded. "Yes."

"It was like a rope, pulling me back to you," he said, pressing his forehead against mine. "I had to fight it to leave, to climb down that tower. I wanted to stay, I wanted to climb back into that bed with you, just to feel you. I don't understand this, any of it."

"Me neither." I turned my face into the crook of his neck.

"I went and asked the priestess about it," he said with a short laugh. "I went into a fucking temple, can you imagine? Me? She didn't know what to think." He nudged my face with his nose, so I was looking up at him. "Do you know what she told me? That you're mine."

"I am. I am yours." My hands flexed on his chest. "I want you, so much. I need you."

"It's going to drive me insane." Rook's eyes searched my face. "A Night Demon with a Fae for a mate, Lada has a sense of humor."

"Or a sense of danger," I replied, "this could get you killed."

"I'm a dead man anyway." Rook brought his mouth closer to mine, our lips almost touching. "I promised you a kiss once, and I didn't give it to you. And if I kiss you now, you'll be in my blood, and I'll never be rid of you."

"Do you want to be rid of me, Rook?"

"Never. Never again." A shuddering breath passed his lips, and he shook his head. "I haven't kissed anyone in years. I never wanted to. But these…" His thumb brushed along my lower lip. "These lips, they command my heart now."

"I want you to tell me what is going on here, right now." Regan's voice accompanied the flinging open of the stable door, guards flanking him as he glared at us. "What is the meaning of this?"

"One of your guards tried to attack the Princess," Rook said, pushing me behind him as Regan and the guards entered the stables. "I did what I had to do."

"He claims he caught you in here violating her," Regan said, and all eyes turned to me as I burst out laughing.

I stepped out from behind Rook. "He's lying. No such thing happened. Rook was merely comforting me."

"He seems to do a lot of that," Regan said, eyeing Rook critically.

"Well, perhaps if you'd ever been a prisoner you'd understand why that was necessary," I replied. "Now, I expect us to be left alone to prepare for the trial tomorrow, is that understood?"

"Absolutely not," Regan said, gesturing to me to step away. "You come with me now, Highness. You've trained enough for today, you need to rest."

I wanted to argue, but instead I moved past Rook with a sigh. His hand shot out and gripped my arm. "Rook," I said quietly, "let me go."

"No." His voice was low, so only I could hear it.

"Please," I said, looking up at him. "I don't want them to hurt you." I put my hand over his. "I need you."

My words seemed to shake him from his trance, and his hand dropped from my arm. His blue eyes fixed on me, and he put a hand to his chest.

"Yours." He whispered.

The silver thread between us swung around itself, becoming thicker with every passing second, unseen by anyone else in the room, but so strong that it almost blinded me. I walked out of the stable, and I felt Rook's eyes on me the entire way, the Bond palpable, trying to draw me back to him.

"I wish to go to the Temple," I said to Regan, who turned on his heel and gave me an impatient stare. "You object to my faith, sir?" I raised an eyebrow. "That is most disappointing."

Regan said nothing, simply threw his hands up and stormed ahead. I followed him around the perimeter of the arena, through a gated archway, and out onto the grass. The golden roof of the temple gleamed in the brilliant sunlight, and the guards fell away, hanging back as I approached the steps. Regan paused at the temple entrance, and his face was earnest as he turned to me.

"Your Highness, I would like you to know that I have a tremendous amount of respect for you," he said, keeping his voice low, his eyes darting to the guards that remained at the edge of the lawn. "Your father was a good King, and he and I were friends at one time."

"Is that so?" I didn't care what Regan thought. "How interesting."

"Norahi has a reputation." Regan took a hesitant breath, pursing his lips. "I know he seems - he seems amicable. But I would like to warn you, Your Highness. He's not what he seems."

"He has been a good friend to me these past weeks, and I think highly of him."

Regan rolled his shoulders, that thin neck bobbing in the frothy collar of his robes. "Your Highness, the Night Demons are known for ensorcelling women, even the Fae. You are not immune to his -"

"That's enough." I strode into the temple. "I will be left alone in my prayers, thank you Regan." Rage swirled in my belly as I crossed the tiled floor towards the altar. I sank to my knees, looking up at the golden statue of Lada, perched on the right corner of the wooden precipice.

"Why?" I asked her. "Why him?" There would be no answers of course. There was no answer to give. I clasped my hands in front of me, and took a deep breath. *Let me live long enough to find out why, and let me be strong enough to win. Then I'll get us out of here. Both of us.*

Chapter 19

Elara

Rain pelted down from the iron sky as the guards escorted me across the ground towards the Pit. My braids dripped down my armor, and water ran into the collar of my leathers. And my hands were fucking shaking.

I hadn't known what was at stake last time. This time I knew. This time I knew my father would be chained up somewhere in that Pit, in some arena of Theron's imagining. I didn't know what I would be facing to save him. I felt sick, the hearty breakfast Drusilla had ordered me sitting heavily in my stomach.

Rook was waiting at the door of the armory, his ax in hand, his soaked linen shirt clinging to his body. He gave me a smile, but immediately sensed my anxiety, and his brow crinkled. "Good morning, princess."

I merely nodded. I couldn't speak. I walked past him, into the armory, and there lay Arankos in the wooden chest. It began to hum as I drew closer. The guards all backed away.

"One of them touched it," Rook said behind me. "He's had to be restrained to stop him from hurting himself."

I snorted. "That'll teach them."

"Indeed." He stood by my side, and I looked up at him. He smiled, leaning on his ax. "You see your father today, you should smile."

A terrible screech broke out in the distance, and the crowd in the stands above us cheered and whooped wildly. I could see from Rook's expression that the alarm in my face was obvious. "What the fuck was that?" I asked.

Rook put a hand on my shoulder. "It'll be alright. You can do this."

"What was that?" I asked again.

The iron gate at the far end of the armory opened, and the guards edged forward to escort me into the Pit.

Rook backed away from me, his expression tortured. "You're fast, remember that. You run, and you don't stop." The guards were ushering him out, and he clenched his jaw. "Stay away from them when they scream!" The guards pushed him out amidst demands he shut up, and the concern on his face as the door closed in front of him sent panic heaving down my spine.

If Rook was worried, it had to be bad.

Stay away from them when they scream. Who the fuck were they?

I was once again led down the tunnel, to the heavy door that led out into the Pit. My mouth was dry, along with my eyes, because I was too terrified to even blink. There was another scream, screeching, blood-curdling, and so fucking close. Arankos slipped in my hand as I held it, my palms sweating. Fuck. Fuck. I was going to die today.

The iron door slid upwards, and before me lay the Pit. But this time it wasn't a lush, humid jungle. I walked out into a labyrinth, towering black slate blocks all around me. It was disorienting at first, the endless cascade of rain making some of the sheer black faces almost mirror-like. It was hard to tell where some columns ended and another began, until I took a few more steps forward. Moving through this maze at speed was going to be difficult.

The terrible weather hadn't stopped the Velesians from turning out in their droves to watch me die. The shouts and cheers of the crowd were amplified, bouncing around and creating an echo that only made my surroundings even more intimidating. Deep puddles had formed at my feet, and my boots sloshed through them. The ground felt slick underfoot. Running was definitely going to be a problem. I felt deeply uneasy as I looked up into the stands, blinking against the raindrops.

Theron was sitting at the edge of the royal box, a black crown set with blood-red gems on his head. Rook was beside him, and the fear on his face tore me apart.

Theron raised his arms, and the crowd quieted somewhat, just as another shrill scream echoed across the black maze I found myself in.

"Our brave royal guest has entered the Pit once again!" He announced. "And today the prize is even greater - the King of Peyrus!" The crowd booed, and rage snaked down my shoulders, blazing through my fingertips as I gripped Arankos tighter. Theron made a grand gesture of disapproval, shaking his head and wagging his fingers around him. "Now, now, good people of Veles, we must be courteous to our guests!"

"May I know the enemy I face today?" I asked, furious at the waver in my voice.

"But of course!" Theron raised his arms, and a crescendo

of screams echoed all around me. Whatever had screamed before, it had company.

Lots of company.

Stay away from them when they scream.

Fuck fuck fuck.

"Your foe today is the Banshee." The crowd cheered at his words. "That terrible scream you hear, it carries more than you might expect."

Stay away from them when they scream.

"As last time," Theron went on, "either you reach your father first. Or the Banshee does. And do be careful, dear one. You really don't want to fall."

I turned and ran, my feet kicking up the rain as I went. The labyrinth became darker and darker as I moved through it, the walls rising and falling and seeming to spring up in front of me every time I turned.

The crowd suddenly became louder, and I was sure one of those fucking things was getting closer to me. I had never seen a banshee before, only heard the stories as a child. I had thought for a time they weren't even real, but no, they were here. They were after me.

I turned, weaving through the maze, trying to keep my bearings. I threw my eyes up into the stands, yes I was moving forward, no I wasn't, I'd doubled back too far. *Fuck, MOVE.* I had to keep going forward.

I turned right and hit a dead end. The crowd whooped and cried out, and I turned to go another way.

One of these fucking things was right in front of me.

Its hair was wiry and black, long talons at the end of even longer fingers. Its eyes were just two bulging black orbs in a wrinkled white face. It almost seemed to float as it moved towards me, its feet not visible underneath the tattered black robes that trailed around its withered body.

I was so frightened I couldn't move for a moment. Its head moved unnaturally as it came closer, its finger pointing at me. Its mouth opened to reveal haphazard sharp teeth, a pointy black tongue flickering out over where the lips should be.

I backed against the black slate wall, gripping Arankos. I didn't know how to kill this thing, did it even have a heart? Did it bleed?

Suddenly, the mouth tore open so far it shouldn't have been possible, and it screamed.

The banshee's scream was drowned out by a scream of my own. The searing pain in the left side of my head was so strong it felt as though a hot poker had been shoved straight through my ear drum. The pain sent me blind, and was met by another searing burn across my face.

I collapsed to the ground, blinking furiously, trying to see. The grey at the edges of my vision cleared enough to see the remnants of a green cloud that had burst from the banshee's face when it screamed at me. My ears were ringing so loudly I felt sick. My hand flew up to my cheek, where I felt the skin blistering.

I scrambled away, realizing I'd dropped my sword, my grip slipping in the rain. I finally got a firm grasp on the hilt, swinging it around towards the banshee, who was looking down at me. But only its head was turned towards me. Its fucking head was on backwards.

I sprang to my feet and swung my sword as it began to walk backwards - forwards, whatever fucking direction, face first at least. That terrible, lipless mouth began to open again, and I knew I had to stop it before it let out another one of those debilitating shrieks. The taloned hand shot out to grab me, but was stopped as Arankos sliced it right off.

The banshee's head fell back, and I jammed my shoulder up against the left side of my head to try and lessen the shrill pain echoing through my skull. The scream directed at the sky erupted with another plume of green gas. I swung again, and the banshee's head hit the wall with a thud. The body crumbled in on itself almost instantly.

The crowd cheered, and I moved forward, pushing on, making myself move. I had to reach my father before one of these fucking things did.

The skin on the side of my face burned, like it was being eaten away. I thanked Mokosh it hadn't gotten my eye. That would have been a disaster. *Stay away from them when they scream* - yes, that was good advice.

The labyrinth seemed to tower higher and higher the further I advanced. I couldn't hear anything but the cheers of the crowd and my own footsteps as they thundered through the puddles. I rounded a corner too quickly and slipped, falling onto my side. Shit, I had to be more careful. I had to be more aware, more deliberate. I couldn't afford to hit the ground when these things were floating around.

The ground rumbled underfoot, and the wall beside me began to move as I ran past it. I didn't understand what was happening until I ran full pelt into a wall that sprang up before me. I was thrown on to my back, and black spots took over my vision as I tried to catch my breath. The labyrinth was changing.

Elara, you need to get up. That was Rook's voice. I could hear it, in my bones, in my head. His voice was tight, and I could sense his fear. *Elara, move, now, they're coming.* I forced myself to my feet. Rook could see what I couldn't. He could warn me. I focused on the silver thread, the bond between us.

Help me, I said and felt his apprehension.

I looked up into the stands, trying to get my bearings, trying to figure out how far I had moved. I had to be more than halfway now. I had to be almost there.

I rounded a corner and nearly ran into another banshee. It floated above the ground, soundlessly, like a ghost. It didn't seem to recognise that I was there, it hadn't heard me. Maybe they were deaf. Maybe they only had those glistening black eyes to rely on. I sliced Arankos through the air before the banshee realized I was upon it, and the head rolled away, accompanied with a spurt of black blood that hit my face. I gasped, expecting another acid burn, but all I felt was ice. Their blood was like ice water, like being struck with snow. I wiped it away with the back of my hand, jumping over the bag of bones that remained on the ground, and pushed on.

The rain was pooling in the labyrinth. It was up to my ankles now, the slate so slick underfoot it made running almost impossible.

There's one behind you. Rook's voice was so loud it made me jump, and I spun around to face a banshee that was twice as big as the others. It towered over me, its spindly hands extending towards me. I swung Arankos, taking off two fingers, but it didn't stop. It kept advancing. Another lunge with my blade, and black blood went flying up the slate wall as more fingers fell away from the banshee's hand. But instead of flinching or pulling back or doing anything else, it rushed at me, its bloodied hands seizing my shoulders.

I drew back my sword and drove it into the banshee's torso amidst a sickening crunch, like I was stabbing into a pile of broken twigs. The banshee merely flinched, then tore its mouth open. Its fingers had a hold of me, an iron grip. I pulled my sword out and tipped it upwards, driving it into the banshee's jaw just as its chest sucked in to scream in my face. The already bulging eyes seemed to roll in their sockets, and the banshee's tongue lolled out next to the sword that had impaled its mouth. I withdrew the blade, and the banshee collapsed into the puddle beneath it. Black blood clouded the water around my feet. I'd killed three. How many more could there be? I kept running.

I was close now. I had to be. I would reach my father in a moment.

The rumbling began again, and the walls around me shifted.

The cries of the crowd seemed to reach a crescendo, and I looked up to see their gazes all fixed to something that lay ahead of me. I ran faster, my feet sliding against the wet ground. I was nearly there.

The labyrinth widened out, the walls falling away beside me.

And then I saw my father. On his knees on a platform ahead, heavy chains holding down his hands. He looked so weak, so helpless, his long white hair sticking to his cheeks. His shoulders raised slightly as he saw me pelting towards him.

"Elara?" His voice rang out. "Elara? Oh Gods, Elara!"

I watched in horror as a banshee rose behind him.

"No!" Why weren't my feet moving faster. Why was I so fucking slow? My father seemed to be moving further and further away from me.

The banshee opened its mouth, wide, so impossibly wide, and it screamed. "No!" I came to a skidding halt as I crashed to my knees just short of the plume of green smoke. Arankos fell into the water around me, and I stared, disbelieving, at the last spot I'd seen my father. I'd failed. I'd fucking failed. He'd died.

The labyrinth dissolved around me, giving way to wet sand. I couldn't breathe. Water ran into my eyes, my mouth, as I kneeled on the ground, my fingers clawed into my thighs.I hadn't been fast enough. My father had been killed, burned and tortured by that fucking green smoke.

The smoke cleared, and my father's eyes stared at me. He

blinked, looking around him, at the barrier around him, that shimmered and undulated as the green smoke drew back from it. The banshee was gone.

The crowd burst into applause.

I didn't understand. I'd failed. Why was my father still alive?

I heard clapping to my right.

"Elara, oh dear, I am sorry!" Theron's voice was dripping with false concern. I didn't turn to look at him, my eyes staying on my father. "You did try so hard, didn't you?"

"Elara?" My father shook his head. "My sweetheart, what are you doing here?" He looked at Theron. "Why is my daughter here? What are you doing with her?"

"Your daughter has agreed to be a part of these games here in order to earn back her kingdom." Theron smiled magnanimously at my father. "She is such a brave warrior."

My father opened his mouth to speak, then his eyes widened, his gaze shifting past Theron ever so slightly. I followed the line of his sight, and saw Rook standing behind Theron. "What is he doing here?" My father asked, and he looked back at me with alarm. "Elara, you stay away from him, do you hear me? Do you hear -"

Theron clapped his hands, his golden wings rustling loudly as he extended them. "Enough of this!" He pointed to two guards, then to my father. "Take King Vayr back to his cell, to await another trial in the morning."

I was still kneeling on the ground. "What do you mean, another trial?" I looked up at him, the rain catching on my lashes. "I failed."

Theron leaned down, his brows furrowing as he smiled. "Oh dear one, you did not think me so cruel, did you? But of course I will give you a second chance."

I was so flooded with relief I thought I would be sick. "You will?"

Theron tutted, and reached out to stroke my cheek with the back of his finger. "Elara, my dear, I'm not a monster." He straightened, his hands clasped behind his back. "And it shall be a very simple trial, I promise you. Do not be afraid. Nothing can be worse than a banshee, surely?"

I turned back to my father, who was being unchained by the guards. "I'll save you, Papa."

His eyes kept darting from Rook back to me. "My darling girl, please, please be careful." He fought the guards for only a moment before they seized him roughly, dragging him away.

Rook was suddenly kneeling beside me in the rain. "Are you alright? Fuck, your ear is bleeding."

"Their screams," I gasped. "Their screams, they h-hurt m-my ear."

"I'm sure they did. Fucking Nav." He tipped my head to inspect the burned side of my face. "She needs a healer," he barked over his shoulder, "this is deep."

"But of course my friend," Theron said, and he clapped Rook on the back. "You know what's best." He leaned down, and nudged Rook. "Well done too, ey? You're doing the most wonderful job keeping our pretty guest distracted." His green eyes met mine, and he winked. "Night Demons are so very good with the females." Theron strolled away from us, back towards the stands, out of the rain.

Rook's eyes were steely as I looked back at him. The stab of betrayal was so great that I slumped sideways, putting out a hand to catch myself. Rook reached out to try and help, and I pushed him away.

"Don't fucking touch me." It hurt to talk, the skin on my jaw tender and raw.

"Elara," Rook said, his voice low, taut, "I didn't -"

"Don't touch me. Don't come anywhere near me."

He grabbed me by the arms, pulling me to him. "Stop this. I would never do that to you."

"Why should I believe you?" I flailed against him weakly, overcome with the near-loss of my father and the pain in my cheek and the fucking devastating stab of betrayal as the thread between us pulled me closer to him. The fucking thread he'd created, that he'd somehow made to serve his master.

"Why would you believe him?" Rook hissed, his eyes wide, a look of helplessness encroaching on his face. "Elara, *please*, I care for you, I would never-"

"You nearly cost me my father!" I shoved him violently, and crawled away from him. "Just fuck off. Don't talk to me. They warned me, they all warned me." I laughed bitterly. "You heard my father." I looked up at him, and shook my head even as his brow furrowed with visible pain. "Don't come fucking near me."

A guard approached and pulled me to my feet. "Come on now, to the healer with you." He jostled me when I didn't move fast enough.

"Hey," Rook barked. "You be careful with her!"

"Or what?" The guard sneered, and pushed me towards the stands. "Come on then, princess, let's get that mangy face of yours seen to." He scoffed. "People keep calling you beautiful. You're nothing but a fucking one-eared freak." He shoved me forward as stars danced in my vision and I stumbled over my feet. "Keep it moving, bitch."

There was an almighty clang, and I was knocked sideways as the guard was struck by something. I stumbled, falling to my hands and knees. There was blood on my hands. I looked over my shoulder to see Rook standing there, his ax in the ground in front of him. Between what had once been a whole guard. He was now split in two.

Rook's eyes were fixed on me, his shoulders heaving.

"I didn't." He growled.

Guards rushed forward and seized Rook, tearing the bloody ax from his hands, and his eyes stayed on me the whole time, only breaking away when he was dragged out of the Pit.

Chapter 20

Elara

I cursed the dreams that chased me from sleep as dawn broke through my window. My hands clawed into my pillow as the ache, the aching need for Rook broke away from me. It faded along with the feeling of his hands, his mouth, the thread that tethered my soul to his. Fuck it all to Nav. Fuck everything. Tears burned my eyes.

"Why?" I whispered, begging Lada for an answer. Lada, someone, anyone. I didn't understand. I didn't want to understand. I wanted it all to go away. I hugged myself under the white sheets, my hands brushing over every place that still burned with his touch, desperate to push it away.

Elara.

No. I squeezed my eyes shut, pushing him out of my mind. I didn't want him there. I didn't want him anywhere near me. I hoped they'd locked him up for killing that guard, maybe they'd fucking execute him.

The look on my father's face as he'd seen Rook haunted me. He was terrified, as though he knew Rook wanted to do me harm. I pressed my face into the pillow as a sob escaped me. Fucking Nav, I was meant to save my father today, and I was crying in my bed over some fucking Night Demon instead. Rook had done his job well. Fuck him. Fuck Theron.

I sat up in the bed and angrily wiped my face with my hands. I wouldn't let myself waver, I'd show them. I'd do it today. I was prepared. I held my hands out in front of me, telling them to stop shaking. I wasn't going to do this today, I wasn't going to be terrified and anxious. I would win.

The door to Drusilla's chamber opened and she hurried into the room, tutting and fussing when she saw my tear-stained face. "Does it still hurt?" She asked, perching beside me on the bed, inspecting my cheek.

I shook my head. "No, it's healed. I can't feel it at all anymore."

Drusilla took my hand and gave me a hopeful smile. "Now, my lamb, you'll be alright. I know yesterday was rather frightening, but his majesty has given you a second chance. And you will win."

"Yes, I will." I sniffed a little, willing the tears to subside. "It was just a shock." In so many ways.

Drusilla set about laying out my leathers. "Now, a good breakfast as per usual, and then we shall -"

"Do you know what happened to Rook?" The question tore from me before I could stop myself. It shouldn't have mattered. I shouldn't have cared. I knew that he was still alive, he was there in my head, filled with false anguish.

Drusilla stopped short and regarded me with surprise. "Rook? Oh, you mean because of the guard? Nothing happened, you don't need to worry about him."

"He killed a guard and nothing happened?"

"Of course not," Drusilla replied absently, shrugging as she unstrapped the pauldron from my armor. "Why should it?"

"He killed someone," I said emphatically.

Drusilla laughed. "A guard is not a Someone in this palace, my lamb. Theron values Rook more than some sniveling guard."

The inhumanity of this place made my stomach churn.

The maid came in - red hair, big tits - and she avoided my eyes this time. Instead of envy, I felt pity. A stupid girl, just like me. Taken in by the big, strong, handsome warrior. I was such a fool.

I struggled with my breakfast, which I never had before. But there was more at stake now. I knew Theron would not give me another chance to save my father, and if I lost again today, I couldn't bear to think what this would mean. My father's death? My own? The loss of my kingdom? What would they do to my mother?

I pushed it all away. Failure was not an option today.

I choked down as much food as I could, and then let Drusilla help me get dressed. She braided my hair, drawing it back from my face. I turned my head in the mirror, looking at the scars on my jaw, my missing ear.

"I wonder what Theron has in store for me today," I said quietly.

Drusilla clutched my shoulders and smiled at my reflection. "You will win today. It won't be a horrid banshee, that much we know for certain, ey?" She gave me a squeeze, and then the door opened behind her.

Regan stepped in, his gaze critical. "Your Highness, they are ready for you."

We took a different path towards the Pit, and I looked towards the doors of the armory. "I need my weapon," I said to Regan's back as he strode ahead of me.

"There is no need for a weapon today, Highness." He barely glanced over his shoulder as he said it.

No need for a weapon? What kind of trial could possibly require no weapon? I balked as I thought of having to engage in hand to hand combat with some creature who was much bigger than I was. My confidence faltered with every step I took closer to the Pit. The sun shone brilliantly overhead, and sweat formed on the back of my neck. The crowd was cheering and whistling as we walked into an arched tunnel underneath the Pit.

Regan escorted me to a barred entrance, then spun to face me, his hands clasped behind his back. "Now, Your Highness, you will wait here until the door opens, yes?"

I nodded. "Of course."

Regan and the guards left the chamber, and the heavy door fell closed after them. I clenched and unclenched my fists as I waited for the barred door to open, sweat forming on my palms. Butterflies erupted in my stomach. I had never gone into combat unarmed. Suddenly the door flew open behind me, and I looked over my shoulder to see Rook storming into the room.

"I told you to stay the fuck away from me!" I held a hand up to stop him, but he thundered towards me and seized me in his arms.

"It's a time trial," he hissed, "the floor of the pit will give way underneath you, you have a set amount of time to get across it."

I tried to shake him off. "Get away from me!"

"I don't have much time!" His eyes were wild. "No matter what gets in your way, you do not stop, do you hear me? You keep moving. You can cross the pit in half the time they've given you, so do. Not. Stop. You can make it in time. When you reach your father, throw the chains on the trap before it closes on him."

"Why are you telling me this?" I asked.

He clutched me to him, pressing his lips against my forehead. "Do not stop." He released me and hurried out of the room.

I watched the door close behind him. *Do not stop. Keep moving. Be quick.* The barred door began to rise haltingly into the ceiling with a metallic rattle. I walked slowly forward, down the darkened tunnel. The door at the far end began to rise, allowing the brilliant sunshine to stream in.

Do not stop.

Do not stop.

I proceeded to the entrance to the Pit, and blinked as my eyes adjusted to the sunlight. The crowd was deafening, cheering and chanting.

The Pit was a bare landscape of sand. It reminded me of the stories I'd heard of the Wastes, the endless, barren landscape that stretched out across the eastern side of Korbiriya - nothing but sand, and death. It reflected the harsh sunlight, and I squinted, trying to take in my surroundings.

I could see the path ahead of me, extending across the Pit, towards a raised platform. No - two platforms. Anxiety prickled at my lips, and I tried to rub it away with the back of my hand. On one platform was my father, chained down by his hands and feet. On the other - oh Gods, oh *fucking Gods.* My stomach churned as I looked up at Theron, who raised his hands for silence.

"Good people of Veles, we are once again here to see our esteemed royal guest, the princess of Peyrus, save her Kingdom!" Theron looked around the stands with a wide smile as cheers rose from the heaving crowd. He gestured to the platforms. "In order to make this trial much more interesting, we have given the princess two targets."

Two targets. Two fucking targets. It was then that I noticed the woman at Theron's side, her face streaked with tears, her hands bound to the chair she sat in. Her long black hair was disheveled, her violet eyes iridescent in her smooth brown face. Her gaze was one of sheer desperation.

"One target is, of course, the King of Peyrus!" Theron gazed about indulgently as the crowd fucking booed my father. "Now, good citizens, the other target is a Velesian child, whose mother sits here beside me." He looked down at me with a predatory grin. "Princess Elara, you have a choice before you. Either you save your father, or you save this poor woman's child."

The woman began to wail, a sound that strangled the breath from my throat. She slumped forward in her chair, her shoulders racked with sobs.

My eyes moved to Rook, whose jaw was set as he gazed back at me.

Both. His command echoed through my mind.

I nodded, only slightly, so no one else would see it. Both. I could do both.

"Now, Your Highness," Theron said, spreading his arms wide, "I would advise you to hurry." The ground underfoot rumbled, and a horn sounded to my right.

I sprinted ahead as the rumbling continued, and the crowd cried out in surprise. No one expected me to move this fast.

I could save them both. The tiny figure on the platform was barely visible, it was so small. I could save them both.

A roar to my left caught me off guard, and a lion was racing across the sand towards me. Rook had told me not to stop.

There was a loud crash behind me, and I knew the floor was starting to give way. Sand rained down on me, peppering my hair and face.

The lion advanced and sprang into the air. I pushed harder, moving faster, and it missed me by a foot. There was another crash, and the lion's roar faded as it tumbled into the collapsing floor.

I'd made it more than halfway. I was nearly there. My father's head was raised, and I could see blood running down his forehead. They'd beaten him. Rage coursed through me, and I willed my limbs to move even faster.

A roar sounded right behind me, and I cried out as something slashed my back. I stumbled forward, turning onto my back in time to see the lion rising into the air to pounce on me. I scrambled backwards, narrowly avoiding its immense paws. The ground rumbled again, and my fingers clawed into the sand as I tried to propel myself back faster. The lion's paws shot out to swipe at my leg, landing a gash in my calf. I bit back a scream, tears pricking at my eyes,and kicked the lion in the snout with my other foot.

It jerked backwards, pawing at its face, then the ground beneath it gave way. It fell to its death, leaving me teetering on the edge of a yawning precipice. I struggled to my feet, the gash in my leg searing with pain. Shit.

I pushed on, running as fast as I could. I felt blood running down my back. Fuck fuck fuck.

"Elara!" My father was so close. "Elara!"

I'd almost made it. 50 feet. 20. 10.

I threw myself onto the chains, pulling them up and throwing them onto the spiked iron door that lay, spring-loaded, beside my father. I didn't even meet his eyes as I turned on my heel and ran for the other platform.

My father's cries were drowned out by the elated shrieks of the crowd as I sprinted for the crying child. I could make it. I'd not lost that much time with the lion.

50 feet. 20. 10. 5. The child raised his tiny head, tears tracking trails through the sand on his face.

Four feet.

And the door slammed shut.

A hot, wet spray hit my face. All that was left of the tiny figure was blood, and a little hand, reaching out towards me.

Someone was screaming, and it wasn't until my throat became raw and tight that I realized it was me.

Chapter 21

Rook

The door opened after two sharp knocks, and I was met with Drusilla's pale face. "I didn't know what else to do," she said quietly, waving me into the room and swiftly pushing the door closed behind me. "She won't get out of the tub."

"How long has she been in there?"

"Since she was carried back up here." Drusilla wrung her hands, then threw them up helplessly. "She refused a healer, and she's scrubbed herself to the bone. I've tried speaking to her, but she's just sat in the tub, and won't speak. I didn't know who else to call for."

I nodded. "It's alright, you did the right thing. Come on, take me to her." I followed Drusilla to the bathroom.

Elara sat in the tub, staring at the water's surface. Her skin was red, her eyes blank. She didn't move at all as we entered the room. My heart ached as I looked at her, feeling the icy depths of her own despair.

"Now then, love," I said quietly as I kneeled beside her.

"You're going to get cold if you stay in there much longer." I reached out and gently caressed her bare shoulder.

"I can't get the blood off." Her voice was hollow and distant, her lips barely moving as she spoke. "I can't… I can't get it off."

Drusilla leaned on the edge of the tub. "My lamb, you've scrubbed yourself raw. I promise you, it's all gone."

Elara's head shivered a little, the weakest sign of disagreement. "No. It's there. I can feel it."

"Elara -" Drusilla broke off helplessly.

I raised my hand . "Now, it's alright. I'll have another look." I lowered my head to try and meet Elara's gaze. "Come on, love, let me look you over." She let me lean her forward, and I ran my fingertips over her shoulders. "Nothing here." I pulled her towards me, tilting her head slightly. "Ah, here's some in your hair and on your face." I gestured to her clean skin, and smiled. "Shall I wash it off? Then you'll be all clean."

"You swear it?" Her lip trembled as her head fell back against my shoulder.

"I promise you, it will all be gone." I lifted a pitcher from beside the bath, turning her head gently. "Now close your eyes, I don't want any of this blood getting in them."

As soon as her eyes closed, her breathing became rapid, and suddenly she was retching, flailing in the water. I quickly took her in my arms, and she collapsed against me, heaving, breathless sobs breaking from her.

"I couldn't save him." Her fingers tore into my shirt. "I couldn't save him. He was so small, I was so close, Rook. Why couldn't I save him?"

"I've got you, my love." I smoothed my hand over her hair. "I've got you. It's over, it's all over."

She shook her head against my shoulder. "Not over. Not over." She choked on her sobs. "Not over."

I scooped her out of the tub, not caring that I was now soaked. Drusilla tucked a towel around her, and I carried her into the bedroom. I sat down in one of the enormous leather armchairs while Drusilla stoked the fire until it raged.

I tucked a blanket around Elara, rubbing her all over, desperate to get some warmth back into her shivering frame. Her ribs contracted as she coughed out one sob after another.

Drusilla held her hands to her mouth as she watched us, and she shook her head as her eyes met mine. "What do we do?"

"Nothing." I stroked Elara's hair, holding her against me as she began to wail. "She needs to let it out."

Drusilla's eyes flashed to the door. "If the guards see you two like this-"

"They'll die." I nodded towards the door to her room. "You go on, lock the door, and you're not a part of this anymore."

She hesitated, then turned away from me with a heavy sigh and scurried into her room. The lock slid home with a metallic scrape, and then it was just me, holding the shivering princess.

She continued to thrash and cry in my arms, and I simply held her. She clawed at my chest, wrapped her arms around my neck, then let her head fall back, all the while sobbing and asking *Why why why*. I had to assure her several times that her hands had no blood on them, holding them up in front of her red-rimmed eyes, only for her to collapse into hopeless sobs again.

I don't know how long we sat like that, but by the time exhaustion took her, the sun had set behind the mountains and we were both completely dry. I thought she had fallen asleep, but when I looked down, she was lying against my chest, her hand over my heart, eyes staring at nothing.

"He's broken me," she finally said. "He's broken me, Rook."

I kissed the top of her head, stroking her shoulder. "No, my love. You're too strong for that."

She shook her head against my chest. "He has. He's done it."

I lifted her chin and broke her stare into nothingness. Her eyes were glazed with weariness when they met mine. "There is pain, certainly. But you are still there. You are still whole. I can feel it." I clutched my hand over hers on my chest. "Here. I can feel you, all of you, right here."

"He lied about you, didn't he?"

"Of course he did." I pressed a kiss to her forehead, and she whimpered. "I couldn't do that to you. I *wouldn't* do that to you."

"I'm sorry I believed him." The sobs began to bubble up again. "I'm sorry I believed him over you."

"It's alright, my love. It's alright now."

"I wanted to die." Her fingertips clawed into my collar-bone, as though she was trying to anchor herself somehow. "I wanted the bond to go away, I wanted you gone. But it was awful, it *hurt* so much…"

I wrapped my arms around her, and held her tightly. "I could feel it, your anger and your pain. And then something else." She gazed up at me. "It was like you were calling to me, in the night. It was torture, not being with you."

"I dreamed of you." She raised a cold hand to my face. "I begged Lada for an answer, why you? Why us?"

I smiled. "And what answer did she give you?"

"Just more dreams of you." She buried her face in my neck. "The dreams, they're agony."

"How so, my love?"

"Because when I wake up, you're not there." She quivered in my arms as she began to cry again. "The longing, Rook, it's unbearable."

Yes, it is. My longing for her was going to drive me insane. I cradled her head in my hand. "I want you to tell me about these dreams."

She drew back, regarding me with raised eyebrows. "What do you mean?"

"Tell me about these dreams."

"Now?"

"Yes now."

She sniffled and shifted on my lap, sitting up a little more. "B-but you know what they are. You have them too. Why now?"

"You need to think about something else, anything else, than what you've been through. Tell me what you dream about me. Tell me how it feels for you."

Her eyes dropped, and she swallowed hard, pushing her hair out of her face. "It's always different. Sometimes you're-" Her eyes flashed up to mine. "Sometimes you're rough, and wild. You say things to me no one has ever said to me before. You *do* things to me I didn't know…. And then other times…" She reached out and traced her thumb over my lower lip. "It's just your mouth, all over me, kissing me everywhere."

"And which do you prefer?"

Her eyes lit up as they met mine, life coming back into them, flaming with a tiny spark of desire. "I like both." Then her lip began to quiver. "But it doesn't matter, because I wake up, and you're - you're-" Her body quaked as she cried. "Oh Gods, please, do something, anything. I don't want to feel this way anym-"

My lips crashed into hers, cutting off her words. *Oh fucking*

Gods. The simmering flame in my chest exploded into a raging wildfire as my hands slid into her hair, and she melted against me. Her lips parted, her tongue meeting mine without hesitation. My mind was almost blank with desire, consumed with nothing but her taste and her scent and the feeling of *finally* kissing her.

Without breaking the kiss, she scrambled on top of me, straddling me and seizing my face in her hands. I felt the blanket fall down around her waist, and my hands raked down the sides of her body, over her warm skin, the soft mounds of her breasts.

"You're not broken," I murmured against her lips. "Every part of you is perfect. All of you."

"I want you, so much." She sighed as I kissed her neck, her head tipping back. Her hands moved down my chest, pushing my shirt open. "Please, Rook."

I took a deep breath as her hands moved down over my stomach. Gods, I wanted her. And when she ground herself against me, my arousal more than obvious, my resolve nearly faltered. But I didn't want it to be like this. I wanted to take my time with her, to make it more than just a quick fuck fuelled by misery.

"Don't say no to me again." She looked at me, shaking her head.

"I'm not saying no to you, princess." I didn't think I'd ever be able to bring myself to say no to her ever again.

"Then please-"

I pulled her to me, kissing her deeply. She whimpered against me as my hand moved between her legs, and she sucked in a breath as my finger dipped inside her. She pulled back from my mouth, her breath shuddering as she gripped my shoulders. She rolled her hips, her clit meeting the pad of my thumb, and she hesitated for only a moment before she repeated the motion with a moan.

I threaded my other hand into her hair, her forehead against mine as she ground herself against my fingers.

"I want your cock," she murmured. "Please Rook, please." She suppressed a cry as I slid another finger inside her.

Fucking *Gods*, she felt exquisite - hot and wet, and so fucking tight. She leaned back, clasping on to my shoulders, and the sight of her naked body right in front of me, her golden hair lit by the fire - she was burning, just for me. I wanted nothing more than to be inside her, but I bit back my longing, simply watching her as she built towards her climax. She threw her head back and let out a soft moan.

"That's it," I murmured, caressing her thigh. "That feels good, doesn't it, my love?"

"Y-yes." She gasped. "Rook, I'm going to-" She broke off, covering her mouth with her hands. I held her steady, gripping her hip as her movements became faster, smaller, jerking herself against my fingers as she tightened around me.

Even through the haze of lust that had overtaken me, I wondered if she'd never experienced this before. My innocent little princess.

"You're going to come for me." I crooked my fingers, pushing against that swollen bud deep inside her, and her thighs trembled. Her cries were muffled by her hands, and then her whole body was undulating, pulsating on my hand. Her hands dropped from her mouth, and she collapsed against my chest, panting. My thumb circled her clit slowly, drawing out every last trembling moment.

She gasped, her hands pawing at my chest. She tossed her head a little, and shivered, letting out a high-pitched *Ah*. Her brows pinched together, and she burrowed into my neck. "I'm going to come again," she breathed.

"I know." I continued my slow, lazy circles, and just as her body had subsided, she broke over me again, trembling against my chest and muffling her moan in my neck. I looked down at her hooded eyes, her rosy, parted lips. "Enough?"

She nodded, biting her lip. "Mhmm."

I withdrew my fingers and she shivered, wrapping herself around me.

"Fucking Nav," she whispered.

"I could watch you come like that for hours." I traced kisses along her forehead. "You're so beautiful."

"Why didn't you fuck me?" She looked into my eyes, still trying to catch her breath. "I wanted you to."

"I wanted to make you feel good, my love, just you. And it did feel good, didn't it?"

Her face lit up with a small, shy smile. "Yes. It's - I mean, I've never… It's never been like that for me before."

"No?" I slid my hand into her hair, drawing her face close to mine.

"No. Even though I wanted more. I-I want you inside me. I want to feel that with you inside me." She stroked my chest with her fingertips. "Please?"

I laughed softly. "Now? It wouldn't last anywhere near as long as I'd like, with how I'm feeling right now." I was so fucking hard I knew it would only take a few strokes inside that sweet wet cunt to end me. "I want to be able to take my time with you, princess."

"But-" She broke off as I pinched her nipple between my fingertips, her eyes clenched shut as her mouth fell open in a moan. "That's not fair."

I chuckled, kissing her neck. "I'll do whatever I need to do to distract you, my innocent little Fae."

"Is that so?" She bucked against me, grinding herself

against my throbbing cock, and I had to bite back a loud groan. "Two can play that game."

I gripped the back of her head and grinned at her. "Do that again and I'll throw you on the floor and eat that cunt of yours til you can't breathe."

Her eyes widened for a second, then her lips lifted into a grin, and she bucked her hips again. "Is that a promise?"

I hissed in a breath. "So fucking innocent, hmm?" I clutched her to me, my fingers running down her back then quickly stopped as I felt the gashes the lion had left behind. "Shit, did I hurt you?"

She shook her head. "No, and don't change the subject." She pinned my shoulders against the armchair and kissed me greedily, her hips working me, the heat of her cunt seeping against my cock through my trousers. *Oh fucking Gods, this is going to end me.*

There was a loud bang on the door, and Elara jumped, shrinking into my arms as she began to tremble again.

"Norahi, the King wants to see you!" The guard's voice was muffled, but I could hear the irritation all the same.

Elara's eyes were wild as she looked up at me. "Please don't leave me," she whispered.

I rose to my feet with her in my arms. "It's alright, love." I carried her to the bed. "You need to rest anyway."

She clung on to me, not letting me put her down. "No, no, no, please don't -"

"Elara." I drew back from her, looking into her eyes, which were wide with terror. "Listen to me. I'll be back, very very soon. I promise. You get some rest, alright?"

Her lip trembled as I put her down, wrapping the blankets around her. "Al-alright."

"Norahi!" The guard slammed his fist into the door again. "Get a move on!"

"Coming!" I bellowed. I kissed Elara's forehead, and stroked her cheek with my thumb. "Sleep. I'll be back soon."

She nodded, and with one last kiss on her shoulder, I walked to the door, throwing it open to the guard's exasperated face.

"Took bloody long enough," he said. "Go on then, King's in his study. Said someone wants to see you."

Chapter 22

Rook

The guard opened the door to Theron's study, and I stepped in to see Theron sitting on his desk, his arms crossed over his chest. He regarded me with a cocked eyebrow, looking me up and down.

"Good evening, Rook."

I bowed my head. "Sire." I caught movement out of the corner of my eye, and looked up - straight into the face of Elara's father. I looked back at Theron. "What is he doing here?"

Theron laughed out loud as Vayr's glowering gaze remained on me. "High Lord Vayr has requested an audience with you, Rook. I am sorry to tear you away from your other engagements, I'm told you were - where were you again?" He looked from Vayr, back to me, his brows knit together, shooting up as he snapped his fingers. "Ah yes, I'm told you were brought here directly from Princess Elara's bedside."

Vayr's eyes widened with fury, and he charged at me. "You, you depraved fucking -"

"I was *comforting* her after she saved your life today, you old bastard."

Vayr stopped short at my words, his hands balled into fists at his sides. "You have no business being anywhere near her."

"And you have no business telling me what I'm to do," I replied.

"How is the Princess?" Theron asked casually, rising from his desk.

"She's upset." I met his gaze and tried not to let my rage show. "She's suffered a great deal."

Theron stroked his chin and nodded. "Yes, failure is not easy to stomach when you are used to victory." He shrugged. "At least she tried."

I inhaled through my nose, determined to steady myself. "Yes, she did."

"And her injuries?" Theron seemed almost bored.

"She will heal, I'm sure."

"Excellent." Theron gave Vayr a wide smile. "Lucky she's so resilient, ey?"

"Sire, may I ask why I'm here?"

"Got somewhere else to be?" Theron guffawed at my question and shook his head. "In such a hurry, Rook, anyone would think you had a warm bed and a naked female waiting for you."

Vayr turned on me again. "I swear to you, Norahi, if you go anywhere near my daughter I will end you."

"Do you know what I do with your daughter?" I raised my eyebrows when he didn't respond, his mouth set in a hard line. "I train your daughter so she doesn't fucking *die* down in that Pit."

"Fuck you, Norahi." He turned back to Theron, his finger darting in my direction. "This *demon* isn't to come anywhere near my daughter."

Theron's lips twitched pensively, and he narrowed his eyes as he looked at Vayr. "That sounded a lot like a command, My Lord."

Vayr quickly bowed his head. "Apologies, Sire. I am merely a father eager to protect his daughter."

"That's really rather noble of you," Theron said, rubbing his hands together. "I am not yet a father myself, but I do understand the urge to protect my offspring." His eyes flickered to me, and I dropped my gaze to the floor. "Oh yes, any male who has heard the cries of his child would know *exactly* how far a father would go to protect their own."

My heart wrenched in my chest, and I clenched my teeth together.

There was a knock at the door, and it opened to a guard. "Sire, Regan is ready to see you."

Theron waved in acknowledgement. "Ah yes, I have a little matter to see to, if you would both excuse me. I trust you'll not murder each other while I'm gone?" His gaze passed between us, and with a satisfied smirk and a flick of his wings, he walked out of the study.

Vayr rounded on me almost instantly, his eyes flaming with fury. "What were you doing in my daughter's room?"

"You fucking fool," I snarled through gritted teeth, darting a finger towards the door. "There are listening ears right outside that door."

He took a step closer to me and mercifully lowered his voice. "I want to know what you were doing in there."

"I told you, I was comforting her."

"Oh I know all about how your kind comfort *females*." He wrinkled his nose in disgust. "I can fucking smell it on you."

"Smell what?"

"*Depravity*." He bared his teeth. "I can scent it on you, like a fucking animal in heat. If I found out you've defiled her-"

I seized him by the collar. "Listen to me, I am the only friend your daughter has in this place, and if you cared about her at all, you would do well to keep your *fucking mouth shut*."

Vayr scoffed, struggling against my hands. "Her *friend*? Does she know, Norahi? Does she know what you threatened to do?"

I shoved him away from me. "You are in no position to accuse me of anything."

"I have never lied to my daughter."

"Keeping the truth from her is so different, is it?" I hissed out a breath. "You utter fucking bastard. She has no *idea* about *anything*."

Vayr crossed his arms over his chest. "Well, since you and she are so close, why don't you tell her what you said you'd do? Since you are the bastion of honesty, Prince Rook of House Norahi, tell her what our last words to each other were. See how far your *friendship* gets you."

An anxious knot formed in my stomach. "Fuck you, Vayr."

"You stay the fuck away from my daughter."

I couldn't look at him, a cold sweat breaking out on the back of my neck as I remembered our last meeting. That moment of utter betrayal, listening to his reasoning, his justification for leaving us. For abandoning us to the Seraph forces. My fingernails bit into my palms as I swallowed down the urge to tell him exactly what I'd just done with his daughter, that only moments ago I'd made her come on my lap. *Twice*.

But I beat those thoughts down. I wouldn't weaponise my feelings for Elara against her family, and I certainly wouldn't taint what I felt for her by making it some dirty act of vengeance. I'd touched her because I wanted her, because I cared for her deeply. Because she was *mine*.

The door opened, and Theron and Regan stepped in. Regan looked questioningly from Vayr, back to me, and shook his head.

"Ah, you two haven't killed each other yet!" Theron smiled jovially. "How wonderful. Now, we have prepared a banquet for you, High Lord Vayr. A royal visitor deserves a proper welcome, don't you think?"

Vayr pointed at me. "And what about him?"

Theron's eyebrows lifted, and he sighed. "Did you hear what I just said? I believe a Thank You is in order, don't you?" He frowned, rubbing his chin. "I do find it interesting that you have not once asked about your wife. You do seem rather more concerned with what my friend here is doing with your daughter than what has happened to your own dear wife."

Vayr sputtered then, and seeing the old bastard caught out gave me a deep sense of satisfaction. I crossed my arms over my chest as he bowed his head again.

"Your Majesty, your kindness is truly overwhelming, and I do not ask after my wife as I trust you implicitly."

Theron burst out laughing, clapping Regan on the back. "Now *that* is an answer, wouldn't you say? Oh yes." His gaze moved back to Vayr with a smirk. "You can tell those that have had to grovel in order to keep their status. They become so very good at it."

Vayr hesitated. "Sire, I only meant-"

"Ah it's of no matter." Theron waved his hand dismissively and looked at Regan. "The Princess, her room is kept under guard, is it not?"

"It is," Regan replied.

"And the only interaction she has with another is when she is training with Rook, is that right?"

"Indeed, Sire." Regan's eyes flicked to me for just a

moment. "Although it hasn't been entirely without its troubles."

Theron looked at me with a conspiratorial smile. "I'm told you were rather brazen that day. What was it you said?"

I rubbed the back of my hand against my upper lip. "I don't recall."

"No? Are you sure?" Theron's head swiveled from me to Vayr. "The guard's story was that he caught Norahi assaulting your daughter in the stables."

"That's a lie." I snapped, and Regan tutted loudly. "I-I didn't assault her." I kept my eyes on the ground, the anxiety that had pricked at my lips now spreading down the back of my neck.

"No, it would seem she was in your arms rather willingly." Theron's tone was languid, clearly enjoying his little game. "Lured you in there, did she?"

"No." My jaw was going to shatter if I clenched it any harder. "She-she needed comfort."

"There's that word again." Theron wagged a finger. "Comfort. Tell us, Rook. How do you *comfort* the princess?"

My lungs were tight in my chest, and I jerked involuntarily as Theron clapped a hand against the desk. "Now I recall what you said 'I'll fuck her in here if I want to', isn't that right?" His eyes glinted with malice as I met them. "Comfort indeed."

Vayr's rage boiled over, and he ran at me, throwing a fist which I easily caught in my hand. "You *fucking degenerate*!" He was almost foaming at the lips, his violet eyes bloodshot. "You touch my daughter and I will -"

"Do calm yourself," Theron said loudly, his wings spreading at his back. "I can assure you, Rook is living under the standards of the Accord. He's a very good boy, aren't you, Rook?"

The mark on my arm burned as I met Theron's eyes. *A very good boy*. I thought of Elara, of her rage at the word Mate, her hatred of being labeled like she was an animal. And here Theron was speaking to me as though I was a little dog, like he was patting me on the head.

"I know when to act, and when to remain silent," I said.

Regan's mouth was set in such a hard line his lips had gone white, and Theron seemed to not be able to measure my response for a moment. Eventually he merely shrugged, and turned back to Vayr.

"I assure you that Rook and your daughter will be kept apart, besides the necessary training. They have no reason to meet outside of the arena anyhow." His lips curled as he looked at me. "Although those chess games in the library for mental fortitude are probably necessary."

He knew everything. I was aware of that. But knowing every single move I made was under such close scrutiny... It made me wonder for one panic-stricken moment if he knew about my visits to the tower. No one knew I was still able to climb so easily, that scaling the sheer wall was as easy as walking up a flight of stairs for a Night Demon. It was the one power I'd strangely been left with, and the uneasiness I felt as Theron continued to leer at me made me wonder if it was on purpose.

Vayr was still glaring at me, and I gave my shoulders a shake. "I'm sure the High Lord will understand that I am merely trying to help the daughter he claims to love so dearly."

"Fuck you, Norahi." He jabbed a finger in my direction. "I made the right decision all those years ago. I'm only sorry your body wasn't on that wagon, too."

That was too much. That crossed a line he knew the moment the words left his mouth that he shouldn't have crossed. He took two instinctive steps back as I rushed at him, grabbing him by the collar and hoisting him into the air. Regan was urging me to stop, to put him down, and Theron merely laughed.

"You *ever* mention that again and I will tear your fucking head off," I snarled. "I will fucking *end you* if I ever hear you speak of it again. Their blood is on your hands as much-"

I broke off quickly, dropping him so that he had to stumble to stop himself falling to the ground. I took a deep breath, running my hands over my head. Rage made the air in my lungs stale, my stomach twisting with nausea. *That wagon. That fucking wagon, with the squeaky wheel. The clattering of my chains. Her voice, haunting me, begging me. Help me, Rook. It hurts. Please.*

"I think our friend has had enough for this evening." Theron's tone was clipped as he approached me, placing a hand on my shoulder. "It's late, and we all need to rest. I shall see you both at the banquet tomorrow night."

I didn't wait for a guard to take me back to my chambers. I hurried down the passageway, my vision blurred as I blinked away tears. I stumbled into my room and slammed the door behind me. I sank to the floor, pressing my hands to the cold stones, sucking in one breath after another, trying to regain my balance, trying not to break into a sobbing heap on the ground.

Help me, Rook. It hurts. They're hurting me.

I pressed the heels of my hands into my eyes until my skull began to ache. "Why her?" I asked the room. "Why *his* daughter? Why?"

Perhaps it was serendipity. The one who'd cost me everything now had to turn over his most precious belonging to me.

No. I refused to think of her that way. She was *mine*. She was not my restitution, and I was not her punishment. She was mine and I was hers because the Gods had decided it to be so. I wouldn't let Vayr destroy it for me.

I went to the basin and splashed my face with cold water. Then I sat and waited for the guards to grow quiet outside.

The moon passed behind a cloud as I soundlessly climbed out of my window, dropping down to the ground beneath me. I listened for a patrol, but their careless, ambling footsteps were nowhere within earshot.

I rounded the palace walls, under the cover of darkness, until I reached the western corner. Elara's tower rose into the navy blue sky. The torches flickered along the wall that stretched between the tower and the castle walls, but the vines that trailed along the stones provided enough cover that I could scale the tower unseen.

I pushed open the window, throwing my legs over the window sill and landing in her room. I paused for a moment, listening for Drusilla or movement of the guards outside. But it was late, and all was quiet. The only sounds were the crackling of the fire and Elara's shallow breaths.

I walked to the bed and looked down at her as she slept. She was lying on her side, the blanket clutched under her chin. Her pale hair splayed out behind her, her rosy lips parted ever so slightly.

She was perfect.

I climbed into the bed, laying against her back. She murmured softly, stilling as I pulled her into my chest. I kissed her soft golden hair, over and over, breathing in her delicate scent.

She was *mine*.

And even though I knew it was dangerous, even though I

knew I shouldn't, I closed my eyes, and allowed sleep to take me. Because all I fucking wanted was to sleep peacefully with her in my arms. Right then, it was the most precious gift I could have ever received.

Because I knew, within myself, that there was no way in Nav it would ever last.

Chapter 23

Elara

The sun was beating down on me, sweat and blood blurring my vision as I ran. I was getting closer, ever closer to the boy, the tiny boy who was crying for his mother. A lion roared behind me. Theron was laughing.

I'd almost reached the boy, I was almost there. Then the spiked iron door snapped shut on him, reducing his fragile frame to nothing but blood. I screamed.

My hands flew out and hit something hard, and I screamed again. "No!" I cried. "No, no!" I writhed in the grasp of whatever was holding me, and my back flashed with pain as the gashes pulled and stung from the movement.

"Elara, it's me." Rook's voice rumbled in my ear, vibrating through his chest as he held me close. "My love, I'm here. I'm here."

The panic doubled me over, and I collapsed in his arms, sobbing. "I couldn't save him," I cried, "I couldn't help him."

"It's over," Rook said, his hand cradling the back of my head. "You're safe, it's over. It's over."

I was still naked from when Rook had deposited me in the

bed before he left. My skin was slick with sweat, and I couldn't stop trembling. Rook clutched me to him, his fingers tracing slow circles over the back of my neck.

"I'm here, princess," he murmured. "I'm here. It was just a dream."

My fingers curled around his shirt, gripping on to him. "I thought you weren't here. I th-thought I was alone."

He kissed my forehead. "You're never alone. I promise you. I came back as soon as I could." He rocked me in his arms, taking one deep breath after another, as though coaxing my body to do the same. It worked, because finally his warmth seeped into my quivering bones, and my breathing became even.

My hand splayed across his chest, across the exposed patch of smooth skin. I looked up at him, and he smiled.

"Better?"

I nodded. "Much." I wrapped my arms around his neck and kissed him, feeling a small thrill as his lips opened for my tongue.

"I could kiss you for all eternity," he said when we parted. He stroked the hair out of my face, and his eyes flickered down over my naked body. "Especially when you're like this."

"That would be fine by me." I nuzzled into him and sighed. "Where did you go? What did Theron want?" He tensed, and I looked back up at him. "Rook?"

He inhaled heavily, and took my hand in his. "I don't know if you want to know this."

"Did something happen?" I could hear the panic in my own voice.

"No, no, it was…" He stroked my cheek with the back of his fingers, his eyes avoiding mine. "Your father, he requested an audience with me."

"My father?" I shook my head. "What did he want with you?"

"My love, I need to tell you something. And I need you to know I never would have done what I said I was going to do. But..." He trailed off, and seemed to steel himself. "Your father seems to think this matter would change how you feel about me."

"He knows?"

"No, it's..." He trailed off again, and made almost a grunt of frustration. "He *suspects*, and that's probably bad enough."

I climbed off his lap, kneeling on the bed in front of him. "Rook, you're being cryptic. I don't understand-"

"I threatened to kill you."

I was confused for a moment. "I know. I mean... we *tried* to kill each other. A few times. I still don't-"

"No." Rook snapped, running a hand through his hair. He still couldn't look at me. "Not now, not here. Years ago, when your father said he was withdrawing the Peyrusian army from Isambard. That he would... Abandon us. He said he had to do what he could to protect you. And I-I..." He looked at me helplessly, regret twisting his features. "I said I'd take his reason for abandoning us away. I said I'd kill you."

"Oh." I held his gaze, dismissing the flicker of hurt that washed through me.

"I didn't mean it." He seized my hand in his. "I swear it. I was angry, and afraid, and I wanted to hurt him, the way he was hurting my people. I could never have imagined that you, and me..."

I clasped his hand, and reached out to stroke his cheek. "Many things are said in anger, my love."

Rook leaned into my touch, closing his eyes. "Fucking Nav. I'm so sorry. I never would have-" He broke off and seized me in his arms, pulling me on top of him, burying his face in the crook of my neck. "I'm so, so sorry."

I stroked his hair gently. "And I suppose my father told you to stay away from me now?"

"Yes." He laid his cheek against my chest. "It was farcical. Threatening me, asking for assurances from Theron. He's completely fucking ignorant as to what's going on here."

I let out a bitter laugh. "It wouldn't be the first time my father had been totally ignorant as to what was good for me."

Rook gazed up at me, his brow furrowed. "I take it you're not especially close then."

"No, never. He wanted a son, and made it very clear I'd fallen well short of his expectations. But you already knew that, didn't you?" I stroked his cheek and gave him a weak smile when he didn't respond. "It's alright."

"No it's not." Rook wrapped his arms around my waist. "He should have thanked the Gods every day for giving him a daughter like you." He leaned up to kiss me, and I became keenly aware of the fact that I was, for the second time that evening, straddling Rook completely naked. I ground against him and a growl grumbled through his chest. "Oh princess, what's this now?"

I smiled at him and bit my lip, prompting him to raise his hand and seize my chin between his thumb and finger.

"Behave yourself." He raised his eyebrows. "I'm not going to fuck you tonight, if that's what you're thinking." He laughed when I pouted, and removed me from his lap. "Come on princess, we need to get you dressed." He rose from the bed, walking to the armoire. "Theron has called a banquet to celebrate your victory, and to welcome his royal guest."

I made a noise of disgust, and shuffled to the edge of the bed. "How have you survived here, all these years?"

"Tenacity." Rook retrieved a nightgown from one of the

drawers, and turned back to me. He stopped short, taking me in. "And what do you think you're doing?"

I feigned innocence, but I had perched myself on the edge of the bed with my legs spread with a very clear intention. I leaned back on my hands, and tossed my hair over my shoulder. "Why? Do you see something you like?"

"You're a fucking tease," he said, but the tenor of his voice had suddenly shifted. I felt a thrill of power as he walked slowly back towards me. Even Rook was only a male. Even he could only maintain control for so long.

He stopped in front of me, the nightgown in his hands dropping to the floor. I gazed up at him, and he stifled a groan. "You look at me like that, and I won't be able to stop myself."

"What makes you think I'd want you to stop?" I reached out for him, gripping on to the waistband of his trousers, holding his gaze.

"Your back," he said slowly. "I wouldn't want to hurt your back."

"I don't have to be lying on my back for you to fuck me, you know."

He grinned, and cupped my face with his hand, stroking my cheek with his thumb. "That is true."

"Take off your shirt."

He cocked an eyebrow. "Such a demanding princess."

I palmed his cock through his trousers, and his jaw clenched as another growl echoed through his chest. He tore his shirt off over his head, and I gazed at his body in the firelight. I brushed my fingers over the scars that adorned his skin, over the muscles of his stomach that began to contract as his breathing sped up. His skin was hot under my touch, and I had to take a deep breath to calm myself.

"Alright?" He asked, stroking my cheek tenderly.

I nodded. "Yes."

"Nervous?" His brow furrowed with concern for a moment.

"No. Not with you." I was anything but nervous.

Keeping my eyes fixed on his, I undid his trousers and pushed them down his legs. His freed cock bounced against my chest, and I wrapped my hand around him. Gods, he was huge. I ran my fingertips over the bumps I'd been told about, the thick, rippled ridge that ran along the underside.

"Do these feel good for you too, or are they just for me?" I asked, feathering my hand over him.

"Just for you?" He asked with a grin.

"Well, your body is mine, isn't it? All of it." I gripped him harder, and he hissed in a breath. "Just for me?"

"Mmmm." Lust flamed in his eyes. "It is. All of me, mind, body and heart, princess."

I lowered my eyes to his cock, and a small part of me felt a little intimidated at the sheer size of him. I'd seen plenty of penises in my time, soldiers weren't exactly private about bathing when in camp. But Rook's was beautiful, if such a thing as a beautiful cock could exist. I pumped my hand along his length, and a small bead of moisture leaked from the tip.

The groan he let out as I licked that small bead away set a flame of desire roaring through my body. I took him in my mouth - as much of him as I could manage at least - and gazed up at him as I flicked my tongue.

"Oh fuck," he gasped, his head falling back. His hand splayed across the back of my head, haltingly, not wanting to push me down onto him further. "I've dreamed of that tongue of yours."

I'd never done this before, so I licked and sucked carefully, the heat between my thighs growing more and more intense with every sound he made. I drew him as far down my throat as I could comfortably take him, and he shuddered, pushing back on my shoulders.

"Stop, stop."

I pulled back quickly, looking up at him. "Did I hurt you?"

He laughed breathlessly, dropping to his knees in front of me. "You definitely didn't hurt me, my love. But if you want me to fuck you, you'll need to stop." He hooked his hands around my thighs and laid his head against my stomach. "Now, I need to make sure this perfect little cunt is ready to take me."

"What do you - *OH.*" I clapped my hand over my mouth to suppress the cry of surprise and pleasure that burst from me as Rook buried his mouth between my thighs. I fell back on the bed, my back arching as Rook's tongue lapped at my clit, his hands holding me steady.

I kept my hand clamped down over my mouth, my other hand clawing into the sheets. His tongue explored me, my body jerking in response to the circles he traced, my thighs shaking as he rolled up and down, over and over.

I moaned against my hand, my stomach quivering as my climax built, heat tearing through my belly, more intense even than it had been when I'd ridden Rook's hand earlier. I writhed, unable to move away from him as his hands held me to him.

The bolt within me exploded so suddenly it caught me off guard, and I broke, quivering violently, my thighs clenched either side of Rook's head. My hand fell from my mouth as I gasped for breath, sure he'd done me in. How was he going to fuck me after that? I was a spent and ruined mess on the bed, biting my lip to suppress yet another moan as he gently kissed my thighs.

"So beautiful," he murmured. "You taste so fucking good." He rose over me, leaning on his fists on the bed. "The idea was that you don't end up on your back tonight, princess."

"I know," I replied breathily, "it's fine, it doesn't hurt much."

"It's not meant to hurt at all." He lowered his mouth to my neck, kissing me hungrily. "Now," he breathed against my ear. "Get on your knees."

I surprised myself with the urgency with which I scrambled to do as he said, crawling up the bed. He leaned over me, taking my hands and placing them on the headboard. He pushed my hair aside, nipping at the nape of my neck.

"Now, princess," he murmured, cupping my breast in his hand, "I'm going to take my time with you, and be very gentle."

"Don't be gentle," I panted, rolling my hips, desperate to close the distance between us. "Please, Rook-"

He seized my hair in his fist, pulling my head up. His teeth raked along my jawline. "My needy little Fae." He chuckled. "If you need me to stop, you tell me, alright?"

I nodded. "Yes."

He jerked my head back harder, so his lips were against my forehead. "You promise?"

"I promise, I promise." His cock press against my leg, hot and hard, and so close to where I wanted him. "Please, please, I want to feel you inside me, please, Rook."

He growled as his fingertips raked against my scalp. "Hearing you beg for me. *Fuck*." His fingers traced teasingly between my thighs. "You're dripping for me, aren't you, princess?"

"Ye-yes," I gasped.

My hips jerked as he pushed his cock between my thighs, running easily through the slickness he found there. A guttural moan broke from me as the bumps that adorned his cock rubbed against my clit, which was still swollen and throbbing from the assault of his tongue. My nails dug into the wood of the headboard, and I felt sure I was about to unravel again.

"Rook," I pleaded. "I want you inside me, please."

"Patience." He continued the slow rhythm of his hips, the white-hot pressure in my lower belly building again with each stroke.

"Please." I turned my head to look over my shoulder at him as my thighs began to tremble violently. "Please, Rook."

He rocked his hips faster. "The harder you come for me, the better it is. These-" He pushed the bumps of his cock harder against my clit with a flick of his wrist, chuckling again as I bit back a moan. "Aren't just for you. I want you to come so hard you can't remember anyone's name but mine. Because then these -" Another flick of his hand, and I shuddered as my climax tore through me, biting my lip so hard I was sure I was going to make myself bleed. "Are so sensitive that when I spill inside you, I'll see fucking stars."

My shoulders heaved as my body subsided, my head hanging between my arms. Rook seized my chin in his hand, his hot breath washing over my lips.

"Now, princess, you're ready for me?"

I nodded, my hair sticking to the beads of sweat that had formed on my face. "Y-yes."

I gasped as Rook began to ease himself inside me. He stopped, kissing me gently, and I realized I was trembling.

"Like I said," he murmured against my lips. "Slowly, my love." He pushed a little more, and a small whimper escaped my lips as I began to stretch around him. "Does that hurt?"

I tossed my head back, clenching my eyes shut. "No. Just… *oh.* It's… full. I don't know. Don't stop." As he'd promised, he took his time, pausing to kiss my neck, to whisper sweet words in my ear. There was no suppressing the moan that broke from me as Rook's hips finally sat flush against me.

"*Fuck.* So fucking tight." He kissed me, letting me just feel him, allowing me to adjust to his size. "You're shaking. Am I hurting you?"

"*No.*" I squirmed against him, my eyes still firmly closed. "I don't..." It was too much. It didn't hurt, but I was overwhelmed with wanting him, my body still reeling from the heights he had already driven it to. I wanted more, *more*, and yet it was all so consuming, so much to be bonded with him, joined with him in every sense, that all I could do was shake my head against his shoulder.

"Elara." His voice was so soft, so tender, and I opened my eyes to meet his gaze. "I want you to take a deep breath."

I inhaled sharply, and he ran a hand down my back.

"A *deep* breath, my love." He stroked my back again, and with the next breath, I relaxed a little more against him. He caressed my jaw, tracing my scars with his fingertips. "It's you, and me. That's all there is. That's all that matters. Nothing else."

Nothing else. I nodded. "I want you to move." I wriggled my hips, and he groaned. "I want you to move now."

He kissed me again, pulling out gently, almost to the tip, then plunging back into me. The jolt of pleasure that raced up my spine was so intense that my mind went stark white for a moment.There was nothing but him and his breath and his heat and the ecstatic stretch of my body. I gripped onto the headboard, feeling every deep, slow thrust, his eyes locked on mine.

"Do you feel how well you take me, princess?" He smiled, his breathing rapid now, longing and desire rolling off him in waves, crashing into my chest over the Bond. "It's as though the gods made this pretty little cunt just for my cock."

He rolled his hips harder against me, and I gasped, my back arching. Instantly he slowed, his hand stroking my cheek.

"If you ease off, I'll take your ax to you," I snapped, and he laughed softly before resuming his rhythm.

I prayed to whichever gods would listen that Drusilla was a deep sleeper. I hoped the doors were made of thick oak, and that the guards were suitably distracted. Because no matter how hard I tried, I wasn't going to be able to be quiet with Rook. Every stroke sent that rippled ridge up against a point inside me that set every inch of me on fire. I was trembling so violently that he had to lean over me, his hand on mine on the headboard, his enormous body pinning me into place.

His hand moved over my breast, pulling my nipple between his calloused fingertips, and I bucked at the touch, gasping as he drove deeper inside me. I turned my head towards him, my mouth seeking out his. His teeth nipped at my lips, his rapid breaths washing over me.

"You're exquisite," he murmured. "All of you. You feel so fucking good."

I quivered, pressing my head back against his shoulder. "Fuck."

"That's my girl." He groaned against my neck.

"Rook, the guards." I could barely speak, my body cresting to that peak again. "They'll - they'll hear us."

"I'm not stopping." He wrapped a hand around my throat, holding me tightly against him. "I'm not stopping until I feel you come on my cock, princess." He hammered into me, pushing me closer and closer to that precipice. My neck vibrated in his hand as another moan threatened to break from me. "That's it, come for me. I want to come with you."

My hands slipped down the headboard, and I buried my face in the pillows. My hips were now canted sharply, Rook's arm sliding around them so he could slip even deeper inside me. He held me steady, his thrusts almost punishing now. The sound of skin on skin filled the room, and I screamed into the pillow as the sweet pressure between my thighs broke. White heat rushed through every nerve in my body as I throbbed around Rook's cock.

His pace didn't slow, the ache of my body clenching down on him as he moved drawing out every second of my climax. He tensed, stilling against me, then groaned as his cock began to pump inside me. He kept me angled up until he stopped trembling, his other hand running up and down the slope of my back as he murmured my name, like a prayer, like a blessing.

Finally he withdrew from me, running his hands over my lower back. "*Fuck*," he breathed. "Are you alright?"

I slowly stretched out my legs, and rolled on to my side. Rook lay down beside me, reaching out a hand to place it on my chest, over my thundering heartbeat. His eyes were full of concern.

"Of course I'm alright," I replied.

"I didn't hurt you?"

I laughed breathlessly. "No. Not at all." I moved into his arms, nuzzling into his broad chest.

"I didn't want to be too rough with you, despite you insisting I not be gentle." He ran his fingertips up and down my spine, chuckling. "Such a greedy little Fae."

"You weren't rough, not at all." I tipped my head up to look into his eyes. "It was perfect. *You* were perfect."

He smiled widely. "That's the nicest thing anyone's ever said to me." He kissed the tip of my nose, then sighed. "What have you done to me, Elara?"

"So, it was good for you too then?"

"If my response left any doubt in your mind then maybe I'll need to do it again." He laughed when my eyes widened a little. "Maybe not right away." He kissed me deeply, his fingers laced in my hair. "I've been aching for you, for weeks now. Those dreams were torturous for me too."

"I thought they made you want to kill me?"

He grinned. "And *I* distinctly remember you saying that you pitied the maid who knew my cock. Still feel the same way?"

I swatted him in the chest, and that pleasing, rumbling laugh rolled through his body.

"Those dreams drove me mad, little Fae. Mad with longing, for you." He rolled onto his back, taking me with him so I lay on his chest. He pushed the hair out of my face, his hands cradling my head. "I think I love you, princess."

I inhaled sharply. "Oh gods."

"Sorry." He kissed me quickly. "Probably not the time to say something with quite so much gravity."

"It's alright. This is all just…" I sighed. "It's confusing." I laid my head against his forehead.

"Not confusing at all, my love. You're my -" He paused, frowning. "What do I call you? If you cannot abide the word Mate."

"Bonded. I am your Bonded, and you are mine."

"Your Bonded." He said the words slowly. "I like that. Much better than Mate. We Night Demons don't believe in all this, you know?"

"No?"

He shook his head. "We call it a violation of free will. Ironic, considering we still have arranged marriages."

My eyebrows shot up in surprise. "You do?"

"Mmm. Even mine was-" He broke off quickly, and exhaled heavily as he tipped his head back on the pillow. "Never mind."

I put my hands on his chest. "Your marriage? You were married?"

His eyes met mine. "I don't want to talk about it now."

"Where is your wife?"

He pulled me down to him, kissing me tenderly. "Not now, my love. That's a story for another day."

I wondered when would be a good day to discuss Rook's wife. A feeling of dread crept up on me as I wondered where she could be, what had happened to her. Isambard had been destroyed, and I had no idea what had happened to Rook's family. I didn't want to ask him now. It was the wrong time.

"You'll have to leave soon, won't you?"

"Yes, unfortunately." His arms encircled me. "What I wouldn't give to be able to just lie here with you, to wake up with you in my arms."

"I want that too." I pressed myself against his naked body, against his warmth. "I hate being left with only dreams of you."

"So do I." He looked sad suddenly, his eyes downcast. "You know, that once you've passed these trials, and you will pass them, you know…" He trailed off. Yes, I knew. I knew what he was saying.

I straddled him and seized his face in my hands. "I'm not leaving you here."

He attempted a smile. "I'm afraid you won't have much choice."

"What did you say to me that day in the stables?" I asked, stroking his cheeks with my thumbs. "Remember what you said? If you believe you can't, you're right. If you believe you can, you're right."

"I'm a slave, my love." His hands pushed the hair back from my face, drawing me down against his forehead. "But if I can see you be free -"

"Stop it." Tears sprang to my eyes again. "Just stop. I'm not fucking leaving you here. Do you hear me? I'll kill anyone who tries to stop me. You're coming with me when I leave."

He attempted a smile, but his eyes were still heavy with sadness. "See? I told you. The Gods help the world if we ever fall in love."

"And we have." Tears spilled down my cheeks onto his face, and he turned his mouth to gently kiss them away. "I'll burn this place down to get you out of here, I swear it."

"So you love me too then?"

I swallowed hard. "You know I do." I put my hand on his chest, over his heart. "Mine?"

"Yours." His voice was gruff as he clutched me to him. "Yours. Forever. All of me."

"Tell me about Isambard," I said, stroking his cheek. "Tell me about your home."

He propped an arm behind his head, his other hand tracing small circles on my bare shoulder as I nuzzled in against his neck. "The ocean," he began, "it glitters, like diamonds, when the sun rises. It's the clearest water you've ever seen, turquoise. And it's always warm."

I sighed. "That sounds wonderful."

"At dusk, the twin moons rise above it, and it's so beautiful."

"You'll have to take me swimming there, one night." I said, smiling as he chuckled.

"I suppose I will, yes." He sighed, his fingers continuing their small circles on my naked skin. "The city itself is… it *was* beautiful. Blue buildings, golden roofs. It was a sight to behold. The trees aren't green, like they are here. They're yellow. Golden leaves, all year."

"That sounds magical."

He leaned forward to plant a kiss on my head. "It is." His

hand fell away from my shoulder. "I should go. It'll be dawn soon."

I climbed off him, watching as he retrieved his clothing from the floor. "I suppose I'll see you at training then."

Rook gave me an exasperated glance. "I think you're joking, aren't you?"

"Why?"

He leaned on his fists on the bed. "You're hurt, and you need to heal. Your back is in a state. Besides," he said with a grin, "I think we've had enough training tonight."

"Is fucking training?"

"The best kind there is." He kissed me tenderly, all the longing and desire to stay with me more than obvious. "I'll see you at this monstrous banquet."

I sighed. "Fuck."

"Indeed." He straightened up, his hands flexing a little as he gazed at me. He opened his mouth to speak, then shook his head with a sigh. He moved towards the window, and I rose from the bed to follow him. He turned and took me in his arms. "I'm sorry."

I frowned. "What for?"

"All of this." He jerked his head vaguely. "I can't protect you from it. And I'm sorry."

I shook my head. "It's not your fault. Please, don't blame yourself."

He gave me a sad smile. "My fierce little Fae." He kissed me once more before easing himself out of my grasp and hoisting himself out the window onto the tower wall. "Try and sleep," he whispered, and then he dropped out of sight.

Chapter 24

Elara

Drusilla shook her head as she looked me up and down. "Red, I just don't know."

I allowed myself a small smile as I regarded my reflection in the mirror. Red, like the blood of my enemies. I had to give myself some small measure of control in this ridiculous situation. My stomach dropped a little as I thought of seeing my father - my father, who had warned Rook to stay away from me. I wasn't going to tell him about the Bond, that much was certain.

If my father found out I was bonded to Rook, much less that I'd taken him to my bed and given him my body, there was no doubt in my mind Rook would be put to death for violating the Accord. Theron would make an example of him, favored assassin or no. The sharp tug at my heart as I thought of anyone hurting Rook was so acute it took my breath away. I'd meant what I said - I would burn Veles to the ground if I had to. I wouldn't leave him here. I couldn't.

Drusilla gave me a single earring, a series of long dangling chains adorned with black pearls. They stood out against the curtain of my pale hair, and I was pleased with my appearance. Regal. Strong. I wouldn't be cowed by Theron.

Or my father.

I tried to imagine the confrontation between Rook and my father, when the Peyrusian soldiers had abandoned Isambard, and had retreated to leave the city to be destroyed. I couldn't blame Rook for what he had threatened. He had told me he'd lost everything. I still didn't know exactly what that meant, and I was afraid to ask. But whatever had occurred, I couldn't see fault in his rage, nor me being the object of it.

The door to my chamber opened, and Regan walked in. He looked me up and down, and gave me a wide smile. "Your highness, you look stunning."

"Thank you, Regan."

He gave me a sympathetic smile. "I do find it admirable that you won't hide your deformity."

I bristled at this. "My what?" I snapped.

His eyes widened instantly, and he began to sputter as he bowed his head atop that ridiculously thin neck. "Oh, Your Highness, forgive me, I meant no offense."

I ran a hand over the side of my head, where Drusilla had pinned my hair back to fall over my right shoulder. I wasn't going to hide my scars. I saw no need to. I thought of Rook kissing them, telling me how perfect I was. He had never shied away from my scars, touching them and kissing them. He was not put off by them, and I refused to see them as anything but a part of me.

"Perhaps we can go now," I said, walking towards Regan, who was still bent double, his face bright red. "I would like to see my father."

Regan could barely speak, spluttering and apologizing as he led the way down the passageway. I didn't listen to him, to his simpering. I had no desire to.

The banquet hall was abuzz with conversation as we approached. I held my head high as Regan announced my arrival, and the room fell silent. It was unnerving, but I didn't let it show. My father sat at the head table beside Theron, and I approached, bowing my head. "Sire," I said to Theron, whose eyes roved up and down my body.

"Your Highness," he said, his white teeth bared as he grinned at me, "you look truly ravishing tonight. What a color on you." He turned to my father. "Your daughter is such a beauty. You must be endlessly proud of her."

My father's eyes were fixed on me, and they widened a little as they moved to the left side of my head. "Yes, she is, Sire. A true beauty, just like her mother."

I bowed my head again. "I thank you for the compliments."

My father turned to Theron. "I wonder, Your Majesty, may I have a moment alone with my daughter? It has been an age since I last saw her, and I would so like to speak with her."

Theron looked from my father to me and back again, his lips twitching in a display of theatrical pensiveness. Finally, he clapped my father on the shoulder and laughed. "But of course, Your Grace!" He gestured to a guard. "Please, follow my man here, he will take you to a room where you may visit with your daughter." His eyes moved back to me. "She is so very precious."

"Indeed," my father replied uncertainly, rising to his feet. He moved to my side and took my hand, gazing at me with his violet eyes. "So very precious."

I clutched on to his hand as we followed the guard. I scanned the room as we walked, the many eyes of the courtiers following our every move. It was then I spotted Rook, leaning against a wall at the far end of the room, his blue eyes fixed on me. He was dressed in formal attire, a black jacket with a high neck and golden embroidery on the sleeves, along with tight black trousers. His curly dark hair spilled over his forehead, and he looked so regal and beautiful. His brow was furrowed as he watched me walk with my father. I could sense his worry, and my palms began to sweat.

"Here," the guard said, opening a narrow oak door to reveal a small side room, with tall windows. A fire crackled in a hearth in the corner of the room, and it was almost oppressively warm. My father and I stepped in, and both watched as the door fell closed behind us.

My father descended on me, throwing his arms around me. "Sweetheart," he said, his voice gruff, "oh Gods, sweetheart." He held my face in his hands, and shook his head. "What did they do to you?"

"It wasn't them," I said, putting my hand over his, where my ear had once been. "It happened in Grixos."

"What were you thinking?" He asked. "What were you thinking, going off like that?"

"I wanted to go with Keir," I replied.

"And he is dead now I suppose?"

I nodded, and bit my lip. "He fell in Grixos. I held him as he died."

"I'm so sorry, Elara." My father hugged me to him again. "I know you loved him deeply."

"I did."

He looked at me earnestly. "Are you alright?"

"Of course I'm not alright," I replied in a harsher tone than I intended. "I'm a prisoner here, and Theron has me entering a death pit to try and earn back our kingdom."

"Your mother?" He asked, clutching my hands. "You saved her?"

"Yes, I saved her. But Esther..." I trailed off as I remembered that terrible day.

"Oh Gods." My father shook his head. "May Mokosh guide her safely to Nav."

I swallowed hard, blinking. "What happened in Peyrus?" I glanced up at him when he didn't answer immediately. "Is it all gone?"

My father sighed heavily, looking thoughtfully down at my hands. "The forces moved so quickly. We had no time to put up shields, nothing." He patted one of my hands firmly, as though to comfort himself as much as to comfort me. "It was terrible. And quick." His eyes were mournful as they met mine again. "It is all gone, sweetheart."

My home was gone. My chest felt tight, and I fought the tight bodice of my dress to draw in a deep breath. "So, where has Mama been sent to?"

"I don't know," my father replied, and I was shocked to see tears in his eyes. "Theron won't tell me."

I laughed bitterly. "Yes, that is Theron's specialty. Being ominous and cryptic."

"Surely he isn't going to send you back into that arena?"

"I don't think there's any telling what he's going to do," I said with a sigh. "But if it truly is all gone, and he's still not letting me go, he has a plan, and I don't think it's one that will end favorably for me."

My father clutched my shoulders. "Have no fear, sweetheart. I will negotiate your release. I've done it once before, and I will do it again."

"Before?" I asked, meeting his gaze. "When you left Isambard to be destroyed?"

My father released my shoulders and took a half a step back. "Norahi has been at you already, hasn't he?"

"I don't need anyone to have been *at me* to know what happened at the end of the Uprising, Father."

He scoffed. "No, but I can tell a skewed version of events when I see one."

"I wouldn't know a skewed version of events at all since this is the first version I've ever even been privy to."

My father pointed a finger in my face. "I protected you."

"You *sheltered* me!" I took a deep breath, steadying myself. "I am your heir. I was not prepared, in any way, for life as a queen. How could you do this to me?"

My father crossed his arms over his chest. "I don't know what that demon has told you-"

"The truth, it would appear, and he is the first one to have deemed me worthy of it."

My father hissed through gritted teeth. "I did what I had to do to protect you, to secure your freedom."

"My freedom?" I gestured around the room. "What freedom is that, father? What did your betrayal of Isambard win you? Veles still declared war on you, and you still lost your kingdom, and your daughter still ended up Theron's captive."

"Norahi threatened to kill you, has he told you that?" My father's ire was rising, I could see it as his violet eyes began to glow brighter in his pale face. "Did he tell you that he threatened the life of my only child?"

"He has, as a matter of fact, and considering the circumstances I can't blame him."

My father moved closer to me again, his eyes narrowing. "And when exactly did he tell you this? Because when I saw him last night I was very much under the impression that you did not yet know."

"That's hardly important right now."

My father's eyes widened. "No."

"What?"

He looked so angry for a moment I thought he would strike me. "You've not been with him, have you?" When I didn't answer, he leaned closer, his eyes wild. "I want you to tell me, have you been with him?"

"I will tell you no such thing," I replied defiantly.

"You are my child and you will answer me now." My father's voice had dropped to a dangerous snarl. "He came to you last night, didn't he? He was in your room, in your bed."

"You have no right whatsoever to know anything of such an intimate nature, father."

"He's had you, hasn't he?" He turned away from me and threw his arms up. "Fucking bastard of a fucking degenerate demon, I'm going to fucking tear him to pieces."

"No you won't."

His head snapped back towards me. "Do you already carry his child?"

I laughed bitterly. "You're being preposterous now."

"You will tell me!"

"No!" I cried. "You will stop this! I am locked up here, in your enemy's castle, a prisoner, and you're here asking me who I have taken to my bed? *That* is your concern? Your only child, and this is what you're in here shouting at me about?"

My father pointed a finger at me, jerking it in the air. "Norahi is not to touch you, or he dies."

"Anyone who harms him will fall under my blade."

My father's jaw fell open as he scoffed in outrage. "You would threaten your own blood?"

"He *is* my blood," I growled through gritted teeth.

My father's eyes widened and he stumbled a little, away from me, his hands falling to his sides. "No." He shook his head. "That's not possible. It's not -" He flew at me, his fingers digging into my upper arms as he shook me. "You have not bonded yourself to him?"

"Lada chooses those as she sees fit, you know very well I had no control over it and neither did Rook."

"Rook?" My father was aghast, veins bulging in his temple. "*Rook?*" He spat the name out like poison, and shook me harder. "Have you given your body to him? I demand you tell me now."

I shoved him away from me. "How dare you ask me that."

"So you have." His finger came up again, pointing at me. "You have. You opened your legs for a fucking Night Demon."

"You're disgusting." I shook my head. "You claim to be of the Faith and then question the Bond?"

"A Fae, and a Night Demon? Bonded?" He raked his hands through his white hair. "It is obscene, unheard of."

"Well it has happened." I hadn't wanted to tell him, and I knew this could get dangerous very, very quickly, for both Rook and myself. "If you want your Kingdom back, if you *ever* want to see me be free again, you will say *nothing*."

"If he touches you -"

"I've already told you what will happen if any harm comes to him. Now, we should get back to the banquet." I walked to the door, raising my hand to the handle, stopped by my father's hand. I turned to look up into his eyes, which were full of fury.

"I expected better of you." His words were sodden with disappointment.

I gave him a bitter smile. "And I of you." I shrugged him off me, and opened the door, back into the din of the banquet hall. The bodice of my dress had suddenly seemed to shrink by several sizes, and the air in the banquet hall was thick, like the air in that fucking jungle had been.

I stumbled through the crowd of courtiers, gasping for air, desperate for a window, a door, anything. I finally crossed the room and found an open door, ignoring the guard who barked at me as I moved past him, out into the courtyard.

I moved as far away as I could from the din of the

courtiers, leaning against a stone pillar with one hand. The air out here was hot, but not as thick and oppressive as it had been inside. Sweat rolled down my neck, and I brushed it away with my hand.

"Are you alright?"

I looked up to see Rook approaching slowly, eyeing me uncertainly. He glanced over his shoulder as though to check if we'd been followed, then turned back to me, his brow furrowed with concern.

"Are you alright?" He asked again.

I shook my head. "I think I just threatened to kill my father."

Rook's eyes widened for a moment. "You did what?"

"He said… He told me to -" I broke off as he drew closer, leaning against the pillar beside me. "I think you can guess what he said."

Rook crossed his arms over his chest. "Yes, I suppose I can." The corner of his mouth pulled up in a crooked grin. "And you threatened his life over it?"

I tipped my head back to the sky, closing my eyes as my lungs finally seemed to fill with air. "I did." I slowly looked back at him. "He knows about the Bond, and he was furious."

Rook flexed his shoulders and laughed awkwardly. "I suppose he was probably as surprised as we were."

"I swore him to secrecy, and since he wants his Kingdom back…" I balked. It was all gone. "Since he wants to have his freedom, and to see my mother again, I suppose he shall behave himself."

Rook glanced over his shoulder briefly. "I should go back in, I'm not supposed to be out here."

"I'll see you tonight?" I asked hopefully.

He cocked an eyebrow. "Want me back in your bed already?"

My throat was dry as I nodded. "I want you to tear this dress off me and claim what is yours."

Rook's eyes flamed, and his fingers flexed against his muscular arms. "You have no idea what those words do to me."

I suddenly felt powerful, seeing his desire for me so plain on his face. "Perhaps I will make you beg for me tonight."

His eyes went feral for just a moment, hooded with predatorial lust. He took a deep breath, straightened his back, and gave me a smile. "Perhaps you shall." He bowed his head, then turned and strode back into the banquet hall.

I crossed the courtyard slowly, letting the evening breeze cool the sweat on my skin. Despite everything that I was facing, the danger, the trials, all of it - being with Rook was the only reprieve I knew, the only comfort I had. I smiled to myself as I thought of the previous night, and I shivered with anticipation at what the night ahead might bring.

"You look stunning tonight."

The voice made me jump, and I turned to my right to see Theron gazing at me. His wings rustled softly in the breeze as he approached me. He looked hauntingly handsome, his brown skin glowing against the white of his shirt, baring a triangle of his smooth torso. I saw for the first time the gold tattoos that adorned his chest. But his eyes still made me uneasy, glistening cruelly.

I gave him a brief nod and a smile. "I thank you."

He held a fluted glass in his hand, and took a sip of the sparkling liquid within it. "You and your father had a good talk I hope."

"We did," I replied, "though we did both wonder where my mother had been sent."

"Fiachra," Theron said quickly, almost too quickly. As though his response had been rehearsed. "She is extremely comfortable there, and all is well." He bared his white teeth in a grin. "You mustn't worry so much, dear one. She is perfectly safe."

I didn't believe him, but returned his smile nonetheless. "Thank you."

"But of course." He gazed up at the changing dusk sky above us. "Are you happy here, Elara?"

The question was so absurd I laughed, a laugh that quickly dissipated when those eerie green eyes turned back to me. "I beg your pardon, Sire. I had just thought your entire purpose in keeping me here was to torture me. I had no idea I should be happy here."

Theron chuckled. "Torture." He considered the word for a moment, swinging the glass in his hand lightly back and forth between his fingers. "I do not mean to torture you, Elara. I mean to motivate you."

"Motivate me to what end?"

"Why, to become my wife of course." The easy smile that spread across his face at the words made my mouth run dry. My face must have betrayed my shock, because his eyes roved over it, his eyebrow lifting. "There are conditions to this bargain, Elara. If you marry me, and live as my wife, all this *torture* will see an end."

"I had thought the conditions of this bargain were that I should win back my freedom."

"Bargains can change." Theron's voice dropped low. "I think only of your happiness."

I cleared my throat. "So I shall live my life as a captive no matter what."

"If you wish to see it so, then yes." Theron sighed, shaking his head, suddenly seeming exasperated. He stepped closer to me, and gazed down at me. He raised a hand to my shoulder, resting it there gently. "I am not a monster, Elara. I would be a good husband to you."

"But I would never be free."

Theron's eyes narrowed. "What is freedom, dear one? Returning home to a land in ruin? Being sold off by your pathetic father to some foreign prince, to share his bed until you've produced an heir, and then never be looked at again?" He raised a finger to my cheek, stroking it gently, and my blood ran cold. "I would be a caring, decent husband. Nothing like my father was." He spread his wings and curled them around us, cocooning us in. "No, I would treat you like the Queen you are. I would share your bed every night, and never make you regret a single moment you lay naked in my arms."

My throat constricted, almost painfully, as I looked up into his green eyes. Sweat began to form on the back of my neck again. The very idea of being naked in Theron's arms made my stomach churn.

Theron lowered his mouth to mine a little more. "You would look so beautiful," he said, reaching out and brushing his fingers over my stomach, "round and swollen with my child."

I ceased to breathe for a moment. "Your child?" It was all I could manage to get out as sheer terror kept me frozen in the rustling prison of his wings.

"Why of course, dear one." He grazed my cheek with his lips. "The Heir to my throne."

I was going to be sick. I inhaled sharply. "When will you announce the next trial?"

A flash of irritation burst across his face, but then he grinned, his eyes hooded, like a striking viper. He raised an eyebrow, and gripped the side of my face with a firm hand, tilting my head back. "You are so determined, aren't you?"

His thumb caressed my cheek. "So brave. So fierce. And so, so stupid." His thumb moved further, tracing over my lower lip, his eyes coming to rest there too. "It could all be so easy, Elara."

"You and I have a very different definition of easy."

Theron chuckled. "We do indeed." He lowered his mouth to my ear. "You are a sight to behold down in that arena, fighting on so bravely." He pulled back a little so he could look into my eyes. "I will have to be more creative, I think."

I mustered the last bit of bravery I had and steeled my gaze. "I am not afraid of you."

He threw his head back and laughed. "It's such a shame you're so stubborn." He grinned widely, baring his white teeth. "All that fire, that ferocity. I imagine you would provide me with a great deal of pleasure in my bed." With a loud whoosh, his wings were drawn in at his back. "Do come inside when you're ready, dear one. I have an announcement to make."

My hands were trembling as I watched him sidle back into the banquet hall. The breath I'd tried so hard to steady was now torn from my lungs, and the weight of the situation in which I found myself fell back upon my shoulders. I'd lied when I'd said I wasn't afraid of him - of course I was, especially now the goal was unknown. What else was there to fight for?

Keir's face swam before me, grinning, pushing his mottled blond hair from his forehead. "You're royally fucked," he'd say jovially, his violet eyes sparkling. He'd said it before the battle in Grixos too.

He'd say it to me now, if he were still here, still alive. And he'd be absolutely right.

Shit.

I walked back into the hall slowly, hoping the sweat on the

back of my neck wasn't rolling down into the dress and staining the silk, betraying exactly how scared I was. I took my place beside my father, who stared at me. I looked straight ahead, avoiding his gaze entirely. I saw Rook crossing the room, his gaze flickering towards me for only a moment before he took his place at a table nearby. My father tensed noticeably next to me.

Theron rose to his feet, his golden wings spread behind him. He raised his hands for silence, and all eyes in the room turned to him.

"Good people of Veles," he said, "I welcome our royal guest, King Vayr of Peyrus."

Polite applause sounded around the room, accompanied by displeased looks and murmuring. We were solidly on enemy ground. I dared a sideways glance at my father, and saw he had gone pale.

"The princess of Peyrus, her royal highness Princess Elara, has secured her father's freedom, and I commend her brave and valiant efforts." He looked down at me. "I do understand the trial was quite difficult, such a limited time, even for one as fast as you." He shook his head sadly. "That poor child."

My stomach lurched, and my fingers clawed into the silk skirt over my thighs. My eyes moved over to Rook, whose gaze was fixed on me. He gave me a brief nod as he sensed my distress. I took a deep breath, keeping my eyes on him as Theron continued to talk.

"The Princess shall engage in another trial, tomorrow!" Theron raised his hands to enthusiastic cheers from the courtiers.

"Tomorrow?" My father asked, his voice barely audible over the noise in the hall. "Your Majesty, my daughter has barely healed and -"

Theron's green eyes flashed down to look at my father, and

he grinned. "Oh, do not concern yourself, Your Grace. This trial will not require anything of your daughter besides her attendance."

My father turned to look at me, and he shook his head, his brow furrowed. "But what could possibly be won?" He was asking me, Theron, anyone, anyone who would have an answer.

Theron's eyes moved over to me, and his grin turned my stomach. "This trial will prove your daughter's powers of endurance, your Grace."

Endurance. I tried to keep my breathing even. "And what shall I be required to endure, Your Majesty?" I asked.

Theron raised his eyebrows and shrugged. "You will see in good time, dear one. Now." He clapped his hands, and servants began to carry out silver platters piled high with food. "It is time for us to dine and celebrate your victory." He raised a goblet to me, and I was sure I was going to faint.

I bowed my head to him briefly. "Thank you, Your Majesty."

Food was placed before me, and I forced myself to eat something, just a small amount. Just a little. I could feel Theron's gaze on me, testing me, waiting for any tiny hint of fear, of relinquishment. I would give him no such satisfaction.

"Please, Your Majesty," my father said, leaning closer to Theron as the king took his seat. "Please, we must be able to come to some sort of understanding. A treaty."

Theron met my father's eyes with a look of boredom and amusement. "A treaty? On what terms?"

"My daughter, please, she must be allowed to have her freedom."

"Why?" Theron asked, taking a sip from his goblet.

"She is a Princess, she is my daughter." My father's voice faltered.

Theron lifted his goblet, and pointed a finger in Rook's direction. "He is a Prince, what does it matter?"

My father spluttered and stammered, trying to find the words, but Theron held up a hand for silence.

"Your Grace, you have nothing to offer me," he said in a low voice, "you are a King with no kingdom, and you have made it rather clear that your heir has fallen very much short of your expectations."

My father's gaze flashed to mine for a moment. "I love my daughter, and am very proud -"

"It is no secret in this realm that you are more than disappointed that you failed to produce a male heir," Theron interjected, "do not make excuses to me now. You should be pleased that your daughter has the prospect of a good marriage before her."

My chest constricted, and anger seeped into my veins as my father's eyes met mine helplessly. Theron was right - my father had nothing with which to negotiate my release, and he never would.

The evening gave way to the dark of the night, and it remained oppressively hot. Lightning began to flash in the distance, a deep roll of thunder sounding as the hall began to clear of courtiers. Regan appeared to escort me back to my room, and I turned to my father. I knew I was saying goodbye to him, and I had no idea when I would see him again. I should try and be tender, to at least part on good terms.

But his eyes were hard as they met mine, and as he took me in his arms to say farewell, he whispered in my ear, "Stay away from him, like I told you to."

"Never."

As I was escorted along the stone passageway back to my room, thunder growled overhead, and I wondered if that would be the last word I ever said to my father.

Chapter 25

Elara

"Dress already off then?" The voice followed the soft creak of the window falling open, and I raised my head from the pillow to watch Rook climb into my room. He was dripping, soaked with the rain that now fell outside, carried in by the summer storm.

"Drusilla insisted," I told him, sitting up to watch him strip his wet clothes from his muscular body. The firelight illuminated his skin, and desire flooded my groin. "Hurry up," I chided, and he chuckled.

"I thought I was going to be begging for you tonight, princess," he said, climbing into the bed beside me and growling appreciatively when he found me already naked.

"I don't have the energy to make you beg." I wrapped my arms around his neck, moaning into his mouth as he kissed me slowly.

He rolled me onto my back, leaning over me, his curls dripping rain across his forehead. "You're so warm," he murmured, lowering his mouth to my neck, brushing one delicate kiss after another from my ear to my collarbone. "I hope you're not too sore after last night."

"We heal fast, remember?" I wrapped my legs around his waist, rocking my hips against him, but Rook pinned me down, holding me still.

"In a rush, are we?" He asked, moving his mouth across my throat to begin kissing up the other side of my neck.

"I just need you," I said with a sigh, closing my eyes as bliss flooded my body.

"Mmm," Rook growled, his kisses trailing down my chest, between my breasts. His mouth moved over my tattoo, his breath hot on my skin. "You still haven't told me what this tattoo means."

"I'm the Heir to the Sun Throne," I told him, my hips jerking up towards him, aching to feel more of him.

"Ah, so you are the sun, and I am the moon and stars." His lips worked harder against my skin, his kisses becoming more desirous. "How fitting."

"Yes, it is." I gasped as his fingers traced over my nipples.

He moved down towards my hips, his lips and tongue tracing over my skin. "Fuck, you smell good, princess." His mouth kept moving down, down, and then his hands pushed my thighs apart, and he growled low in his throat.

My back arched as his tongue moved between my legs, slowly at first, just the tip moving over my clit. "Oh Gods," I murmured. Rook's hands held my hips down, but as his tongue moved faster, lapping up more of me, I bucked against his mouth, and he chuckled.

"Even after last night, your sweet little cunt is still so needy for me, my love."

A flush rose in my cheeks. "You just feel so good."

He crawled back up and kissed my neck ferociously. "If you want to fuck my mouth, there's a better way to do it."

With a swift movement he'd rolled onto his back with me on top of him, and he guided me up onto his face. "There now," he said, brushing his lips against the delicate skin of my inner thigh, "you can ride my tongue as hard as you want."

I steadied myself on the headboard as Rook pulled me down hungrily onto his face, licking and sucking like he was possessed. I tried to pull back a little, afraid I'd smother him, but all this served to do was for Rook to press harder against my thighs to keep me in place.

And fuck, his tongue felt so good. He moved over and around my clit, finding the tiniest sensitive points that I didn't even know existed. His tongue swirled down, to my entrance, inside me, then back up again, over my clit, over and over.

I abandoned all worries about smothering him, and rolled my hips on his face. He groaned against me, his lips locked over me, that tongue of his expertly eliciting moan after moan from my mouth. My thighs began to tremble, and the sweet pressure in my belly was so intense I felt like I was going to explode.

Then Rook's hands moved from my thighs to my breasts, pulling my nipples hard between his calloused fingertips. That was enough to send me spiraling, my whole body felt like it was on fire. My hips bucked harder, Rook's tongue swirling around my clit.

I clutched my hands to my mouth, my head thrown back as my climax crashed through me violently, riding his tongue until I couldn't bear it any longer. I pulled away from him, sliding down his chest to collapse on him.

"Oh Gods," I moaned. "Oh fuck."

"We're not done yet," he said, his breathing quick against my ear. "Turn around."

I weakly rose to arrange myself on him so I was straddling him, facing the end of the bed.

"Now, you're going to ride my cock."

A thrill rushed through me as I moved to lower myself on to him. Rook held my thighs firmly. "Slowly, princess. I want to watch you take me."

I whimpered, biting my lip as I slowly, slowly moved down his thick length. By the time he was seated fully inside me, my head was swimming and I was sure only a few movements at this angle would have me coming again.

Rook's hand's moved over my ass. "This view is fucking perfect. The things I want to do to this perfect ass of yours."

I rocked on him gently, looking over my shoulder at him. "And what things are those?"

He let out a low laugh. "We'll work up to that, my love."

I circled my hips on him, moaning as that ridge rubbed up against where I wanted him. "Is that good for you?"

"Everything you do is good for me." His hands dug into my hips. "I want you to fuck me for yourself. Rub yourself on me the way it feels good for you. Use my cock to make yourself come, princess."

I rolled and ground myself on him, and fucking gods he felt incredible. He was so deep inside me at this angle, claiming me, claiming every inch of me for himself. My climax was still sending delicious heat coursing through me, and I knew it wouldn't take much to reach it again.

I pinched my nipples between my fingers, rolling my hips.

"Here, let me," Rook said, and he leaned up behind me.

I cried out, the change in angle driving him even deeper within me, deeper than I thought possible. His hand moved over my breast, rolling it so my nipple grazed against his rough palm.

I rested my hands on his thighs, bucking my hips back against him. My face flushed with heat, and I bit my lip, whimpering as I cursed the fucking room, the guards and

Drusilla just a door away from us. I wanted to scream Rook's name, I wanted to moan and cry out as loudly as I fucking well pleased.

My fingers dug into his skin as my body quaked. My climax crested over me again, and a small cry escaped my lips. I leaned back into him, a thin sheen of sweat forming on my skin as my breath rasped out of me.

"Oh fuck," he groaned, "feeling you come is fucking magical." His fingers continued to tease my nipple between them, and his other hand moved between my thighs. "I want to feel you come again." He began to stroke my clit with his finger, and I shook my head.

"Oh gods, Rook." I gritted my teeth, my hands shaking as they dug into my thighs. "I can't." I bit back a moan, my body so sensitive and wound so tightly that every movement almost hurt. "Please."

"Do you want me to stop?" He growled into my ear. His strokes were slower, but harder, and fucking gods the last thing I wanted for him now was to stop.

"*No.*" I curled an arm around his neck, panting against his cheek. "Don't stop."

"You're going to come for me again, princess, and then I'm going to fill you up." His breathing was rapid, and he groaned as I began to tighten around him. "*Fuck.* Such a good fucking girl. That's it. *Fuck.*" He hissed in a breath, circling my clit furiously with two fingers. "This wet little cunt is mine, isn't it, princess? You're going to come so hard for me now, aren't you?"

I was shivering violently, his words sending desire rippling through me. I was his, every muscle in my body pulled taut just for him, because of him. Our thighs were slick with my arousal, sliding between us as I squirmed and bucked on top of him. I threw my head back against Rook's shoulder, and he seized my chin, pushing two fingers against the seam of my lips. I opened my mouth, taking them in and letting him gag me, stifling my moans.

And then he drove me over that edge, my lips vibrating around his fingers as I came. My climax drew out Rook's own, and he moaned into my hair as he pumped inside me. We both shivered and tried to catch our breath, covered in sweat and each other's scent. Rook wrapped his arms around my waist, tracing his lips over my shoulders as he whispered sweet words to me, *beautiful, perfect, mine*.

Finally, the sweat had cooled on our skin, and I slumped off him, onto the bed.

He curled up beside me, taking me in his arms. I couldn't speak, all I could manage was a moan as I nuzzled against him.

"Yes, I agree," he replied, stroking my hair. "Fucking Nav, princess."

His heartbeat thundered against my cheek. I was so overcome with delirium that I almost said it, but I quickly pressed my mouth against his chest instead.

"You want more already?" He put a hand under my chin, tipping my face up to his.

I shook my head. "I think if I come again I'll melt into the bed."

"Oh but what a way to go, ey?"

I laughed breathlessly. "I had no idea it could be like this."

"It's not like this with just anybody. You bring out the best in me."

"And you in me. Making me come three times."

He huffed out a breath. "Only three? Give me a few minutes and we'll rectify that."

I kissed his chest, breathing in his scent. "Rook, is it… Is it possible that you've made me pregnant?"

He tensed, looking down at me with a frown. "You think me so irresponsible, my love?"

"My father asked if I'm carrying your child."

Rook's brow crinkled for a moment. "I see. And what did you tell him?"

"That he was being preposterous." I lifted my mouth to his, kissing him gently. "But it's possible, isn't it?"

Rook sighed, stroking my cheek. "My innocent little princess. I haven't made you pregnant. Of that I can be certain."

"How do you know?" I asked, my eyebrows raised.

Rook lifted his arm, showing me the slave tattoo on his forearm. "This is how I know." He tucked a hand behind his head and stared at the canopy above the bed. "That mark has magic woven into it. And that magic holds true while Theron is King. I cannot fly, I cannot use my powers, and, amongst other things, I cannot breed."

I bristled at the word breed, and climbed higher onto Rook's chest to look into his eyes. "You can't have children?"

"Not while that mark is there, and the magic is active." He raised his hand to my cheek, stroking it gently. "So, you can rest assured that you will not have to bear my child."

I lay my head on his chest. "I'm so sorry, Rook."

"I am too." He shrugged when I looked back up at him. "For you, to be bonded to someone like me."

"Say that again and I'll slap you," I said, throwing myself on him and kissing him hungrily. "I don't care."

"You don't care that we'll never be able to have a child?"

"No," I said, kissing him again, and again, wishing they would leave behind a lasting mark to remind him how much I loved him.

Rook sighed. "I do love you, Elara."

"The only relief I have is when I'm in your arms," I said.

"It's the same for me, my love," he said as I lay my head back on his chest. "You are the only thing that has made sense in my life, for a very long time."

"Are you ever going to tell me about your… your life in Isambard?" I didn't want to say the word wife. I didn't want the moment to be painful for him, and maybe, just maybe I didn't want to admit that I was jealous. I hated myself for it.

Rook's fingers traced small patterns over my bare shoulder. "I will, princess. One day. Not today though. You have enough on your mind."

"Yes, I certainly do," I said with a heavy sigh.

"How are you feeling about tomorrow?" He asked, his fingers picking up a strand of my hair and twirling it between them.

"Anxious. I don't know what to expect." I looked up at him, at his beautiful blue eyes glowing in the dim light. "Theron said if I married him it would all be over."

Rook made a sound low in his throat, a threatening snarl. "Did he now? And what did you tell him?"

"I told him to announce the next trial and that I wasn't afraid of him."

Rook laughed, seizing me in his arms and rolling me onto my back. "My fierce little Fae, you're fucking extraordinary, you know that?"

His mouth moved along my jawline, down my neck, and I closed my eyes, surrendering to the feeling of his mouth exploring my body, as I had dreamed so many times.

"Please," I murmured, "I need you again."

"I thought you'd never ask." He pushed his cock inside me, finding me still slick from his climax and all my own. But this time, he was gentle and slow, holding me tightly in his arms as he rocked his hips against me.

His mouth was tender, kissing me softly, and I whimpered

as I felt my climax rising. He held me as my body quivered, as I moaned into the crook of his neck. He held me as he shuddered, murmuring my name as he came inside me.

Then we lay together, holding each other for a long time, until our eyes became heavy.

"I need to go before I fall asleep," he whispered, kissing me. "Mokosh knows I'd love to stay here with you."

"One day," I replied, stroking his cheek. "One day we will sleep in the same bed every night and wake up together every morning."

He smiled at me, tracing a finger along the scars on my jaw. "That is a lovely future to dream of, my love."

Chapter 26

Elara

Drusilla had picked out a flowing lilac gown, and it felt strange to be wearing such a fine dress when I was going to the Pit. I sat down at the dressing table and saw with alarm the mark on my neck. Shit. My kisses may not have marked Rook but his had certainly marked me.

My eyes flashed up to meet Drusilla's, and she hesitated for only a moment.

"A bruise, is it, my lamb?" She asked, picking up a small porcelain pot and soft round-headed brush. "I'll have that covered up in no time."

I said nothing, merely smiled and watched her swirl a soft white powder over the love bite. It thankfully was barely visible once she was done, and she went on with my hair, winding it up into a soft style on my head, decorating it with tiny rows of white pearls.

"You're being careful, aren't you, my dear?" She asked me as her nimble fingers worked.

"Careful?" I willed my voice to remain nonchalant.

"Yes, careful." She met my eyes in the mirror. "I've found

the window unlatched many a morning. It's none of my business, and I don't want to stand in the way of anything, but you must be careful."

I nodded. "I am very careful, don't worry."

Drusilla sighed and continued to work on my hair. Once she was finished, she handed me a dangling diamond earring, and placed a delicate silver chain around my neck.

"There now, you look wonderful," she said.

"Thank you Drusilla," I replied, rising from the stool. "I'm not entirely sure why I'm in my finery today, but I suppose the King has a plan for me."

She eyed me nervously, then dropped into a brief curtsey before scurrying back to her room. Everything was setting my nerves on edge, and I told myself her behavior had nothing to do with the trial. But I was sure now, I was certain that Drusilla knew about Rook and I, and as much as the thought filled me with trepidation, I was also relieved that I could rely on her silence.

There was a knock on the door, and then Regan admitted himself to the chamber. He looked me up and down. "Oh, Your Highness," he said, clasping his hands together, "you are a true beauty."

"Thank you, Regan," I replied, "not my usual attire for entering the Pit, but I suppose a special test of endurance calls for a special dress."

"Indeed. Shall we?" He gestured to the door, and I followed him once again along the stone passageways, out into the courtyard, and across the grounds towards the Pit. As usual, we were surrounded by guards, though they seemed to perceive me as less of a threat in my flowing gown, and did not keep quite such a tight distance.

The sky was overcast, and a breeze blew through the bright green leaves overhead, threatening a storm later.

Anxiety prickled at my scalp as I was escorted to the grand main entrance of the Pit, led up into the stands, along with the teeming, cheering crowds. Theron's royal box that I had only ever observed from below was furnished with plush red velvet chairs, its position right at the edge of the stands giving the best view of what went on below.

The Pit looked much as it had the day I'd saved my father, and my stomach twisted into a knot. I couldn't think about it. Not now. Not today. I gazed across the sandy expanse, the only difference being that there were no platforms, no spring-loaded spiked steel doors at the far end. There was only a singular platform in the center of the Pit, with a round hole in the middle of it.

The crowd cheered as Theron appeared, looking regal all in black, his golden wings spread behind him. He leered at me as he approached, his eyes almost hungry as they roved over my body. He waved to his subjects as he made his way to his seat beside me.

Rook was following him, and I balked for a moment. His hair had been cut, close to his scalp. He gave me a warm smile, and merely nodded when he saw my surprise. He had his ax in his hand, and placed it upright between his legs when he sat, leaning on it like a cane.

"Your highness," Theron purred as he took his place beside me. He took my hand and raised it to his lips, and my skin crawled. "You look truly delectable today. A vision indeed." He leaned closer. "You're right, these dresses really do show me all the curves and edges I dream of in the dark of the night."

Rook's grip on his ax shifted audibly, the butt of the haft grinding into the ground. I didn't look at him, but I could feel his anger. I gave Theron a weak smile. "Thank you, Sire. These dresses are truly stunning."

"You are what makes them stunning," he said, raising a finger to my cheek, "and the thought of what lies beneath them is all the more tantalizing."

I felt the wrench of Rook's fury so tangibly it almost took my breath away. I turned away from Theron abruptly and looked down into the Pit. "And what shall we be observing today, Your Majesty?"

"Have you ever heard of the Arachne, dear one?" Theron asked, leaning back in his chair.

"No, Sire."

"They're a fascinating creature, enormous, a cross between a crab and a spider," he said, the excitement in his voice setting my teeth on edge. "They have spines, on their legs, filled with poison, and a mouth capable of crushing a person, instantly, with no problems."

"Sounds terrifying," I replied. I clutched my hands together to stop them shaking. "And we shall be observing this creature?"

"Indeed, observing it hunting some prey."

My head snapped towards him. "Prey? What will be its prey?"

Theron laughed heartily. "Oh, do not worry so, dear one, all is well."

"Sire, please, what will be its prey?" I clutched my hands together, my fingernails biting painfully into the palm of my hand.

Theron reached out to put his hand on my leg, and I willed myself not to recoil, even as his touch made bile rise in my throat. "You will see, dear one," he said, his voice low, barely audible over the din of the crowd, who had now begun to chant impatiently. "You will see."

Theron rose to his feet, and held his hands up for silence,

which was met with cheers and whoops from his subjects. He looked down at me smiling widely.

"Good people of Veles," he called when his attention moved back to the surrounding stands, "we are here today to witness the spectacle of the Arachne, and its prey! Princess Elara will today be our honored guest, and will be allowed to simply observe, rather than fight so bravely as she has up until now."

The crowd clapped and cheered, then began to chant again, urging the tournament to begin. Theron threw his hands up in a gesture of mock defeat, and sank back into the chair beside me.

"Let the games begin, ey?" He asked.

There was a loud rumbling noise, followed by an ear-piercing roar. I jumped as the creature came into view, and the crowd went positively rabid around me. I'd never seen anything like this before.

It had eight legs, though the first set were much smaller and indeed looked like a crab's claws. Its black shell was covered in red-tipped spines, and two beady eyes waved from the top of its head. It raced around the Pit, the footfalls of those scuttling legs echoing like thunder. It tore open its mouth, dripping and red, and roared again.

Theron clapped and laughed. "Oh my, what a creature! Truly magnificent, isn't it?" He turned to me, smiling widely, a maniacal gleam in his eyes. "Are you impressed, dear one?"

Lightning flashed overhead, meeting the Arachne's next terrifying shriek as it stampeded around the arena, seeking its prey. My blood ran cold as I wondered who Theron could possibly throw into the Pit, what leverage he possibly still had now that my parents were safe.

When I did not respond, Theron rose to his feet and clapped his hands together. "Bring out the target!" He called.

I kept my eyes fixed on the podium, waiting for something, someone, to emerge. Thunder rumbled, mingling with the sounds of the Arachne as it continued its death scuttle on the sand below, the sounds of the teeming crowd around me.

A pole began to rise out of the hole in the Podium, slowly, slowly. I felt faint. I wanted to look away, but I couldn't. Fear gripped my throat.

A figure was leaning against the pole, lifting its hands to shield against the sudden light. It staggered, trying to catch itself on the pole. It was dressed in grimy linens, a simple shirt and pants, its feet bare.

Mottled blond hair fell across their face. They moved their hands, and gazed around them, their violet eyes iridescent even from here.

It was Keir.

A scream tore from me as I leapt to my feet. The guards all moved as one to catch me, but I was too fast for them. I heard Rook call for me to stop, *STOP*. But I launched myself over the barricade, tumbling down into the sand with a heavy thud.

I scrambled to my feet and ran across the sand amidst shrieks and chanting from the Velesian crowd..

"Keir!" I cried. "Keir!"

He turned to look at me, confusion crossing his face. He stumbled forward, reaching out a hand. He was alive, he was *ALIVE*, oh Gods how had I been so stupid? Theron had corrupted the Bond somehow, and hidden him from me. Keir was alive, and he was here, reaching out for me.

"Elara?"

I threw my arms around him. "You're alive," I cried, nuzzling into the crook of his neck.

"Elara, you're here," he murmured, putting his arms around me. "You're here, oh Gods, I was so worried."

It was only then that I noted how cold his skin was. It was like ice against my face, no blood flowing beneath its surface. I drew back a little and took in his appearance. His eyes were glowing, but unfocused. His lips were blanched white.

"Elara?" He asked, raising a hand to my face.

The ground beneath us began to quake, and I spun around to see the Arachne racing towards us. I was unarmed. I had no weapon at all. I looked around frantically. There was nothing, nothing I could use.

I turned back to Keir, clutching his face in my hands.

"I'm sorry," I whispered, laying my forehead against his, flinching as his ice cold skin touched mine.

"We finally get to die together, I suppose," he said.

I clutched on to him. Yes, we would finally die together. I closed my eyes, ready to feel the Arachne's dripping mouth tear us apart.

It roared and shrieked, getting closer. I clenched my eyes shut.

There was a screech and a loud thud, followed by an almighty crack. I heard the Arachne's legs thunder on the ground, away from us, and the crowd erupted into a chant I couldn't decipher.

I turned to see what had happened, and there stood Rook, brandishing his battle ax, which was covered in the green blood of the Arachne. The creature was scuttling back and forth, that red mouth torn open as it screeched, lamenting its cracked right claw.

Rook advanced on the creature, arcing his ax towards it. The Arachne opened its other claw as Rook drew closer, roaring, sending black dots of spittle flying through the air. Rook rushed at it, swinging the ax into the underside of its leg.

The Arachne reared up, screeching furiously as it flicked one of its back legs in Rook's direction. I cried out as the spine-covered leg slashed Rook across the stomach, sending him through the air, skidding to a halt in the sand. He clutched a hand to the seeping wound, blood pouring from between his fingers.

He got back to his feet, and roared loudly at the creature, which was now tottering about almost drunkenly, trying to balance on its remaining good legs. It puts its head down, and ran at Rook. Rook met the attack, swinging the ax around and around.

The Arachne's charge ended almost instantly, as Rook's ax landed square in its skull. It dropped to the sandy floor of the Pit in a shower of dust, green blood running in rivulets along the floor. Rook's shoulders were heaving as he looked over at me.

I realized tears were running down my cheeks, and the Bond between us pulled tight. The Bond I did not feel with Keir anymore, but the bleeding Night Demon who had just saved my life.

"I'm sorry." I shook my head. "I'm so sorry."

Rook's eyes moved to my right, and his face darkened. "Elara," he said, "you need to step away."

"Fr-from what?"

He pointed his ax. "Move away, now."

I opened my mouth to speak, and then I heard the gurgling sound next to me. I turned slowly, my blood running cold. I came face to face with Keir, whose eyes were now black, his skin a haphazard pattern of black veins on deathly pale skin. His lips were still blanched white, but the tongue that lolled sickeningly from his mouth was black.

He stumbled towards me, gurgling and gasping. I backed away, my feet catching on my dress.

"Keir?" I asked.

He didn't respond, he merely gurgled and moved closer, ever closer.

"Elara, get behind me," Rook commanded. The crowd had fallen oddly silent as they watched this spectacle unfold. "Elara." His voice became more stern."Get behind me, right now."

I edged towards him, keeping my eyes on the stumbling figure that looked like Keir, but wasn't. Grief washed over me. What had they done to him?

I reached Rook's side, and he pushed me behind him. He looked over his shoulder at me, his expression mournful. "Don't look, princess."

"At what?"

Keir's gurgles had become louder, and now his hands extended out towards me as he gnashed his teeth together. My eyes moved back up to Rook's face.

"At what?" I asked again. "You're going to kill him, aren't you?"

"It's not really him," Rook said quietly. "I'll make it quick. Just, please don't look."

I nodded, then turned my back, crossing my arms over my chest as I began to shiver violently. Keir became louder, and he growled. I heard Rook's heavy footfalls through the sand, and then Keir shrieked. A split second later, there was the sound of Rook's ax falling and the sickening sound of wet flesh splitting open.

The crowd went wild, cheering and chanting Rook's name. I clutched my hand to my mouth, willing myself not to throw up. Keir had been killed, all over again. They'd made him into some monster and I'd been willing to die alongside him. This was what I had been expected to endure.

Rook was at my side, and I looked up at him. "Is it done?" I whispered.

He merely nodded, then winced, clutching a hand to his stomach again.

"Oh Gods, you're hurt." I put my arm around his waist, and began to lead him back to the stands.

"I'm alright," he said. "I am, really." But even as he said it, blood gushed from the wound.

Theron rose to his feet, arms spread wide, wings spread even wider. "Our very own hero has entered the arena!" He announced, and the crowd chanted Rook's name again.

Guards rushed forth, and yanked Rook away from me. "Come on now, Norahi," one of them said, "let's get you seen to."

"He needs a healer immediately," I said, but they were already dragging him away.

I looked up at Theron, who was smiling down at me. I wanted to kill him. I wanted to claw his fucking eyes out. He wanted to make me suffer. He had no one left to torture me with. I didn't even want to guess what he'd do next.

He gestured to me. "Looks like you need a new dress, dear one."

I looked down, and saw the splatters of blood on the lilac fabric, the torn skirt where I had stumbled and caught it with my shoes. My stomach churned.

I was so fucking sick of blood.

Chapter 27

Elara

Regan entered my chamber just as I'd finished getting dressed. The simple blue cotton dress was a welcome relief from the flowing silk gown, especially as the summer storm had made the afternoon oppressively humid.

"Your Highness," Regan said, bowing his head, "how are you feeling after today's events?"

"I think you can probably imagine," I replied.

"Indeed." Regan met my eyes with a sympathetic smile. "The King has asked if there is anything that may be provided to you to make you more comfortable this afternoon."

"I wish to see Norahi, immediately."

Regan seemed taken aback by the request, and cocked an eyebrow. "Madam, I do not understand how -"

"Norahi risked his life to save me this day and I will offer him my gratitude in person, now I would kindly ask you to escort me to his chambers immediately." My voice was even more commanding than I intended.

Regan was caught so off guard that he merely stood aside

and allowed me to pass through the doorway, before he followed me out, then took the lead.

We walked down the stone corridors, then came to a winding staircase. We entered a darker part of the castle with a lower ceiling, the narrow windows wedged just below the ceiling letting in precious little light.

We arrived at an arched wooden door, where two guards stood.

"Is the healer with Norahi presently?" Regan asked.

The guard leaned lazily against the wall and shrugged. "Refused one apparently."

I rolled my eyes. "Of course he has." I took a step towards the door and the guards instantly straightened to bar my way.

"Move this instant." I ordered.

They were both surprised, and their eyes moved to Regan. "Your Grace, what do we-"

"You will move aside immediately," I interjected. "If Norahi has refused a healer he will not refuse me now stand aside and let me pass."

They jerked aside like naughty schoolboys and I pushed through the door into Rook's room. I heard Regan take a step, and I turned to close the door in his face. I didn't care if I was being insolent, no one would challenge me right now.

"Hello love," came the voice from the corner of the room. Rook was sitting in a wooden tub by the window. He smiled as I approached, though his smile was pained.

"Don't Hello Love me. I'm told you refused a healer." I raised my eyebrows. "Now who's a fucking idiot?"

Rook rolled his eyes. "I thought you'd come to coddle me a little, not give me guff."

I reached the side of the tub and gasped when I saw the wound, heavily leeching blood into the bathwater. I shook my head as I met Rook's eyes. "Fucking gods, Rook, you're going to bleed out."

"Don't be ridiculous," Rook said, waving his hand dismissively. "I've had much worse."

"Get out of the tub now," I ordered, holding out a towel. When he didn't move immediately, I glared and shoved the towel at him. "*Now,* Rook!"

"Gods, woman," he muttered, wincing as he got to his feet and wobbled his way over the edge of the bathtub. "No wonder the guards let you in, you're terrifying when you're like this."

"Sit down." I snapped.

Rook wrapped the towel around his hips and sat down on a padded bench at the end of his bed. He leaned back on the bed with one hand, and sucked in a breath as the wound poured more blood.

"You need a healer," I said.

Rook waved me away again. "No, I don't trust them. They'll try and poison me or something."

"Oh for fuck's sake," I grumbled, and looked around the room. On top of an armoire there was a wooden box with glass bottles in it, and I walked over to inspect the contents. It was haphazard, but I found marigold tincture, gauze and linen bandages.

"Regular little witch, aren't you?" Rook joked, wincing as I set about stuffing the wound with the gauze soaked in marigold.

"Isn't that what you said to me when we first met?" My eyes flickered up to his. "I had to be on the battlefield. I can at least stop you from bleeding out, which is important right now."

"It's not just you Fae that heal fast, you know." He

sounded almost indignant. "In fact we Night Demons probably heal even faster than you."

"Not fast enough like this," I scolded him. He sucked loudly on his teeth as I jabbed more gauze into the wound. "And now is not the time to be competitive."

I worked in silence, and he gasped and winced a few times before I finally wrapped the linen bandages around his torso to keep the gauze in place. "There now," I said, kneeling at his feet. "We at least have some hope that you won't die on me today."

"Yes, there's been enough of that today," he said, and his eyes were filled with sadness as they met mine. He lifted a hand to my cheek. "Near deaths too, enough to last me a lifetime."

I clutched his hand to my face, turning to press my lips into his palm. "I'm sorry," I murmured, shaking my head. "I'm so sorry. I don't know what came over me. I don't know why I was so stupid."

"Yes you do. You know exactly why you jumped into that Pit. And so do I." He sighed, gazing out the window at the darkening, stormy afternoon. "I understood it. Which is why I jumped right in after you."

"You understood it?"

He looked back down at me. "Yes." He curled his fingers around mine and lay our joined hands in his lap. He gazed at them, his brow furrowed. "I told you, I had a wife once."

"Yes, you did."

"Celeste," he said softly. "It was an arranged marriage, but it didn't matter. We were good friends, had been since childhood. It didn't bother us to be husband and wife." He ran a finger along my knuckles. "She was a good wife, and she would have been a good queen."

Thunder rumbled softly in the distance, and I shifted my

legs to the side so I could sit properly at Rook's feet.

"After the Peyrusian army left," Rook went on, "it didn't take the Velesians long to invade Isambard. The battle was over in less than two days. We didn't stand a chance. They'd robbed us of our power, there was nothing we could do."

"Your power?" I asked.

"The Umbra Furorem. Dark Fury." He scoffed. "One of the few paths of magic Theron managed to corrupt. Without it, we were defenseless. So the Seraph stormed Isambard, and claimed the city. Within a day, they'd signed the Accord, making us a restricted race. Limiting our movements. And -" He swallowed hard. "And decreeing that no further Night Demons would be born."

I felt a shiver down my spine. "Oh Gods."

"That first night, the Velesian forces made their way through Isambard, slaughtering any Night Demon they found that was with child, any infant that was under a year old." His gaze moved back to the window as lightning flashed. "The screaming, it was terrible. I'll never forget it." He clutched my hand harder. "Celeste was, oh Gods, days off giving birth to our first child. I tried to hide her in the castle. My mother, she tried to smuggle her out, tried to protect her. But..."

I tried not to breathe too loudly even as my heart thundered in my chest. I had suspected that the story of his wife was a terrible one with a sad ending. Tears bit at my eyes as Rook's face contorted with pain.

"They caught them," Rook said. "The Velesians, they discovered my mother and my wife. So they laid my father and I in chains, and forced us to watch as they killed them." He took a shuddering breath. "They were screaming for us. Celeste was begging them to spare her for the - the baby's sake." He winced. "But they killed them both."

"Oh Rook," I said, my voice cracking, "I'm so sorry."

"They chained me to a wagon," he went on. "A wagon which contained Celeste's body. I walked behind that wagon, all the way from Isambard to Veles." He clenched his eyes shut for a moment. "I cannot even begin to tell you the tricks my mind played on me, the number of times I was sure I saw her breathing, that I was sure she was whispering my name, begging me to help her. I heard her voice, I still hear it in my nightmares, telling me that it hurt. That everything hurt." He shook his head. "But of course she was dead. And then we got here, and I was taken to the dungeons, chained to the wall." His eyes met mine. "And my wife was taken to the necromancers."

My stomach dropped. "They did the same thing to her that they did to Keir?"

Rooks' thumb traced circles over my knuckles. "They came to the dungeon door, I could hear a strange sound, I couldn't place what it was. And they held this tiny bundle up to me. I didn't understand at first, but then I saw it. The black curly hair, and a tiny little fist, flailing about as this little bundle cried."

I gasped, and put my head on his lap. *Oh fucking Gods.* Bile rose in my throat and I clutched tighter onto Rook's hand.

"The necromancers had sliced open my wife's belly and reanimated our -" He cleared his throat. "Our son. He was so tiny. So helpless. They put him on the floor outside my cell, and left him there for a week."

I clenched my eyes shut, quashing the tears that wanted to fall.

"For a week, I listened to him screaming, and listened to him dying." Rook's voice had become vacant and hollow. "I fought against those chains. Gods, did I fight them. I broke both my arms, my shoulders, most of my ribs, every bone in my hands, trying to get out of those chains. I called out to him. I tried singing to him. Anything, anything to try and soothe his cries. To do what a father…" He broke off, sucking in a shuddering breath. "And then I heard them kill him, for the final time. Those desperate screams just… stopped."

I looked up at him. "Oh Rook." I didn't know what else to say. Words were useless and pale in the face of suffering such as this. What could I possibly say?

He inhaled deeply. "After that, I was broken. I was nothing. A shell, for years. I was Theron's assassin, a killer. Nothing more." His gaze met mine, and he raised a hand to my cheek. "And then, my enemy's daughter showed up. I thought I'd hate you, I should have hated you. I wanted to. I wanted to make you suffer for all the suffering I had borne. I wanted to despise you as much as I despised your father. But I couldn't. There was air in my lungs again. For the first time in years. Someone looked at me, spoke to me, *me*. Not a Night Demon, not a ghoul, not a killer. Me. I found myself again. In you." He pulled me up to sit beside him on the bench, and put his arm around me.

"What was your son's name?" I asked quietly.

Rook pressed his face against the side of my head, and his shoulders quivered. "Orion," he whispered. "We'd picked out the name Orion, for a boy."

I smiled as I sniffled. "That's such a beautiful name."

"I've never spoken it out loud before." Rook tipped my face up to his. "Thank you. Thank you for asking me. Thank you for - for making him real, for the first time."

I leaned my forehead against his cheek, a tear rolling down my face. "Thank you for saving me today."

"I had no other choice," he replied, brushing his lips against my temple. "You're my heart, princess. Without you, there is no air, no life." He put a hand under my chin, lifting my mouth to meet his, and kissed me deeply.

"We have to be careful," I said, my eyes remaining closed as we parted. I curled my fingers around his. "Regan is just outside."

"Probably gathering the cavalry to get you out of here," Rook said, "they're all terrified of you now."

"Good." I nuzzled into him.

Rook moved to hold me tighter and winced. "Fucking Nav, that Arachne was a right bitch of a thing to get hit by."

"I really wish you'd let a healer see you."

"No, it's alright," he said, smiling at me. "I'll be all healed tomorrow morning, you wait and see."

"Theron said I could have something to comfort me." I held Rook's face in my hands. "I want to ask him if we can go for a ride together, out into the forest."

"You think he'll let that happen?" Rook asked, cocking his eyebrow cynically.

"I'll tell him I'm going mad, locked up in the palace, and need fresh air and exercise." I was almost giddy at the prospect. "He can put a binding spell on us, we won't be able to go far. But we'll be able to be alone."

"That is a rather tantalizing prospect," he said.

There was a sharp knock on the door. "Your highness," came Regan's voice, "I think a suitable amount of time has passed."

"I'm coming!" I looked back at Rook and rolled my eyes.

"I hate this place," he muttered, tracing a hand down my back.

I stroked Rook's cheek and kissed him gently. "We'll be out of here soon, I swear it."

He smiled weakly. "Of course we will, my love."

"Get some rest," I said, backing towards the door as thunder growled loudly overhead.

He nodded. "You too."

I tore open the door to find Regan and four guards waiting anxiously.

"Please get a message to the King," I said as haughtily as I could, "that I wish to go riding tomorrow afternoon."

"Riding?" Regan asked incredulously. "Outside the castle grounds?"

"Yes, I'm going mad in this place, weeks and weeks on end. I need some fresh air and proper exercise." I clasped my hands together, drawing myself up to my full height to make it clear I would take no argument. "I am more than willing to have a binding spell placed on me, to ensure I cannot go too far and that I will be back in the castle grounds by sundown."

Regan looked for a moment as though he wanted to protest, but then his skinny shoulders merely slumped, and he sighed. "Very well, Your Highness."

I gave him a brief nod. "And Norahi will accompany me."

Regan's eyebrows shot up. "Madam, you wish to be alone with Norahi?"

"I wish to be well-protected while I am outside the safety of the castle." I turned to look at the guards with a cocked eyebrow. "And since I could best most of your guards myself, I do not see much point in sending them with me. I need Veles's finest warrior, and that is Norahi."

Regan almost groaned with exasperation. "Your father made it clear that he didn't want you anywhere near Norahi."

"My father would want me safe. Now, see to it that I will be able to have the comfort the King wishes for me to have and that two horses are made ready for us tomorrow afternoon."

I stormed off down the passageway, back to my room. Regan didn't even attempt to follow me, and for the first time in, I didn't even know how long, I was excited. Genuinely, thrillingly excited.

Chapter 28

Rook

To everyone's shock - and certainly to mine, most of all - Theron agreed to let me go out riding with Elara for the afternoon. I couldn't help but question his motives at first, but I couldn't entertain the idea that more sinister intentions were at play. Not when I had hours of time outside of the fucking palace ahead of me, time alone with Elara.

I was escorted down to the courtyard, where my large black stallion had been saddled and readied for me. The stablehands were preparing a smaller palomino for Elara, one of them hauling a side saddle over his shoulder. I shook my head as I gestured to it.

"I suggest you get her a proper saddle or she'll whip you," I said. "She's a soldier and I can tell you right now she won't be wearing a dress."

Sure enough, Elara appeared a moment after Regan appeared in the courtyard, wearing form-fitting brown riding leathers and a linen camisole. The look of disgust on her face when she saw the side saddle made me laugh out loud.

She met my eyes with a look of confusion and amusement. "Do the Velesian ladies really ride like that?"

I shrugged. "Not everyone has thighs as powerful as yours."

She grinned, then concern overtook her face. "Are you healed?" She took a few hurried steps towards me. "The wound, did it close up?"

"Your battlefield witchcraft was splendid," I assured her. "It's healed up perfectly."

"Oh good." She took my hand. "I was so worried."

Regan cleared his throat loudly. "If you two are quite finished." He stepped between us, holding out both his hands. "I will place the binding on you both now."

Elara and I each placed a hand in his, and a low hum emanated from Regan's fingertips. A shimmering golden thread appeared, winding itself around our wrists, before settling into place. It buzzed against my skin, but not unpleasantly.

"You must both be back within the palace grounds before sundown," Regan said as he released us.

"Or what?" I asked with a grin.

Regan's glare was thunderous. "Don't test me, Norahi. The King has made his decision and I don't need to agree with it."

"No you don't," Elara said lightly, turning to her horse as the stablehands finished fitting her saddle. "Now, shall we?" She smiled at me widely.

"We shall."

We mounted our horses, and I laughed as Elara waved airily to Regan as we trotted out of the courtyard.

"You're a true queen, you know that?" I asked as we rode towards the gates.

Elara shrugged. "Just trying to be friendly."

The guards eyed us wearily as we approached, taking their time to open the gates with visible irritation.

"Thank you!" Elara called cheerfully as we passed.

The horses' hooves clattered on the wooden drawbridge as we crossed the moat, a warm summer breeze meeting our faces as it washed over the surrounding soft green fields. Elara took a deep breath, her head tipping back as her eyes closed.

"Where to?" She asked.

"You lead the way," I replied. "I'd like to see what kind of a rider you are."

"Don't you already know that?" Her eyes were sparkling. She poked her tongue out at me before spurring her horse on, taking off into a gallop across the fields. Her form was impressive, and her command of an animal she'd never ridden before was truly remarkable.

I urged my stallion on with a dig of my heels, feeling lighter and lighter with each stride of the creature's legs. I hadn't left the palace for anything but running Theron's murderous errands, to haul off and kill whichever creature that had drawn his ire, in years. This almost felt like freedom. Just for a few hours.

The creeping feeling of being baited by Theron swam at the edge of my consciousness, but I batted it away. Not now. I wasn't going to let doubt ruin these few hours for me.

Elara pulled on her horse's reins, directing it towards the lush green forest that spread out to our left. My horse finally caught up with hers just short of the tree line, and we both slowed our pace as we began to pass through the iridescent green foliage.

Elara inhaled deeply through her nose. "Oh it's a relief to be out here." She looked over at me, her cheeks flushed red and her hair coming loose from the pin holding it out of her face. "I was going mad in that place."

"It will do that to you." I reached across the space between us. "Are you alright?"

She sighed heavily. "Yes. I feel as though I shouldn't be, after… But I am." She gazed up into the sun-dappled canopy. "It wasn't really him. I know that now."

"No, it wasn't."

"I'm sorry." Her eyes were sad as they moved back to mine.

"What are you sorry for, my love?"

She shrugged, clutching my hand harder. "For not listening to you. For being so incredibly fucking stupid. You got hurt because of me." She blinked rapidly. "Please don't think I - I was choosing him over you. It wasn't like that. I panicked."

I brought my horse to a stop, and hers followed suit. I climbed out of the saddle and pulled her down to the ground with me.

"My love, I know." I pushed the stray wisps of her silky hair out of her face. "I told you, I understand. I don't doubt you, or your feelings for me, or the Bond, not for a moment. *Ever*. Alright?"

"I'm sorry you had to kill him." Her lip quivered.

"I'm sorry you had to watch him die again."

She threw her arms around my neck, burying her face against my shoulder. "It wasn't him. It wasn't really him."

"No, it wasn't." I pressed my lips against her temple, holding her tightly.

"I feel like I should be in pieces," she said, pulling back from me. "I feel like I should be destroyed. I'm sad, but I feel like… Like I already mourned him. And I know a part of me always will, but…" She gazed up at me. "I feel guilty."

"Why, princess?"

"Because I'm happy I'm with you."

I smiled at her. "Keir would want you to be happy. He would want you to be safe, and loved."

"I had a dream, one night." Her fingers brushed over my chest. "That I was lying down with him, and he told me to go ahead, and be happy in the sunshine, and that he'd be alright." A smile ghosted over her lips. "And then… then when I looked up again… It was your chest I was lying on."

I clutched her to me, and kissed her forehead. *Gods, I love you*. "Then perhaps Keir knew how much I'd adore you."

She nuzzled into me with a sigh. "Perhaps he did."

"Come on now," I said, stepping away from her to take the horses' reins. "Let's walk and see where this forest takes us."

We walked on in silence, listening to the birds sing from the branches of the towering birch trees. The gentle summer's breeze tugged on the vibrant leaves, and the soft forest floor muffled our steps and the heavy footfalls of the horses.

The trees thinned, and we found ourselves in a sunbathed clearing. A stream bubbled over smooth, shiny rocks, surrounded by mossy banks. Elara gasped happily and smiled up at me.

"Well this is rather pretty, isn't it?" She asked.

I chuckled as I began to tie the horses to a tree. "Yes it is." By the time I turned around, Elara had already set about removing her clothes. "And what are you doing, princess?"

She raised her eyebrows, but the curl of her lips betrayed her feigned innocence. "I wanted to put my feet in the water." She was down to nothing but her camisole, and she stretched her arms over her head, watching me carefully as I saw she was completely naked from the waist down. "It's so hot today." She began to back away towards the water as her eyes met mine. She shrieked as I darted towards her, her hair coming loose as she bolted for the stream.

She was faster than me, splashing through the shallows

well before I reached the water's edge. She turned and grinned at me triumphantly.

"Beat you."

I began to strip off my own clothes, throwing them down on the mossy bank. "Just you wait."

"Are you going to punish me now?" Her tone was full of teasing and challenge. Her eyes took me in as I stood on the bank naked.

"Oh you know it." I stormed into the water, seizing her in my arms. She laughed as I picked her up, her legs locking around my waist. I pulled the pin from her hair, so it tumbled down her back. She was smiling so widely, she looked so carefree in that moment. My throat constricted, and I pulled her close, so her forehead was against mine. "You're so beautiful."

She wrapped her arms around my neck. "So are you," she murmured in my ear. "I've been wet all morning, just thinking about being out here with you today."

I laughed out loud. "Ah, my sweet innocent little Fae, so it wasn't just a ride you were wanting then?"

"Oh no, I did." She nibbled on my earlobe. "I just wanted to ride you somewhere I could comfortably scream your name."

I was instantly hard at her words. Fucking gods, what she did to me. I carried her to the mossy bank kneeling down with her on top of me. She wriggled and squirmed as she kissed me, her hips bucking against me.

"In a hurry?" I asked against her mouth.

Her legs squeezed around my waist. "I want to feel you."

"Oh and you shall, all of me, princess." I lay her down on her back, taking her in, memorizing the curve of her hips and the swell of her breasts, the angles of her collarbones as my lips traced over them. Her legs fell open for me, and she shivered and moaned as my mouth roved over her.. The sun had heated her skin, intensifying the scent of roses and rainwater that she always carried with her.

I kneeled between her thighs, her delicious cunt glistening in the sun, dripping with arousal. Just for me. All of her, just for me. I couldn't decide whether to plunge my tongue or my cock into her first. I fisted myself, teasing her entrance with just my tip, groaning at just how good she felt, slick and hot.

She rolled her hips, trying to guide me inside her, but I held her down, rubbing myself up and down, driving us higher and higher until we were both panting with need and anticipation.

"Rook." Her voice was almost gravelly with desire. "Please."

"I want you to touch yourself," I told her, and her eyes flew open with surprise.

"Wh-what?"

I guided her hand down between her legs. "I want you to touch yourself."

"But why?"

I leaned over her, resting on my forearm. "You touch yourself thinking of me at night, don't you?" I traced my lips along her jawline, and she sighed. "I know you do, I feel it. I feel you make yourself come thinking of me. And I want to see it. I want to see you stroke that wet cunt of yours for me."

She let out a soft moan, and as I rose back to my knees, she began to move her hand, two fingers moving over her clit in slow circles. She looked down at my cock, which my hand was still firmly curled around.

"You too." Her eyes met mine. "I want to see you too."

"What do you want to see?" I asked her.

"I want to see you touch yourself," she said, gasping. "But don't come. I want that."

"Oh you do, do you?"

She nodded, her breathing becoming more rapid. "That feeling when you - *Ah* - when you come inside me. It's…" She broke off in a moan. "It's ecstasy."

I growled as I began to pump myself, watching her stomach quiver as her fingers began to move faster. Watching her fingers glisten in all that sweetness that was pouring from her body. I had to slow my pace, otherwise I'd spill all over her. As much as the thought of watching the hot spurts of my climax lash her body aroused me, I wasn't going to deny her what she wanted.

Her other hand moved over her breast, pinching the rosy nipple between her fingers. She moaned loudly, trying to clench her thighs together, but my own legs blocked her.

"I want you open, princess," I said. "I want you spread out for me. I want to see everything."

Her back arched, her fingers moving faster, stopping for only a moment to dip inside herself, seeking out more slick-ness. She resumed her circles, her knees falling back so she was completely on display for me. I almost lost my resolve and drove into her right then, into that swollen, pink cunt that was on the brink of climax.

"Look at you," I gritted out. "Look how fucking perfect you are. You look so beautiful, coming just for me."

"*Rook.*" She cried out as she came, shaking and panting and arching off the ground. I had to stop stroking my cock, otherwise it would have been over. She held out her arms for me, her eyes closed. "Please, I feel so empty. Please."

I leaned over her, hitching her leg over my hip and sinking into her. She clawed into the mossy earth beneath her, her head thrown back. She was so wet, she took me easily, her body still contracting and shaking against me, around me.

Her hands came up to hold my face, her eyes opening to meet mine. They stayed locked on me, wide and wanting, and *mine*. Like a brand to my chest, that gaze told me everything. The Bond between us sent flames licking up my throat, and with a loud groan the pressure at the base of my spine ignited. I came so hard I couldn't breathe, shredded near in half from relief and desire. As much as she needed me to come inside her, that's how much I needed it too. I collapsed on my forearms, my forehead resting against hers, and she sighed happily.

"You were right," she murmured.

"About what?"

Her mouth claimed mine, catching my lip between her teeth. "The gods did make my pretty little cunt just for you."

I inhaled sharply. "*Fuck*."

"What's the matter?" She wriggled her hips, moving her slickness and heat around on my still-throbbing cock.

I groaned. "Keep doing that and I'll be out here fucking you until well past sundown."

She laughed, wrapping her arms and legs around me, kissing my neck. "That would be fine with me."

I shook my head, rolling off her, my back connecting with the warm mossy ground. Instantly she was under my arm, snuggling against me, and I held her close. The sun was hot and we were both slick with sweat.

"If I closed my eyes now, I could almost imagine we were in Isambard," I said, stroking her soft hair. "On a beach. The water nearby."

"You'd fuck me on a beach in Isambard?"

I laughed. "You are the greediest little creature I've ever met." I swatted her ass, and she giggled. "*No*. I mean, yes I would, I'd fuck you on every beach in Isambard. *But*, what I meant was, right now I could almost imagine we were there, not here."

She sighed, her fingers drawing circles on my chest. "What do you miss most about home? Besides your family of course."

"The food."

She looked up at me and smiled. "The *food*?"

"Mmm, the northern Kingdoms and their fucking potatoes. If I never see another potato in my life I'll be glad for it." I tucked a hand behind my head. "Eating a ripe mango on the beach, splitting open a watermelon still warm from the sun. Bliss."

"I've never eaten anything like that before." She rested her chin on my chest. "Tell me more, about this fantasy of us on a beach."

I closed my eyes, allowing myself to drift away on the fantasy. "Your skin would be browned from the sun, making your eyes even bluer. You'd wear white flowing dresses, like all the Isambardian ladies do, and there'd be flowers in your hair. We'd swim every day in the water."

She sighed. "I'm not much of a swimmer."

"Then I'll teach you, my love. You'll be diving into those depths before you know it."

She remained silent, and I opened my eyes to see her gazing at me thoughtfully. "What would your family say?"

I frowned. "About what?"

"You, and me." She lowered her eyes. "I'm a Fae, how would the Night Demons feel about their prince having me as his Bonded?"

I rolled her swiftly onto her back, kissing her with a deep, searing kiss. A mark on her mouth, on her tongue. "They would love you. Because you are a part of me, and you make me happier than I could have ever conceived of being." I traced my fingers along her jawline, along the scar that had faded to a blushing pink now. "Not all parents are like yours. My father would welcome you with open arms."

She nodded, leaning into the touch of my hand with a small sigh. "I hope so."

"I know so. I have a little sister, Nesryn, and gods she'd be thrilled having you around."

Elara smiled shyly. "I always wanted a little sister."

"Come on," I said, pulling her to her feet. "Let's go and cool off in the water."

We splashed through the shallows, walking down the stream until we came to a deeper pool surrounded by tiny waterfalls that babbled as they spilled over the smooth gray stones. I sat with my back against one, and Elara placed herself in my lap, leaning back against my chest.

"And what about you?" I asked, pushing her hair aside so I could stroke her neck. "What do you miss most about Peyrus?"

She was quiet for a moment, turning her head to lean it against my shoulder. "The forest. On a misty day, the trees would look almost black. I'd go for walks, and it was as though I was the last creature on earth. The mist swallowed all sound, all light. It was like it was just me." She laughed bitterly. "I had no idea then how true that would be."

"What do you mean, my love?"

She sniffled a little, shifting in my lap. "All my kin are dead. My parents are who knows where. I'm unlikely to ever have a child. I am quite possibly the last of my kind. I'm alone now."

I tilted her head up with my fingers, meeting her eyes. "You are never alone. Never. We will watch this world burn together if we must, it can all fall apart around us. But you will never be alone."

She brought her lips to mine. "Thank you."

"I love you, princess. With every part of me. Forever."

She turned around in my arms to wrap herself around

me. I ran my cooled hands up and down her back, and she melted against me.

"Are you ever going to tell me you love me?"

She pulled back suddenly, and she looked hurt. "You know I do."

"But why won't you say it?" I regretted bringing it up instantly. It didn't matter. She was right. I knew it. "I'm sorry, but I just want to understand why."

"Because it's a farewell." Her lip trembled a little, her gaze dropping from mine. "It's nothing but a goodbye. No one has ever told me they loved me except in farewell. Keir said it when he was called to battle, and again as he died. My parents *never* said it. And I don't - I don't want -"

She paddled through the water, away from me, and I heard a sob tear from her. *Fucking fool.* I cursed myself silently.

"Elara, wait." I moved through the water after her, reaching her quickly and pinning her against a towering boulder.

"Let me go, Rook." She dug her chin determinedly into her shoulder, refusing to look at me.

"I'm sorry, my love. It doesn't matter."

"It does matter," she snapped. "It does matter, because otherwise you wouldn't say it. I'm sorry, alright? I'm sorry I'm so broken. I'm sorry I can't-"

I cut her off with a kiss, forcing my tongue against the edge of her lips. She flailed against me, slapping my chest and trying to free her mouth from mine.

"*No*, Rook." She pushed back, still not looking at me. "It matters to you, and I can't give you what you want."

"And what am I supposed to say?" I framed her chin with my hand, forcing her to look at me. Her eyes were full of sadness and fury, a dull fire that roiled away in those soft blue depths. "You sit here, saying you'll never be able to have a child, and why is that? Because you're bonded to a cursed demon."

Her eyes widened. "I never said that."

"You don't have to." Hopelessness crashed through me. I'd not given any thought to it, not until now. Not until she'd said those words. Not until we'd discussed my son the day before. My eyes dropped to her belly, and I clenched my jaw against the draining ache. "I want a child. I want a child with *you* one day. I want to be a father. And I know you want to be a mother. And this curse, this fucking *curse* on my arm, all of *this* -" I gestured around us with an angry hand before meeting her eyes again. "It means we'll never have that. You'll never feel safe enough to tell me you love me, to speak openly and freely. We've had to sneak away just so we can fuck without smothering our faces in pillows, for fuck's sake." I ran my hands through the water, turning away from her and heading back to the banks of the stream.

She followed me, her hands clasping onto my shoulders and forcing me to turn around. "Rook, stop." She seized my face in her hands. "We'll get out of here. One day, somehow, we'll be home. In *our* home. Remember? We'll wake up together, every morning. I'll wake you with the words you want to hear. And you'll put your hands on my belly, feeling our child kick, because he's heard your voice and loves it most of all."

My eyes burned as I looked down at her, at her beautiful, desperate face. I wanted her to promise me. I wanted to hear her say it even though I knew it was impossible, even though I was asking something of her she could never promise to give me. "Do you swear it?"

"I promise you. That is our future. I've seen it. I don't know how, I don't know when. But it will be." She threw her arms around my neck, and I lifted her into my arms. Her legs wrapped around my waist, and she kissed me sweetly, urgently, as though every kiss she laid on my mouth was the last. I held her to me, her skin cool from the water, beads of it dripping from her long hair down my arms. "I'm sorry." She whispered between her shower of kisses. "I'm so sorry."

"Don't be." I murmured. "We'll be home soon."

Her kisses changed as her skin heated against me, her tongue seeking mine hungrily. I carried her down to the ground, kneeling underneath her as she braced her feet against the mossy floor, and with a jerk of her hips she'd taken me inside her.

There was nothing slow or drawn out now. She rocked herself furiously on me, holding on to my shoulders as she rode me. It was a promise, the most intimate way she could show me she loved me, the most exposed and vulnerable she would ever be. It was raw and sharp, dragging through my chest as her heart beat next to mine. Her eyes stayed on me as she panted, as she moaned and drew me out of myself.

"Rook," she whimpered. "Tell me you're mine."

"I'm yours, princess."

Her head fell back, and she sobbed her way through a violent climax, stilling as I released inside her. Her chest jerked as she cried and tried to breathe, and then she collapsed against me, hot tears running down my skin.

She laughed after a while, brushing the backs of her hands across her face. "Keir always used to tell me I never cried, and I feel like all I do with you is cry."

I clutched her to me. "I don't care. I want you to share everything with me. Tears, laughter, anger, hope, joy, all of it. All of you."

"I ruined the afternoon."

I shook my head. "No, my love, you didn't. Not one moment with you could ever be ruined."

She raised her head a little. "The sun's starting to get low."

"Mmm. There's a ball tonight too. We should get back soon."

Her head shot up. "A *ball*?"

"The dragons are coming." I brushed the hair off her forehead, and wiped away the last of her errant tears with my thumb. "Coming out of their lands to beg for favor."

Elara's lips tilted into a crooked grin. "Dragons? Like… like you?"

"More like cousins of mine," I said, grimacing. "True dragons are vile creatures. Slippery. I don't trust them. And Caedmon, the one coming tonight, he's especially odious."

Elara rolled her eyes with a sigh. "I suppose Theron will want to show me off like some oddity."

"No doubt." I kissed her jaw. "But anyone who looks at you in a way I don't like won't see the dawn."

"What's it like to fly?"

I leaned back on my hands, gazing up at the sky. "It's incredible. Being purely weightless, moving with the wind. I miss it. Along with a great many other things."

She took my hand, gazing at it intently. "And the shadows?"

I laughed softly. "I was wondering if you'd ever ask about that."

Her eyes met mine. "What can you do with them?"

"I can turn the day to night." I ran my hand down her chest. "I can create a wall of darkness so thick that it's almost impenetrable, but I can see, as though it was brightest daylight." She sucked in a sharp breath as my thumb grazed over her nipple. "I can press the air from someone's lungs. I can fill their entire body with nothing but night." I squeezed her nipple between my fingers, and her eyes fluttered closed as she sighed. I lifted her wrist to my mouth, raking my teeth along her soft skin. "I could bind these wrists to the bed." I smacked her ass with my other hand, and she let out a sound that lay somewhere between surprise and pleasure, pressing herself against my chest. "I'd have you bound with this perfect ass in the air while you begged me to claim you."

She moaned against my neck as I gripped her hips, rolling her against me. "I thought we needed to get back." She was panting, rocking herself back and forth.

"We do." I nibbled her earlobe, and she shivered. "I told you, you've cast a spell on me. You're in my blood, and you're all I can think of." I wanted to throw her down on the ground and drive myself into her one more time before we had to return.

But the buzzing of the golden bindings on my arm suddenly brought me back to reality. The sun was beginning to sink down towards the horizon. I cast a gaze out over Elara's shoulder, towards the vast forest that stretched out behind us, and wondered just how far we'd get before the bindings would hex us. What would happen if they did.

Elara wrapped her arms around me. "Soon." She murmured. "We'll be home soon, my love."

I pressed my face into the soft crook of her neck, my lips resting against the steady rhythm of her pulse. "Yes. We will be."

I said it too quickly. A promise I didn't know I could keep. A promise I had forced her to make. A future I didn't know how to grasp. But I had to hope, as I held her in my arms and felt the silver coil that held between us heat my blood, that one day I would have everything she had promised me.

Chapter 29

Elara

I was surprised to see Theron when the door to my chamber opened, and even more surprised when I saw that we seemed to have matching outfits. His sapphire blue velvet suit perfectly matched the color of my silk dress, and the heavy gold chain around my waist was almost identical to the one he wore around his neck.

He leaned against the door frame, looking me up and down appreciatively. "I do always love it when you wear blue, dear one." He sounded so adoring.

I gave him a polite smile as I threaded a filigree earring into my earlobe. "Thank you, Sire."

He walked into the room, withdrawing a small box from his pocket. "I have something for you."

"You do?" I said, willing him not to come too close. "How thoughtful."

He opened the small box, and inside it lay a gold ring, set with an enormous yellow diamond. "A Velesian diamond," he said, smiling warmly. "They are incredibly rare and as such, very valuable."

"You wish for me to wear it tonight?" I asked lightly.

Theron cocked an eyebrow. "I wish for you to wear it always, dear one. It is a gift." He retrieved the ring, letting the box drop to the floor, and took my hand. "And perhaps I might make the announcement that it will be more than that?"

I watched as he slid the ring on to my left hand. It was a little big, but not so that it would fall off easily. I felt dread rising in me as my eyes met his. "More than that, Sire?"

"I was rather hoping we could announce our engagement this evening," he said, not letting go of my hand.

I tried to keep my breathing even. "You still believe I will marry you, Sire, even though I have now earned my freedom?"

Theron's eyebrows shot up. "You believe you have earned your freedom now?"

"Certainly," I replied. "My parents are safe, you have again killed my Betrothed and my home is destroyed, what more is there for me to win back?"

He pulled me close to him so suddenly I saw Drusilla jump out of the corner of my eye. She scurried out of the room and into her chamber, leaving me alone with this man who was now looking at me with an almost crazed expression.

"You continue to insist on testing me, don't you?" He said in a low voice.

"I am merely adhering to the parameters of this bargain you set down when you captured me," I replied. "What else is left? I have nothing else to win. Nothing else to gain."

"Then perhaps the parameters of the agreement have shifted." His green eyes narrowed. "Perhaps it is no longer about what you have to win, but what you are willing to lose?"

His words sent panic down my spine. "What do you mean?"

A smile broke across his face. "Come now, dear one, do not worry yourself. The ball awaits." He led me out of my chambers, down the passageway, swinging my hand as he had that night he had shown me the temple.

And I did not feel any safer in his presence tonight than I had that night.

"Have you ever met a dragon before?" He asked me as we walked.

"No Sire, I was of the understanding that they kept to themselves," I replied.

Theron chuckled. "They are a solitary race indeed, though they do come out every now and then to try and get back into my good graces."

"I imagine that is no easy feat," I replied, wishing he would release my hand. I couldn't stand the feeling of his icy skin against mine. Were all the Seraphim this cold, I wondered.

Theron chuckled, and I thought I was going to faint as he pulled me closer, clasping my arm in his. His fingers caressed my hand as it lay on his arm, and he smiled down at me indulgently. "I'm not a monster, Elara, I've told you this before." He stopped walking, and leaned down to me. Before I could even respond, or jerk away, anything, he kissed me, tenderly.

Nausea gripped me. I looked into his eyes, and he leaned in to kiss me again. This time I ducked my head, so my lips were just out of reach. He threw his head back and laughed.

"Come now, dear one," he said, dragging me along the passageway again, "we will be late."

Music met us as we walked into the enormous ballroom. The courtiers were, for once, not dressed in their usual burgundy and black, but rather a kaleidoscope of color.

Everything stopped as Theron and I entered, and Regan stood by the door, clearing his throat. "Our King, Theron, and his royal guest, Princess Elara of Peyrus!" He announced loudly.

Polite applause sounded, and the crowd parted so that Theron and I could cross the room to where the throne stood. A smaller golden chair, upholstered with rich blue velvet, had been placed beside it. Between the ring, the throne, and Theron's arm clasping onto mine, it was very clear what kind of message he was hoping to send to everyone present.

My eyes darted around the room, looking for Rook. I could feel he was close by. Theron's grip on me tightened, and I told myself he couldn't possibly know what I was thinking, but it unnerved me all the same.

Theron led me up the two steps to the throne, and with a grand sweep of his wings he turned around so we were both facing the crowd. He animatedly took my hand from his arm, and raised it to his lips. His eyes flashed up to mine as he did so, and I felt a flare of envy at the base of my neck.

That was Rook.

I took my seat beside Theron, and when I raised my eyes back to the room, they immediately met Rook's. He was approaching the throne, and he looked so handsome I had to suppress a gasp.

He was wearing a long white jacket with a high collar and swirling golden embroidery down the sleeves. White pants encased his legs, and there was a thick golden cuff hooked around his left ear. When he reached the throne and raised his hand to his forehead as he bowed to Theron, I saw the golden rings that adorned his fingers. Everything about him was regal.

"My King," Rook said, straightening from his bow, "it is an honor to attend the ball this evening."

Theron's wings swished as he settled in his throne. "But of course, my friend. I would not dream of keeping you hidden from the many ladies who are so eager to meet you at these events."

Rook's eyes flashed to me as he no doubt felt my own surge of envy at Theron's words. Once again, as though he could sense precisely what thought had passed between Rook and I, Theron spun to me with a grin on his face.

"I did tell you, did I not, dear one, about Rook's prowess?"

My cheeks flushed violently and my eyes dropped to my lap. "Sire, I do not think -"

"Seen any ladies you like the look of yet, Rook?" Theron turned back to Rook with a jovial laugh. "There are so many pretty ones here this evening."

"None that can match Princess Elara's beauty, sadly."

His eyes were on me as I raised my head. Oh Gods, that was too brazen. I swallowed hard and tried to smile.

"That is very kind of you to say." My voice wouldn't waver. It couldn't.

Theron looked back and forth between us, the toxic smile remaining plastered to his face. "You two really do think very highly of each other, don't you?"

"We do." Rook's gaze darkened, and I almost jumped when his eyes changed from the bright glowing blue I was used to, to a deep, burning navy. "The Princess is one of the most extraordinary beings I have ever had the honor of meeting."

Theron raised his eyebrows as he looked back at me. "Well, that is high praise indeed, Elara. Though I would tend to agree with it. You are certainly something very, very special." His green eyes roved over my chest, and sweat prickled at the back of my head. "How was your ride this afternoon?"

I met his gaze with a casual shrug. "It was very pleasant," I replied, "It did me good to get some fresh air."

"Plenty of exercise too, I hope? A ride is so very good for getting the blood pumping."

I didn't have time to acknowledge the creeping feeling of dread as his green eyes bored into me. A trumpet sounded outside the Hall, and all eyes turned to the door. Regan stepped forward and cleared his throat.

"The High Lord Caedmon of Tyval," he announced loudly, then stepped back into a bow. The crowd murmured as they parted, and then a man strode in that made my skin crawl more violently than even Theron.

I couldn't say what it was about him that made him so immediately unpleasant, but the way he gazed around the room, like he owned it, like we were all there to see him especially, was sickening. He had long red hair which was pulled back into a series of messy, matted braids, and his skin was almost unnaturally white. Except for his face - that was so ruddy it looked like he'd simply consumed too much wine.

It wasn't until he drew close to the throne and his eyes settled on me that I saw the most terrifying feature. His eyes were bright yellow, and the pupil was not round, it was a long, black slit. Just as you'd expect a dragon's eyes to look.

"Your Majesty," Caedmon drawled, his gaze staying on me, "you did not tell me you had such a pleasing lady at your side." He bowed deeply to us both.

"Princess Elara is our esteemed royal guest," Theron said as he waved Caedmon out of his bow. "I do believe you knew her father well at one time."

Caedmon's lecherous grin made my skin crawl. "I had the pleasure of being at this delightful creature's Blessing Day." His eyes moved to Theron. "I do believe your parents were there that day too, though you were not in attendance."

Theron's mouth twitched. "They were indeed." He looked over at me. "It was such a special day."

"The lady has certainly grown in a rather pleasing way, has she not?" Caedmon's eyes moved over me.

Rook was still standing nearby, watching the entire scene transpire, his eyes moving from Caedmon to me, and with every word Caedmon spoke, his gaze became more lethal. As though sensing the animosity being directed at him, Caedmon turned and spread his arms wide.

"Norahi, you're still here too then!" He said with a chuckle. "How's slavery treating you?"

Rook's eyes were still that deep navy blue, and he tilted his head with a cynical grin. "I'd say about as well as it's treating you, My Lord. Your lands are still barren are they not?"

Caedmon laughed, baring a mouth of sharp, browned teeth. He gestured to Rook with his taloned fingers. "You'd know all about being barren, wouldn't you, Norahi?" Caedmon turned back to Theron. "Unless of course the King has decided to release you from the Accord?"

Theron rubbed a finger across his lip as he grinned. "Certainly not."

"Ah." Caedmon clasped his hands behind his back as he turned back to Rook. "Still not allowed to fuck then, is that right?"

"You still seem to have a rather vested interest in my cock, Your Grace." Rook raised an eyebrow, looking Caedmon up and down. "Is that a hint of envy I detect?"

Caedmon's laugh rasped out of him. "I know the needs of a male and I know what happens when those needs are not met." He gestured to me. "I'm told you're this delightful creature's training partner. Must be agony, feeling that body in your arms and not being able to do a thing further."

"That's enough!"

Three sets of very surprised eyes turned to me as I sprang

out of my chair. Fury blazed through me as I looked at Caedmon.

"How dare you insult a member of the King's court in this way," I said, becoming aware of more sets of eyes turning my way as the courtiers around us began to listen in. "And to speak this way in front of a lady? My Lord, I do not know what kind of manners are taught to a dragon but they cannot be of any note if this is how you speak."

Theron laughed out loud and clapped his hands together. "Caedmon, I believe you have met your match."

Rook's gaze was one of dismay and admiration, and he shook his head a little as I glanced over at him.

Caedmon let out a rasping, throaty chuckle, but his eyes betrayed him. He was livid. "She is a delight, Your Majesty. A true delight."

"I am nothing of the sort," I replied, my head snapping back to meet Caedmon's disgusting yellow eyes. "You insult this house, this court and me with your words, and you should be ashamed."

Theron burst into applause, joined by a few courtiers. Caedmon's smile wavered a little, and he bowed deeply as I took my seat.

"Forgive me, madam," he said, "and forgive me, Sire. I came to establish our friendship and instead insulted your royal house."

Theron reached over and took my hand, his eyes staying on Caedmon. "I accept your apology, and I'm sure my -" He broke off and looked at me, his eyes widening in theatrical shock. "Oh dear, we didn't want to announce it yet, did we?"

Rook's fury flared so heavily I gasped. Theron completely misunderstood my reaction, and swiftly raised my hand to his lips.

"It's alright, dear one, we will hold off a little longer," he assured me. Music started to play, and Theron held his hand out, gesturing to Rook. "Rook, come, why don't you and the Princess open the dancing for us?"

Rook didn't hesitate for a moment, stepping forward to take my hand from Theron. His grip was tight on mine as he led me onto the dance floor, and the crowd parted to let us pass. I felt the stare of a thousand eyes on me and it was so deeply uncomfortable.

But then Rook put his arms around me, and I gazed up at him as I put my hand on his shoulder, and then he was sweeping me across the dance floor. Everything else seemed to melt away as he gazed down at me with those startling navy eyes.

"You're rather light on your feet," I said to him, trying not to think about the barest touch of his hand against the skin that was visible in the low-cut back of the dress.

He smiled down at me. "How do you think I climb that tower every night?"

I suppressed my smile. "You know Theron is just showing us off," I said, looking around the room at the watching courtiers. "Showing his people his possessions."

"Mmm." Rook's response rumbled low in his chest. "I saw the lovely ring he gifted you, and the announcement he wishes to make?"

I rolled my eyes. "Never mind about that, just more of his games."

"I don't like these games," he replied, his hand holding me tighter, "but I do rather like holding you in my arms like this."

Other couples began to join us, gliding past us as we continued to dance.

"I would have thought you had rather a lot of holding me in your arms this afternoon," I said quietly.

Rook grinned, the dimples on either side of his mouth

showing again. "I think you would know by now, my love, that you are all I desire to have in my arms, for all eternity." He lowered his mouth a little, brushing his lips ever so delicately against my forehead.

"You need to be careful," I replied. "There are a thousand eyes on us." I looked back up at him. "Why are your eyes so dark? What have you done to them?"

Rook's fingers brushed over my back. "I have dimmed them so as not to scare those attending," he replied, "Theron commands it." He cocked his head. "You do not like it?"

"I love your eyes," I replied, "no matter the color."

I felt a growl reverberate through his chest. "I want to kiss you right now."

"Where?" I asked, grinning up at him.

He lowered his mouth to my ear. "Everywhere."

Shivers went down my spine.

A couple bumped into us and I was suddenly pulled back into the room, into the moment of where we were. My gaze swept past Theron as we continued to dance, and my heart sank as I saw his eyes fixed on us.

"I am so tired of being watched," I said, fighting the urge to lay my head against Rook's chest.

Rook pulled me closer to him, and my head fell against his shoulder. "You'll be free soon, princess." His fingers brushed over my back again, slow and soft.

I said nothing. I wanted to believe it, and I could hear that Rook wanted to as well. But at this point, neither of us did. Theron's ring burned like fire on my hand, a reminder that he had a far more insidious plan in mind. *What are you prepared to lose?*

I shivered, and Rook's gaze as it settled on me was one of concern.

"Alright?"

I nodded. "Just enjoying this."

The music ended, and Rook led me from the dance floor. "Wine?" He asked.

"Yes, please." I watched as he walked away, and then an unpleasant sensation prickled up my back. I turned and came face to face with Lord Caedmon. His eyes were positively terrifying this close.

"Your Highness," he said, holding out a taloned hand. "I am so pleased to make your acquaintance personally."

My skin crawled as I placed my hand in his, and I felt dizzy as he kissed it. "Indeed, Your Grace. I have never met a dragon."

"Your father and I were good friends once," Caedmon said as he straightened. His hand remained curled around mine, his clammy skin turning my stomach.

"Yes, you said so."

"He had high hopes of you making a good marriage," Caedmon said, and his eyes strayed to the side of my face. He grimaced a little, and shook his head. "Such a shame."

"What is a shame?" I challenged him, pulling my hand from his.

He raised a hand, gesturing to my scars. "Fae ears are so pretty, and now you look like - well, like this." He sucked on his teeth. "So terrible to see such a pretty face mutilated in such a way. But then if the cunt still works adequately, perhaps you will still be of use to someone."

In a flash, Rook was behind Caedmon, a dagger at the dragon's throat. I cried out, and the courtiers around us fell into shocked silence as they observed the scene.

"Say that again," Rook snarled.

Caedmon's eyes bulged a little, and he raised both hands slowly. "Say what again?"

"I want you to say what you just said to the Princess

again," Rook said, baring his teeth. "I want to see just how many words you can get out before I lay open that useless fucking throat of yours."

"Rook, don't!" I shook my head as Rook's eyes met mine. "Please."

Caedmon's expression shifted from fear to a sickening grin. "Oh, I see now," he said, chortling. His eyes turned to the side, towards Rook. "Taken up with a Fae, have we, Norahi? I heard their cunts taste like sweetest honey, is that true?"

Rook growled and pressed the dagger harder against Caedmon's throat. "You're a fucking disgrace."

"*I* am a disgrace, am I?" Caedmon tilted his head slightly, giving Rook a strained sideways glance. "You killed my son when he was just a boy."

I gasped a little, and Rook's blazing eyes widened. "Your son was as evil as you are," Rook snarled into Caedmon's ear.

"ROOK." Theron strode towards us, his wings stretched out beside him. "What is the meaning of this?"

Rook turned his gaze to Theron, his eyes glowing bright blue. "This reptilian sack of refuse insulted your royal guest, and I will not have it in your court."

Theron crossed his arms over his chest and looked at Caedmon. "What did you say?"

Caedmon laughed, his hands still held up as Rook's grasp remained firm. "The Princess and I were merely having a small joke. And then her lover took issue with it."

I couldn't help the look of dismay on my face as Theron's eyes flashed to mine. His lips curled into a grin for a split second, before he focused back on the scene unfolding before us.

"Rook, please unhand His Grace," Theron said slowly.

Rook's gaze was lethal, but he withdrew the dagger and stepped back from the dragon.

"What did you say?" Theron asked again.

"He said as long as my cunt wasn't mutilated I'd still be of use to someone," I said. A few courtiers gasped, and Rook's eyes flamed again.

Caedmon's mouth fell open into a rasping laugh, and he turned to Theron. "See? A mere jo-"

Theron's hand moved so fast it made me jump. Caedmon's head snapped to the side as Theron's fist connected with his cheek, and he stumbled a few steps before losing his balance and collapsing to his knees.

"How dare you," Theron hissed. The ballroom had fallen almost completely silent by this point, all eyes turned to us. "How dare you speak to a Princess in this manner."

Caedmon rubbed his jaw as he looked up at Theron, attempting a smile. "Sire, I -"

"You came here to seek my good grace," Theron interjected, towering over the dragon who remained on the ground. "You came here to make some pathetic attempt to snivel your way into gaining back more power, calling yourself my ally, and then you make accusations against a man I consider a friend and insult my guest in such a way?"

Caedmon's face dropped, and he scrambled to his feet. He bowed to Theron. "Your Majesty, you are my King, and I am forever your ally, you have no need to ever question my loyalty."

"You come into my house and speak so to a Princess?" Theron scoffed. "You will apologize to Her Highness and then you will remove yourself from the palace immediately, and go back to your lands to think how you may attempt to make amends with me."

If Caedmon wanted to protest he did not show it, instead

dropping into a bow directed at me immediately. "Your Highness, please accept my sincerest apologies, my behavior was deplorable and it will never happen again."

Theron looked at me. "Do you accept this apology?"

"No."

My response brought a gasp from the room, and Rook's face settled into a satisfied smile.

"No?" Theron asked, his eyebrows shooting up in surprise.

"Words are meaningless," I went on. "His Grace is only apologizing because he wishes to please you, My Lord. It has nothing to do with me." I glared at Caedmon. "This is the kind of man who will say whatever he pleases to a woman so long as no one is around to hear it, and I have no interest in accepting an apology from an odious creature like that."

Theron turned his head to Rook, who was still smiling as he shrugged. "She's right," Rook said. "I told Your Majesty the dragons were bad news."

Theron nodded. "You did, my friend. You were right, as always." He fixed his green eyes back on Caedmon. "You will leave my house this instant." With a wave of his hand, two guards rushed forward and escorted a trembling Caedmon from the room. The courtiers didn't know where to look.

Theron moved to my side, putting a hand under my elbow. "Dear one, I am so sorry." He lowered his mouth and kissed my cheek tenderly, eliciting a sigh from the crowd. "Come, let us enjoy the evening." With another wave of his hand, the music started again, and Theron led me on to the dance floor.

I looked over my shoulder, and Rook's gaze was once again one of fury. He dimmed his eyes, back to that dark navy. A lady approached him, and my stomach lurched when I saw her run her hand across his chest. Rook's face contorted a little, and he tried to smile, but his discomfort was so obvious it almost caused me pain.

Theron seemed to notice where my gaze was fixed as he put his arms around me, leading me into the dance as the music swelled around us. He laughed and shook his head. "The ladies certainly love a Night Demon."

"It's nothing but depraved curiosity," I replied. "He clearly doesn't enjoy the attention."

"He seems to enjoy yours, though."

My eyes snapped up to meet his, and a shiver ran down my spine. "What do you mean?"

"You and Rook," he said slowly, "you are close, are you not?"

"We are friends," I replied curtly.

"Friends." He mulled over the word, and I hated it when he did that. "It must have been a shock to hear what Caedmon said about his son."

I shook my head. "I am sure that whatever occurred, Rook had his reasons."

"Sixteen years old," Theron said languidly. "Caedmon's only child no less. They called him the Heir of Pain." He laughed softly. "Such a reputation to have at a young age."

"Then perhaps Rook did do this Realm a favour by killing him."

"Perhaps." Theron's gaze was pensive. "You and Rook, you trust each other, don't you?" The emphasis he placed on the word trust madc my lips prickle.

"We do, Sire."

Theron continued to sweep me around on the dancefloor, his gaze pensive. "Trust is such a delicate thing, is it not? So easily lost."

"Certainly." I hated being this close to him, feeling his body pressed against mine. As we moved I saw Rook dancing with the lady who had touched him, and I could once again sense his discomfort, like a searing pain across my forehead.

"Then I would certainly hope nothing you do would ever cause Rook to lose his trust in you." Theron's voice brought me back, into his arms, dancing across this fucking dance floor with him. "Rook has lost so much already, you see."

I bristled with anger. "He certainly has."

"He told you the tragic story of his wife, did he?" Theron shook his head, and I wanted to kill him. "Poor Rook. He has lost so very much."

I stumbled a little, and Theron clutched me tighter.

"Oh dear one, are you alright?" He asked, his voice tight with concern.

I couldn't speak, feeling the combination of Rook's anxiety and my own rage swelling at the base of my neck. Theron's proximity didn't help, the icy feeling of his hands on my skin making me want to crawl out of my own skin.

Theron quickly escorted me from the dance floor and clicked his fingers, gesturing for a servant to bring a glass of wine. I didn't want to drink it, the smell alone made my stomach turn but I gulped it down anyway. Perhaps the alcohol would stop the spiraling feeling that was now clouding my vision.

"Are you well?" Theron asked, clasping my shoulders in his hands. "You have gone so pale, dear one."

"I'm - I'm fine." I tried to steady my breath, clutching a hand to my stomach. "I need some air."

"Of course," Theron said, clutching my arm under his and guiding me outside onto the balcony.

The night air was warm, and the moon hung above us, illuminating the grounds in iridescent blue light. I pulled my arm from Theron's and leaned heavily on the railing, my shoulders heaving.

"You're rather overcome, aren't you, dear one?" He leaned on the bannister, his brow furrowed as he looked down at me.

"I am like a caged animal," I replied, "the captivity, it's becoming too much."

Theron sighed. "Yes, I imagine someone like you would not do well like this. So strong, so spirited."

"Why will you not let me go?" I asked, meeting his eyes. "What else can you possibly hope to achieve by keeping me prisoner here? Do you enjoy seeing me like this?"

"Certainly not, Elara."

Fuck I hated it when he said my name. I squeezed my eyes shut, sucking in another breath. "Then why?"

Theron's mouth twitched, and he crossed his arms over his chest. His golden wings looked silver in this light, shimmering behind him as they rustled in the night air. "The powers of the Sun throne were never explained to you, were they?"

"The what?" I asked, shaking my head. "The powers of the Sun throne? There are no powers, Sire. It is merely a title."

Theron shook his head, chuckling. "Your father really is the most egregious monster."

"My father?"

"Did you ever wonder why your father was so angry about not having a male heir?" Theron asked, turning to shift his gaze onto the gardens sprawling beneath us. "You were the first female heir to be born in generations, and he lamented your birth to every other ruler in this land, for years."

I tried not to acknowledge the sting of his words. My father had raged at my mother plenty of times when I was growing up, berating her for her failure to provide him with a son.

"Lots of kings want a son," I replied, "that's nothing unusual."

"Certainly not," Theron said, "but in your case the disappointment stretches even further. Because once you marry, your powers will be bestowed upon you, and your betrothed, of course. And your father was very adamant who he did not want this power to be passed on to."

My head was spinning. I opened my mouth to speak, to seek more explanation, but then the night erupted into flame as a dragon flew overhead. Flames licked into the inky sky, roaring above us.

Theron laughed out loud. "And there goes Caedmon," he said, "back to his barren wastelands to lick his wounds after being bested by a Fae Princess."

I had never seen a dragon before, and I watched with grim fascination as the enormous scaled creature disappeared into the night.

Suddenly, Theron had taken me into his arms, and I gasped as he brought his mouth down on mine. I was so shocked for a moment that I did not even fight, merely froze as he kissed me. With a jolt, I pushed my hands against his chest, and his release of me was just as sudden, sending me stumbling backwards.

"You continue to fight me then?" He asked. It was a challenge. His eyes were narrowed as he stepped closer to me, those shimmering silver-black wings spread wide behind him,

"I will never stop fighting you," I replied. "I was promised my freedom in exchange for these fucking trials, and now you seem determined to go back on your word."

"You know, Elara, I thought you would have been smarter than this," he said, his voice dropping low. "I think you underestimate my feelings for you."

I couldn't help but laugh. "Your feelings? You continue to

tell me you're not a monster, and yet you seem determined to prove otherwise. This is your courtship, is it? Nearly killing me at your pleasure?"

He seized my arms, his fingers clawing painfully into my skin. "Listen to me now," he said, his teeth glinting in the moonlight, "this can all end at your word. You can save anyone else from suffering, from dying, if you agree to be mine now. If you continue to refuse, I will not be responsible for what happens next."

"You're never going to let me go, are you?" I spat back at him. "You never intended to. This was always your plan. Well then hear this - nothing you do could ever motivate me to marry you. I would rather crawl across broken glass into the gates of Nav than share your bed."

"Then that can be arranged." He grasped my chin roughly, his face almost right up against mine. "If it is further anguish you seek, then that can be provided. But do not say I did not warn you."

He released me abruptly and stalked back into the ballroom, and I struggled to breathe as his words sank in. I looked up at the sky, and begged someone, anyone, to help me.

But even as I sent my prayers up into the sky that still smoked with the remains of Caedmon's flames, I knew no one was listening.

Chapter 30

Rook

I lay naked on the bed, unmoving as the lady that had paid Theron for my time hurriedly pulled on her clothes. I wanted to tear my skin off. I was covered in her scent and I felt positively filthy. She ran a hand through her hair, arranging it back into place as she cast a lecherous glance over me.

"Well, that was quite an experience. Worth every piece of gold." She purred.

I stared at the ceiling. "Thank you."

My response seemed to throw her off, and she scoffed as she pushed through the door, slamming it behind her. I clenched my eyes shut, shutting out the ornate room that had been made into nothing more than a fucking brothel. The room where I was expected to take ladies of foreign courts and fuck them. Indulge their curiosity about my body, about my abilities.

There were times when I'd managed to enjoy it. After enough alcohol and months of deprivation, touching another had been pleasing. But I'd never kissed any of them. I'd never looked into their faces as they came. I'd fucked them from behind, or let them ride me. Anything to avoid intimacy. Because that's not what this was.

But now it was simply torture.

Not even imagining I'd been with Elara had helped. The lady had tried several times to mount me, and I'd managed to avoid that. I'd fucked her with my hand, and when she continued to mewl and pout I finally used my tongue. She'd tasted acrid and stale, her scent making me nauseous. But she'd come quickly, screaming as she flailed amongst the silk sheets.

The only satisfaction I'd felt was forcing my cock down her privileged throat, seeing the tears leak from the corners of those fucking eyes that looked at me like a piece of meat. I'd flooded her mouth with my release, and she'd desperately wiped it off her chin, clearly disappointed I'd not done that inside her.

Never again. I pressed my fists to my eyes. I didn't want to do this ever again. I didn't want to be whored out ever again. I rolled onto my stomach, retching heavily. I didn't care if I threw up on this bed, on its fine velvets and silks. I hated it.

With shaking hands, I dressed, rushing out into the passageway and past the cruel, judging gazes of the guards. They'd heard everything. They knew what that room was for. Shame burned at the base of my neck, tears biting at my eyes. By the time I was back in my chamber, my lungs were contracting painfully as I tried desperately to breathe.

I picked up a bottle of liquor that I'd smuggled into my room at some point, pulling the cork out with my teeth and spitting it on the floor before I downed so much of the biting alcohol my throat was numb. I wanted to wash away that taste, that fucking awful taste of that female. I tore off my clothes that reeked of her, and threw them into the corner of the room.

The bath I drew myself was so hot that it scalded my skin as I sank into it. I scrubbed at my skin until it was raw, until everything hurt. And still I felt so desperately and awfully unclean.

There was a sharp knock at the door, followed by a muffled bellow of *The King*, and suddenly Theron had swept into my room. He was still dressed in his attire from the ball, save for his crown, and the slight way to his step told me he'd imbibed too much wine.

"Good evening, my friend," he drawled, sidling to the tub. "And, how was our noble guest?"

"Fine." I still felt sick, her taste clinging to the roof of my mouth.

Theron guffawed, sitting on the window sill, his arms crossed over his chest. "*Fine*?"

"Yes, fine." I wanted to cry, or scream, or smash in the side of the tub. My chest was tight and I felt as though my skin was 10 sizes too small. Sweat broke out on my upper lip from the heat of the water. I felt as if I'd go mad if Theron didn't leave instantly.

But he didn't leave, of course. He ran a thumb across his lower lip, watching me carefully. "She was a little confused." He said finally.

"A little old to be pure, isn't she?"

Theron laughed out loud. "Indeed. Old enough to be your mother, I suppose. But in any case, she was a little confused as to why she did not get to know your cock."

"She and her mouth knew my cock very well, Sire." I had to bite back the cynicism that threatened to color my words. "She wanted me to fuck her so I did."

"But not with your cock."

Bile rose in my throat. "Sire, if you please, I'm tired, and-"

"Why didn't you fuck her, Rook?"

I exhaled heavily, rising out of the tub and meeting his eyes. "Why do you care?"

He raised an eyebrow. "I beg your pardon?"

"I asked, why do you care? She paid you handsomely, I made her come so hard she tore shreds into your fine silk sheets. I ask again, *Sire*, why you care so much that I didn't impale her with my cock."

His eyes flamed. "You are tasked to keep the visiting ladies to this court happy, Rook."

"I am tasked with whoring myself out to sate their curiosity."

Theron slammed a hand into the window sill. We both stood still, venomous gazes fixed on each other. If he wanted to kill me, right now, he could. I was naked in a bath and totally at his mercy. There was less than nothing I could do.

Then that cruel grin snaked across his face, his green eyes glittering in the dim light of the lamp overhead. "I have business for you to attend to, in the Lowlands. You leave in the morning."

I gritted my teeth. "What kind of business?"

"*Business*." He took a step towards me. "You would do well not to question me, my friend. You know I have a tremendous amount of respect for you. But do not test the limits of that respect. When I hand you a task, I expect you to honor that task and fulfill it as *I* see fit. A rogue Night Demon who will not do as he's told is no good to me."

"Are you saying I'm replaceable?"

"I'm saying you're expendable," Theron snapped. "The next time you're handed a lady to fuck, you *fuck her* so I don't have to listen to her mewling about her neglected cunt, do you understand me?"

I wanted to snap back at him, to tell him to go and fuck the lady himself. But the retort died on my tongue as the knot in my stomach wrenched. I just wanted him to go away. My head dropped.

"Yes, Sire."

Theron's wings rustled as he pushed himself away from the window. "Good. The carriage will be waiting for you at dawn."

Alone again, I dried myself and dressed. I needed to see Elara. I needed to hold her, to drench myself in her sweetness and erase everything that had occurred that evening. I needed to convince myself that we'd be free soon. That this torment had an end. That this wasn't the life that lay ahead of me forever.

I packed a satchel for the coming days while I waited for it to grow quiet outside. It had to be the early hours of the morning. I didn't have much time before I had to get to the carriage, maybe two hours if I was lucky. But it didn't matter. I had to see her.

I waited and waited. The sounds of the guards didn't die down. The laughter and chatter of guests in the castle gardens carried on and on. I became more and more anxious. My hands wouldn't stop shaking.

Go away I cursed silently at the voices outside. *Go away so I can see her. I need her.*

But by the time the grounds fell silent and the readily-flowing alcohol lulled everyone to sleep, dawn had begun to break on the horizon. There was no time now. I'd be gone for days. I was leaving her here alone. I was overcome with such an overwhelming sense of grief that I hung my head in my hands and wept.

Please, I begged. *Please, if you're real, if you brought us together, please get us out of here. Please. I'll do anything.*

She smiled up at me widely. "He's kicking again. Here." She moved my hand, to the top of her swollen belly. I felt the insistent nudging of tiny feet.

"Oh Gods." I laughed in disbelief. "He's so strong."

"Or she."

"Or she. I don't care."

She sighed as she leaned against me. "I'm so happy." She looked up at me.

Her eye was missing.

I gasped. "Oh gods, Elara."

"What?" She raised a hand to my face. Her little finger was gone, blood dripping from the rough stump left behind. "Rook?"

The patch of skin where her tattoo had been was bleeding through the white linen of her dress.

I ran a hand over her bald head. "Fuck, Elara, what has he done to you?" She was bleeding, everywhere. Blood poured from her belly, as though someone had slashed it from within.

"Rook." She tipped her head, her lips trembling, both sockets now empty of her beautiful blue eyes. "Rook, where are you?"

The jolt of the carriage woke me, and I gasped, trying to catch my breath as the nightmarish image of Elara's bleeding body and hollowed eye sockets swam before me.

I'd been gone three days, barely able to sleep, unable to do anything but worry what was happening to her in that castle.

She was alright of course. I heard her voice in my head, I felt the glow of warmth in my chest as her heart beat steadily beside mine. She missed me, but that was all. She was safe. No harm had come to her.

Yet since I'd left Veles, I'd had nothing but endless nightmares. Elara having all the wounds of the heirs inflicted upon her. Elara giving birth to a child only for Theron to crush its skull under his boot. Returning to Veles to find Elara hanging from her tower, her neck snapped so that her head hung at a sickening angle, her glazed, dead eyes gazing at me.

I was ready to lose my mind. The business I'd been sent away on had been a joke, collecting papers from landholders and nothing more. A servant's errand. It had been an excuse to get me away from her. To punish me for not doing his bidding. For not being his devoted little slave any longer.

He'd broken me once before. He'd tamed my spirit into a cage where it had festered and died, rotting for years into nothingness. But now, with Elara's breath and life inside me, I was renewed. I was no longer his dead-eyed thug, and Theron could see that. Uneasiness crept over my shoulders like a cascade of ice. He couldn't know. He *couldn't.*

I looked out of the window of the carriage to see familiar mountains and forests around us. We were almost back at the palace. I felt the sharp stab of anticipation, desperate to see her. I'd sneak to the tower that night. I would. I had to see her. If I didn't, I'd go mad.

The carriage rolled into the castle grounds, and I didn't wait for it to stop before I threw open the door, stumbling towards the palace entrance. Regan was waiting for me, eyeing me with something between irritation and boredom.

"A successful trip, Norahi?" He asked, holding out a hand to take the papers I shoved at him without meeting his eyes.

"Yes. Now if you'll excuse me -"

"She's not in her room," he told me, and I stopped short. He regarded me with raised eyebrows as I turned back to face him.

"What's that?" I felt ridiculous feigning ignorance, and Regan sighed heavily.

"She's in the temple, as she has been every afternoon since the ball." He narrowed his eyes. "She seems to be praying rather hard for something. Perhaps you should go and ask her what it is."

I gave no credence to the thoughts that plagued me as I stormed to the temple. I had no time to wonder why Regan would tell me where she was, much less why he would tell me what she had been doing while I was gone. I didn't trust anyone here.

I hurried up the temple steps as the sun began to set, the smell of incense meeting me.

My heart swelled as I saw her, kneeling in front of Lada's altar in the corner. Elara sensed my presence at the same moment, rising to her feet and spinning around to look at me, the blue veil covering her hair falling to the floor. Her eyes were both sad and full of joy, and I rushed across the tiles to take her in my arms.

"Oh gods," she breathed against my neck. "I missed you."

I drew back, taking her face in my hands, looking her over, then running my hands over her shoulders, between her breasts, over her belly - all the places that blood had poured from her in my dreams. Her lip trembled as I did, understanding completely my urgency. And then - *oh gods* - I realized she'd had the same dreams.

"Are you alright?" I asked, then shook my head, crushing her against me again, breathing in the sweet scent of her hair.

"Are you?" She gazed up at me. "That lady, at the ball. She… You and she… He makes you do that, doesn't he?" A tear rolled off her lashes.

I swept it away with my thumb and shook my head. "It doesn't matter."

"Yes it does." She pressed her hands to my chest. "Whatever hurts you, hurts me. I felt your anguish, my love."

"I don't want to talk about it." I laced my fingers through her hair, cradling her to my chest. "It's over, and I'm here with you, and that's all that matters. Remember? That's all there is. You, and me."

She sobbed quietly in my arms, and I simply held her, pressing kisses to that soft golden hair.

"Theron threatened me," she murmured after a while, her face red and tear-streaked as she looked up at me. "He said things were going to get worse, so much worse. And that it would be all my fault. Because I refused him again."

"This is *not* your fault. Anything he does, anything at all, that is not your fault. None of this."

She shook her head emphatically. "I can't give in to him. I *won't.*"

"No, you won't, and I won't let you." I brought my mouth down on hers, tasting the saltwater on her trembling lips, knowing how dangerous this was, knowing that at any moment a guard could discover us. But she was so sweet and warm, and I could not resist her. I decided that any punishment I'd bear would be worth it for those few moments of tasting the one being in this Realm that belonged entirely to me.

The kiss made her cry even harder, her fingers curling around the collar of my shirt and dragging me into her. I never wanted to let go. I never wanted to step away. And yet I knew this wasn't over. I knew I'd have to watch her fight again in the Pit, and I'd be powerless to help her.

If Theron meant to make matters worse, he'd find a way to sink to new levels of depravity. The thought made my blood heat with rage. How the fuck was I going to protect her from all of this?

There was a cough, and I drew back quickly. I looked up to see the priestess entering the temple, gazing intently in the other direction.

I clutched Elara's face in my hands, and pressed a kiss to her forehead. "I'll see you tonight."

She inhaled deeply through her nose, shaking her head. "You can't, Theron has placed extra guards around my tower. I hear them all night, talking and laughing. It's too dangerous."

I gritted my teeth. *Fucking Theron*. "It's alright, my love. I'll see you in the training arena."

She nodded, still crying, and pressed my hand to her chest. "Yours. Remember?"

"Always, princess. As I am yours."

I tore myself away from her and left her, still weeping, in the temple, resigning myself to the reverberating anguish of my nightmares as I threw my travel-weary body into my bed.

I'd lied to her, of course. It wasn't just her, and me. There was an entire world around us, determined to keep us apart, to tear her to shreds, and to break me down again.

I'll see her free. If it's the last thing I do in this lifetime. I shall see her be free.

Chapter 31

Elara

I ran across the training arena, directly at Rook, leaping at him as he raised his hands. My legs wrapped around his neck, slinging him to the ground where he landed in a shower of dust. He grappled my thighs, swinging me flat on my back, pinning me to the ground with his body.

"That was impressive," he said, panting. "Where did you learn to do that?"

"Watching you," I replied, my chest heaving. "Told you I was learning all about hand-to-hand combat."

"Well it was one hell of a move," he said. "You're getting really good at this."

"I suppose I need to be. So I don't… Don't fucking d-die." Suddenly I couldn't breathe.

Rook's eyes widened with alarm, and he hauled me into a sitting position. "Elara, come on, deep breaths." He rubbed a hand over my back. "Deep breaths now."

"I-I c-can't-" I choked out a sob, clutching my hands to my head. "I-I'm so afr-afraid. I c-can't do this anymore." I threw my arms around his neck, not caring that the guards were watching this all unfold before them. "H-he never meant to let me g-go." I wailed into Rook's chest as hopelessness tore through me.

Rook drew back, holding my face in his hands. "Look at me. Look at me now."

I opened my eyes slowly, and met his steely gaze.

"You are the strongest creature I've ever met." His voice had dropped low, curved with urgency. "You are unlike *anyone* I've ever met. And you *will* be free. You *will* fight, and you *will* win, and you will show him exactly who he threw into that Pit."

"B-but-"

"You are Elara Osunon. You are the Sun, remember? You were born to be *free*, and no one is going to take that destiny from you."

"I can't do this," I said, my voice faltering. "I can't do this anymore."

Rook's fingers stroked my forehead. "Yes you can. You *can*." He smiled at me as I began to shake my head. "My fierce little Fae, you will set this world on fire if you have to. I know you will."

"Norahi." Regan's voice echoed across the training arena.

I wanted to scream or throw something. We both turned to look at Regan as he walked across the sandy ground.

"Getting cozy again, are we?" Regan asked, though his cynical gaze softened quickly when a sob escaped me. "Oh dear, has something happened?"

Rook put an arm around my shoulders. "Anguish, Regan. It comes with the territory of being a prisoner."

"Ah. I am sorry." Regan clasped his spindly fingers before him. "Well, then I hate to be the bearer of bad news, but the King has requested an audience with you both."

"What the fuck for?" I spat out, sweat running down my back.

"To announce the next trial." Regan replied, his voice dropping a little.

I sobbed into Rook's chest, clutching on to his neck. He got up with me in his arms, carrying me into the shade. "Come on now, love," he said, brushing his lips against my forehead while his back was to Regan. "A drink of water and then we'll face him together."

"I can't." My voice was little more than a squeak as Rook put me down on the ground. "I can't do this anymore. He's going to do something terrible."

Rook filled a cup with water and pressed it into my hand. "You aren't doing this, my love. We are. Together. Now drink, and dry your tears. I will be right by your side."

My hand shook as I raised the cup to my lips, water running down my chin as I drank. Rook reached out and wiped the water away with a smile. I gulped down a shuddering breath, and nodded as I met his eyes.

"Alright. Together."

Regan led us to the throne room, and I was shocked to discover it was almost empty but for a few guards. The empty room felt somehow even more ominous than it did when filled with courtiers. Our footsteps echoed on the stone floor as we approached Theron's throne, where he sat, arms casually draped beside him.

"How was training today?" He asked once Rook and I were standing before him.

"I'm hardly training her." Rook gave me a brief sideways glance. "She's a fierce warrior."

"Yes, anyone who has watched her in the Pit would know that is the case," Theron said admiringly. But his eyes betrayed something else as he looked at me - he was angry. He appeared almost unhinged. His gaze moved back to Rook. "Do you trust the Princess, Rook?"

Rook shifted on his feet, clearly surprised by the question. "I beg your pardon, Sire?"

"It's a simple enough question, Rook." Theron sounded almost irritated. "I asked if you trust the Princess."

"I do," Rook replied. "Of course I do."

"With your life?" Theron asked.

Rook nodded. "Certainly."

Theron raised his eyebrows. "And the lives of others?"

"Yes." Rook's voice boomed off the stone walls around us.

"Even though that poor child died at her hands?" Theron's lips pulled into a sneer. "You would trust her with another's life even in the light of that failure?"

Rook's hands flexed behind his back as he rolled his shoulders. "When faced with the impossible, it is not a failure not to deliver, Sire."

My chest was so taut with panic I didn't know where to look. My legs felt like jelly underneath me as I tried to suppress the image of that small child dying under that iron door.

Theron's laugh echoed around us. "I admire you, Rook," he said, rising to his feet. "Your faith in Elara is truly remarkable." His eyes moved to me. "It must be so heartening, dear one, to have the faith and trust of your training partner."

"It is." I choked the words out, trying to ignore the roaring in my ears.

"Even one who you were sure was determined to kill you not so long ago. How quickly things can change."

I tried to swallow but it was as though my throat was swollen shut. "Indeed."

"It would be such a shame to lose that trust, would it not?" Theron asked, a sickening grin spreading across his face. "I ask you again, Rook, would you trust Elara with the lives of others?"

"Yes, without hesitation."

Theron nodded. "Good, then we shall test that theory. Bring her in!" He called to the guards at the far end of the throne room who hurried out of the oak doors.

Rook and I turned to look at each other, and I felt sure I was about to faint.

"It's alright," he whispered.

The guards came back in, and I heard Rook's sharp intake of breath.

"Oh Gods," he murmured.

I watched as the guards hauled in a girl, surely not older than 16, with long curly black hair. Her skin was deep brown and smooth, just like… just like….

"Nesryn," Rook gasped.

The girl's eyes widened as they settled on Rook, and she began to sob. "Rook!" She struggled against the hands of the guards. "Rook!"

"Sire, please," Rook said, turning to Theron and taking two steps towards him. "She is just a girl. She has nothing to do with this."

"I thought you trusted Elara?" Theron shrugged. "What difference is it if it's your sister in the Pit? If the princess is indeed such a force to be reckoned with, then your sister will be just fine. " He waved his hands, and the guards let Nesryn go.

Rook rushed to her side, taking her in his arms. "Oh Gods, Nesryn, are you alright?"

She collapsed against him, sobbing. "I was so frightened. They took me from the palace and Papa tried to stop them but -" Her voice broke off as she began to cry harder.

"It's alright, little one," Rook said, cradling her to him. "I'm here, it's alright."

Sheer panic gripped me. I looked at Theron's leering smile and shook my head.

"Please do not do this," I said, barely able to get the words out.

"Let me fight with her." Rook's voice boomed against the walls as Nesryn continued to wail in his arms. "Please, Sire, you say I am your friend, let me fight alongside the Princess."

Theron considered this for a moment as he regarded Rook from narrowed eyes. "Why?" He asked with a shrug.

"Because Nesryn is not her responsibility, she is mine," Rook said. "There is nothing Elara can gain from winning this trial."

"Elara?" Theron raised his eyebrows. "It's Elara now, is it? How very interesting. In any case, the princess shall enter the pit alone, and shall fight to save your sister and prove herself worthy of your trust."

Rook's eyes flashed to me. "She does not need to prove anything. She has my trust, and my faith. Unreservedly."

"Well that is sweet." Theron smiled widely at me.

"Do not do this!" Rook's voice was filled with pain. "I beg of you, she is a child."

"I am your King!" Theron's cat eyes flashed with rage. "You are in no position to ask anything of me, and certainly in no position to question me. Your sister will go into the Pit and the wielder of Arankos will go in and show us once again just what a fine warrior she is."

"Your Majesty, *please*." Rook appeared on the verge of tears.

Theron stormed towards me, seizing me by my hair as I cried out. He kicked my knees out from under me, standing behind me as I crashed to the floor. I heard the scrape of metal and suddenly there was a blade to my throat.

Rook's eyes widened, and Nesryn covered her face with her hands as she shrieked.

"NO!" Rook cried.

"I ask you one last time," Theron snarled, "do you trust her?"

"I do! I do!" Rook held out a hand. "Please -"

"If you do not trust her I may as well kill her right now." Theron pressed the blade harder against my neck, biting into my skin.

"Please don't!" Rook released Nesryn and took a step towards us, his hands up in surrender. "Please, Sire, I trust her. I swear it."

"Do you believe she can save your sister?"

"Yes!" Rook's gaze was pleading, and I gasped as Theron pulled my head back harder. "Please, Sire, don't hurt her. I trust her, I do."

My head was tilted back so far I could see Theron's face. He stared down at me, his eyes wide and wild.

"If you're going to kill me," I rasped, "you should just get it over with."

Rook cried out, and I heard him fall to his knees. "*No!*"

Theron's gaze was positively triumphant as it settled back on Rook. "It is truly heartwarming to see just how much you mean to each other." He shoved me away from him, and I barely caught myself before my head connected with the floor. "You will go into the Pit tomorrow and you will attempt to save the last remaining Princess of Isambard." He snapped his fingers, and the guards dragged a screaming Nesryn from the room.

"It's alright, little one!" Rook called after her, his shoulders heaving. "Don't be afraid. It's alright!" He turned back to look at Theron, and his eyes dimmed from blue to positively black. His hands were clawed at his sides.

Theron regarded him with amusement. "And what do you want to do now, Rook?"

Rook stalked across the chamber, and for a moment I panicked, thinking he was about to hit Theron, or worse. Instead he stopped short, his face like thunder, and dropped to his knees beside me. He tilted my head back, inspecting the graze the dagger had left behind on my throat,

"I'm alright," I assured him, "it's just a scratch."

"You're bleeding," he said, clasping my face in his hands.

"The Princess needs to prepare for tomorrow," Theron said, snapping his fingers again, and I was determined to crack those fucking fingers clean off his hand one day. "Take her back to her room and have her seen to."

"No need," Rook growled, scooping me up in his arms and staring Theron down as he rose to his feet. "I will tend to her."

The tension in the room crackled, and for a moment I thought Theron would protest. Instead, his face broke into a smile, and he gestured towards the door.

"Whatever you say, my friend." With a swish of his wings, he turned and strode out of the throne room.

Rook gazed down at me with a furrowed brow, and pressed a kiss to my temple. "Come now, let's get you out of here."

"I'm fine," I whispered, even as I slumped against his chest and began to shiver. The weight of what had occurred bore down on me with such force my head began to ache.

Rook ferried me through the palace, down the passageways and up into my room in the tower.

"Here, let me down," I said, before he could kick the door

in again the way he had the day I had almost fainted in the training yard.

He placed me on my feet hesitantly, his eyes still that violent black. I pushed open the door of the chamber, stumbling in as my legs failed me, and his hand was instantly at my back, guiding me inside.

"Sit down," he commanded, pointing to the armchair in front of the fire.

"Rook, I-"

"*SIT DOWN.*" His voice had an edge of almost-hysteria to it as his eyes met mine, slowly fading from black back to blue.

I sat down in the chair and watched as he retrieved gauze and ointment from the dressing table, crossing the room to fall to his knees in front of me. He took a deep shuddering breath as his eyes settled on me.

"I'm fine," I said again, reaching out to stroke his cheek.

He clenched his eyes shut. "I want to kill him," he said quietly. "I want to kill him and I fucking can't." His eyes flew open, and he cleared his throat. He dabbed some ointment onto the gauze, and leaned over to swipe it gently against the graze on my neck. His eyes flashed up to mine as I winced. "Alright?"

I nodded. "Yes, it just stings." I sighed as Rook continued to clean the wound. "He knows, Rook."

"No he doesn't," Rook said quickly. "He doesn't. He thinks something may happen, and he's jealous, and he wants you for himself. That's why Nesryn is here. He's trying to drive a wedge between us, and that's all."

"He knows." I closed my eyes, leaning my head back against the velvet upholstery of the armchair.

"He can't know." Rook's hands dropped from my neck and were suddenly clutching mine. When I looked down, his head had fallen to his chest, his shoulders shuddering as he tried to breathe. "He *can't* know."

"I'm so sorry he's dragged Nesryn into this," I said softly, running my hands over his head.

He lay his head in my lap, clasping on to my legs. "She's a child. She's just a child. She's my little sister. I haven't seen her in years, and now he's doing this."

"I'm going to save her," I said. "I will. I swear to you."

"I know." He didn't look up at me, just stayed slumped over my legs, letting me stroke his hair.

"Rook." I took his face in my hands, and his mournful gaze made my heart ache. "I swear to you, I will. I'll save her."

"And who will save you?" He asked, before pulling me down off the armchair and into his arms. "I have to sit and watch you fight, I have to sit there, unable to save you, unable to do fucking *anything*. Because of this fucking mark on my fucking arm."

"It stops you hurting him, doesn't it?"

He sighed heavily. "Yes. Anything I do to him, I do to myself." He tipped my head back, looking into my eyes. "And if you die in that arena, I will run him through, even if it means my own death."

"Don't say such things." I clutched onto him.

"I told you already, without you, there is no breath, no life for me." He smiled sadly, and put a hand to his chest. "Here, right here, it's where I feel you. It's where you've tethered me to your soul. And without you, that space would consume me until I was nothing but an empty void again, my love."

I shook my head, nuzzling into him. "If anything happens to me, you live. You live for both of us."

"Elara -"

"Promise me!"

He flinched, looking down at me.

"You told me I was stupid for wanting to die with Keir," I said, cupping his cheek in my hand. "You told me he should have wanted me safe. And you were right. And I want you to promise me you will live, no matter what happens to me. You will LIVE. For me, for both of us."

He kissed me deeply then, holding me in his arms, cradling me against him, not caring if Drusilla or the guards happened upon us. It felt too much like a farewell kiss, and I pushed away the flicker of fear I felt.

Theron was not going to make this trial easy.

I had the overwhelming feeling that I was about to die.

Chapter 32

Elara

Theron gave away nothing about the trial. Once Rook left my chamber, I did not see him again, and he did not appear as I was escorted to the Pit. I could sense his fear and his anxiety, and also the handle he was trying to keep on it. To stop me from being afraid, no doubt.

The sky was dark gray, and lightning flashed in the distance over the towering mountain range. I heard thunder rumbling as we approached the armory. I rolled my shoulders, straightening my back, holding my head high. I wasn't going to give one single Velesian the pleasure of seeing just how terrified I was.

Regan's face didn't help. His brows were pulled so far down that I could barely see his eyes. He opened his mouth to speak as he escorted me to the entrance of the tunnel, but instead just shook his head and put a hand on my shoulder.

It was bad. It was really, really bad.

I clutched the hilt of Arankos in my hand, taking a deep breath. The ground quaked heavily beneath my feet. I clenched my eyes shut, trying to keep my breathing steady.

This was like any other battle, just like Rook said. I didn't have to think about it. I simply had to defeat whatever was in there, and it would be over.

I advanced down the tunnel towards the entrance of the Pit, and the ground shook again. Arankos slipped in my grip, my palms beginning to sweat.

I'm here. It was Rook's voice, floating through my mind. *I'm here. You can do this. I know you're afraid. But you can do this.*

I puffed out a breath. *Will you kiss me if I win?*

For all eternity. Now show Theron what you're made of.

I clung on to his words, hard and with every fiber of my being, and tried to focus. Nesryn was in there. She was a child, and she was terrified. She needed me. She was relying on me. I had to save her.

The metal door scraped and shuddered as it rose from the ground. The quaking of the ground underfoot continued as I walked out into the Pit. It was a thick, lush forest today, much like the ones back in Peyrus. Towering pine trees surrounded me, and the floor was soft and mossy.

I stepped out slowly, taking in my surroundings. Trees. I hated trees. Too much cover. And they were so tall. I didn't like this at all.

It was then that I realized the crowd was silent. I turned in a slow circle, looking around at the stands. They were full of Velesians, all eyes fixed on me. But silent. Barely a murmur.

I looked up into the royal box, and Theron was on his feet, dressed all in black, a black crown on his slicked-back hair. Rook sat beside him, bound in place by thick chains around his arms and torso.

"Your Highness!" Theron exclaimed, raising his hands. Still not a whisper from the crowd. My scalp prickled. "You have come here today to save the Princess of Isambard, is that so?"

"I have, Sire," I replied, feeling the first drops of rain land on my forehead. "I will lay waste to whatever obstacle you have put in my way."

Theron laughed loudly. "Yes, I am sure you will. But today the trial is slightly different. The Princess is not secured somewhere, you must find her first." He leaned on the railing, his wings spread behind him. "Before whatever else is in here finds her of course. I would suggest you be somewhat quiet. It has excellent hearing."

Rook's face was set with worry as he looked at me, but he attempted a small smile and gave me a nod. *You can do this.*

The ground shook gently beneath me as I turned to look at the forest around me. Find Nesryn first. Where would I have hidden had it been me?

I advanced slowly, trying to orient myself. Unlike when the Pit had been turned into the jungle, the trees did not part, they stayed upright like sentries as I walked under them. The eerie silence of the crowd made me feel ill.

Every breath I took seemed too loud as the Pit became darker and darker around me. I held Arankos ready, placing my feet carefully, ready for the Pit to give way under me or for-

A rush of teeth and claws pounced over me, coming out of the complete silence to my right. I was thrown to the ground with a hard thud. I spun onto my back, watching as the wolf doubled back on itself to charge at me again. I raised my sword just as it leapt at me, skewering it between the ribs.

There was a sharp yelp, and the wolf slumped over me. I shoved it away from me, pulling my sword from its body, and backed away from it. I had to be more careful. If these wolves had excellent hearing and could move so fast and silently, I needed my wits about me.

Gods, where was Nesryn? Where was she hiding that she

was staying out of reach of these wolves? I hoped she'd received the same training Rook had been privy to. She'd need it in here.

I edged forward as rain began to fall harder. I blinked it off my lashes, wiping my brow with the back of my hand.

There was a thundering of paws behind me, and I turned in time to see the wolf crouch down as it prepared to leap. With a roar, it launched itself at me, and I swung my blade into its snout. It yelped and gnashed its teeth as blood dripped from its injured mouth.

A growl came from its chest as it ran at me again, and when I swung this time I missed. The wolf's teeth latched on to my arm, and I cried out, hammering down on its nose with my closed fist. It pulled back its lips and bit down harder.

I gritted my teeth as I stretched to reach my sword, which had fallen from my hand, my fingertips barely brushing against the hilt. The wolf bit down harder, and I heard a bone snap.

A gurgled scream escaped me, and I heard another set of paws coming towards me. The wolf loosened its grip for a split second as it drew back to bite down again, and I seized the moment to pull away just far enough to grip my weapon. I plunged it into the back of the wolf's skull, and its black eyes rolled back in its head almost instantly.

I rolled over to watch the other wolf advancing in a run, its belly low to the ground. Its yellow eyes shone, teeth bared as it snarled at me. I struggled to my feet, and gripped my weapon, groaning as my left arm protested. The bone was definitely broken, and blood ran from my armor, thick and bright red.

Balance your weapon. I remembered what Rook had said to me that day. I knew my sword. I adjusted my grip on the hilt with my right hand, bringing my hand as close to the blade as I comfortably could.

The wolf continued its slow advance, ears pinned back as it scented my blood.

"Come on, then," I said, clutching my broken arm to my side. "Come and get me."

The wolf snarled, spittle dripping from its lips.

"Come on!" I raised my sword, slowly at first, feeling its weight settle in my hand.

The wolf howled, then with a growl shot through the trees directly at me. I heaved my sword towards it, and felt a sudden stop as the blade landed in the animal's gut.

It panted sickeningly, and slumped to the ground, its limbs twitching as it died. I backed away, into a tree and tried to catch my breath. I had no time to celebrate the fact I'd managed to wield Arankos one-handed. There'd be time for that later.

It was hard to see the sky as the canopy closed in, but I pushed myself off the tree and moved forwards. I had to find her, she had to be here somewhere. I spied a tree with a swollen trunk. That looked like a good hiding place. My eyes scanned left and right as I advanced on it, straining to hear any sign of any more wolves.

"Nesryn?" I whispered as I reached the tree. "Nesryn, are you here?"

Fingertips emerged around the edge of the trunk's opening, and a terrified face appeared. Oh thank the Gods, she was alright. Nesryn clambered out when she saw me, and huddled close to me.

"There are wolves," she said quietly.

"I know, sweetheart," I replied. "Stay close to me, we'll get you out of here."

I turned, and Nesryn put a hand on my shoulder, staying

close to my back as we began to move out of the darkness of the forest. She flinched as we heard another wolf howling, not too far away.

"It's alright," I said, glancing over my shoulder at her.

A wolf was advancing right behind us.

With my broken arm, I grabbed Nesryn and pushed her out of the way at the same time that the wolf leapt at us. I swung Arankos, missing the wolf completely. Pain sent white stars floating through my vision, and the weight of my sword falling jerked me forward.

Nesryn screamed as the wolf turned tail and began to lunge at her. I stumbled after it, hoisting the sword into an arc, swinging it down into the wolf's back. It threw its head back as it yelped, and Nesryn clawed away from it along the mossy forest floor.

The wolf snapped wildly, trying to catch the sword that was stuck in its back. I tried to pull the blade free, but I kept losing my grip as the wolf writhed under me.

Instead, I pushed down with my full weight, pain tearing through my broken arm. The wolf spluttered and howled, and I heaved with my whole body, twisting the blade until I heard the loud snap of the animal's spine.

The wolf fell sideways as a long breath left its body, taking me with it. We crashed to the ground, and I gasped. My vision was going gray as I tried to pull myself out from underneath the wolf's deadweight. Nesryn crawled towards me, shaking violently.

"My sword," I said, gesturing to the blade still wedged in the wolf's back. "Help me get my sword out."

She nodded, and we both gripped the hilt, pulling it out of the bleeding carcass. I leaned on her arm as I pulled my leg out from underneath the dead creature, struggling to my feet.

"You're Elara, aren't you?"

I smiled weakly. "Yes, sweetheart, I am."

"My brother, he cares for you deeply, doesn't he?" She asked, her eyes lighting up just a little. "I could see it yesterday."

"Yes, he does," I replied. "Now come, we have to get you out of here."

She looked down at my arm. "You're hurt."

"Let's get you out of here, and then we'll worry about me." I tried to give her a reassuring smile but blood was pouring out of my arm and I was starting to feel light-headed.

We moved through the forest, back in the direction of the stands, at least I hoped so. It was so dark amongst the trees now. Nesryn shivered as her hand stayed on my shoulder, and thunder began to rumble loudly overhead.

The shaking underfoot returned.

"What's that?" Nesryn asked.

"It's probably just the Pit," I replied, "it moves and Theron changes it with magic. Don't worry, we'll have you out of here in just a moment."

The quaking became louder as the edge of the treeline came into view. I dragged Arankos along the ground, holding my broken, bleeding arm close to my body. I tried to stay alert for wolves, but it was becoming harder and harder to focus.

Even though the sky had darkened above us, the light when we emerged from the dark of the forest caught me off guard, and I blinked rapidly as I looked up at Theron in the royal box.

He rose to his feet, and smiled down at me. "Ah, you have retrieved the Princess. Well done."

Rook's face was twisted with alarm as his eyes settled on me. Nesryn began to cry quietly beside me.

"I have," I called back, "now let us out -"

"You have not yet completed the trial," Theron interjected, and the rhythmic quaking began again.

"What do you mean?" I asked, my voice failing me on the last word.

Rook's head turned, and his entire face exploded with shock. His eyes snapped back to meet mine.

"*RUN*!" He called.

I turned towards the cause of his alarm, in the direction of that terrible, rhythmic thudding, and my heart stopped.

A giant was pelting towards us. It was at least 20 feet tall, its enormous feet thudding into the ground as it came ever closer. Its face was pinched and strange, its enormous black eyes appearing almost unseeing. Its nose twitched as it seemed to scent us, and its lips lolled open in a bone-chilling groan as it began to pick up pace.

Nesryn screamed, and I spun around, shoving her away from me.

"Run!" I told her, pointing to the far end of the Pit. "Run and stay hidden!"

She took off, running backwards at first, her wide eyes on the giant behind me, before she burst into a sprint, disappearing into the dense forest.

I could hear Rook screaming at me, over the Bond, from the stands above me, telling me to go, telling me to *run*. But I turned to face the giant, tightening my grip around my sword. I gritted my teeth as I adjusted my grip, repeating the words over and over - *balance the blade. Balance the blade. Know your weapon. Balance the blade.*

Arankos hummed in my hand, just as it had the day I'd thought I was going to die on the battlefield in Grixos. Perhaps today its prediction would be more accurate.

The giant was close, so close now, the ground shaking so hard it was hard to keep my footing.

I clutched my broken arm close to my body, heaving Arankos up with a cry as pain shot through the left side of my body. When the giant was within striking distance, I leapt towards him.

The giant's eyes followed the arc of my movements through the air towards him, surprised and amused at the same time. He lifted one of his enormous hands, as though to try and swat me out of the air, but instead my blade sliced through his thumb.

The giant wailed, the sound almost splitting my ear drums, as I landed hard on the ground behind him. The sound of the thumb falling was like the thud of a felled tree.

The giant was stumbling, clutching his bleeding hand, dark red rivulets flowing onto the mossy floor around us. I seized the chance and charged at him, slicing through the tendon in the back of his left leg.

Another bellow from the giant, and he started forward, in the direction Nesryn had run. I heard Nesryn scream, at the same time the giant did, his enormous round head turning in that direction.

He began to amble towards Nesryn's distressed cries, and I pushed myself forward, using Arankos like a crutch. My arm was still bleeding profusely, and I felt so dizzy I could barely see.

But I had to save her.

"Hey!" I called. "Hey you! You come back here!"

The giant didn't even pause.

"Hey!" I dropped my sword to pick up a rock my foot had nudged against, and hurled it at the back of his head. "Hey, you come back here and face me!"

The giant continued to amble forwards, towards where Nesryn had screamed.

"Hey!" I scooped down to pick up my sword, almost unable to straighten back up as my vision went gray.

Elara, it's going to kill you. Rook's voice was full of anguish as it sounded in my mind. But I couldn't stop. I couldn't hide. There was no choice.

"Hey, you moronic, overgrown fuck!" I summoned the last of my strength, hauling my sword along with me as I broke into a run. My body screamed at me to stop, pain shooting through me so sharp it took my breath away.

But as I launched myself at the giant, it finally turned towards me. With a scream, I wrapped both my hands around the hilt of my sword, pointing the tip of the blade straight down.

The giant didn't have time to react, taking a small stumbling step backwards, but not far enough to escape my reach. I landed on its swollen chest, and sank my sword right into the base of its throat.

There was a loud popping sound, followed by bubbling, bright red blood, and the giant stumbled sideways. I held fast as the crowd erupted into cheers, and felt Rook's relief flood my body.

I'd killed it. It was going to die.

It crashed to its knees, and I bit through the pain radiating through my arm to keep a hold of the sword. I looked over my shoulder at Theron, who was leaning on the bannister of the royal box. His expression was one of pure shock, his wings dropped low at his back. He hadn't scared me.

"I won." I knew he couldn't hear me. It didn't matter. I couldn't help but laugh through my pain. "I *won*."

I wasn't sure for a moment what had happened. There was a rush of wind and suddenly all feeling left my body. My vision went white, and I was falling to the ground.

The giant had crushed me between its hands. I looked up

at its black eyes as everything seemed to slow down, as it watched me plummet down, down, down. The crowd erupted in surprised shouts, but Rook's voice drowned out everything. He screamed and raged as the wind rushed past my ears, and I only knew I'd hit the ground because that rushing stopped.

It was as though my body was no more. There was just a haze of white, and Rook telling me I couldn't die. My vision failed me. Then there was nothing.

Chapter 33

Rook

In the time it took Elara to fall from the Giant's throat to the ground, I wished for death precisely three times.

I begged whatever gods were out there to extinguish my life right along with hers.

I pleaded for them to let her dying heart consume mine and drag me to Nav with her.

I bargained for the strength to break free of my chains and snap Theron's neck, even if it meant leaving her at the Gates of Nav and languishing forever in whatever state a cursed soul found itself after death.

Because I was absolutely certain, as I watched her fall, that she was dead.

She hit the ground, limbs spread from her body, head tilted at a sickening angle. I was bellowing, screaming at the guards to release me. I fought against the chains binding me until the steel tore into my skin and my arms bled.

Still Theron stood and watched, his face contorting between shock and an infuriating neutrality that made me want to carve out his fucking eyeballs.

"HELP HER!" I cried, bucking and twisting to get out of the fucking chains. "THERON! HELP HER! SHE NEEDS HELP!"

His head turned towards me, but his eyes did not. "She killed it," he said. "She fucking killed a Giant."

"THERON!" I wanted to slap him, punch him, *anything* to break him out of this fucking trance as Elara lay in a mangled heap beneath us. "THERON! FUCKING HELP HER!"

The crowd around us seemed to catch on to my cries, and suddenly a chant of *Help her, help her, help her* began to erupt from the stands.

Theron stumbled a little, catching himself on the railing of the royal box. His head sunk between his shoulders, and a pallor had crept over the back of his neck. He shook his head, his lips moving as he muttered words I couldn't hear over the din of the crowd.

"THERON!" I roared, and finally his head snapped up to look around him.

His confused gaze landed on me, and he waved a hand in my direction. One of the guards rushed forward and released me from my chains, barely removing the last binding before I shoved him out of the way and vaulted myself down into the Pit.

"Elara!" I dashed across the ground, furious at myself for not being able to move as fast as she could. Every stride towards her felt like I was moving barely an inch. "Elara!" She didn't move at all.

I skidded to my knees beside her, and reached out before jerking my hands back, unsure if moving her would hurt her more. I gently took her face in my hands, and saw with relief the flutter of her throat as she breathed. Bones protruded from her arm, blood cascading down the shredded casing of her armor. Thick black coils had started to whorl over her skin from where the venom of the Hadrian wolves Theron had so proudly sourced was now poisoning her blood.

"Elara?" I stroked her cheeks with my fingers. "Elara? Wake up. Please, please, fucking gods, wake up."

A small, strangled sob sounded behind me, and I looked over my shoulder to see a shivering Nesryn hugging her arms around herself. She stared down at Elara's inert frame with wide eyes.

"Is she dead?" She asked quietly.

"No," I said, turning back to Elara. "She's breathing, but…" She wasn't waking up. If she wasn't dead now, I had an awful feeling that in a few short hours, she would be.

Suddenly, healers were beside me, pushing me out of the way so they could lift Elara's broken body onto a stretcher.

"You bring her back!" I commanded, rising to my feet. "You don't let her die."

The healers waved me off, muttering and shaking their heads. I watched as they carried Elara from the Pit, amidst cheers from the Velesians. The fucking Velesians had enjoyed their spectacle, and now they'd go to their homes, perhaps wondering for a few minutes whether or not the brave little Peyrusian princess would live. Then they'd go back about their day, as though she was nothing. As though she was no one important. As though she wasn't my Bonded, the entire reason for my existence, the only thing now tethering me to this life.

Nesryn clutched onto my arm, big tears rolling down her cheeks. "Rook, she was so brave," she murmured. "She protected me. She saved me. She must live."

I patted her hand, still staring at the door the healers had carried Elara through. I only realised I was shaking when Nesryn clutched me tighter and began to cry into my arm. I held her to me, stroking her hair, my eyes still fixed on that door.

"It's alright, little one," I told her. "It's alright. She's strong. She'll live. She has to."

The heart beside mine was beating. Slowly, but it was there. She was still alive.

Don't leave me. You can't leave me. Please.

"Norahi!" The voice made Nesryn and I both snap our attention away from our grief. A guard gestured for us to follow him. "Come on then, king wants to see you."

I kept my arms protectively around my little sister as we were escorted to the throne room. She clung on to me, and through the haze of my despair I was aware that her hair now tickled my chin. She was so much taller than when I'd been taken away.

I looked down at her wide, terrified eyes, glowing a soft cornflower blue, and a lump formed in my throat. She looked so much like my mother. I sniffled, stroking a finger under her chin and attempted to give her a smile.

"Are you alright?" I asked, chiding myself for not having asked her sooner.

She nodded, returning my smile with trembling lips. "Hello, big brother." She sniffled, clutching onto the lapel of my jacket. "You've changed a little."

I gave a laugh, tears blurring my vision. "So have you, little one."

"Father sends his love," she whispered as we were ushered into the stone chamber where Theron sat on his ebony throne.

"Send my love to him too. Tell him I am well." I replied, and gently kissed her forehead. "It's going to be alright. They'll send you home. I'm sure of it."

Nesryn continued to tremble as we approached Theron, whose eyes were fixed on something in the distance. Only when we were right in front of him did his weary gaze land on us. His wings were pulled in tightly at his back, and he opened his mouth to speak, only to sigh heavily.

Nesryn glanced up at me, frowning.

"Your Majesty," I said when Theron remained silent. "You sent for us."

Theron nodded, rubbing a hand across his brow. "I did, didn't I? Yes…" He rose to his feet, and waved to a guard. "The princess may be returned to Isambard now."

I pushed Nesryn behind me. "I want assurances that she will not be harmed."

"Of course she won't be," Theron replied, pinching the bridge of his nose. "There is a Night Demon escort waiting at the western gate, and they will have an escort as far as the borderlands."

"You swear it?"

A few days ago, Theron would have scolded this display of rebellion. He would have reminded me of my place. Those green eyes would have been full of threatening malice. But today, he merely looked at me wearily, his shoulders drawn up as he sighed.

"No harm will come to your sister. You have my word, my friend." He raised a hand, and guards moved towards us.

Nesryn huddled into me with a panicked sob. "I love you, brother."

"I love you, too." I hugged her to me. "I will see you soon. I will. Tell our father I will see him soon."

I stepped back, letting the guards escort her out. Before I knew it, she was gone and out of sight. The tension of the past two days dissipated, and I was overcome with sadness and anger. My sister had been dragged here, terrified, only for Theron to now be a useless, simpering heap in his throne.

But it was over. Nesryn was safe, and Elara's heart continued to beat slowly, weakly, next to mine.

Theron walked past me, still pale, eyes still unable to focus. "That was quite something, wasn't it?" He said quietly.

"Was it?" My rage threatened to boil over.

"I never thought…" He cleared his throat. "I never thought, for a moment, that she'd actually engage. It's a Giant. A fucking *Giant*."

"And she's a warrior." I clenched my teeth so hard my jaw ached. "She doesn't run from a battle."

But Theron wasn't listening to me, tearing the crown from his head and sending it clattering along the stone floor. "She's insane. She should have begged for mercy. She should have thrown herself at my feet. That was my intention."

"Well, in that, you failed." Another statement, that days ago would have been met with a patronizing scowl and a reminder of my place, was now simply met with a look of defeat.

"I did." Theron exhaled heavily. "You were right, as always. She's strong. More so than I could have ever expected."

"Let's hope she survives." My words were laced with venom, and Theron straightened his shoulders, my meaning more than clear.

"We'll see to it that she does." Theron stormed across the throne room, past Regan who held up a hand as he tried to speak. "Not now, Regan," Theron snapped, flicking a hand sharply in his direction. "I'm not to be disturbed."

Regan looked almost helpless as his eyes moved to me, and he shrugged. "He's rather out of sorts."

I didn't care to discuss Theron's wellbeing. "Where is she?"

"In the infirmary, beside the healer's chambers. She's alive, from what I'm told."

"She'd fucking better be."

Regan's hand shot out to stop me as I passed him. "Rook, I'm sorry about your sister."

I jerked my arm out of his grasp. "She's fine. She's safe. For once your king's bloodlust didn't require a child to die."

Regan flinched, but I didn't wait to engage in any more conversation, rushing through the corridors to get to her. The Bond was there, but softer, almost pliable, as she hovered somewhere in a place between life and death.

The door to the infirmary was open, and three healers were working on her. I steadied myself against the door frame as the shock of her blood-stained skin, her ruined arm, washed over me. I inhaled sharply, and pushed into the room.

"How is she?" I asked.

The healers ignored me, continuing their work

"Someone tell me!" I bellowed, and everyone in the room jerked to a brief stop. While the other healers exchanged hesitant glances and returned to their work, one approached me tentatively, as though I was set to detonate at any moment.

"Her arm is broken in several places, and the wolf venom is making healing… difficult." He wrung his hands before him. "We are doing all we can, I assure you."

"The Giant," I said with a gasp. "He crushed her. What-what damage did that do?"

"Her ribs are broken, and one of her lungs is not functioning." His tone was slow and measured, still afraid, no doubt, that I'd destroy every being in the room if I did not like his answer. "She is breathing, but it is difficult."

"Will she live?" Asking the question sent a dagger of ice into my gut, because the healer's eyes crinkled into an expression of mild defeat. I wasn't sure I was prepared for the answer.

"We must hope," he said softly, and ducked his head before returning to the table and Elara's mangled body.

I sank into a chair by the window, watching, willing Elara's eyes to open. I found myself praying to those gods again, the ones she was convinced were real, the ones who'd brought us together.

Please, let her live. Do not take her from me.

The coppery smell of blood was slowly replaced by healing ointments, and Elara was washed clean. I winced as the bones in her arm were set, feeling the snapping and grinding echoing through my jaw. I wasn't squeamish, I never had been. Blood, broken bones, severed limbs - none of this had ever bothered me. But this was happening to *her*. This was *her* body that was wrecked and ruined, her chest sucking in with every breath she took. It was torture to observe.

Her heart continued to beat next to mine, wavering every now and then as though blowing away on a soft breeze. I pressed my hands to my chest as though I could protect her, keep her contained there. As long as her heart remained next to mine, she was safe.

Finally, her bones were set, her wounds dressed, and the healers covered her in warm blankets.

The one who had spoken to me approached me with raised eyebrows. "She is not out of the woods yet. We must hope her body is able to heal."

"I will stay with her."

The healer gave a sharp nod of assent, wiping his hands on a cloth that hung from his wide leather belt. "Make sure she stays warm, and keeps breathing. If anything changes, call for one of us. We won't be far away."

"When will she wake up?"

He placed a hand on my shoulder. "We must pray the Gods see fit to return her." He nodded his head towards my bleeding arms. "Do those need seeing to?"

I shrugged him off. "Don't worry about me."

The room emptied, the door closed, and I was alone with her. I moved the chair to the side of the bed, and reached out to take her hand. I pressed my lips to the back of it, smelling nothing but the harsh scent of the tinctures the healers had used on her. Her scent of roses was under there somewhere. Her hand warmed in mine.

"Don't you die on me, Osunon," I murmured. "I won't let you."

I held her hand against my forehead. "If you're listening," I muttered to the Gods, "if you can hear me - you can't have her. Not yet. You can't have her. She's mine."

Chapter 34

Elara

All I was aware of was pain. Throbbing through my chest, through my arms, beating at my temples as I tried to open my eyes. At least I knew I wasn't in Nav, because I was still sure there was no pain to be felt there.

Light overwhelmed me as I slowly woke. I wriggled my toes tentatively, relieved that I could feel them. I flexed my left hand and winced as shockwaves radiated through my nerves. I still wasn't healed. It can't have been that long since the trial. Gods fuck it all.

I opened my eyes and blinked twice, three times, trying to focus. My vision cleared enough for me to see a figure seated beside me, arms crossed over their chest, head slumped forward. I could sense that it was Rook.

I tried to reach out to touch him, but the pain from moving even my right arm was so sharp that I sucked in a breath and let out a low groan.

Rook awoke instantly, dropping to his knees beside the bed I lay on. He leaned over me, his brow furrowed with concern.

His face was almost ashen, and his blue eyes were dim with fatigue.

"Elara?" He stroked my forehead gently. "My love, it's me, I'm here."

I managed a weak smile. "You look terrible."

He exhaled heavily and kissed my temple. "Oh my love, I thought I'd lost you." He smiled through his tears. "You're a brave little fucker, have I told you that?"

"Going to take more than a mangy giant to take me down," I replied, turning my head gingerly to move closer to him.

"Yes, well you certainly showed him." Rook lay his head on the pillow beside me with a sigh. "I thought they'd have to stitch you back together. You were so broken when they carried you - you…" He broke off, his voice strained.

"Is Nesryn alright?"

"Yes, she's safe." He pressed another kiss to my cheek. "Back in Isambard with my father, thanks to you."

"Good." I coughed as my voice fought its way through my dry throat. "That's good."

Rook got to his feet. "You need water, you must be parched."

"How long have I been asleep?" I asked, watching as he poured water from a clay pitcher. I realized for the first time I wasn't in my room, rather in a dim stone chamber, on a wooden bed. It must have been the infirmary, I decided.

"Three days since the trial," Rook said slowly, moving back to my bedside. He gently supported my aching head and held the cup to my lips so I could sip the cool water. "I was so sure - I was sure you'd died." He looked into my eyes and shook his head. "I wasn't sure I'd be able to keep my promise to you. I thought you'd died, and I wanted to die too."

I lifted my hand to touch him, wincing as pain snapped at my ribs. "I'm here."

He took my hand and pressed it to his cheek, then leaned over me and placed a delicate kiss on my lips. "My love, the sun of my life." He smiled as he leaned his forehead against mine. "Theron was speechless."

I let out a laugh, gritting my teeth. "Ah fuck." I tried to raise my head and look down at myself. "Why am I taking so long to heal?"

"Hadrian Wolves," Rook said, moving around the bed to inspect my left arm. I saw for the first time the gnarled black scars on my forearm, from where the wolf had bitten me. "They have venom in those fangs of theirs, and Fae are especially susceptible to it."

I groaned. "Of course."

"Theron really thought he'd scare you into marrying him." Rook cocked an eyebrow at me. "But you, my fierce little Fae, won't be cowed, will you?"

"And give up your cock?" I asked with a grin. "Never."

Rook burst out laughing, and I was relieved to see some color return to his cheeks. "Greedy little Fae, you asked for a *kiss* if you won, not a fuck."

"Since when am I ever satisfied with just a kiss?"

He shook his head, still smiling, and I wanted nothing more than to throw myself in his arms and kiss the dimples in his cheeks. "Greedy, *greedy* Fae. You will have to wait until you're recovered before you have the pleasure of more-than-a-kiss again, love."

"Surely I'll be perfectly well again in a day or two." I tried to move and whimpered as pain rushed through me.

Rook's smile instantly dropped. "Now, you need to rest. Enough talking."

"I don't want to stop talking."

"Of course you don't," Rook chided, "You're a stubborn ass."

I smiled, suppressing a laugh because I didn't want to hurt again. Rook sat beside me, holding my hand gently.

"I wonder what Theron will do next," I said quietly.

"I think he knows he's exhausted his bag of tricks," Rook said. "He was utterly defeated after the trial. I've never seen him like that before. It was as though he was in a trance."

"I suppose I showed him." A glimmer of satisfaction bloomed in my chest at the thought of a defeated Theron.

"You certainly did. He thought you'd be throwing yourself at his feet begging for mercy and instead you catapulted yourself straight into a Giant's-" He choked a little clutching my hand, and sucked in a breath. "I never want to see you like that again. It was terrible."

I curled my fingers tighter around Rook's. "It's alright. I'm alive. I beat these trials just like you said I would." I sighed. "Perhaps now I shall have my freedom after all. *Our* freedom."

Rook smiled weakly. "Yes, perhaps now you shall."

The door opened with a loud creak, and Rook's hand remained around mine as Regan stepped into the chamber. He regarded us both critically for a moment before he moved to the bedside, his hand clasped behind his back.

"You're awake then, Your Highness," he said.

"You don't need to sound so thrilled, Regan," I replied.

"I am more than relieved you're alive," he retorted, frowning. "Merely wondering how much longer you think you can last."

Rook tensed noticeably, the fire returning to his glowing eyes. He lifted his chin as he turned to face Regan, his shoulders rolling back as he straightened. "And what is that supposed to mean?"

Regan lifted his hands with a sigh. "I am concerned for the Princess, nothing more."

"I hope that Theron will honor his word," I said. "I was supposed to earn back my home, and now that it is destroyed, does he hope to terrorize me with the remainders of the other kingdoms?"

Regan's mouth twitched, and I couldn't tell if he was annoyed or concerned. "I will let His Majesty know you're awake, and will arrange for you to be moved back to your chambers to recover there in comfort."

"Thank you."

Regan's eyes moved back to mine and Rook's entwined fingers. "Norahi, perhaps you should go and rest. You've been here all this time, surely you're exhausted."

"I'll leave her once she's safely back in her chambers," Rook replied in a low voice. "Until then, I do not leave her side."

"Norahi, you know this cannot -"

"I'm not leaving her." Rook's eyes flamed as he looked back down at me. "Ever."

Regan pursed his lips, as though considering his next words. Instead of saying anything further, he merely turned on his heel and left the room.

I raised my eyebrows as soon as the door fell closed. "Ever?" I clasped onto his hand. "Is that a promise?"

"An oath, princess." He lowered his mouth to mine and kissed me gently, tentatively so as not to cause me any more pain. "I love you, Elara."

"I know." I winced as I lifted my right arm, but the pain was not so bad that I couldn't lay my hand on the back of his neck, drawing him down to me again. "I know."

Rook held his oath, staying with me as long as the guards would allow, every day after I was returned to my chamber. The Hadrian Wolves had left me with an arm of black scars, and I tried not to despair whenever I looked in the mirror. My body was now riddled with the marks of battle.

None of this bothered Rook in the slightest. He kissed every single scar, and told me every day how beautiful, how perfect I was. He would sneak back into my room after dark, to simply hold me, to tell me stories of Isambard, to tell me how it felt to fly. I would fall asleep to the sound of his voice, my cheek on his warm chest, and woke to his knock at my door every morning right after dawn.

He wasn't shy about caring for me, even in front of Drusilla. A shift had occurred, a new freedom in how we expressed our devotion and love for each other. It was almost as though we anticipated that any day now Theron would grant me my freedom. I still didn't know how to convince him to let Rook go with me. I'd considered telling him of the Bond, appealing to his good nature, but then I reminded myself who I was thinking about - Theron had no heart nor good nature to appeal to.

But I was determined to find a way. Somehow, I would walk out of Veles with Rook by my side. I was never going to leave him. I would die first.

A week after I left the infirmary, I was healed and able to move without any pain. Drusilla tutted as she looked at my arm after my bath.

"Those bloody wolves," she said, shaking her head. "They certainly got you."

"At least I still have my arm."

"Yes, well," she said, rolling her eyes and sighing. "I suppose we must count our blessings." She put my robe around me, and followed me out into the chamber.

Rook was sitting in the armchair in front of the fireplace, his eyes roving over me. "Hello, love."

Drusilla let out an exasperated sigh. "You two may as well announce your engagement, like a pair of lovesick younglings."

Rook grinned as he rose to his feet. "Perhaps we should do that." He moved towards me, putting an arm around my waist. "Care to be my wife?"

I smiled and nodded. "If this is a proposal, I accept."

Drusilla let out something akin to a squeak and scurried for her chambers. "I won't be a part of this, I'll leave you two alone." The door swung shut behind her, and we were alone.

Rook immediately seized me in his arms and carried me to the bed. I broke out in giggles, wrapping my arms around his neck.

"What are you doing?" I asked.

He placed me on the bed and kissed me deeply, propping himself up so as not to hurt me. He still treated me like I was made of glass, no matter how many times I told him I felt fine.

"The healer said you still need to be careful," he murmured against my lips. "But I can't go any longer without hearing you moaning my name."

He tore open my robe and dragged his tongue over my nipple. My gasp quickly turned into a moan, my back bowing, pressing my body against him. Desire flooded me, and I pawed at his clothes, wanting to feel his warm skin on mine.

It felt so dangerous to do this, in broad daylight, when Drusilla could walk in at any moment. But Rook's fingers moved between my thighs, swirling over my clit and plunging into the liquid heat that pooled at his touch, and every worry left me.

"Take off your clothes." I tugged his shirt loose from his trousers. "I need you to fuck me."

The words had scarcely left my mouth, and he was already setting about stripping off, until his body was naked and warm against me. He hesitated as he hovered over me, and with a frustrated grunt I pulled him down to me with my legs and arms, tangling around him.

"Would you stop worrying?" I said with a sigh.

"I don't want to -"

I silenced him with a kiss, my fingertips clawing at his shoulders, clutching him to me, suddenly overwhelmed with urgency. His uncertainty seemed to dissolve, and his mouth moved from mine down my throat, back to my nipple, covering my breast as he sucked.

I cried out, and he lifted his head at the same time that he plunged into me, seating himself fully inside me with one hard thrust. My head fell back on the pillow, and his hand was instantly behind my head, lifting me back to him.

"You look at me, princess," he said with a gasp. "You keep your eyes on me."

I whimpered as he withdrew then filled me again, as though he was claiming me all over again. Every time it felt like this, like my body was giving itself to him for the very first time, remembering the smell of his skin and the heat of his body, the sharp raking of his fingertips at the nape of my neck.

He kissed me ferociously, and I allowed myself a long moan, smothered by his lips and his tongue.

We didn't have much time, but it didn't matter. Our desire

and longing for each other drove us to that climax quickly, and he pressed his forehead to mine as we met each other there. I bit my lips together as I trembled violently underneath him, the heat between my thighs threatening to consume me.

Rook groaned into my neck, one hot breath after another washing across me as he subsided.

"Oh, fucking Gods," he said finally with a breathless chuckle. He raised his head to gaze down at me. "Did I hurt you?"

I rolled my eyes, my chest still heaving. "You most certainly didn't hurt me."

"Well, good. You're not so broken after all." He grinned as he withdrew from me. "Shame we don't have more time, I'd like to do that again." He plunged himself back into me, and I was so surprised I couldn't suppress the cry that broke from me.

"Oh you bastard," I bit out, shivering. He began to move again, how was this possible? My body was not anywhere near subsided yet, and the deep warmth in my belly grew quickly as he moved deeper and deeper within me. "You're going to drive me mad."

I propped myself up on my elbows, looking down between us, watching our bodies join over and over again. Rook smiled against my cheek.

"You see, princess? I told you, you take me so well."

I let out a breathy laugh which hissed into a gasp as he drove into me again. Watching him enter my body like this was incredible, and sent my arousal into a dizzying spiral.

My head fell back and all I could say was, "Harder."

He obliged immediately, catching my mouth again, tasting my moans as my body rose, impossibly, headily, towards yet another climax.

There were sudden exclamations and calls for attention

outside my door, and my body cried out in disappointment as Rook withdrew and climbed off me. It took me two breaths to realize what was happening before I too scrambled off the bed.

"Fuck, that sounds like Theron is coming." He hurriedly pulled on his trousers and shirt as I fled to the bathroom. The bathroom door flew open a second after I slammed it shut, and Rook threw a gown at me, which I caught with a startled laugh. "Get dressed."

Sure enough, I heard Theron's voice a minute later, and realized then that my heart wasn't only pounding because of my activities with Rook. Theron had nearly caught us. We had become too reckless. My freedom still wasn't guaranteed. We had to be careful.

I pulled the green dress on, and quickly ran a brush through my hair, hoping I did not look too wild. I cast a glance into the mirror, at my shuddering chest and my rosy cheeks. I took a deep breath, willing myself to calm down, and pushed through the door back into the chamber.

Rook gave me a smile as I emerged, and Theron regarded me with a look that caught me off guard at first.

"Your Highness," he said, bowing his head. Oh Gods. What the fuck was this? He was speaking to me reverently, almost sheepishly, his wings drawn close to his back.

My eyes moved to Rook, my eyebrows raised questioningly. He shrugged lightly and leaned back against the window frame, his arms crossed over his chest.

"Your Majesty," I said slowly, looking back at Theron. "To what do I owe the pleasure?"

He straightened and smiled. "I wanted to congratulate you on your spectacular triumph in the Pit." He exhaled through pursed lips, shaking his head. "I never should have doubted you, not for a moment. The finest Seraph warriors have fallen at the hands of a giant, and yet you defeated one, alone, and injured. You are truly a marvel, Elara."

"Thank you, Your Majesty." I gave him a brief nod. "You are too kind."

Theron took a step towards me, almost hesitating. He clasped his hands before him, and sighed. "I do hope you will accept my admiration, and my friendship."

"Your friendship?" I didn't know where to look.

"Indeed." Another step towards me, his stance still one of hesitation. "I see now there is nothing for me to gain here. You have told me what you seek, and what you will not accept."

My heart began to hammer against my ribcage again, so violently it threatened to jerk me off my feet. "Your Majesty, do you mean…?" I trailed off, the question hanging thickly in the air.

Theron smiled amicably. "Once you are recovered, and able to travel, we will negotiate your release, dear one."

If it hadn't been for Rook's low chuckle from the window, I would have thought I was dreaming. I would have asked him to repeat himself. How many months had I been here? Had it only been months? The relief that flooded me was so encompassing I felt faint.

"My release?" I asked, unable to stop myself smiling.

"Your release." Theron nodded on a heavy exhale, his eyes kind as he smiled at me. "I know when I have won, and when I have lost, Elara."

I couldn't help but gaze over at Rook. "Your Majesty, there is something I would wish to discuss with you. I don't know what I can say to convince you, but-"

"In time," Theron interjected, nodding. His eyes moved to Rook. "I will do all I can to ensure that what has been brought together shall not be torn apart."

Rook's face betrayed every emotion he did not verbalize,

and he merely nodded, his arms staying firmly across his chest. "Thank you, Your Majesty." Even these words caught in his throat, and I felt his own relief, coupled with intense disbelief, washing over my shoulders like a waterfall.

Theron's smile landed back on me. "Now, my dear, the healers will see to you to ensure you make a full recovery, and then we will speak." He moved closer to me, and held out his hand. I took it hesitantly, and he raised it to his lips. "All will be well, Elara."

With a final nod, he left the room. The door fell closed, as though in slow motion. When it finally landed in the frame, Rook and I turned to stare at each other. I don't know how many breaths and heartbeats passed before we finally stumbled into each other's arms, laughing through our tears.

Rook cradled my face in his hands. "You're extraordinary," he said, smiling widely, "my love, my bonded." He kissed me, our tears mingling on our lips. "Sun of my life."

"We're going to be free." I clasped on to his hands. "I told you. I told you I wasn't leaving you here."

"You did, my love, you did." He drew me close to him, and I nuzzled into his chest. "I didn't doubt you, not for a moment."

"Liar."

He chuckled, putting a finger under my chin and gazing down at me. "You're going to love Isambard."

"Of course I will. It is our home. I don't even know it, and yet I know I will love it." I stroked his cheek. "Because it is a part of you."

He broke into yet another smile, those dimples showing either side of his perfect mouth. "Yes, my love. It is. A part of us." As he kissed me, the door opened, and I heard Drusilla tutting.

"And now they're kissing, my word, I just don't know."

I turned to her with a smile. "He is letting us go," I told her tearfully, Rook pressing a kiss to my temple. "Theron, he was just here. He told us he would negotiate my-" My eyes snapped up to Rook's, and I laughed breathlessly. "*Our* release. He would discuss our release."

There was silence from the other side of the room, and when I turned to look back at Drusilla, her brows were drawn together.

"Theron said that?" She asked slowly.

"He did," Rook replied, holding me close. "We just need to wait for Elara to recover fully, and then we will be going home." He sighed. "Home."

I leaned against his chest again, listening to his heart beat. "Home."

Drusilla cleared her throat and moved to the fireplace, retrieving the undergarments that were hanging in front of the fire to dry. "Yes, well that is wonderful, my lamb. And speaking of your recovery, the healer has recommended you bathe in the hot springs."

"The hot springs?" I asked.

Drusilla nodded. "Yes, there is a cave system underneath the palace, and the hot springs down there are said to have healing properties. It was suggested that they'd be beneficial for you, and since Theron wants you properly healed for… your journey…"

Rook smiled down at me. "That sounds like just what you need."

I sighed as I wrapped my arms around his neck. "Perhaps you could come with me."

"You're meant to be recovering," he murmured into my ear, "and if I have you naked in a hot spring…"

I swatted at his back, laughing. "You're a brute."

He drew back from me and smiled. "Go down and enjoy

your bath, it will do you good. I have some matters of my own to attend to." He kissed me again, and another soft tut came from Drusilla. "I will see you tonight," he whispered in my ear.

"I certainly hope so." I replied, our hands staying joined as he backed towards the door, Finally our fingers dropped from one another's, and his smile stayed on me until he left the room, and the door fell closed before him.

Drusilla rolled her eyes and shook her head when I regarded her with a grin. "Oh, to be young and in love again," she muttered.

"I am deliriously happy, Drusilla," I replied, falling down into the armchair in front of the fire. "Not two weeks ago I almost died, and now I am here, and happy."

"Yes, and I am happy for you as well, my lamb," she said, but her tone did not match her words.

I was tempted for a moment to ask her what the matter was, why her face remained creased into a frown, even as I sighed with contentment. But instead I gazed out of the window at the warm afternoon light.

In a few days, I would be healed, and then I would be free. We would be free. I closed my eyes as I thought of the beach in Isambard, the turquoise water Rook had mentioned. Soon we would swim under the twin moons.

Only a few more days.

Chapter 35

Elara

The healer escorted me through the passageways and catacombs, into the bowels of the palace. It smelled strongly of minerals, the air so thick with iron that it was like running my tongue along the blade of a knife. But it was warm and pleasant, the walls dotted with torches that lit the way in warm, flickering light.

The walls around us seemed to almost hum with energy, and the sound was intensely soothing. Perhaps the healer was right, and these caves were magical. He'd told me earnestly about the powers of the caves and the waters therein, and now I had no choice but to believe him.

The stone was warm under my bare feet, my thin robe becoming quickly sticky with humidity. I had wound my hair up and pinned it on the top of my head, and the tendrils that had escaped now curled in the damp air.

We moved down a carved stone staircase, and a turquoise glow met us, reflecting off the walls in undulating lines. The staircase opened up to a flat, golden rock, and beyond that lay the glowing blue water that was meant to heal me completely.

"It is not very deep," the healer said to me, gesturing to the water's surface. "Up to your shoulders at its deepest point. But it will do you good. Try and stay submerged for as long as possible." He looked down at my arm that bore the black pocked bite marks the Hadrian wolf had left behind, then smiled at me warmly. "Might even heal up some of those scars, Your Highness."

I nodded. "Perhaps, I will have to see just how magical these waters are."

With a brief bow of his head, the healer padded back up the stone stairs and out of sight. I inhaled the thick air deeply, feeling droplets catch in my nose and mouth. It was not an entirely unpleasant feeling.

I peeled off my robe, which clung lightly to my body, and moved down more stairs that disappeared under the water's surface. The water was warmer than I expected, hot even, but it felt so good as it traveled slowly up my legs. Even though I was healed, my muscles still ached a little, and I couldn't help but groan as I moved further into the depths. Oh Gods it felt nice.

The floor of the springs was a little slick, and I had to paddle a little to move deeper into the caves. I remembered Rook's promise to teach me to swim, and smiled. Perhaps this would be an opportunity to practice my swimming. I willed my body to float, which it did easily in these waters. I propelled myself slowly with my legs, using my arms to sweep myself forward. I hadn't been swimming in years, and this was simply heavenly.

Another few strokes and I moved underneath a crystalline archway, its craggy surface glittering in the flickering torch-light. I turned onto my back and floated on the water's surface, taking in the myriad colors of the gems above me, like an arching sunset.

It was so quiet, and I closed my eyes, feeling the water lapping at my limbs. There was a slight tingle on my skin, and I wondered if that was indeed the magic the healer had spoken of. I exhaled, the sound echoing through my head as my ears remained submerged under the water.

There was a swishing sound nearby, followed by another, then another, growing louder. It was movement, someone pushing through water and drawing closer. I smiled to myself. Rook had followed me down after all.

"You're incorrigible, do you know that?" I opened my eyes.

Theron grinned down at me.

I started up in the water then immediately submerged myself up to my neck to hide my body from him.

"Not who you were expecting?" He asked, cocking an eyebrow. He was very obviously naked, the water rippling low on his hips. His wings were drawn close to his back, the golden tattoos over his chest clearly visible. He ran a hand through his hair, which was curling in the humidity of the cave.

"I - I had thought -" I stammered, breaking off as he moved closer to me.

"You needn't hide yourself from me, dear one," he said in a low voice. "It is just a body. I have seen plenty of breasts in my life." He inhaled through gritted teeth as he took yet another slow step closer to me. "Though admittedly, your breasts are particularly beautiful."

"I am merely trying to maintain my modesty, Your Majesty." I was keenly aware of being backed into a small alcove of the cave, the craggy walls closing in around me.

Theron chuckled. "Your modesty. Yes, such an important quality to have in a maid like you."

His tone chilled me to my core. He lowered himself into

the water so we were eye to eye, and continued to move towards me.

"We were interrupted, the night of the ball," he said. "When we were speaking about the Sun Throne."

I nodded, unsure if sweat was now breaking out on my top lip or if this corner of the cave had just become much, much warmer. "You claimed the Sun Throne had powers, and I told you it did not."

"Mmm." Theron's voice hummed across the water, and he tipped his head back into the water, wetting down his hair. "Your father raged for years after your birth, lamenting his inability to have another child." He gave me a sideways glance. "You almost killed your mother, coming out of her, did you know that?"

I swallowed hard. "I had been told she was unable to have any more children."

"Your father fucked every chambermaid he could after your birth," Theron said, waving his hands lazily through the iridescent blue water. "He so hoped he would produce a son, even an illegitimate one, that he could claim, much like my father had done with me."

My stomach was in a knot. "Is that so?" I asked. "Are the powers of the Sun throne so dangerous in the hands of a woman?"

Theron laughed. "Your father was afraid of who they would be shared with, dear one. You see, there was a prophecy spoken out, the day you were born." He looked at me with slightly narrowed eyes, which glowed in the light of the cave, a sickly, unnatural green. "You were born under an eclipse. And the prophecy stated, that the child of the Sun, born under the darkened moon, would unite the Realm." He moved closer again, caging me into the stone alcove, his wings spreading a little to block out the flimmer of the torchlight. "You, Elara, are destined to be the one true queen of Korbiriya. All of it. And as such, your husband would be the one true king."

I shook my head, suppressing the shiver that ran down my spine. "That's impossible."

Theron shrugged. "A great many things are possible. Under this prophecy, well, your father was faced with a dilemma. Every Kingdom offered their heir, desperate to claim the power of the Sun Throne for themselves. Even House Norahi, would you believe it?" His mouth curled into a vicious grin. "Rook could have already been your husband, you could already have borne him a horde of little Night Demons, had your father not been a prejudiced fool."

A shuddering breath left me, and caught in my throat. I coughed, sucking in the wet air rising from the steaming water. "My father never told me," I whispered, "my mother didn't either."

"No, they wouldn't have. Because what they did next caused the Uprising."

I frowned. "What are you talking about?"

Theron grinned, and moved so close that we were almost touching. His eyes moved over my face, resting on my lips.

"They promised you to my brother."

The floor seemed to tip sideways underneath me. I shook my head, willing my breathing to normalize, for my lungs to fill entirely with air. "That isn't possible," I replied. "That *isn't* possible, My father is of the Faith, he believed-"

I cried out as Theron's hands thudded against the cave wall either side of me. I realized for the first time just how big he was.

"Your father was a fucking fool," Theron hissed. "So desperate to keep the powers of the Sun Throne away from the Night Demons and the Bloodborn, so eager to see his enemies perish even if it meant giving power to the greatest tyrant this realm had ever seen. You call me a monster - I am nothing compared to Tannis. He would have ruined this Realm, enslaved every race to do his bidding." His lips curled in disgust. "It is no wonder that the people united, and rose against Veles, determined to remove Tannis before he could claim you for his bride."

I felt I was going to suffocate, caged in by his arms like this, and with a gasp I tried to push past him, back out into the open cave. But Theron was too fast, seizing me in his arms and pushing me back against the cave wall. His naked body was pressed against mine, and panic whirred through me so violently my vision clouded for a moment. I stared up at him, and he smiled back.

"I'm not done yet, dear one." He backed away, only a few inches. "There is more of the story to tell."

"How did you become King?" I asked, my voice barely audible over the rushing in my ears.

"It is so easy to claim power over the oppressed." Theron grinned. "The Seraph troops were treated so poorly under Tannis, indeed, the whole kingdom had become tired of him. My father -" He scoffed. "The useless brute, in his eyes Tannis could do no wrong. He did nothing, stood by and watched while Tannis killed and punished and beat them down. So then, when I offered them something, even the smallest scrap, they fell to my feet." He brought his face close to mine, his hot breath washing over my lips. "Give a starving man food, you are his master. Give a homeless man shelter, you are his king." His eyes bore into mine. "Give a weak man power, and you are his God."

"And you did not want to claim me for yourself?" I asked, trying to sound defiant despite my legs threatening to buckle beneath me.

Theron's eyebrows shot up. "Oh but I did, dear one. That

was the bargain." Under the water, his hands bracketed my waist. "Your father insisted I had to wait, because you were still a girl. He promised me that when you turned 21, you would be mine."

"No, they would never - they wouldn't give me to you. I had a - a Mate. They knew of him, they knew…" I was going to faint, the sharp stab of betrayal piercing me to my core.

"I had no choice but to declare war on Peyrus, in an attempt to claim you." Theron's grip on me tightened. "And then I was informed that you were on the battlefield, delivered straight into my waiting arms. Such…" He brought his face down to the side of my face, the tip of his nose tracing my jawline. "Serendipity."

"You said you were going to let me go." My voice croaked out of me as hopelessness crashed onto my shoulders. "Today, you said - you said-" Tears bit at my eyes. "You told us-"

"Mmmm, I did, didn't I?" He raised his head and smirked. "You, and your mate."

My eyes widened. "My - my what?"

"Did you think I didn't know?" Theron raised a hand to my cheek, stroking it gently with the backs of his fingers. "I confess, at first I thought it was just fucking. When your chambermaid informed me of the moans and cries of ecstasy coming from your chamber, I did not think it was anything more than a stupid young girl being taken in by a voracious predator. The Night Demons are so very dangerous, you see."

I slumped back against the cave wall. Drusilla had heard us. She'd heard us, and betrayed me. Of course she had. Stupid, stupid little girl. I clenched my eyes shut as Theron went on.

"I was tempted to kill Rook for taking your maidenhead." His voice was thick now, dripping with poison. "But then the most extraordinary thing happened. The Ladaian priestess in my service, she informed me…" He hand cupped the back of my head, firmly, and I opened my eyes to meet his. "She informed me that there was a Bond. And suddenly, I found myself in a rather fortuitous position."

"And what position was that?" I asked weakly.

"I had your whole world in my hands." His eyes, like a cat, like a viper's, narrowed. "Winning back your parents, your broken kingdom, what good was that? But now, well now…" He pressed himself against me, and I suppressed a sob as I felt his hard cock against my stomach. "Now, I own you. Both of you. For you do not want any harm to come to him, and he is helpless to stop any harm from coming to you."

"What if I kill you in your sleep?" Tears blurred my eyes. "What if I run you through in our marriage bed?"

"Then you will kill him." Theron lowered his mouth to mine. "Whatever happens to me, happens to him. Whatever he does to me, he will do to himself." His lips curled back into that sickening grin. "There are consequences, dear one. Consequences to ever saying no to me. If you refuse me, I will cause him insurmountable pain while you watch."

A tear ran down my cheek, scalding hot. "You said you would let us go."

Theron tutted, forcing me up out of the water, leaning me against the rough stone wall. "I have such a gift, do I not? For attaining trust?" His eyes moved down to my chest, and he exhaled heavily. "So beautiful." His eyes flamed as they moved back to meet mine. "Do you consent to be my wife?"

"No." I bit the word out through gritted teeth, raising my hands to push against his chest.

One of his hands curled around my throat, and Theron slammed me back against the cave wall. "I ask you again, with the knowledge of what I just swore to, should you ever dare refuse me." His hand crushed my windpipe, and my breath rasped out of my lips. "Do you consent to be my wife?"

I struggled against his hand, desperate for air, the oppressive heat of the cave suffocating me further. "N-No."

Theron released my throat and seized my hair, yanking my head back. "Which of his limbs do you suppose he will miss the least?" He snarled. "How much blood do you suppose a night demon can lose before he succumbs? Shall we test his ability to heal?"

The sob I had been fighting to suppress finally tore from me. "Please, don't."

"Shall I add his eyes to my collection? Or one at least, I wouldn't want him to miss out on seeing our marital joy." His voice was maniacal now,

I shook my head, more and more hot tears pouring down my cheeks. "Please-"

"Or perhaps I shall haul his beloved sister back, and see just how quickly those wolves devour the sweet little princess?"

More sobs bubbled up my throat. "Please no, no, *no.* Don't hurt them. Please… please."

His face softened slightly, and he cocked an eyebrow. "So I ask you again - what is your answer?"

I closed my eyes. I had no choice. I was a prisoner, ever a prisoner. I had to protect him. This was the only thing I could do. Theron wouldn't stop. He would come up with ever more depraved ways to torture Rook and his family. I couldn't let that happen.

I nodded, biting my lip to stop it from trembling.

"Yes?" Theron asked, his mouth by my ear.

"Yes." I whispered.

"Finally, you make a wise decision." He released my hair to drop his hands to my waist, spinning me so my front slammed into the craggy cave wall. He kicked my legs apart, then his hands were on my hips, lifting me up so my skin dragged along the stone.

"What are you doing?" I asked, clawing into the rock in a panic. "Please, please don't-" I cut off with a cry as I felt his tip at my entrance.

"I told you," he said, his hot breath on my ear, "there are consequences to saying no to me."

I squeezed my eyes shut, awaiting his intrusion into my body. "Please," I whimpered one last time, sending a prayer out into the hot cave, that someone, anyone might save me. "Please don't. I don't want you to-"

But then it was too late. With a loud groan, Theron pushed into me. I gasped, wishing I could somehow retreat within myself. If my eyes were clenched tightly enough, perhaps I could imagine myself out of this place, out of this cave.

"Oh Elara," he murmured, "I've dreamed of this moment. *Fuck*, you feel so incredible."

I sobbed as he thrust again. I couldn't imagine myself out of it. It was really happening. I could do nothing to stop it.

"I did wonder," he asked quietly, his tongue darting out to lick the length of my ear, "will he feel this? Will Rook sense this is happening to you? Your distress?" He kissed my neck. "Your fear?"

My lips were trembling so violently I couldn't speak. My body was cold despite the warm water. My fingertips were slick on the cave wall, no doubt coated in blood as I scrambled against them, trying to somehow keep my bearings. I could barely move. My body was seized in disbelief. All I could do was nod.

Theron chuckled softly. "Good."

Chapter 36

Elara

My face was soaked with tears. That was all I was aware of. That was all I could sense. I wasn't crying, or wailing, or sobbing. There was just an endless flow of tears ran down my cheeks. I stared at the wall, unmoving. Moving meant pain, and I didn't want to feel that anymore.

I didn't remember how I had returned to my chambers the night before. I had just woken up there, and stared at the wall. Drusilla tutted and fussed, but I didn't respond.

A hand landed on my shoulder, and I flinched, shoving it away.

"Don't touch me."

"My lamb, you've been lying here all day," she said urgently. "Come now, you must have a bath."

"So I can wash him away?"

Drusilla made a small, helpless sound, her footsteps pacing back and forth beside the bed. "I'll run you a bath." She said finally, her voice cracking.

Bitch. Traitorous fucking bitch. Tears burned my eyes as I

sat up, pain shooting through my groin. My fingertips were raw from that stony cave wall, from scrambling against it as I tried to escape Theron's grasp.

Bile rose in my throat, and I stumbled to the ceramic basin on the dressing table, retching drily. Drusilla was suddenly at my back, tutting and stroking. I shrugged her off, the tears not stopping, continuing their neverending cascade down my cheeks.

"Fuck off."

"Elara, I'm sorry."

I turned on her. "Do you know what he did to me?"

Drusilla's face twisted with pain. "I never expected he would-"

"How could you do this to me?"

"He threatened my son!" Drusilla clutched her hands to her mouth, shaking her head. "I am so sorry, Elara. I had no choice. My son, he's small, he's not strong. Theron said he'd force him into the infantry if I didn't… If I didn't…"

I watched her cry, and I wanted to feel pity, I wanted to try and understand. I should have lifted a hand to her shoulder to comfort her. I should have seen that she was nothing more than a servant who had no more power in this cursed palace than I did. I should have tried to alleviate her guilt, somehow.

But I was too numb for that. Instead I turned away from her and walked into the bathroom, pushing the door closed behind me.

I gingerly lifted my nightgown off over my head, and whimpered when I looked down at myself. My breasts were covered in grazes, my hips and thighs bruised. I looked in the mirror and saw the purple handprint around my throat. The left side of my face was covered in scratches, from where the craggy cave wall had caught my skin. I wasn't healing, my body and my very being seized in an awful kind of stasis, trapped in that cave. Imprisoned. Drowning.

I lowered myself into the bathtub, whimpering as the water touched my groin. Suddenly I couldn't breathe. I was shaking violently as the feeling of the warm water on my limbs brought everything crashing back down on me. Everything hurt. I felt like he'd torn me open. Even through the haze of disbelief, my body confirmed that it had really happened. It hadn't been a nightmare, and I wasn't about to wake up. The nightmare was very, very real.

There was a sudden commotion outside, yelling, the voices of guards, doors being slammed. There was a loud thud on the other side of the bathroom door and Drusilla cried out, asking "What are you doing here?"

More shouts from the guards, and then I felt it, smashing through the numbness that had me in its clutches.

It was Rook, descending over me like a storm cloud. His bewilderment, his fear and anger - they made me feel ill.

The door flew open and then he was there, staring at me, shaking his head.

"My love?" His eyes took me in, widening with every passing second. His jaw clenched, and as more cries came from the guards, he bolted the door behind him and rushed to the side of the tub. "Elara, what happened? Oh fucking *gods*, who did this to you?"

I tried to move away from him. "Rook, you need to go."

The confusion that crossed his face crushed me. "Elara, please, what happened? I nearly went mad last night." He put his hand behind my head, trying to draw me close. I refused to look at him, my lip trembling. "My love, please, I couldn't find you, and then I felt - my love, look at me. *LOOK AT ME.*"

I turned to him slowly, the tears still not stopping. My eyes met his. "You need to go."

"I don't understand." He brought his other hand to my face. "What was that? What happened to you?"

"Theron knows." I winced as I shifted in the warm water, and Rook's eyes flashed down to my throat, across my chest, then back up to mine.

"What do you mean?" His voice dropped, low and lethal. "Elara, what did he do?"

I shook my head. "Please don't make me say it."

Rook's eyes darkened. "Did he…" He trailed off, and I felt the bubbling rage well up inside myself, burning under my rib cage painfully. "He did this to you?"

"I have to marry him," I said, pushing Rook's hands away and slumping over the side of the bathtub. "I have no choice. He'll hurt you if I don't. And I can't -"

Rook was in front of me, his face desperate. "Elara, what are you talking about? *Marry* him? You're mine, you're *mine*, and he said we'd be free. Wh-what did he do to you?"

"Once I give him an heir, perhaps then, I can negotiate your release."

Rook coughed in disbelief. "An *heir*?" He held my shoulders gently. "My love, tell me what he did."

I put my arms around his neck and began to sob. "You need to go. Please, I don't want him to hurt you."

Rook drew back a little and looked down into my face. "What did he do?"

"I cannot live in a world where you are not," I said.

He cradled my face in his enormous hands. "I need you to tell me what he did."

"He knew." I shook my head. "He knew the whole time."

"What did he know?"

"What you are to me." I heaved in a breath, panic threatening to crush the air from my lungs. "He knows, he's always known. He let us be close, he let us fall in love. He wanted us close so it would hurt so much more." A gasping sob escaped me."He just gave us hope. We were fools, Rook. He was never going to let us go. It was all a game to him." I pressed my eyes shut, trying to erase the look of anguish and bewilderment in Rook's face. "You need to leave me. This is the only thing I can do to keep you safe."

Rook pressed his forehead against mine. "I'm going to fucking kill him."

My eyes flew open. "No! You have to promise me, swear to me, you won't do anything." I clutched on to him. "You promised me you would live for both of us, swear to me, swear to me that you will keep that promise."

There was an eruption of sound on the other side of the door, guards yelling and banging on the door.

I kissed Rook tenderly. "You need to go."

"I won't." He held me to him. "My oath, princess, have you forgotten it?"

"Please." I nuzzled into his neck, one last time, breathing him in, bidding a silent farewell to the other half of me. "I need you to live."

"And I need you," he murmured as the thudding against the door grew louder. "How am I meant to go on without you?"

I clung on to him. "Think of that beach, the turquoise water, the twin moons rising above us. Think of me, and I will meet you there." I pulled back and looked into his eyes. "In our dreams, I will meet you there. In that place where we will wake up together every morning."

Rook's face crumpled. "Elara, *no*."

They were trying to break down the door, the loud rhythmic beating of an ax tearing through the wood. Rook let out a heavy breath through gritted teeth.

"I will save you," he said, "I will. One way or another. I

will take you home." I began to sob louder, and he pressed a kiss against my quivering lips. "I love you. And I will love you for all eternity."

The door splintered and swung open, a flurry of guards rushing into the room. I cried out as they seized Rook, dragging him from the room, his eyes staying on me.

"I swear it," he said over the guards shouts, "I swear to you, my love."

I fell over the side of the tub, wailing as the sound of the guards drifted away down the passageway. Drusilla hovered near the doorway, but her shoulders fell in defeat and she turned away, back into the bedchamber.

I stayed in the water until the cold bit into my skin. All I could feel was the hollow thump of Rook's anguish, anchored in the center of my chest. My fingers still burned with the feeling of him, that last touch forever etched on my skin.

My chambers were swiftly moved from my isolated room in the tower to the rooms adjoining Theron's. As the guards opened the immense double doors before me, revealing this new prison, I stood rooted to the spot, staring into the brightly lit room, dappled with warm sunlight.

It may as well have been a tundra. I shivered as I crossed the threshold, and my wrists burned as though shackled. As soon as my feet touched the floor, on the other side of that life where I'd once had hope and now had nothing, I felt something within me die. A small spark, a fleeting ember that only days before had promised to burn brightly, sputtered and went out. It left behind only coals, cold, empty, and endless black.

I raised my head to take in my surroundings. The room was lovely, of course. Everything was grand and lavish, gossamer curtains and fine velvet furnishings, along with an armoire no doubt full of new dresses. When my eyes landed on the four poster bed in the center of the room I nearly began retching again.

I threw open the window once the servants had finally left, and gulped down the warm summer air. I gazed out over the castle grounds, wondering where Rook was. I could feel him, like a tempest raging below my heart. I tried to shut him out. It would do neither of us any good to remain attached, to cling on to the Bond. The best I could hope for was to become pregnant as quickly as possible, and give Theron his heir. Then I would have some leverage, perhaps, some favor with him.

Then Rook could be free. Even if I could not be. I laughed bitterly. How quickly our positions had been reversed.

Another wave of nausea gripped me as I realized that the seraph heir may have already taken root in my belly. Tears stung my eyes as I thought of that night in the cave. My fingers trembled as they gripped on to the window frame. Gods I hated him. I hated everything about him.

As though my loathing had summoned him, the door opened, and Theron stepped into the room. I turned, glaring over my shoulder at him, saying nothing.

"Dear one," he said, casting an approving glance around the room, "I think these rooms are rather fitting for a queen, don't you?"

"A queen or a slave?" I spat out.

Theron laughed jovially. "Are you still a little cross with me?" He sauntered across the room, smiling at me indulgently. "Now, dearest, that is not how it must always be, you know?"

"Yes, in fact I do know."

His eyes flamed as he understood my meaning. "Is his cock so much more pleasing than mine?"

"I find willingness tends to make the act more pleasant." I looked back out over the gardens, my eyes slamming shut as I recoiled at Theron's touch on my back.

"Then perhaps next time you should not resist me." His breath was hot on my ear.

"Fuck you." I attempted to move away from him, but he grasped me roughly and pulled me back to him. His green eyes bore into mine.

"I told you what the consequences of saying no to me are, did I not?"

"And what are the consequences of telling you to fuck off and die?" I hissed.

Theron bared his teeth in a venomous grin. "Perhaps we should see how all this fire and spark may be used to please me in my bed, madam."

"Go on then." I leaned against him, lifting my chin defiantly. "Defile me again if you so please. Do not think for one moment that I will ever give myself to you willingly."

He gripped my hair, his nails raking at my scalp. "Then I will take what I wish."

I bit back tears, hoping he did not see the trembling of my lips. I tried to wrench out of his grasp, but his fingers held firm. His eyes remained locked on mine, his lips curling into a smirk.

"Was he such a good lover?" He asked slowly.

"That's all you can think of, isn't it?" I spat at him. "That is the singular thought in your mind, that he had my body."

"He took what was mine to possess."

"He didn't *take* anything." My lips twisted into a smile as tears ran down my cheeks. "I begged for him. I begged him to fuck me."

Theron's eyes narrowed. "Oh you did, did you? Begged like a hungry little whore, hmm?" He yanked my hair harder. "Rook was only too happy to oblige, of course."

"It was *bliss.*" I sneered at him as his eyes blazed. "*You* had to force yourself on me in a fucking cave, where no one could hear me, where I was completely at your mercy. Do not for one moment ever *dream* of comparing yourself to him. You will *never* have what he had."

Theron released me roughly, stepping back from me with a swish of his wings. He clasped his hands behind his back and gazed out the window, a slow smile spreading across his face.

"But I do not need to have what he had, dear one. For now I shall have what he will never know again, and in plain sight too." He turned back to gaze at me, tilting his head slightly. "He will watch you marry me. He will watch your belly grow with my child. He will be forced to see all of it. And *that* will give me more satisfaction than if you opened those legs of yours willingly."

Nausea washed over me as I turned away from him, clutching a hand to my stomach. "You're a fucking vile monster."

"I have organized a celebration, tomorrow night," Theron went on, ignoring me entirely. "An engagement party, if you will. I expect you to dry those pathetic tears by then, and show the kingdom what a pretty face you can have when you're not moping."

"Fuck off." I crossed the room and climbed into bed, pulling the covers over my head.

"You will be ready," he said, and his footsteps moved across the hardwood floor, coming to a stop beside me. "Perhaps I shall visit you tonight, dear one. First I have some business to attend to."

I buried my face in the pillow to muffle my sobs. Finally, his footsteps retreated, and the door closed behind him. I was alone in this ridiculously ornate room, crying so hard I couldn't breathe.

I didn't know what to do. I was so overwhelmed with hopelessness, with crushing defeat, I felt faint.

Elara. Rook's voice brushed against my mind, soft like silk. *My love. I cannot bear this.*

I pushed him away, and cried until I made myself sick, stumbling from the bed to retch in the basin again. My throat was raw and my eyes burned. There was nothing, *nothing* I could do. I could not even keep my body from Theron. Everything I had was his. Everything I was and had ever been was now his. He'd laid claim to it all - Keir's life and indeed his death, my home, my parents, my love for Rook, all of it. Nothing now belonged to me. It all merely existed for him to cause more pain, to twist and torture in whatever way he saw fit.

Still I felt Rook in my chest, like a fire storm, raging in a sea of despair. The Bond between us was no longer pulled taut - it threatened to tear me apart, straining at my rib cage.

Perhaps this is what it would feel like to die of a broken heart.

Chapter 37

Rook

A breeze blew in through the shattered window, reminding me that I'd smashed it sometime in the night. The chair I'd hurled in my rage lay in three pieces on the stone floor. Thunder rumbled as the sky darkened.

Elara's despair thumped in my chest, but every time I reached out to her, she slipped through my fingers, like sand, like mist. She was trying to protect me. Trying to shield me from her anguish.

As though that could ever work. I felt her tears like they were my own, a hot, steady stream down my face. I clutched a hand to my chest, as though she would be able to feel it, feel my hand reaching out to comfort her.

Fucking Gods, I just wanted to hold her.

My head fell back against the bed, and from my position on the floor I could see the approaching storm, gathering outside the broken window. I'd been locked in my chambers since I'd stormed Elara's room, since I'd seen her beautiful face peppered with bruises, her eyes filled with terror and sadness. Since I'd discovered exactly what had stolen my breath that night when I had run from room to room, trying to find her. When pain had flooded my body, and her screams had been so loud I couldn't hear anything else.

I clasped my head in my hands. Blood trickled down my arm, reminding me of the knife I'd taken to myself, slicing and thrashing at the fucking mark Theron had placed on me. I'd tried to cut it away before, I knew it was useless. It reformed every single time I tried to cut it away. Burned it away. It didn't matter. Nothing worked.

I gritted my teeth as I opened my hand, the tiniest of shadows dancing across my palm. As they grew, a searing pain clawed at the backs of my eyeballs, and I roared. But I kept trying, the pool of black floating higher and higher above me. They undulated, stuttering as the agony tearing through my head became so intense I could barely see.

With a guttural cry I let the shadows fall, and I slammed my fist into the stone floor, recoiling for only a moment before I was on my knees slamming my knuckles into the stones over and over. I only stopped when the wet slap of blood brought me to my senses.

Hurting myself wouldn't help her. It wouldn't help me. But it was all I could do.

There was a sharp rap on the door, and a guard stepped through it, standing to attention as Theron swept in. His gaze moved around the room, and a satisfied smirk spread across his face.

"Rough night, my friend?" He asked, tilting his head as he looked down at my bloody hands and arms.

Wordlessly, I rose my feet. I held his gaze, smearing my hand across my face, leaving long, thick trails of blood behind.

"You're either brave or stupid to fucking show your face in here."

Theron bared his white teeth as he laughed. "Am I supposed to be intimidated?"

"I know what you did to her." White hot rage swelled in my chest.

Theron shrugged, strolling past me to the open window, ducking down to glance out at the dark gray clouds. "And? What are you going to do about it? You know, it's almost a little boring, facing you, knowing you can't do a single fucking thing to hurt me."

Remember your promise. You swore you wouldn't hurt him. You promised her.

"You really thought I didn't know, didn't you?" He turned to face me, spreading his wings so he could lean against the window frame, crossing his arms over his chest.

"Know what?"

"That she is your Mate, my friend." His mouth twitched, an eyebrow lifting. "As I said to the princess, I thought it was just fucking. We all know how much you enjoy that." His eyes narrowed. "But no, it was much more than that, wasn't it?"

"Yes." Blood was running down my fingers, dripping onto the floor. My hands had started to ache, but not just with the pain of pounding them into the stones. No, they ached with the need to squeeze the very life out of Theron's body, crush his windpipe until those venomous green eyes went glassy and vacant.

"Extraordinary." Theron stroked his chin thoughtfully. "I never could have guessed that such a gift could be handed to me. I certainly won't make the same mistake I made last time."

"Last time?"

He nodded as a flash of lightning illuminated the room. "Giving your enemy nothing to lose is an unwise move. Killing your wife, and not just your wife, but your *son* as well. That was a mistake. I was foolish. I mean, it broke you certainly." His mouth twitched. "But it did not… Bridle you. Not the way I would wish."

My hands balled painfully into fists, the broken flesh stretching across my knuckles. "Don't talk about my wife or my son."

"I had her brought to me, did you know?" He chuckled. "Celeste. When they carried her into the palace. She was laid out for my inspection. You were a lucky man, Rook. She was a true beauty. Those breasts of hers." He gave a low whistle. "Perfection."

"Enough."

"There is something about the female form, is there not, when it finds itself in a state of fertility." Theron sucked in a breath and growled low in his throat. "I confess, it's something I look forward to. Fucking my Queen while she is round with my child."

I wanted to turn away from him, but I was frozen to the spot, watching the delight on his face grow with each passing second. I wanted to smash his fucking head into the wall until there was nothing left but blood and brain matter.

"It must be hard for you," he went on. "Knowing my seed may have taken hold already, when yours merely lay inside her uselessly. Knowing that the only child you will ever know is dead, buried here somewhere." His eyebrows shot up suddenly. "Oh, I do wonder what that will feel like for you, when your Mate is carrying another's child? Surely that will be torturous?" He took two sidling steps towards me, tilting his head pensively. "As torturous as it must have been when you felt me take her."

I had sworn it to her. I had promised her I wouldn't hurt myself. I wouldn't hurt Theron. But with every venomous word that dropped from his lips, my rage became more blinding, more all-consuming. My fists were shaking at my sides.

"It was a dream, finally taking her." Theron stepped closer to me again. "Such soft skin."

"Stop."

"That mouth…" He grinned, licking his lip. "Delicious."

"Stop this." Red seeped at the corners of my vision. Shadows danced across my fingertips, the slave mark burning on my arm, the clawing pain at the back of my eyes returning.

"Her cunt is so fucking tight." He was right in front of me now. "You wouldn't believe how wet she was for me."

"Enough." My shoulders were heaving as shadows moved up my arms.

"And the sounds she makes when she comes." Theron exhaled heavily. "Magical."

With a roar, my hands were around his neck. Theron recoiled for only a second as I slammed him into the ground. I fought the searing pain that burned in my head as I wound my shadows around his throat, the sharp tug of Elara's anguish in the center of my chest spurring me on.

"I'M GOING TO FUCKING KILL YOU!" I bellowed, fighting for breath as I pulled the shadows tight around Therons' neck.

He grinned even as he spluttered, as he saw my own eyes widen as I tried to breathe. The pain in my head threatened to split my skull, but I held tight. If I died killing him, then so be it. Elara would be free of him at least.

The door flew open, guards running into the room. I summoned another shadow and threw it in front of them, doubling over as the pain tore through my body. My limbs burned as though on fire, and I tasted blood, feeling it run down my chin.

Theron's eyes were wide now, bloodshot as he suffocated. His tongue lolled out of his mouth as he gasped for breath.

My own vision was going gray, my mind failing as agony claimed me. I began coughing up more blood, my lungs draining of air right along with Theron's.

Then she was there, in my head, screaming. Begging me to stop. Pleading with me. She could feel it happening. She could feel me dying. She could feel me breaking my promise to her.

A sharp pain in my side stopped everything. My shadows fell, and Theron rasped and hacked underneath me. I fell back from him, onto the floor, and looked down at the dagger lodged between my ribs. I met his eyes, and his chest heaved as he leered at me triumphantly.

"She truly brings out the best in you, doesn't she, my friend?"

Guards crowded Theron as I slumped to the cold stones. I pulled the dagger from my side, and felt a sharp pain in my chest. It hurt to breathe. Blood poured from the wound onto the cold stone floor, and Elara's sobs echoed in my head.

I'm sorry. I wasn't strong enough.

I clenched my eyes shut.I was a fool. I'd made her a promise, and now I'd simply left her alone. I'd broken my oath.

I'm sorry. I love you.

And still she screamed and raged, begging me to live.

Elara had told me how she had woken up in the castle after the battle in Grixos, confused that she was alive, and in pain, and not in Nav. I understood that as I woke, pain shooting through my side.

Regan was looking down at me critically as my eyes opened. "Norahi, you're a fool."

"We've established that," I said with a groan as I tried to sit up.

"Don't," Regan snapped. "Stay where you are, you're still healing."

"Lucky me," I said, trying to raise my arm and wincing. I eyed Regan's displeased face. "I don't know why you're looking at me like that, your King's still alive isn't he?"

"He is, thankfully." Regan turned to the guards standing watch and waved them away. "Leave us."

The guards left the infirmary, the heavy oak door falling closed behind them. Regan turned to me, and the urgency in his face caught me by surprise.

"Elara is safe," he said quietly, "I swear to you, she will be safe. And when the time is right, you will need to get her out of here."

I stared at him, trying to absorb what he was saying. "What are you -"

"The next eclipse, it is coming," Regan interjected, "and with that will come her power. She is the heir to the Sun Throne, you knew that didn't you?"

"Ye-Yes," I stuttered, trying to understand why Theron's advisor was telling me all of this. "But what does that have to do with her power? Peyrus is gone."

"Elara is the one true Queen of Korbiriya, and when she comes into her power, she will be the target of every race wanting to seize that power," Regan said. "She will need your protection. You are her Bonded, the joined sun and moon, just as the prophecy said."

The clouds began to clear from my head, but I still didn't understand. "What prophecy?"

Regan sighed impatiently. "The child of the sun, born

under the darkened moon, shall light up this Realm. She is the Sun, and her beloved is the Moon, and the stars."

My heart skipped a beat. "You mean - you mean you all knew? That she and I are meant to be together?"

"Yes, we knew. But Theron knows too, and that is why we must be exceedingly careful and wait for the right time."

"Theron knew?" My head was still foggy, and my tongue was muddled as I tried to find the words I was looking for. "But, if he knew-"

"The war, on Peyrus." Regan shook his head. "Did you never ask yourself why he declared it? It wasn't for lands, what would he do with those? It was for *her*."

I stared at him, mouth agape. "To claim her for himself?"

"I'm sorry you suffered for this," Regan told me, putting a hand on my shoulder. "I am so, so sorry, Rook. But we need to protect her, and when I give you the signal, you will need to run. You will need to take her, and get as far away from Veles as possible."

The door opened, and one of the healers walked in, a small, frail woman with wiry white hair. Regan straightened up, his demeanor changed, all urgency gone.

"He is healing well, but some help is in order," he said almost indifferently, before giving me a nod and leaving the room.

I lay back on the bed as the healer worked, trying to absorb what Regan had said. I tried desperately to recall a conversation with my father - had it even been a conversation? Perhaps no more than a snide comment. Something about Peyrus, rejecting the gods. *So close to their faith, but they'll refuse this now*. I hadn't understood. I'd had no idea what he meant. But now I knew. I'd been destined to be with Elara, and her father had refused. He'd rejected the prophecy, the gods and his faith.

If I ever saw Vayr again, I'd beat the shit out of him. He'd put Elara in so much danger.

An agonising wave of grief washed over me as it sank in - that I could have been her husband by now. We could have been together, all this time. She would have been safe, and protected. She might have borne a child by now - our child. Gods fuck it all if tears didn't bite at the backs of my eyes.

The healer tutted as she lifted my arm, breaking me from my mournful reverie. "Tried to cut it away again, hmm?" She asked, without a hint of judgment in her voice.

I gave a cynical scoffing laugh. "It was worth a try."

"Don't forget that magic only holds true while he is on the throne," she said slowly.

I looked at her face, as she hummed and kept working, her blue eyes fixed on the wound.

I suddenly felt as though the entire castle was full of double agents and imposters, all merely waiting for the chance to take Theron out and destroy him.

I said nothing as she kept working, the smell of lavender and marigolds filling the air. I closed my eyes and reached out to Elara. Her sadness shivered against me, as though she was trembling in my arms, my blood pulsing right along with hers.

My love. I'm alright. I'm here.

Meet me in the temple when you're recovered, if you can.

I couldn't help but smile at the sound of her voice, washing over me like a breeze through the trees.

I will.

I'd wait for Regan's signal. I'd protect her. I'd get her safe, and we'd leave this wretched palace far behind us. I just had to wait for the signal.

Chapter 38

Rook

As soon as I was on my feet, I was hauled in front of Theron.

The throne room was full of its usual crowd of simpering courtiers, all giving me the obligatory stares of distaste and disappointment.

I shook the guards off and strode the rest of the way to the throne - the thrones, now. My step faltered for only a moment as my eyes settled on Elara, sitting beside Theron on her own ebony throne. Her blue eyes fixed on me, a tiny smile ghosting across her lips.

She was so beautiful she took my breath away. Her hair cascaded loose over her shoulder, a small glittering diadem perched on her head. She was wearing a sapphire blue dress, which made her eyes even more startling. There was an ache in the center of my ribcage as the Bond pulled me towards her, arching and stretching as the need to just touch her overwhelmed me.

Her lips trembled as I stopped in front of the dais, my hands clasped behind my back.

Theron regarded me with a grin. "I'm glad to see you recovered, Your Highness."

My hands flexed as I remembered the feeling of Theron's throat being crushed by my shadows. "Likewise, Your Majesty," I said with a smile. I dipped my head, gesturing to the bruises that were still visible above the collar of his blue jacket. "Shadows do always leave such a lasting mark, don't they?"

Theron lifted an eyebrow as his grin dissipated. "Oh it's nothing, I assure you. I like to wear such injuries, like a badge of honor."

"Indeed." My gaze strayed back to Elara, whose eyes were still fixed on me, her hands clasped in her lap.

"My fiance looks beautiful today, doesn't she?" Theron said, turning to look at her. "We had to cancel our engagement party after our little scrap." He turned back to me. "But now that you are recovered we can proceed with the arrangements."

"How wonderful for you."

Theron laughed out loud. "Now, now, no need for cynicism, Rook." He rubbed his chin, and gave Elara a sideways look. "Dear one, you must be glad to see your Bonded up and recovered again?"

Elara's eyes dropped from my face, to her clasped hands, and she nodded. "I am, Sire."

"Won't you go and give him your hand?" Theron asked, gesturing to me with a nod of his head.

Elara sucked in a breath, wincing. "Sire, I'm sure this isn't necessary."

"Go on." Theron lounged back in his throne, wings spread wide behind him. "Show the court what a Fae Bond looks like. They've never seen such a thing before, not up close like this. What a spectacle."

My fingernails were biting painfully into my palm. Gods I wanted to tear him to fucking shreds, and the mark on my arm burned as those murderous thoughts raced through my head.

With a sigh, Elara rose from the throne and walked towards me slowly. With every step the coil between us wound tighter and tighter, the ache almost taking my breath away. The courtiers were totally silent, as though awaiting an explosion, or fireworks.

Elara stopped in front of me, her eyes lifting to gaze at me. A single tear ran down her cheek as she gave me a small smile.

"My love," I murmured, my hands dropping to my sides, fighting the urge to take her in my arms.

"Are you alright?" She asked me.

I nodded.

Her eyes darted around us, her lip trembling.

"Hey." I smiled at her as her gaze landed back on me. "It's alright."

I extended a hand to her, and she tentatively took it. The feeling of her skin blazed through me, heating my blood, longing and sadness flaring at the back of my skull. Her fingers curled around mine, holding tight, and she took another small step closer to me. Her chin was mere inches from my chest. I wanted to crush those trembling lips under mine, hold her in my arms, feel her skin and smell the delicate scent of roses in the crook of her neck.

Theron broke into applause suddenly, and Elara jumped, that movement jerking her against me. Instinctively, I put my arm around her shoulders, and a collective gasp went up from the courtiers. Elara tried to step out of my grasp, but I couldn't let go of her. I was frozen with her in my arms, and she realized it too, because her head fell against my chest as she began to sob.

"Oh, I must say, this is most curious." Theron rose to his feet. "It truly is something you cannot fight. Look at you now, holding your future Queen like she is your lover, with no fear, right in front of your King."

"What else can you do to her that you have not already done?" I asked. "What else can you do to me?"

Theron shrugged. "I wouldn't doubt my creativity if I was you," he said. "She is strong, but everyone has their breaking point. Everyone has their weakness, and I am rather skilled in discovering precisely what that weakness is."

Elara's hands grasped onto my shirt as another sob burst from her. I clutched her tighter to me, my fingers tracing over the back of her neck gently.

"It's alright," I murmured, lowering my mouth to her ear. "It's alright, my love." More lies. It wasn't alright, it was far from fucking alright. Theron snapped his fingers, and footsteps thundered towards us. Elara's head snapped up to look at me, panic twisting her tear-stained face.

"Rook," she gasped.

"The temple," I murmured. "Meet me there."

Guards tore me away from her, one of them yanking Elara's arm so she stumbled.

"You touch her like that again and I'll break your fucking ribs," I snarled at him.

The guards laughed heartily as they pulled me away. "Give it a rest, Norahi".

The guard who had a hold of Elara jerked her back towards the thrones, and she tried to cover her face with her hands as she cried. The guard held her hands down by her sides.

"You watch while they drag your lover away, you filthy whore," he said to her with a hacking laugh.

My rage flared so violently it felt like my face was on fire, and I threw the guards off me, aware of a bone snapping as I put my foot into someone's leg. I stormed to the guard holding Elara, whose sneer quickly dissipated as he stumbled away from her.

I seized him by the neck. "What the fuck did you say to her?"

He gasped and spluttered, looking to Theron for intervention, but none came. Even the other guards must have been stopped, for no one rushed at me, trying to get me off this simpering fool.

I pounded a fist into the guard's side, feeling bone give away. The guard's eyes widened as he sucked in a croaking breath. I threw him to the ground and stomped on his ribcage, satisfied when I felt more ribs breaking, and then I couldn't stop myself, all the rage and hatred and anger I bore Theron but could not take out on him, making me blind.

By the time I managed to breathe again, by the time my vision cleared of the red haze that had enveloped me, the guard was dead. A bloody, twisted torso, mouth torn open in his last moments of immense pain.

Theron was laughing. I turned to him, blood on my fists, splattered all over my legs. Elara's face was white with shock, her hands trembling.

"You see, dear one?" Theron said, ambling down the stairs of the dais. "This is who your beloved truly is."

"You baited him," Elara said, her shoulders heaving. "You baited both of us. This is all a game to you."

"He's a murderer," Theron spat, his head snapping towards her. "A cold-blooded killer. An animal."

The collective gasp in the throne room as Elara launched herself at Theron was almost deafening. I took a step back in surprise myself, watching as Elara knocked Theron to the ground, her fists pounding into his face.

"HE IS NOT AN ANIMAL!" She screamed. "YOU'RE THE FUCKING ANIMAL! YOU'RE A FUCKING RAPIST AND A MURDERER!" Her fist landed in his throat, and I sank to my knees as the breath was knocked out of me, my hands clutching my neck.

Elara stopped instantly, and her face twisted from anger to anguish. "Oh Gods, what have I done?" She scrambled across the floor towards me. "Rook, my love, I'm sorry, oh Gods, I'm so sorry." She'd almost reached me when the guards seized her, dragging her away from me as she cried out for me.

"I'm alright," I called after her in a broken voice. "It's alright, my love."

Theron sat up, laughing as blood ran down his chin. "Take the Princess back to her quarters," he said, getting to his feet. "And take the prince back to his chambers. Ensure he does not leave, and see to it that the restrictions in his mark now extend to trying to reach out to his beloved over this fucking Bond."

"No!" Elara screamed as they hauled her out of the throne room. "Rook! NO! NO!"

Her voice was in my head, calling out to me as she was taken further and further away. But then the mark began to burn, and the searing pain tearing at the back of my head drowned her voice out.

She sensed my pain, and with a knot of anguish that threatened to cut off my breathing, she let go of me.

Chapter 39

Rook

The silence in my head was terrible. It was worse than hearing her and knowing she was within reach and yet so far away. At least I'd been able to hear her. Now I could merely feel her sadness and hopelessness roiling in my chest like an ocean in a storm, but I couldn't tell her I loved her, that I was alright. Nothing.

I lay on my bed, staring at the ceiling, and thought of nothing but her. Her smile, the high tinkling sound of her laugh. The feeling of her hair running through my fingers. Her breath against my skin. The taste of her lips. The taste of…

With a sigh I rolled on to my side. Rain dripped in through the broken window. I shouldn't have been thinking about sex, not now. But once the thought crept into my head it was all I could think of. Elara's legs wrapped around my waist, her sweat on my skin, her moans as I drove myself into her.

Sex with Elara wasn't just sex. I'd never experienced anything like it before.

It was more than love, more than a physical experience,

more than a feeling or an emotion. I had never lost myself in another person like that. I was joined with her, and she possessed all of me so completely that it hurt.

The sharp wrench in my chest almost distracted me from the growing bulge in my groin, and I groaned with frustration. I wanted to get her out of here. I wanted to hold her in my arms, and make sure she was safe, take her home. And then I wanted to fuck her relentlessly for a week.

My arousal must have been more overwhelming than I realized, because there was a brief flare of confusion in my chest. Elara could still feel what I was feeling. Quickly confusion gave way to something warm and soft, and I sensed her thoughts mirrored my own, tracing over my skin like velvet.

If we couldn't speak to each other, if I couldn't hear her voice and comfort her, at least I could do this. At least I could control my emotions, and pass her my love and desire, not just sadness and anguish. I conjured up every moment I'd been in her bed, the sounds she made, the feeling of her dripping wet cunt around my cock. I palmed myself through my pants, imagining it was her hand.

The heat in my chest swelled and grew, grazing across my ribcage and coursing through my bones. I closed my eyes and saw her hair tumbling down her back as she rode me, feeling her come on me again and again. I rolled onto my stomach and ground into the mattress, the soft haze of her love enveloping me. I wondered where she was, what she was doing. Was she in her own bed, her fingers buried deep inside her as she thought of me, wishing it was my cock instead? Was she in the bath, writhing in the warm water as her hands moved over her rosy nipples, her mouth falling open in a moan?

I imagined taking one of those nipples in my mouth, hearing her gasp as I sucked. Her hand wrapped around me, each tug of her hand along my length drawing me closer and closer to climax as she begged me to fuck her. I remembered rolling her on to her knees, fucking her from behind, my hands raking through her hair. Her shuddering breath as she tried to stay quiet, her lips quivering as she kissed me.

With a grunt I shoved my hand into my pants, pumping myself furiously as I felt something sharp and aching burst within me. "That's my girl," I growled to the empty room. "Come for me."

That soft, sweet inferno consumed me as I released onto the bed with a strangled moan. My cock twitched in my hand, my shoulders heaving as I tried to catch my breath. Her contentment was warm on my shoulders, like sunlight. I smiled to myself, burying my face in my pillow, imagining it was her - her breasts, her thighs, the soft rose-scented crook of her neck.

Thunder rumbled outside, and I turned my head to look at the darkened sky. Tonight was the engagement party, which I, for some unfathomable reason, was expected to attend. I dimmed the thoughts of what Theron was playing at quickly. I wanted to hold on to this, *this*, the warmth and contentment and softness that buzzed in my chest. I imagined her under my arm, her fingers tracing tiny circles on my skin as she shuddered against me, as her body came down from the peak we had just reached together.

Once my breathing had steadied and my skin had cooled, I tore the soiled blanket from the bed, discarding it in the corner. I filled the tub, stripping off my clothes and sinking into the steaming water. I lay my head back, closing my eyes as thunder rumbled loudly overhead.

My mind wandered to what Regan had said to me. I still didn't trust him. For all I knew it was yet another trap, yet another device Theron had engaged to torture me, to give me hope only to have it dashed again. But something in his tone, the urgency in his eyes, allowed me to feel the tiniest sliver of anticipation.

Then the realization that she and I were meant to be together, had been meant for each other all these years bore down on me. Why had my father insisted I marry Celeste, if he knew of the prophecy? My eyes fluttered open. Elara had been bonded to Keir. If she and I had been meant for each other, destined for each other… I chewed my lip as lightning flashed. Something the priestess had said ghosted at the periphery of my mind, but I couldn't quite grasp it.

This didn't make any sense. None of it did. The brutish part of me wondered why my father hadn't simply seized Elara from Peyrus, taken her to Isambard if her father had been so resistant. But that would have been wrong. That would have made us no better than Theron declaring war to try and claim her. But the thought wouldn't let me go, and I wished I could ask my father, have some sort of explanation for what he had done.

I did know now, however, that there was something else at play. Something had been done, and my life, and Elara's, had been meddled with. I just hoped we'd both survive Theron's games so we could find out why.

I was escorted by several guards to the banquet hall, where a lively crowd was gathered. Music played and wine was flowing. Everyone was dressed in white and gold, as was custom for announcements like this. Candles lit every corner of the room, and the windows were lit up by lightning sporadically, as the storm continued to circle outside.

Once in the hall, the guards fell away, leaving me to move through the crowd. I hesitated for a moment, wondering why Theron did not see me as a threat in this room. But after the altercation in the throne room two days previously I didn't want to cause any more trouble. If there was indeed a plan in place, I had to keep calm and wait for the signal, like Regan had said.

I moved towards the thrones, where Theron was sitting and talking animatedly, his body turned towards… Towards her.

She looked like a goddess. Her pale hair hung to her waist in luscious curls, a golden diadem crowning her head. She wore a flowing white gown that exposed her shoulders, and I had to suck in a steadying breath as I imagined tracing my lips over that skin.

Gods she was beautiful.

Her face bore an expression of indifference as Theron talked to her, but then her head turned, her blue eyes landing on me. A small smile spread across her face. Theron followed her gaze, and threw his hands up as he smiled widely.

"Rook! You made it!" He said, rising to his feet, approaching me and clapping me on the shoulder. He looked me up and down approvingly. "You look so well, my friend. Does he not, dear one?" He looked up at Elara, who gave a small nod.

"He does." Elara's face flickered with uncertainty before the mask was back. She looked at Theron haughtily as she rose to her feet. "I'm thirsty, I need some wine."

"But of course." Theron took her hand as she passed him, raising it to his lips. "Why doesn't Rook accompany you?"

I swallowed down my sigh of frustration. His games were

simply exhausting. He wanted to push us together only to pull us apart like his own sick puppet show. It didn't matter that I'd tried to kill him barely a week ago, it didn't matter that two days ago Elara had tried to beat the life out of him - he saw neither of us as a threat.

I didn't betray my emotions, simply took Elara's hand in mine, tucking it under my arm and giving Theron a warm smile.

"I'll look after her, don't worry," I told him. I steered her across the room, towards the windows. I felt her slump a little, melting into me. I leaned down to her ear. "This afternoon was nice."

Her eyes flicked up to meet mine, and her lips parted in shuddering breath. "It was."

"What were you thinking of?" I asked, clutching her hand tighter.

"That afternoon, by the stream," she murmured, bringing her face closer to mine. "And you?"

"Fucking you from behind in your bed," I whispered in her ear, and a small moan broke from her.

"This is torture." She drew back from me with a sigh.

"I'm sorry," I said, the sadness on her face tearing me apart. "I shouldn't have said anything."

She quickly shook her head, gesturing to a servant for wine. "It's not your fault." Her gaze became lethal as it wandered across the room, in Theron's direction. She snatched the proffered goblet of wine from the servant without looking at him and took a large gulp. "Gods I hate him. I hate these games he's playing with us."

I thought for a moment of telling her about Regan, but decided against it. She'd suffered enough, she didn't need her hopes dashed yet again when Regan turned out to be nothing more than Theron's snake in the grass.

Her gaze moved back to my face when I didn't respond, and her brow furrowed as her eyes settled on my lips.

"He hasn't been..." She trailed off, and shook her head. "He hasn't come to see me."

My stomach churned, and her hand burned in mine as I held her tighter. "Good."

A cynical laugh broke from her. "Though tonight that might change. Once he's had his fill of wine, who knows -"

I tugged on her hand and pulled her through the open doors out onto the balcony. No one tried to stop us, I doubted anyone had even seen us. Elara didn't resist, following me out and pushing me against the wall as soon as we were out of sight. I crushed her mouth under mine, my fingers threading through those soft golden curls, groaning as she pressed herself against me.

"Someone will see us in a moment," she murmured, her voice wavering. "They'll come and tear me away from you. They'll lock you up again."

"Let them try." I kissed her again, feeling her melt into my arms, into that space that had been made for her. Her ribs quivered against my arms as she began to cry softly. "Don't cry, love." I smiled down at her, holding her closer.

Her eyes closed, and she pulled me down so my forehead rested against hers. "I can't do this," she murmured. "I can't live like this. I-I..." She trailed off as she sobbed, and buried her face against me. "I can't sleep, because I'm afraid that if I wake up, he'll be in my bed, and..."

Rage boiled up inside me. Rage and helplessness along with the unrelenting desire to choke the life from Theron.

"I wanted to throw myself off the tower last night," Elara went on, and my stomach dropped. I clutched her close, as the images from my nightmares, of her hanging from her tower, swam before my eyes.

"No, no, my love, don't think like that." Such useless words to say to her. I held her chin gently, so she was looking into my eyes, and smiled. "You must live, remember? If I must live for you then you must live for me."

"Rook…" Her face crumpled.

"There is only hope so long as this is beating." I splayed my hand over her heart, feeling it pound against my palm. "As long as there is life, and breath, there is hope. I swore to you I'd get you out of here, and I will." I pressed a kiss to her forehead.

"We should go back," she said quietly, regret edging her words. "They'll notice we're gone."

"I love you," I said.

Her blue eyes fixed on me, and as she opened her mouth the bark of a guard made her jump.

"Ey!" He stormed towards us, and Elara clutched on to me with trembling hands. "What do you think you're doing?"

I pushed Elara behind me and held up a hand. "The King asked me to look after his bride, and she was overwhelmed." I gave him an amicable smile. "You know how delicate the Fae are, she needed some air."

The guard stopped short, my amiability catching him off guard. He leaned on his spear, peering around me at Elara. I was ready to strike, to beat another one of these bastards to a pulp if they so much as sneered at her. But then he pushed his helmet back from his brow and laughed.

"Oh the females," he said, giving me a knowing look. "Lucky they have us around to look after 'em, ey?"

I laughed and nodded, reaching behind me to take Elara's hand. "Indeed."

The guard walked off with a nod, and I turned around to see a tiny smile ghost over Elara's lips. "Delicate Fae, hmm?"

I smiled and planted a kiss on the tip of her nose. "So delicate. So fragile."

"But a great ass, right?" She lifted an eyebrow.

A low growl rumbled in my throat. "Talk about your ass any more and I'll risk death to drag you down into that garden and fuck you senseless."

Her eyes flamed with alarm and desire, and then the smile dropped. "Don't do that." She sighed, wrapping her hand around my arm. "Take me back inside, Theron will be looking for us."

"My love-"

"I'm sorry," she said, gazing up at me. "I can't bear this."

We walked back into the hall, Theron's gaze landing on us almost immediately. His lips curled into that cruel grin again, and my skin crawled. He would bait us endlessly. He was enjoying this new form of torture. My hand tightened over Elara's as I thought of him, crawling into her bed, drunk and....

"Rook." Elara's voice brought me back into the room. She was looking down at my hands, where shadows swirled from my fingertips. Her eyes moved up to mine, and she shook her head. "You'll hurt yourself."

I was about to tell her that it didn't hurt at all, but Theron approached us, and I pulled the shadows in before he saw them.

"Dear one," he said, extending a hand to Elara, who hesitated for a moment before she stepped away from me, the heat of her hand lingering on my skin. Theron lifted Elara's hand to his lips, and again I felt the cool vapor of the shadows whispering from my fingertips. "Come." Theron tucked Elara's hand under his arm. "It is time to announce our engagement."

I watched them walk to the thrones, the Bond pulling me

along uselessly, leaving me standing as close as I could without Theron noticing my presence. I kept my eyes fixed on her, watching her face become passive, the light and laughter leaving her eyes. Barely a few minutes ago she'd looked at me with passion, and now she was merely a shell.

It was like watching her go into the Pit all over again. All I could do was sit by and watch. I tried to control my rage - she didn't need to feel that as well. This was my burden to bear. My eyes flickered to Regan, who was standing near the thrones, conversing with one of the High Council members. I still wondered what sign I was meant to be looking for, when it would come. How fast could I run with her?

I couldn't fly. I hadn't used my wings, much less shifted into my other form, for over 5 years now. I wondered if I'd still be able to, if I'd still know how to extend those leathery, taloned wings and take off into the sky. Since that wasn't possible, what did Regan expect me to do? They'd catch us if we were on foot, they'd catch us on horseback. Elara could - my breath caught in my throat as the thought occurred to me.

Elara could outrun them on her own. I'd be what slowed her down.

As though sensing my thoughts, Regan's eyes met mine. The tiniest shake of his head answered me. Alright. Not today then. I thought of Elara spending another night in her bed, afraid to sleep. That thought alone made me determined that when the time came, she'd have the head start she needed. I'd give her as much time as I could.

Then she'd be free.

Theron raised his arms, and the room quickly fell silent.

"Good people of Veles, I am pleased to have you all gathered here tonight to bear witness to a joyous occasion," he began, and the courtiers broke into excited whispers. Theron turned to look down at Elara. "The princess of Peyrus has agreed to be my wife."

The courtiers broke into applause, and Theron offered Elara his hand. She took it without looking at him, standing beside him, her eyes still vacant. Theron put an arm around her waist and drew her close, placing a kiss on her cheek. The room exploded with happy sighs and a chorus of *Awwws*. I took three steps closer to the dais out of nothing but instinct, then stopped myself.

Theron smiled indulgently at Elara, who continued to refuse to meet his eyes, staring at something just over his shoulder. "Dearest one, you have made me the happiest man in the realm." His eyes flickered towards me for a moment, the corner of his mouth lifting in a satisfied smirk. "Now, we must plan the ceremony! You will be such a beautiful bride."

Elara said nothing, her head dropping a little.

Theron gestured to me then, and I stepped forward. "Rook, I do wonder if you'd volunteer to give the bride away?" His suggestion was met with disdainful sniggers from the courtiers. Elara's shoulder slumped further, and it was as though I could see the life draining out of her, pooling on the floor around her.

I wanted to tear Theron's fucking head off. "Surely that is a duty that should be assigned to her parents?" I said, trying to stop rage coloring my voice.

"They are in Fiachra," Elara said flatly. "That is not so far that they cannot be here to witness… this."

Theron took Elara's hand and sucked on his teeth. "Oh dear, of course, you don't know yet, do you? I am sorry to spoil the evening."

My shoulders tensed as Elara slowly looked up at Theron.

"What do you mean?" She asked.

Theron sighed. "Well, you see, your parents, they were

taking an alternative route to Fiachra. The mountain passes are thick with snow at this time of year."

Lies, fucking lies. It was summer. My heart began to pound in my chest as Elara's panic rose.

"What alternative route?" She asked, her voice wavering. "Where are they?"

"They went via the Wastes," Theron said, his gaze theatrically mournful. "It is such a harsh place, such an unforgiving landscape." He shook his head. "Who could have foreseen that such a tragedy would befall them."

"What happened?" Elara grabbed on to the collar of his jacket. "Where are they?"

"I am so sorry, dear one." Theron's words did not match the icy look he gave her. "I am told your mother succumbed quickly. Your father followed soon after. Lost to the sands."

Elara's scream sent the room into shocked silence. She stumbled back from Theron, hands outstretched at first, before she began to claw at her head, screaming, screaming. Theron clasped his hands behind his back, watching her rage and cry with a look of deep satisfaction.

I rushed towards her, and she collapsed against me. Her head hung limply, and I realized she'd fainted. I scooped her up in my arms, the courtiers all covering their mouths in shock, eyes darting around the room.

Theron met my eyes with a smile. "Such a delicate creature, is she not?"

My chest was heaving, hot with rage. "They're really dead?" I asked.

Theron nodded. "Such an unfortunate accident. A tragedy." He waved his hand. "Take her to her chambers."

I nodded and turned.

"She will need a rest before I visit her tonight." His words followed me as the courtiers parted, letting me pass. I clutched her to me, my breathing quickening, rage tearing its way up my spine.

I thought for a moment of running right then and there. Fuck Regan and his plans. I had to protect her. I couldn't take her back to that room. I couldn’t put her in that bed knowing what was going to happen to her when Theron slunk into the chambers under the cover of darkness.

But then I was surrounded by guards, a spear pressed to my back, and I was escorted through the palace to Elara’s chambers.

“Go on then, Norahi,” a guard said once we’d reached Elara’s bedside.

I held her close, feeling her weight in my arms, the contraction of her ribs as she breathed. I couldn’t put her down, how could I put her down in this bed and leave her here?

“Now.” The guard growled, prodding me in the ribs with his weapon. “I’m not going to say it again.”

I kissed her forehead, my eyes burning. “I’m so sorry, my love.” I put her down gently, then turned to the guard.

“Alright then, out of here.” He commanded.

I’m sorry, Elara.

I grabbed the spear, the guard's eyes widening as he was jerked forward. I twisted, the spear snapping in half at the same time that the guard’s arm was likewise snapped in two. The other guards exclaimed, rushing at me. I shoved the spear into one guard’s neck, pulling it back to slice the blade along another’s throat.

I felt a sharp pain as one guard landed a blade in my side, and I turned on him, pushing the splintered end of the spear into his gut before shoving him at one of his advancing comrades. Once they were impaled, I seized the blade the guard had stuck in my side, jolting it free and landing it in the chest of another guard.

More guards poured into the room, and I roared as my shadows flew from my hands, barely feeling any pain as they enveloped the soldiers. I heard them choking, spluttering as the darkness invaded their lungs and pressed the air from their bodies.

"Enough!" Regan's voice sounded from beyond the shadows, and the slave mark burned violently. "Rook, stop this!"

I gritted my teeth, pulling the shadows towards me and yanking the suffocating bodies of the guards along with them.

"Rook, this isn't helpful!" Regan's voice was sharp and direct, and reminded me of the promise I'd made myself earlier. I would stay calm and not cause trouble until I could run. Until I could buy Elara the time she needed to get as far away from Veles as possible.

The shadows fell to the floor, bouncing from the stones and vanishing. The guards' faces were red, sucking in air, eyes darting around the room as though trying to place what had just happened to them. One of them lunged at me with a strangled cry, and Regan was there, his hand on the guard's shoulder.

"Leave us," he ordered. "And take the dead with you." He snapped as the guards hesitated. They filed out of the room slowly, pulling the bodies out with them, leaving behind scarlet trails of blood on the stone floor.

I became aware of my heaving shoulders, my eyes still stinging with unshed tears. Elara remained unmoving on the bed, her eyes closed. I dipped to my knees and held her hand to my lips.

"I'm sorry, my love."

The door closed behind me, and Regan's footsteps padded closer.

"You must control yourself," Regan said in a low voice.

I rose to my feet, towering over him. "Control myself?" I snarled. "I have to place the woman I love in this bed, knowing what may happen to her when your fucking king comes crawling in here."

"I don't doubt this is painful for you, and I cannot even begin to imagine what this must be doing to her." His eyes flickered briefly to Elara, his gaze softening in that split second. "But you'll be no good to her dead."

"How can I leave her here?" I asked, my voice cracking as helplessness washed over me. "How can I… knowing what he will…" I couldn't say it. I couldn't speak the words.

Regan took a step closer to me. "If it's any comfort at all, I have slipped a contraceptive elixir into her water."

A disbelieving scoff left me. "A fucking *what*?"

"That's all I can do right now," he said urgently, putting a hand on my shoulder. "We have no choice, Rook. We have to do what we must."

"What kind of a fucking plan is this?"

Regan's eyes widened. "Keep your fucking voice down!"

My finger darted in the direction of the bed. "If she is so important, how can you surrender her to *this*? How can you stand by while she is violated? If she is your Queen-"

"This plan is bigger than you or me, even bigger than her." Regan snapped. "I'm sorry, I truly am. I cannot stand how this is playing out. Do you not think me plagued, knowing what she suffers? Knowing what you suffer? I'm not hesitating to torture you. But the time must be right."

"When?" I asked. "Tell me *when*."

"Soon."

"*When*?" I grasped his thin shoulders and shook him. "How much longer am I expected to surrender the woman I love to be raped by your fucking King?"

"Soon." If he said it again I would hit him. "I cannot tell you more. You must... You must control your rage. I have never experienced a Ladaian bond, I have no idea what this is doing to you. But I know for certain, with absolute surety, that if you die, that anguish will end her. We need her." He put a hand on my hand with surprising weight. "And we need *you*. Alive. Both of you. Do you understand?"

Drusilla hurried into the room at that moment, and Regan's hands were already clasped behind his back, the indifferent expression back. Drusilla regarded me uncertainly, edging towards the bed.

"What happened?" She asked, her eyes moving over the blood on the floor.

"The princess had a fainting spell," Regan said, turning to the door. "Norahi and I brought her back, and the guards caused some trouble. See to your mistress, Norahi and I will leave you." He gestured with an open hand to the door, urging me to leave the room.

I turned to look back down at Elara, who slept on, looking like an angel in the cloud of her golden hair. I reached out and ran my fingers down the length of her arm, swallowing all the aching misery that threatened to burst out of me. Regan was right. But leaving her here...

"Norahi." Regan's voice pulled me back from her, away from her, reminding me I had to leave.

My feet were like lead as I backed out of the room, watching Elara's chest rise and fall with every shallow breath.

"Rook," Regan said softly when I stopped, and I realized I was holding on to the door frame. "Please. She needs you alive."

I peeled my unwilling fingers away from the door, and Regan hurriedly closed it before I could storm back in and leap from the window with Elara in my arms. I looked down at him wearily.

"Come now," he said, "you need a healer."

I remember the wound in my side, and shook my head. "I'll be fine."

"You need a healer," he insisted. "Go to your chambers and I will bring one to you."

I nodded, feeling cold and hollow all at the same time. I trudged through the passages to my room, feeling the fight drain from my body. Elara had fought in the Pit for nothing. She had freed her parents, only for Theron to kill them anyway. She had fought for her freedom, only to be Theron's prisoner - worse, his wife. And all I could do was watch.

Back in my chambers, I sat down heavily on the bench at the end of my bed. I held up a hand, summoning the black shadows. With barely any pain. I looked down at my arm, at the slave mark. I brought my arm closer to my face, sure it was just my tired eyes, the dim light of the room.

But no - it had faded. Only a little. Only I would notice, having looked at it every day for five years. But it had faded. I exhaled heavily, wondering what the fuck that could mean.

The healer came, tending to the wound left by the guard, though by that time her attendance was almost unnecessary. New skin had already formed over the wound. She fussed over me with tincture and a motherly warning to stay out of further trouble. Then I was alone again, lying in my bed.

I stared at the darkness, nothing but the faint, dancing moonlight staring back.

Suddenly a weight crashed into my chest, pulling taut and crushing my lungs. Terror. Fear. Ice cold rivulets piercing my veins.

I could do nothing but cry and scream into the darkness surrounding me as I felt Elara being violated yet again. The shadows exploded from my hands, shrouding me in night. I couldn't control them. They swirled and coiled as her anguish reverberated through my body.

I did not sleep that night. Her terror faded into defeat, and I felt her heartbeat falter slightly next to mine. I stayed awake to ensure it did not stop beating. By the time morning came, I was sure I'd shed all the tears I'd ever shed in my lifetime. Her heart felt smaller, as though she was fading away.

As the sun's rays broke through the shattered window, I swore to myself that I would see the light leave Theron's eyes, if it was the last thing I ever did.

Chapter 40

Rook

I spent the next days in a haze of drunkenness. I don't know how much wine I drank, but it was enough to leave me in a mess on the floor, drowning out the sharp pain in my chest every time Theron came anywhere near Elara. The skin on my hands was permanently pink and shiny now, my body struggling to keep up healing from the endless hours I spent pounding my fists into the stone walls.

I could feel her slipping away from me, her soul cracking and shattering, shard after shard falling into a black abyss where I could not reach her.

On the fourth day, the door opened, and Regan stepped in. His nose wrinkled as he looked at me lying on the floor, and even through my bleary-eyed vision I could see the concern on his face.

"Rook, you need to get up and wash," he ordered, his eyes moving to the empty goblet beside me. "Come on, you need to sober up now."

"Why?" I asked, my voice thick. "What could I possibly need to be sober for?"

"This won't help her."

I struggled into a sitting position, draping my arms over my knees. "And being sober will help her, will it?" I shook my head, laughing as the room spun and the floor under me tilted. "I can do nothing but lie here and feel your fucking king violate her, and you want me sober for that?"

"You have to think of her."

I got to my feet as fast as I could, wavering slightly as I towered over Regan's slight frame. "Think of her?" I spat at his feet. "Fucking *think* of her? What do you think I do here all day? What do you think I fucking *do* in here, old man? I *ache* for her. I *die* with her, every single fucking day. Her pain is my pain, and it is all I can do but to think of her." I shoved him in the shoulder, half-heartedly as my blurred vision made my aim weak. "You don't understand anything." I stumbled to the basin and plunged my face into the cold water, scrubbing at my numb face with raw fingertips.

"Rook, she will need you, very soon." Regan had stepped closer, his voice low.

I turned to look at him, steadying myself against the wooden counter. "Stop telling me soon." I gritted my teeth, putting a hand to my chest as I felt another drop of her heart wither, another thread between us twisting painfully. "Soon is not an answer. Tell me fucking *when*."

"Tomorrow." Regan's voice dropped to a whisper.

My stomach dropped, my fingertips clawing painfully into the wood behind me. "Don't toy with me, old man. If you're lying to me-"

"Lord Caedmon has come to offer the king a gift," he interjected, his eyes darting to the door. "Theron will be distracted. When I give the signal, do not hesitate. You take the princess, and you run."

His words had me sober in seconds. "How will we escape? How can I outrun the guards with her?"

Regan shook his head. "No details. You will know." He stepped forward and pulled down the frothy collar of his long black robes. There, on the right side of his skinny neck, was a tattoo. The mark of the sun, no bigger than the tip of my thumb. "Do not trust anyone but the Guild."

"The Guild?" I shook my head.

Regan adjusted his robes, pulling his collar back up. He straightened his back, that indifferent look back on his face. "Until tomorrow." He turned on his heel and left the room.

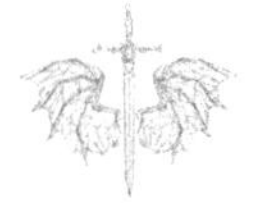

By the time I was summoned the next day, my nerves were frayed. I had not slept that night, looking out at the palace grounds, formulating one escape route after another in my head. Wondering which gate to run to, how many guards there would be. How to get my weapon. How to get Elara her sword. But every single plan ended in failure, and capture.

Fucking Regan. His cryptic messages gave me no comfort nor guidance. There were obviously more players in this game - this mysterious Guild he had mentioned - but anyone could have a sun tattooed on themselves and claim to be an ally. Anyone could be an enemy.

My eyes moved along the line of guards as I was escorted to the throne room, wishing I could see through their armor, see if any of them bore this mark. I tried to analyze each gaze as I passed it - were his eyes softer? Was he blinking, trying to tell me something? I was going to go mad with this.

By the time we reached the throne room I was almost

trembling with anticipation. I had to take several deep breaths before I was admitted. I would give us away otherwise, I would destroy any chance of escape if Theron saw how skittish I was.

I was getting her out of here today. I was going to save her. That was what I had to focus on.

The doors were opened, and I walked in slowly, to the scornful glances of the courtiers. They parted to let me pass, soft whispers and tuts following my steps.

Theron regarded me with amusement, but I barely took any notice. I was too consumed by the sight beside him.

My beloved.

My Bonded.

Her face was ashen, her blue eyes glassy as they gazed at me. The shadows underneath them were deep, as though bruised into her beautiful face. Her lips trembled, her shoulders sagging.

He was killing her. He was killing her spirit, driving her further and further into that place I could not reach.

"Rook!" Theron rose to his feet, golden wings spread behind him. "How are you, old friend?"

"Tired." I did not take my eyes off Elara. Tears began to roll down her face, and as I drew closer I saw the bite marks on her neck. My fingertips cooled as darkness enveloped them.

"Ah that is a shame," Theron said, fingers steepled before him as he watched my approach. "My darling fiancee and I haven't had much sleep either, but for very different reasons, I am sure."

Elara's chin dropped to her chest, and the yearning to take her in my arms coursed over my skin like a flame. The courtiers tittered with amusement, and I wanted to kill every single person in the room. I clenched my hands into a fist as the fading mark on my arm stung, determined to keep my shadows hidden. I still didn't fully understand what was happening, and I did not want to reveal anything at this point. Not when, as Regan had promised, escape was so close.

"Now!" Theron clapped once, and the room fell silent. "Lord Caedmon has kindly offered me a gift to celebrate my engagement, so if you would all follow me, we shall go out into the courtyard."

The courtiers burst into excited chatter, and my eyes scanned the room, looking for Regan. There was no sign of him. Sweat broke out on my upper lip as I followed the others out, two guards flanking me silently. Where the fuck was he? What signal was I waiting for? I felt sick, panic pricking at my lips.

Theron was leading Elara by the hand, and she moved like she was already dead, like her feet were no longer touching the ground. My Bonded was already turning into a ghost.

Not much longer. We'll be out of here soon. I will save you.

Out in the courtyard, Lord Caedmon and his entourage waited. They all bent into low bows as Theron approached, Caedmon rising with a foul smile on his lips. His eyes moved over Elara, with a hungry look that made me want to smash his teeth out of his skull.

"Your Majesty, Your Highness," he drawled. "May I offer my congratulations on your forthcoming nuptials. I wish you both many years of happiness and an abundance of blessings from the Gods."

"Thank you." Theron kissed the back of Elara's hands.

Her eyes remained fixed on the ground. "Thank you." Her voice was hollow. I felt as though a rib had cracked in my own chest.

Not much longer. Not much longer. I gazed again around the courtyard, looking for any sign of Regan. He was still nowhere to be found. My anxiety began to spiral, and Gods I hated that it made Elara look at me. She sensed it, and her eyebrow lifted for the barest of moments before her shoulders drooped again.

Perhaps if the darkness no longer caused me pain…

Theron and Caedmon were engaged in conversation, laughing and joking as though they were old friends and not mortal enemies. They were too engrossed to notice anything but their own words. I tentatively reached out to her, my words traveling the lengths of those silver strands. There was a sting at the back of my eyes, sharp but not unbearable.

Elara.

Her head whipped around to look at me, her lips parted, her eyes wide. Theron began to look up, the sudden movement catching his attention, and her head dropped again, but she could do little to disguise her rapid breathing.

"Are you well, dear one?" Theron asked.

Elara nodded, her eyes fixed on the ground. "It is hot, that is all."

Theron and Caedmon laughed jovially. "Ah the Fae." Theron pressed a kiss to Elara's temple, and she winced. "Such tender creatures." He released Elara to once again speak animatedly with Caedmon, whose entourage now became involved, gesticulating to the sky as they discussed the fantastic gift they had brought for Theron and his new bride.

Elara's head tilted ever so slightly, her eyes moving towards me. *Rook?*

I suppressed a laugh, a sigh of relief, tears, I wasn't sure which. *My love. I missed you so much.*

How is this possible?

My mark is fading. I don't know what is happening.

She lifted her head, and her blue eyes were clearer now as they fixed on me. *Can you summon the darkness?*

I surreptitiously lifted a hand, a tiny puddle of night welling within it.

Then she smiled. A delighted shooting up of her eyebrows, and a smile. I thought my heart would burst as her joy warmed my chest.

I'm getting you out of here. There is a plan in place.

Her eyes fluttered closed with relief. *How? When?*

Wait. And when the time comes, you run. Run and don't stop.

Her eyes opened again, and she gave me a small nod.

A roar from above made us all jump. All eyes flashed to the skies as an enormous shimmering blue dragon flew over our heads. It circled the courtyard, and Theron laughed out loud.

"Oh Caedmon, what a truly brilliant specimen!" He exuded delight as the dragon breathed out a jet of blue flame.

Elara's eyes moved back to me.

Can you do that?

I scoffed. *I'm much more impressive than that sorry looking thing.*

You would say that.

Only because it's true.

Let me guess - you're a giant red dragon.

I grinned at her. *No. Black. And my wings are twice as big.*

Show off.

Gods, the color in her cheeks was coming back. Tears bit at my eyes as I looked at her, as I felt her soul slowly knit itself back together.

At that moment, Regan entered the courtyard. His intense gaze sent a cold shiver down my back. A quick, barely distinguishable jerk of his head confirmed it - we had to move now.

Elara, go.

She understood immediately, stepping sideways behind a duo of entranced courtiers. Theron was still too busy applauding his new scaly pet to notice anything going on around him. He and Caedmon laughed heartily, and I moved around the group of courtiers. Elara took a few more steps backwards, towards Regan.

I glanced around at the guards, who were also too mesmerized by the spectacle above them to notice our trio moving out of the courtyard. I had almost reached her. I was only a few steps away. She reached Regan's side, all of us still looking into the courtyard, checking for confused looks or calls asking what the fuck we were doing.

But none came.

Then her hand was in mine. Cold and small, her delicate fingers dwarfed by mine as our hands entwined. The Bond coiled and pulled tight, almost jerking me forwards, closer to her. She shivered for a moment, feeling it too, but there was no time for anything else.

"Go." Regan stood still as Elara and I moved behind him, through a stone archway and into the open passage that led to the open green, and beyond that - the Gate.

We moved swiftly, Elara's hand clinging to mine as we headed wordlessly along the stones. Regan overtook us, hands clasped behind him. I should have dropped Elara's hand, but I wasn't letting her go now. With Regan ahead of us, no guard should think anything untoward was happening.

So we moved on. I still didn't know what was going to happen. I had no idea how we were going to get out of here, what was awaiting us. I wasn't ready yet to try and unfurl my wings, unsure of what the fading mark would allow me to do. But I could give Elara cover, I could send her on her way.

As though she sensed my thoughts, her fingers held onto mine tighter.

Don't let go. Don't let go of me.

My oath, princess. Have you forgotten it?

Something like a sob escaped her. I couldn't break my

promise. I would run with her. I wouldn't let go of her. I would get her out of here, and safe, to Isambard.

Regan led us down the stone staircase, nodding to the Chief Guard as he passed. The man looked puzzled for only a moment, before he shrugged and resumed his position. Regan walked to the Gate and waved his hand. The guards opened it without so much as a protest.

A flicker of fear passed through me. Why was this so easy? Perhaps I had underestimated Regan's power in the palace. Perhaps there were more members of this Guild than I could have imagined. Either way, we continued to walk unimpeded, into the forecourt. Between us and freedom there now lay only a wooden bridge. A warm breeze blew across the fields, and in the distance we could hear Theron's new pet roaring and breathing fire.

Regan stopped abruptly, and the guards sitting by the bridge looked over at us with mild curiosity. Regan's shoulders lifted as he inhaled, then he turned to face us.

"A lovely day to be by the sea, don't you think?" He asked me, and the corner of his mouth twitched into a grin.

It was then I realized he was speaking my native tongue.

"Run. And do not stop," he went on.

"But how do we -"

"Umbra Furorem." Regan's command was clear.

I looked over at the guards, two of whom had now risen to their feet. Elara clutched on to my arm.

It will get dark. Hold on to me. And run.

She nodded. *Do it.*

The shadows emanated from my hands, and I flung them towards the guards, who barely had time to cry out. Darkness engulfed us, but my eyes saw everything. My dragon eyes. I could see again, like daylight. Elara broke into a sprint beside me, running blind but clutching on to me and moving without a hint of hesitation. Her speed was challenging, but I kept pace. There was wood under our feet, then loose stones. We were on the road.

The swirling darkness remained around us as I unfurled my wings. Pain thumped at my temples, but I gritted my teeth through it. With a loud snap my wings extended behind me, heavy and strange and familiar all at once. I gathered Elara in my arms, and heard her sharp intake of breath as we left the ground.

Oh Gods we were free. I was flying and we were free. The shadows fell away from us, and Elara yelped, clasping on to my neck as the ground below us came into view. It was a long way below us.

"I've got you, it's alright." I smiled down at her, and she returned it slowly. "We're free, my love. I'm taking you home."

She slumped against me and sobbed, her fingertips clawing into my neck. Her relief was so sweet I could taste it, like honey on my tongue.

"It's alright my love." My wings sliced through the air, and we shot through the sky. "We'll be home soon, it's all over."

"Going somewhere?"

The deep voice sounded right behind us, and I looked over my shoulder to see Theron's new pet, the enormous azure dragon, pursuing us over the fields. He bared his teeth at me, grinning, then opened his mouth.

He was going to burn us.

I banked sharply to the left, and Elara shrieked, holding on to me tightly as wind rushed past our ears. The dragon followed easily, swooping and lashing out, slicing a hole through my leathery left wing. This sent me into a drop, and I spun in so we were now facing the huge creature.

"Running away were we?" He asked, flapping his wings as he hovered in front of us.

"Let us go." I clutched Elara to me, desperation and hopelessness crashing so sharply into my gut that I didn't know if it was hers or mine. "You have no quarrel with me, and no loyalty to him."

The dragon seemed to consider this for a moment. "It is true, I have no quarrel with you. I suppose we are cousins, of a sort." He gestured with a taloned claw to my shredded wing. "Sorry about that."

"Please, let us go." Elara looked up at him, tears streaming down her cheeks. "He rapes me. He beats me. Please do not take me back there. Please let us go.

The dragon sighed heavily. "I am sorry to hear that." Then his wings moved in what I suppose would have been a shrug, had he been in human form. "But there is a plan in place, and I have my orders." He swooped towards us.

Elara screamed as I spun in the air and tried desperately to maintain a straight course, throwing the darkness back at the dragon. It was futile. He'd be able to see just as well as I could. It wouldn't buy us any time. The aching in my head was disorienting, and I was losing height, the tops of the dark forest below coming closer and closer.

The dragon sent a flame at us, and it caught the tip of my wing. My feet crashed into the top of a tree, sending us spiraling through the air sideways. Elara slipped out of my grasp, just the tiniest bit, and I held her closer.

"Don't let go!" She cried, burying her face against my neck.

"I've got you, my love." I couldn't outrun the dragon. I couldn't fly with two broken wings. He would catch us.

I swooped into a clearing and… I let go of her. She dropped the few feet to the soft mossy ground and flipped onto her back, eyes wide as she looked up at me.

"Run." I gave her a weak smile. "Run. I'll lead him away."

"No!"

"I love you."

She screamed as I took off into the sky. "Rook! No! No!"

Her cries followed me as I darted through the air, the dragon's roar right at my heels as I tried to rise higher into the sky. Her screams echoed in my head as the dragon sent a flame after me. Her hopeless sobs filled my ears as the flames caught my wing again, the smell of burning flesh filling the air.

"You cannot run from me, demon." The dragon's deep laugh rumbled through the air. "You are weak. You cannot outfly me, or outrun me."

"That's what you think."

He was right of course. My wings were damaged. I was barely able to maintain any sort of altitude. And the pain in my head got worse. But I was buying her time.

Run, my love. Run. RUN.

The dragon's laugh rumbled again. "They already have her, cousin. You are such a fool."

Elara's screams echoed in my head as the dragon's flames lay waste to my wings. I hit the ground, and was aware of nothing after that.

Chapter 41

Rook

The splash of cold water in my face woke me.

I started up, but my arms were stopped short by chains. I blinked away the water that clung to my lashes, and looked up into Theron's smirking face.

"Good morning," he said brightly. "How are we feeling?"

"Where is Elara?"

He threw his head back and laughed. "Oh don't worry about her." He ran his tongue along his teeth and shrugged. "A shame your little plan didn't work. That Regan." He waggled a finger in the air. "Sneaky. Very sneaky. If it hadn't been so incredibly obvious I would have been impressed."

I exhaled heavily, the cuffs biting into my wrists as I flexed my hands into fists. "I don't know what you're talking about."

"The ruse is up." He clasped his hands behind his back, his wings rustling as he stretched them. "No need to pretend. Regan's head is already on a spike on the palace walls. I will say, you made it further than I expected, well done. But your wings were no match for my new dragon. He is rather impressive isn't he?"

"Where is Elara?"

"Worry about where you are, my friend." He gestured vaguely around us. "You're right back where you started. Remember this place?"

I didn't need to look around to know where I was. I remembered the feeling of the rough sandstone at my back, the iron chains around my hands and arms. The smell of the moat only a few feet below the exterior wall.

I was back in my torture chamber, where they'd left me to listen to my infant son scream for days.

I strained forward, aching to tear Theron's throat out. "Fuck you. Where is she?"

"Would you like to see her?" Theron sneered at me, dropping into a crouch so we were face to face. "Shall I bring her to you?"

"Yes."

"And then what?" His eyes were flaming with predatory delight. "What happened last time you were here? Oh yes, you had to listen to your son wailing, just out of reach." He bared his teeth in a sickly grin. "What shall I do when I bring Elara here? What sounds of terror should I subject you to? Hmmm?"

My stomach dropped. "You touch her and I'll -"

"You'll what?" He cocked an eyebrow. "What, Rook? You'll break your arms again, crack your ribs? Lie here, a bruised and mangled mess, while your body heals and I fuck your Mate right over there?" He pointed deliberately to the open cell door. "Is that what you'll do?" He leaned closer, a calculated move, knowing exactly what range I had in these chains. "Tell me, Rook? What does she enjoy?"

My rage was so consuming I couldn't speak. I could barely breathe.

"Oh go on." Theron's voice dropped low. "As an old

friend. What does she like in bed?" He bit his lip, sniggering. "Does she enjoy having that sweet cunt eaten? Does she like fucking your hand? Does she like to ride your cock? Oh, wait!" He raised his eyebrows. "Has she let you claim that perfect ass of hers?"

I roared as I strained against the iron holding me back. "I'm going to fucking end you!"

Theron's eyes lit up. "Oh so you'd not had *that* yet." He stroked his chin. "I have, though. And let me tell you, it was incredible." He chuckled. "They feel so different when they come with your cock in their ass, don't they?"

"I am going to kill you!" Darkness snaked along the iron chains.

Theron watched the shadows move towards him with boredom. "Oh Rook, you really want to try and kill me again? Knowing that if you fail, you'll be leaving her all alone with me?"

"I won't fail. Not this time."

With an exasperated sigh, he withdrew a golden dagger from his side and plunged it into my stomach. I sucked in a breath, and my body jerked violently as he pulled the dagger out. I slumped forward, the chains holding me inert. I watched as blood dripped and pooled on the floor below me.

"You never fucking learn, Rook." Theron rose to his feet. "You just don't understand that I have the upper hand here."

"She. Loves. Me." I coughed, blood moving up my throat. "She. Loves. *Me*. And you will. *Never.* Have. That." Breathing was painful as the wound in my stomach gaped open, pouring blood down my legs.

"I don't need her to love me." Theron's tone dripped with disdain. "I need her to open her legs and bear me a child. Nothing more. That's the difference between you and I. I know what needs to be done, and you still answer to your baser instincts." He scoffed. "Night Demons. The most pathetic, poetic creatures to ever take to the skies." He dropped back to his knees, head dipped so he could meet my eyes. "Now, would you like to see her? Knowing what I will do to her, right in front of you?"

My vision had started to gray. My breathing slowed.

"Rook, I asked you a question."

"Fuck." I rasped in a breath. "You."

"I know you can feel me fucking her." He grabbed my hair and pulled my head up sharply. "Now, would you like to *see* me fucking her?"

"If she has any sense at all," I said, feeling my knees slide in the slick of blood that had gathered underneath me, "she'd run you through while you slept."

Theron laughed. "Ah but she won't do that. She loves you too much. Speaking of which." He licked his lips as he grinned. "When did she first tell you she loved you, hmm?"

How could he know? How could he possibly know? His triumph was complete as defeat twisted my face. He laughed out loud, shoving me away from him and rising to his feet.

"You're a fool, Rook. A fucking fool." He turned on his heel. "Get him a healer. I need him alive and well for his Trial in the Pit."

My head hung as I watched my blood congeal on the stones.

Once again, the healer brought me back from the brink of death.

Once again, I lay in my chambers, clawing at my heart,

feeling it crack and shatter anew as Elara screamed in my head.

Once again, a new day dawned, and when I looked out my window, I saw Regan's head on a spike, the mouth torn open, the eyes picked away by hungry crows.

The old man had failed in his plan. I had no idea who I could trust in this palace. I had no idea if Theron knew of any other informants, if they had now turned since their leader was dead. Had Regan even been the leader?

I smashed my fist into the window frame, letting out a guttural roar. I'd failed. I'd sworn to Elara I'd get her safe, and I hadn't kept my word. I'd let her down and probably made everything so much worse.

I didn't yet know what Theron had planned for me in the Pit. I had nothing to win back, nothing to gain as Elara had once believed. No, this was more torture, just another opportunity to make Elara suffer, and to hurt me.

Rook?

I clenched my eyes shut at the sweet voice.

I'm here. I wished I could reach out and touch her.

Are you alright?

Yes. I'm alright? Are you?

My bleeding came this morning. Theron is furious.

My relief was mixed with yet more fear, more anxiety. She was safe for now, but without Regan sneaking that contraceptive elixir into her water… Drusilla, the fucking snake, certainly wouldn't be amenable to that. *Fuck.* I punched the window frame again.

I'm so sorry, my love.

Don't apologize to me. You tried. They were ready for us, that's all.

Theron is going to throw me into the Pit.

I felt her gasp, and there was a torrent of fear welling in my chest.

What for?

I sighed. *I don't know.*

That dragon said there is a plan. What do you think he meant by that?

I didn't even dare to hope that there was a plan that ended with Elara finding freedom. The dragons had no reason to want her free, if anything they had even more reason to want Elara destroyed than Theron. I didn't trust anyone anymore.

I sank to the floor, draping my arms over my knees.

Rook?

I'm here. I'm here, my love.

Don't die down there.

I couldn't help but smile. *I'm not as strong as you, Osunon.*

Don't you dare die down there.

The door flew open, and guards crowded into the room.

"On your feet, Norahi." One of them gestured sharply. "Up, now. The King has a little game planned for you."

They'd all love to see me fail. They'd all love to see me die. But I was ready to set this entire palace on fire to get her out of here.

I just had to pick my moment.

I was escorted to the armory, where I was provided with leathers. I never fought in leathers, and these ones were tight and uncomfortable. My ax was nowhere to be seen.

"I need a weapon," I said to the guard as the Velesian crowd above us broke into excited cheers.

He waved his hand in the direction of the tunnel that led into the Pit. "It's out there waiting for you."

"Worried I'd lay waste to you all, ey?"

The guard scoffed. "Go on with you then. Have fun dying."

I advanced down the tunnel, into the darkness. I thought of Elara, standing behind this iron door, waiting for it to rise. I thought of the fear she must have felt. The bravery she had shown in the face of death.

Be ready.

There was no response. A terrible thought crossed my mind - what if she wasn't here? What if she was drugged in her chambers, locked up and guarded?

I gave myself a shake as the door began to rise. She was here. She was alright. Theron wouldn't miss an opportunity to torture us. She was merely biding her time. It was going to be alright.

The Pit was a vast desert, tall dunes rising either side of me as I stepped out into the light. The sky had become overcast, heavy gray clouds rolling in. Thunder rumbled in the distance, followed by a roar. I recognised it instantly. A shadow passed over my head, and the rush of wings told me the dragon was circling above.

I walked out, the sand giving way under my feet. My ax lay waiting just beyond the door, and I welcomed its weight in my hands, spinning the rough wooden handle a few times. I turned to look up into the royal box. The last time I had been down here I had saved Elara from that Arachne. Now I stood here alone, looking up at Theron, who was wearing a large golden crown on his head. Elara was in the seat beside him, thick golden strands wrapped around her.

They'd bound her to the chair. They knew she'd throw herself in after me without hesitation. She'd done it before. Theron had learned not to underestimate her.

My eyes met hers, and her face was taut with terror.

The shadow passed over the Pit again, and I looked up to see the blue dragon wind through the sky, flames simmering at his snout.

"Good people of Veles!" Theron's voice boomed across the Pit as he raised his hands for silence. "Today, we have our very own hero, my trusted, traitorous assassin, in the Pit, for our entertainment."

The crowd booed loudly, and when I looked back at Elara's face, I saw pure rage. She strained against her bindings, and looked up at Theron. She bared her teeth at him, like she wanted to tear his throat out at that very moment. He reached out to stroke her cheek, and she snapped at him. Theron jerked his hand back, and his shoulders heaved.

My fierce little Fae. I smiled when she met my eyes again. She wasn't going to go down without a fight.

Neither of us would.

"Today your adversary is a cousin of yours!" Theron gestured to the sky. The blue dragon passed over the Pit again, then came to land in a shower of sand at the far end of the Pit. The dune it landed on gave way under its weight, a cascade of gold accompanying it as it moved towards me.

"Now," Theron went on. "I have never seen a Night Demon under the shower of a dragon's flames, but I am sure it will be a sight to behold. Do you suppose he shall burn well, dear one?" He titled his head, giving Elara a sideways glance as he grinned.

"Not as well as you."

Even if I hadn't heard the words, she mouthed them with such vicious intent I could not have missed them.

Theron laughed loudly, grabbing her chin and giving her head a shake. "Well, let us see shall we?" He turned back to me, raising his hands and giving a single, loud clap. "Let the Trial begin!"

I spun towards the dragon, who continued his advance towards me through the shifting sands. Lightning flashed above, and the first drops of rain landed around me, speckling the ground and sending up that familiar scent of rain on burned ground.

The dragon breathed out a jet of fire, but nowhere near me. He was showing off to Theron. The fire illuminated the eyes of the crowd, who all jumped in surprise, then burst into applause. Yes, he was giving them a good show.

I kept running, and he lowered his snout to the ground as I drew closer.

"Hello again, cousin." He bared his teeth. "Shall we have a little scrap?"

"Wanting to show off?"

"I've no need to show off." He chuckled low in his throat, smoke swirling from his nostrils. "We both know that in this form you cannot best me."

I lunged at him, bringing the ax down as he raised his talons, as though wanting to swat me away. We both missed our target, and I spun under his raised claws, landing the ax in his leg. Fire exploded from the snout above my head, and the heat was so intense I immediately felt sweat break out on the back of my neck.

"Well done!" The dragon ambled sideways, away from me, his thick blue blood tracking through the sand. "You're much faster than you look."

"I've heard that before." I spun the ax in my hands as I followed the dragon, trying to keep my footing up the side of a dune.

The dragon laughed, a deep rumbling sound that was caught by the crash of thunder above. "I'm sure you have. But you should watch out."

There was a rush of wind, and I was thrown suddenly through the air as the dragon's spiked tail struck me square in my stomach. I connected with the ground and skidded on my back through the sand. The ground quaked around me as the dragon rushed towards me.

"I'm more than just claws and fire, cousin." He breathed

out another jet of flames into the sky, and I thought for a moment I heard a horn in the distance. My ears must have been ringing from the impact.

I rose to my feet, brandishing my ax. "Well, why don't you show me what else you can do then?"

The dragon's claws pounded into the ground as he shot towards me, and he brought his wings up, the talons darting towards my face. I ducked down, underneath their reach, and traced a long slice through the right wing, leaving it flapping in the breeze that had sprung up.

"Oh you little bastard!" The dragon choked out a laugh.

I dipped out from underneath his reach, lunging at him again with my ax, but missing as he flapped his wings. He hovered above the ground, and with a shriek he sent a heavy black cloud of smoke towards me.

Out of sheer instinct, I raised my shadows, creating a wall of night between us. The smoke rose against it, and then died. The crowd exclaimed in surprise, and when I looked up at Theron, I was more than pleased to see his eyes wide in shock. Elara was still straining against the golden ropes holding her down.

A shadow skittered through the growing storm, and my eyes darted upwards. But there was nothing.

My attention diverted for a moment, the dragon advanced on me again, snapping his enormous jaws at me. Too late, I swung my ax, only for it to land in his teeth. His mouth slammed shut, and with a shake of his head he sent me flying through the air again, my ax still firmly wedged between his teeth.

"Careful now, cousin." He chuckled, his tongue shifting the ax from his mouth, and it landed on the sandy ground with a thud. "Without a weapon even those fancy shadows of yours won't do you much-"

The shadows exploded from my hands, and I sent those inky tendrils towards the dragon's snout, where they wound around twice, then three times. He protested with a guttural grunt as his mouth was tied shut, and with a jerk of my hand, his head was pulled to the ground.

I advanced on him, holding the darkness steady. His claws scratched crevasses into the sand as he tried to back away from me, but I kept my grip on him.

"Now, cousin," I said, putting a foot on his smoking nose. "You will tell me what this plan is that you spoke of."

His enormous yellow eyes narrowed, and he growled. I pulled harder on his snout.

"Tell me what the plan is."

A shadow passed overhead, and then another. The dragon's eyes lifted to the sky, and he made a noise as though he wanted to speak.

I carefully loosened the grip on his mouth, so he could open just enough to talk.

"I would run now if I were you."

"What do you -" I broke off as something began to cross the stormy skies above us, one shadow after another flitting across the ground. I looked up at Elara, whose eyes were fixed on the skies. Everyone was looking upwards now.

I looked back down at the dragon, who chuckled. "I told you cousin, run. Now. It's about to get rather hot in Veles."

There was a shattering roar overhead, and a dragon swooped down low over the Pit. I stumbled away from the dragon, my shadows releasing him, and he took off without a second's hesitation.

Then everything exploded, into screams and flames.

Chapter 42

Rook

Dragons rained from the sky in a swirl of flames. The Velesians screamed in the stands, climbing over each other in waves of burgundy and black, trying to escape. I grabbed my ax and broke into a run towards the royal box, where Theron stood, staring wide-eyed at the scene unfolding before him.

Elara was fighting furiously against the golden bindings.

Rook! Her voice was filled with panic as it rang through my head. *Rook! I can't get free!*

"I'm coming!" I said the words out loud, my feet pounding into the dry sand. "I'm coming."

Theron's gaze landed on me as I ran towards them, and his eyes flashed down to Elara. Even from this distance I could see him considering his next move. Even in the midst of an attack, even with fire raining down on him, he was still thinking how to hurt, how to torture, how to cause more pain.

Elara seemed to notice too, and she looked up at him, her struggle stopping for a moment. Theron slowly turned back towards me.

Why wasn't I running faster? Why wasn't I as swift on my feet as she was?

Elara's eyes stayed locked on Theron, and then dropped to his hand at his waist. I saw the flash of gold as lightning crackled through the sky.

It was that fucking dagger again.

"No!" I roared. I was close. I was almost there. "Don't you fucking touch her!"

Elara's face twisted with terror and she looked back at me as Theron seized her hair.

"No! Don't you touch her!"

Just as Theron raised the dagger, a dragon crashed onto the roof above the royal box. One moment Elara was there, terrified, and then she was gone, in a ball of flames and debris. The dragon's weight crushed the stands, and it breathed fire above it all, sending a red wall of heat across the surface of the wreckage.

I launched myself at the dragon's neck, and it wasn't expecting me, it didn't even turn its head towards me. The ax sliced through the thick scales easily, and the dragon's body collapsed as its head rolled away into the sands.

"Elara!" I threw the ax down and began to dig, plunging my hands into the burning wood. "Elara! Where are you?"

I could feel she was close. She was here. She had to be here. I could feel her. She was here. She was *here.*

"Elara!"

Hair, like corn silk, and stained with blood, was suddenly under my hand. I pulled away charred remains and broken tiles, and then her face was looking up at me, smeared with soot.

"Oh Gods." I scrambled to pull away the pillar that was pinning her down, my fingertips torn open. "My love, I'm here, I've got you." She coughed as I pulled her out, and I wrapped her in my arms. "I've got you. I've got you."

She held onto me, shaking. "Rook."

"I'm here. Now, come, we have to go." I lifted her into my arms, and exhaled heavily as I extended my wings. The pain in my head returned, but I clenched my teeth together and with a swoop, we were in the air.

A searing pain hit me in the side, and Elara yelped as we were thrown sideways, out of the air. I shielded her in my arms as we hit the ground. Blood was running down my side.

"Rook?" She clutched my face in her hands. "Rook, what happened?"

"Going somewhere?" Caedmon's voice sounded loud and booming. I twisted to look at him advancing.

"Elara," I said, clutching her hands. "Run. Get out of here now. Run."

She shook her head. "I'm not leaving you."

"He'll kill you. Get out of here. I'll follow."

"Rook!"

"*RUN*." I pushed her away and turned towards Caedmon, clutching my side as I rose to my feet. "Looking for a fight, Caedmon?"

"Let's call it revenge for my son." Caedmon's dragon form was truly enormous, and he bared his teeth as he moved closer to me. His eyes flickered towards Elara, who was backing away along the wall.

"Look at me, you ugly fuck." I summoned a pool of darkness before me, and Caedmon's gaze shifted back to me. The wound in my side stung as I extended my arm, but I bit through the pain. "Your son was a useless bastard just like his father, and killing him did this Realm a favor."

Caedmon roared, smoke swirling from the back of his throat. "I'm going to tear you to pieces, Norahi."

"Come and get me then."

Caedmon rushed at me, his taloned wings darting towards me. I lifted my hand, swinging the shadows around one wing and jolting it to the right, causing Caedmon to stumble. With my other hand, I sent a black tendril to tear his other wing to the left. He growled as he pushed forward trying to break free of the shadows.

Out of the corner of my eye I saw Elara edging towards my ax.

What are you doing? I told you to run.

Before she could respond Caedmon tore open his mouth and a flare of flame shot through the air towards me. The darkness dissolved with a hiss as I threw myself back on to the ground, wincing as the impact shattered though the wound in my side.

"Your kind, Norahi," Caedmon said with a sneer, moving towards me with serpentine ease. "Your kind should have been killed off, not just restricted. And now, now that there will be a new order, they will see to it."

"They will, will they?" I asked, pushed myself up on a hand. I grinned at Caedmon, licking the blood off my teeth. "And who is they? More lords who promised you power? More nobles who'll use your strength to their own ends and leave you up on your barren lands to rot for all eternity?"

Caedmon chuckled, his yellow eyes disappearing briefly in a slow blink. "No. This time, the dragons are on the right side. This time, we will have our power. We will stand at the side of the new King, and all shall be right in this Realm."

I got to my feet, and laughed. "Your judgment will always be impeded by your thirst for power."

"Enough of this." He took a deep breath, and unleashed another tornado of flames in my direction.

I leapt out of the way, the flames catching my right arm. I

hit the ground, the gritty sand flying into my wounds. I sent a cloud of night at Caedmon's face, disorienting him long enough to scramble towards Elara, who now had a hold of my ax.

Gods, it was almost as tall as her. She clutched the handle, her white knuckles visible even from this distance. Her eyes flashed from Caedmon, to me, and back. She couldn't throw it, she could barely lift it. Shit.

Caedmon shook his head violently, the shadows around his face dissolving in another flurry of flames. With a snarl he was on top of me, and I cried out as a talon pierced my thigh.

"Rook!" Elara's scream was swallowed by thunder as it crashed directly over us.

"Run!" I twisted my head so I could see her face. One last time. "RUN. GO. NOW."

She shook her head.

GO. I love you. Please, GO.

Caedmon's talon sliced through my leathers, and my fingers clawed into the sand as the skin on my back opened up. Caedmon laughed.

"Ready to die, you fucking decrepit piece of shit?" Caedmon cackled maniacally, a sound infinitely more menacing in his dragon form.

I clenched my eyes shut, and took my last breath.

Caedmon's roar was a mix of human and animal, and he thrashed wildly, yanking his talon from my thigh. I threw myself onto my back, looking up at the dragon that was howling in pain above me. My gaze snapped over to Elara.

Two bloody hands were wrapped around the hilt of my ax, which now lay in the middle of Caedmon's tail. Her eyes were on fire, lit with a lethal blue flame. Blood was splattered across her face, her shoulders heaving.

I looked back up at Caedmon, whose snout flailed in the

air, before turning to look at the source of his pain. He bared his teeth, and a growl rumbled in his chest.

"Fucking bitch," he hissed.

"ELARA, RUN!" I rose to my feet, only to be caught by Caedmon's hind leg, sending me sprawling into the sand. Pain ricocheted through my body as I landed, but I gritted my teeth and pushed myself up, tumbling back to the ground as blood poured from my thigh.

Caedmon was advancing on Elara with alarming speed.

"ELARA! GO, NOW!" I couldn't reach her in time. I was too slow.

But she wasn't running. Instead, I saw her steel herself, lifting that fucking enormous ax, that weighed as much as she did, and with a loud cry she launched herself right at Caedmon's open mouth.

I didn't feel any pain as I pushed myself back up off the ground and sprinted towards them. Elara moved through the air, surprising Caedmon, who reared back for a moment. The ax landed in Caedmon's eye, and Elara lunged, shoving it in even further, as she hung off the side of Caedmon's head. He howled, trying without success to shake her off. Elara held firm, just as she had with the giant. Caedmon howled again, and he swatted at his face with his heavy black talons.

He fell sideways, and Elara let go of the ax, dropping to the ground. Caedmon shifted and writhed, his guttural wails becoming fainter as he moved further along the Pit. He heaved himself over a dune, and amidst a shower of sand and flames, he went still.

I reached Elara's side, where she had landed face down. I rolled her over in my arms, brushing away the sand that was sticking to blood and sweat on her face.

"My love, I'm here, I'm here."

"Rook," she said, with a small smile. "Did I kill him?"

"I think you did. My crazy, fierce little Fae." I laughed. "You never listen to me, do you?"

"I'm sorry, Rook." She winced. "I'm sorry."

I frowned, shaking my head. "What for?"

She looked down, to where her hands were clutching her stomach. I followed her gaze, and when she moved her hands, I was sure my heart stopped.

"His talon," she said weakly. "It - when he - when he tried to get me off him, he…" She broke off, her breathing shuddering. The hole in her stomach was enormous, pouring blood. He'd torn her open. There was no chance she'd be able to heal fast enough.

Disbelief tore through me as I looked back into her face. "My love, what have you done? What have you done?"

"I'm sorry." Her face crumpled, her lip trembling. "I don't want to leave you."

"No, no, you're not going to die." I shook my head, trying to smile. "You're going to be fine. You're not leaving me. I won't let you."

"I love you."

Her words sucked the air right out of my lungs. Not now, not here. Not like this. "Elara, please, you can't leave me."

She lifted a hand to my cheek. "For both of us, remember?"

I clutched that delicate, blood-stained hand to my face, willing her to stay, sure that if I held on tight enough, she would live. "No, no, I can't, not without you. I can't."

But her eyes went blank, the brilliant blue fading in a split second as the light inside her went out. The hand against my face went limp. There was a snap in my chest, as though I had a thousand ribs, a million hearts to break, and they all shattered at once. The Bond frayed and tore, twisting out of my body, and I screamed as I clutched her to me, as I scrambled against my chest with my other hand, trying to hold on to something I couldn't see but was tearing me apart all the same.

She was dead. My beloved, my Bonded.

I roared and raged, shaking her and holding her, stroking her cheek and screaming in her face, begging her not to leave me. Begging her to keep her promise to me. Begging her to give me the future she had sworn would be ours.

"You told me we'd wake up together, remember?" I pressed my forehead to hers, scorching hot tears landing on her face. "You promised me, we'd wake up together every single morning. Now you've broken that promise, and I cannot forgive you for it." I kissed her mouth, her perfect mouth that lay still. "You must come back to me, my love."

But she didn't. She lay in my arms, her head falling against my chest as I wept. Her heart went still next to mine. She was carried away from me, beyond my reach. Away to Nav.

"Bring her back," I begged the sky, the stormy gray sky that carried smoke and embers and the burning remains of Veles as it was laid to waste around me. "Bring her back to me."

I was answered with movement behind me, and I looked over my shoulder to see Theron struggling from the debris. One golden wing hung at a strange angle, clearly snapped from his back, and blood ran from a heavy gash across his forehead.

I kissed Elara's mouth again. "I'll see you soon," I whispered against her lips.

I rose to my feet, walking slowly towards Theron as he struggled to gain his footing, swaying in an unseen breeze. He squinted at me, blinking rapidly. His gaze dropped briefly behind me, to Elara's body, and his eyebrows shot up, betraying the barest hint of grief.

"He killed her." He looked back at me. "They came to destroy my kingdom, and they killed my bride."

"*You* killed her."

Theron scoffed, wincing as he stumbled a little. "I had nothing to do with this. The fucking dragons betrayed me. I should have known." He squeezed his eyes shut, clutching a hand to his forehead. "Fucking dragons."

"You killed her." My foot nudged against something, a dragon's talon in the sand. I bent to pick it up, curling my fingers around it as I continued to advance on Theron.

His eyes opened slowly, and lightning flashed overhead as he seemed to focus on me properly. "And I suppose you mean to kill me now, is that it?" He laughed, staggering again. "Even though it means your own death?"

"You vastly overestimate my desire to live without her."

At those words he was suddenly uncertain, and held out a hand. "Rook, please, I never meant her any harm, I swear it."

"You raped her, you violated her, and you nearly crushed her very spirit." I was only a few feet away now. "You tried to destroy me, you tried to destroy her, and now you will die for it."

"Rook." He stumbled back a little, his eyes wide. "You'll kill yourself!"

"Then I hope you die faster than me, so your dying eyes are the last thing I see." I pounced at him, and we toppled to the ground. Theron tried to hold me off, his hands pushing against my shoulders. He threw a fist, striking me in the jaw, but I barely felt it.

The keening rage and grief drove me on, and I slammed his hand to the ground at the same time that I drove the talon into his throat.

Chapter 43

Rook

I waited for my throat to be torn open. I waited for my blood to fall to the ground in violent, crimson jets, just as it was leaving Theron's neck now. I waited for the feeling of choking, for my vision to gray, to fall spluttering into the sand until the soft warmth of death took me. Took me back to her, to the Gates of Nav, where she would be waiting for me.

But I looked down at Theron, and felt nothing.

His eyes were wide at first, his mouth lolling open as he tried to breathe through the blood. He became quieter and quieter, his body stilling underneath me. His blood poured out of him, until it was merely a trickle. Until his eyes lost all light, and he died.

And still my heart was beating. Still I smelled the burning city around me. Still I heard the storm raging above me and the roaring of dragons in the distance.

I crawled away from him, breathing rapidly. How was this possible? Why wasn't I dying?

I tore away the ragged leathers, and looked at my arm. I

ran a hand over it, blinked again, clenched my eyes shut, and looked back, rubbing the skin again.

The mark was gone.

Grief tore through me. I pounded my fists into the ground, throwing curses at the sky, at the fucking Gods who were mocking me. Now I had my freedom? Now? Fucking NOW?

"I DON'T WANT IT!" I roared. "I DON'T FUCKING WANT IT." Hot tears poured down my cheeks, and I clutched my head in my hands. "It's meaningless. It's fucking meaningless without her."

I crawled across the sand, back to her side, and took her in my arms. Her body was already losing warmth, and I buried my face against her neck. But she didn't smell of roses anymore. She smelled of blood and sand. I stroked the hair out of her face, nudging her cheek with my nose.

"You were supposed to learn to swim, remember? I was going to teach you. We were going to swim under the twin moons together." I kissed her again, and again. "I was going to take you home. I was going to marry you. And now you've left me here alone. You cannot do this to me, Elara. You cannot die for me."

"Rook."

I looked up to see an old woman walking towards me. I knew her, I had seen her before. Yes, she was the healer who had seen me in my chambers. She hurried across the sand towards me.

"What do you want?" I asked as she knelt beside Elara.

Her eyes were mournful as she gazed at the dead princess in my arms. "Oh no."

"Who are you?"

She pulled down the collar of her brown robes, to reveal a

small tattoo at the base of her neck. A tattoo of the sun. "We've failed you both. I am so sorry."

"You're with the Guild?"

She nodded. "I am Hipatia. I am a priestess of the Order, and leader of the Guild."

"Well," I said cynically, sniffling, "it won't do us much good now."

"Tannis has returned." Her eyes were wide as I met them. "Tannis has returned, and you must go, now."

I shook my head. "Tannis was destroyed, years ago."

"No, he was merely weakened. Theron believed he had claimed power completely, as power-hungry fools often do. But Tannis was merely biding his time, until he could return. He still hoped to claim his prize." Her gaze wandered down to Elara. "But now she is beyond all of them. Even you."

An explosion sounded nearby and flames shot up into the gray sky. Hipatia clasped my hand, the wrinkles in her ancient face becoming even deeper.

"You must go, now. Tannis will show no mercy."

I shook my head, holding Elara close. "I don't care. Let them come."

"Don't be a fool!" She jerked in on herself as another explosion sounded, closer still. "There is still much to be done, Rook. You *must* do it. You must go back to Isambard. You have to warn them that Tannis has returned. Take the princess, and go. Fly."

"Why?" I asked, a scoff dropping from my lips. "What for? She's dead. It's too late."

"A life for a life."

"What?" I shook my head. "What do you mean? Whose life?"

An explosion rocked the remaining wall of the Pit, and

debris flew through the air around us. Hipatia rose to her feet, her hands glowing with a strange yellow light.

"Take her, and fly. The Umbra Furorem is rising again, and you must go."

"I still don't understand."

"A life for a life." She said it again, but this time in Malakh, a language I'd learned as a child and had not heard spoken since. "You will know, when the time comes, you will know what to do."

Suddenly, guards were flooding the pit, running at us, wearing a uniform I did not recognise. They were Seraph, their golden wings drawn to their backs as they stormed towards us.

"What the fuck do they want?" I asked.

"Go!"

"But they'll kill you!"

Hipatia looked over her shoulder, her eyes glowing a bright yellow. "You must take her home. *Now*. I don't have time to explain." Hipatia turned to face the guards, raising her hands in front of her and sending a shimmering wave of yellow light towards them. She did not turn back to face me, but over the shouts and calls of the guards she cried, "*NOW, ROOK!*"

I scooped Elara up in my arms. The guards were held back by the shimmering yellow shield that Hipatia continued to manipulate in the air before her. But she wouldn't be able to hold them back for long. It was hopeless. We were outnumbered.

I threw out my wings, and with a single heavy swoop I shot into the thunderous sky. I rose higher and higher, above the flames and the screams and the smoke. Rain met my tear-stained face as I flew, and it took me several minutes to realize I was flying in the wrong direction.

I banked to the left, over the dark forest, towards the mountain range. Over the mountains and past the jungles. And then I would be home.

I looked down at Elara's face. Her eyes were still open, unseeing. I kissed her forehead, feeling fresh tears well up as her cold skin touched my lips.

"I'm taking you home," I whispered to her. "I'm going to take you home, and lay you in the ground where you can see the ocean, where you can see that turquoise water you dreamed of. You'll see it every day now. And I'll meet you in my dreams, just like you said. Just like we promised each other."

On and on I flew, and still she remained lifeless in my arms.

So small, and so very far away.

ACKNOWLEDGMENTS

I am so incredibly blessed to have so many amazing people behind me, cheering me on and making all this possible.

Mark, my amazing husband, without you, none of this would be possible. None of it. Your love and support is unwavering (and yes, I know it's just because you want to be a kept man and buy all the Legos. I love you anyway.)

My Mum, for herding kids and entertaining teething babies so I could answer yet another email and try and work out another plot hole - thank you.

Felica and Deana - I love you both so, so much. Your support is endless and I cannot wait for OCR. Manifest it!

My amazing Street Team - our chats are the best. Unhinged and smutty, as it should be. Let's hype the shit out of this bitch.

My ARC readers - your enthusiasm for this story has been inspiring and moved me to tears more than once (a day). Thank you for taking the time to read and hype this book!

Stephen, Robbie, Marty and Jodi - your artwork brought Rook, Elara, Korbiriya and A Realm of Dark Fury to life in the most beautiful ways. Thank you, thank you, thank you

And finally, as always, the BookTok Community. I don't know how to thank you. You changed my life.

About the Author

RD Baker writes dark fantasy even when she doesn't mean to. It just sort of happens. She is highly caffeinated at all times, always has a book idea that has to be jotted down in her Notes app, and doesn't sleep much. But that's OK.

She lives in the Blue Mountains, Australia, with her family.

Printed in the USA
CPSIA information can be obtained
at www.ICGtesting.com
LVHW092122281223
767345LV00105B/44

9 780645 820782